DRIVING DEAD

DRIVING DEAD

Stephen Collier

Matador
9 Priory Business Park,
Wistow Road, Kibworth Beauchamp,
Leicestershire. LE8 0RX
Tel: 0116 279 2299
Email: books@troubador.co.uk
Web: www.troubador.co.uk/matador
Twitter: @matadorbooks

ISBN 978 1789016 512

British Library Cataloguing in Publication Data.
A catalogue record for this book is available from the British Library.

Printed and bound in Great Britain by 4edge Limited
Typeset in 11pt Adobe Garamond Pro by Troubador Publishing Ltd, Leicester, UK

Matador is an imprint of Troubador Publishing Ltd

For Sarah

1

Jake Jordan sat up.

Instantly awake.

Soaked in sweat.

Rain hammering on the bedroom window.

The images of his exploding police Volvo receding under a vale of departing sleep.

05:40.

2

Lisa

'Come on James, put your shoes and coat on or we'll be late for school again! Look, Olivia's ready. Why are we always waiting for you?'

Lisa was standing by the front door, tapping her foot, waiting for her son.

'Don't shout at him love,' said Richard, as he came out of the kitchen, at the same time brushing the arm of his suit to remove some unseen fluff. He took his overcoat from the coat stand and threw it over his arm, as he made his way into the hallway joining his wife and children.

The keys to the family car were sitting in a bowl on the side table. Richard casually collected them, then threw the jangling bunch at his wife, which she just about caught. 'You'd better drive after the skinful I had last night. I think I'll probably still be over.'

'Really?' Retorted Lisa. 'And I'm not, I suppose?' She grinned, mocking him.

'You didn't have as much as me, that's for sure. Come on James, hurry up! Anyway, you seemed to spend most of the night trying to get rid of Darren, who didn't want to stray too far from you.'

'Yeah, and you weren't much help fending him off either, because you were three sheets to the proverbial wind,' Lisa said without any real rancour, smiling at her husband.

'I told you that you shouldn't have worn that short dress, you know what my work mates are like when they've had too much beer.'

'I wore it for you hun, not your leery mates.'

Richard chuckled. He smoothed his hair in the hallway mirror. 'Being pissed didn't do my chances any good for… well… you know.' He gave his wife a wink.

'Indeed.' Lisa returned her husband's smile, and shook her head slightly, glancing towards the children. 'It was a good night, though, wasn't it? But I can't for the life of me remember how we got home.'

'Come on you two, let's go.' Richard said, his son having stood after putting his shoes on.

With that, he opened the front door, ushering the two children outside. Lisa saw the bottle of water she'd had the previous night and grabbed it from the hallway table, as she closed the door to their family home.

As they left the house, Lisa felt a cool breeze caress her, bringing with it the smell of the late harvest of wheat from the field behind their home.

Gathering the children into the car, she watched Richard make sure that they were secure, before he jumped into the passenger seat. He was such a good dad, she reflected. Despite the ups and downs of family life, Lisa knew that she had chosen well, blessed with a kind and gentle soul.

Getting behind the wheel Lisa turned to her husband, at the same time unscrewing the top of the water bottle. 'Although I didn't have that much to drink last night, I do feel a bit rough this morning,' she murmured to her husband.

'What do you mean, a bit rough?'

'You know, as if it was me that had the skinful and not you. And I've got a thumping headache.'

'You didn't have that much, surely?'

'I know, but I still feel as if I did. The problem is, I can't remember any of it.' A puzzled looked passed over Lisa's face. 'I don't remember the taxi. I don't even remember getting back here, talking to the babysitter or going to bed. It's weird.'

'Do you want me to drive then?'

'No, I'll be all right.' She took a big swig of water.

'Where did you get that bottle of water from anyway?'

'No idea. Tastes a bit funny though.'

'Meaning?' Richard frowned and turned to face his children in the back.

'Tastes a bit salty.' Lisa thought for a moment. 'Must be in my mouth from breakfast.'

'That's odd, anyway, kids are you ready? James put your seatbelt back on please.'

'No! Hurts.'

'James, please, it's for your own good.'

James glowered at his dad, then reluctantly reattached his seatbelt.

Lisa started the engine and reversed the car off the drive. She took another swig of water before driving off, hoping it would quench her raging thirst.

3

Jake shook his head in an attempt to rid himself of the image of his burning police Volvo. He knew this was futile along with the fuzziness of being woken by a hypnagogic jerk once again, and fell back onto his bed, mulling over the interminable nightmare. But thinking about it would do no good. He knew that.

He swung his legs over the side of the bed and sat for a few moments, rubbed his face with his hands then scratched his head, before he peeled off his sweat-soaked shorts and headed for the shower.

The new apartment Jake had rented still had bare walls, as if someone was imminently about to move in… or out. The furniture minimal. He hadn't come out of his divorce with much furniture as most of it was Rosie's anyway. He did get to keep his Rick Wakeman CDs, an old sofa he used to keep in his home office, and the new kettle he'd bought a week before she left.

Was he angry? Yes, he was. Considering that it wasn't even him who'd been having the affair! It was that he had come away with so little of his possessions. So much for civil justice. If it were not for the Bingham Tyler incident twelve months before, Jake would probably still be in his home, none the wiser that his wife was having an affair with her boss. Jake's brother-in-law.

At least Jake had got Tyler to thank for that. Not that he really felt he'd anything to thank Tyler for. All the mandatory counselling sessions Jake had been to didn't stop the stuff running through his head every morning. A dreary radio show came on with the alarm and played in the background while he shaved. He turned on the shower, testing the temperature with the palm of his hand, as he did every morning. The deaths he'd seen during that incident lay heavy on him, and the police force. But it was very rare in the county to see a murdering psychopath deliberately target and slay his victims, and a police officer. Did he feel like a failure? Maybe.

Then there was Kirsty. As her Family Liaison Officer, he saw how deeply affected she had been by the death of her husband. She was, Jake reflected, still very vulnerable.

Standing in his shower, Jake wished that the hot water could magically wash away the last terrible twelve months. He was bitter about having been put on a 'fizzer' by Marland for disobeying his instructions to let the dogs flush Tyler out of the factory.

But Jake went in anyway and found the psychopath, surviving a brutal fight with him. Jake got the blame for allowing Tyler to get away, who then stole Rebecca Burnett's traffic car. Both he and Burnett chased him down to destruction, literally. Brought to his own justice in a collision with a train.

Never mind the fact that Jake also fought for his life in Jim's apartment where Tyler had held Kirsty hostage. Never mind the fact that Tyler, after targeting Jim, targeted her. And what did Jake get? A shit load of trouble from as many bosses that could make a case to screw him to the floor. Sod that.

Did he get any thanks? No.

Did he get promoted? No.

Detective Chief Superintendent Marland though, he got promoted to Assistant Chief Constable. His old crewmate Rebecca? She got promoted to Chief Superintendent in charge of Operations. And Dave Harte? Even he had climbed the greasy pole to Inspector.

Jake had been in the job long enough to understand how the force worked. But the injustice of it all stuck like a fishbone in the gullet. And he was angry.

Trying to relax, Jake let the hot water run down his back. Calming the thoughts racing around his head. He didn't need this every bloody morning.

Switching off the shower, he stepped out and grabbed the towel from behind the door. He growled, 'I was only doing my fucking job!'

He finished drying off vigorously. 'I don't need this shit in my life,' he said, then threw down the towel.

Jake tried to put his feelings back in their box. He had no idea how to stop them.

He put on his uniform, ready for the early start, went to the kitchen and put two slices of bread in the toaster. He flicked on the kettle and spooned some coffee into a mug.

The kettle clicked and popped as it boiled and the toaster ejected the hot toast with a thunk. Slathering butter on the two pieces and pouring water into his coffee mug making a hot black coffee, Jake stared at the sky from his kitchen window. It was grey and leaden and he was unsure if the sun would be able to penetrate the gloom of the day.

When he'd finished, he quickly washed his mug and put it to drain. Collecting his kit, he headed for his car and made his way to the station, only a short five-minute drive away.

4

Lisa

Leaving their village, they joined the A5 at Long Buckby and travelled north. After Long Buckby and the canal bridge, the road opened up to a long straight as it approached the Watford Gap. Seeing the road ahead, Lisa felt she could briefly take a hand from the wheel to ask her husband for the bottle of water again.

Richard, who had been chatting to his children and scolding his son for taking off his seat belt again, took the bottle of water from the cup holder and involuntarily gave it a shake. It bubbled up for a moment then settled, but seemed to take longer than normal to resume its natural appearance. 'It's not flat fizzy water, is it?'

'Wasn't last time I drank from it.'

'Unusual, it has a few bubbles,' he said casually, unscrewing the lid, sniffing it, then passing it to his wife.

She absent-mindedly reached for the bottle her husband was offering her and took another big gulp of water. Despite nearly drinking half the bottle in large mouthfuls, the water did nothing to touch her thirst. Her mouth still felt dry.

They had passed the Watford Gap crossroads and were heading towards Kilsby. After the crossroads and the railway bridge, the road dropped into a hollow before it launched itself again into a left-hand bend at the top of the hill, bounded by lush green trees and hedges. On a sunny day it could be a beautiful drive, but that morning, Lisa was in no mood to enjoy it.

She turned to her husband, looking ashen faced. 'I think you'd better drive. I'm going to stop somewhere. I don't feel too good.'

'All right, there's a layby just up the road. Stop there and I'll take over. If you don't feel well, you'd better go see the doctor.'

With a horrible reckoning, Lisa knew that something wasn't right. In fact something was very wrong. Suddenly she couldn't keep her eyes open. With horror, she felt all the muscles in her body cramp, as it went into an uncontrollable spasm. Her right foot hit the accelerator pedal and lay there like a brick.

5

Jake arrived at the new Multi-Agency Emergency Services Joint Operations Complex on Northampton's Swan Valley. Six years in the building, it was purpose-built to house a new regional control room for all three emergency services, plus Highways England. It stood three storeys high, but by no means could anyone describe it as an architectural masterpiece. From a distance across the valley, it looked like a big red brick dropped randomly on the landscape. There was a huge parking area for police, fire and ambulance vehicles, with an underground garage for repairs. State-of-the-art and, Jake thought, nothing but a big white elephant. The only people who'd moved in to-date were the Road Policing Unit and the Force Vehicle Workshop. Everyone else who was supposed to move in had cold feet about becoming 'one' emergency service, as promoted by the Police and Crime Commissioner.

'A new era in providing emergency services to the people of Northamptonshire,' the PCC had said. Everyone with any sense knew that it was doomed to failure, but the PCC still spent £1.5 million on the project, only for it to be cancelled when the new PCC took office. It made the county a laughing stock.

The entrance to the building still made Jake smile sardonically. It was like walking into the CIA building in the US, with the crests of the force, the fire and ambulance service emblazoned in a marble floor. Talk about the PCC's God complex. Jake took the lift to the second floor. As he stood in the lift, he was aware that the haunting images of his endless nightmare, sitting in the recesses of his mind, were ready to pounce all too easily. Perhaps that was the reason for his permanent headache. The doctor had said it was tension in his neck, likely from sitting at a computer for long periods.

Jake knew the increasing mountain of paperwork, and 'digital reporting', was a literal pain in the neck. He, on the other hand, suspected his persistent headaches were down to the unremitting tension caused by his mental state.

On the way to his office, he poured himself a coffee from the machine, dumped his bag, and flopped down into his chair at his desk. There was no one else in the office. The nightshift was still out and none of his crew had yet appeared, after all he was an hour or so early. He flicked on his desktop and reviewed the entries on tasking and resource management known as STORM and the intelligence system NICHE. All seemed to have had a quiet night. Jake knew that wouldn't last. It never did.

As if on cue, the phone on his desk rang and he answered it. It was the force control room manager. 'Thought you might be in early, Jake.'

'What made you think that then, Ivan?'

'You've got previous for it.'

Jake grunted. 'How can I help you?'

'You've got PC Prentice on duty this morning, haven't you?'

'Yes, but he was celebrating his birthday last night, so I don't know what state he'll be in.' Jake chuckled.

'He won't be in at all.'

'Oh, why?'

'He's at the hospital's A&E.'

'How'd he manage that?'

'He was found by an area car about four a.m., handcuffed to a lamp post.'

'Is he OK?'

'Yeah, just shook up a bit, I think.'

Jake heard Ivan trying to stop himself from chuckling and he could hear the smile in his voice.

'Do we know how it happened?'

'I know, but I'll let him tell you.' He laughed and signed off. Jake was just left with a dial tone in his ear. He looked at his watch. No time to get down there and back for the briefing. He rang the control room to tell them to instruct the early shift to self-brief and let them know where he was.

6

Sometime later, Jake parked his patrol car outside the Emergency Department in the dedicated police bay. He spoke to the receptionist, who also seemed amused by the predicament Prentice was in and indicated where Jake could find him.

They'd put him in a side-room and, as Jake entered, Prentice was halfway through getting dressed. He looked up at Jake, his embarrassment obvious. Failing to meet his supervisor's eye, Prentice mumbled, 'Are you going to take the piss as well, Sarge?'

'Moi?' Jake said with open arms, smiling.

Prentice just grunted. 'Most of the others have. Worst effin' night of my life. Some birthday.'

Jake sat down in a chair by the door and leaned forward with his arms on his knees. He looked across at Prentice who'd sat down in a chair next to the bed to put on his boots.

Jake tried to keep a straight face. 'Is there anything you want to tell me, Chris?'

'See, I knew you couldn't resist taking the "P" as well.'

'I'm just asking after your welfare. Anyway, I thought that you didn't have any clothes?' Jake chuckled.

'Had the nightshift go home and get some uniform for me,' puffed Prentice, struggling with a shirt that for some reason had been turned inside out. 'See? The bastards are still taking the piss when they're not here, turning my shirtsleeves the wrong way around.'

Jake couldn't help but laugh.

'Don't, Sarge, it's not funny.'

'Mmm… it is, Chris.'

'Look,' he said, 'I don't want to miss work as I'm supposed to be on duty.' He looked at his watch, then said, 'Now.'

'Do you want to tell me about it?'

'Not really, no. I think I'd prefer to forget the whole night.'

'Try,' Jake said, more serious.

Prentice gave a big sigh. 'I went out to celebrate my birthday. Thought my mates had my back. Clearly, they hadn't. Next thing I know I'm buck-naked and strapped to a lamppost on Eastlands.

'And how did you get in that position? As it were.'

'I have no idea.'

'How much had you had to drink?'

'Enough, obviously.'

'How are you feeling now?'

'I'm fine. I just want to get back to work and forget about it.'

'You don't want the day off then?'

'Nah, got to get the pisstaking out of the way. Anyway, I'm not actually injured. Don't know why they brought me down here.'

'Only if you're sure.'

Prentice nodded.

At that moment, they heard a commotion outside his room. Poking his head outside, Jake scanned the corridor and located the noise close to the resuscitation room.

'I'll see you in the car,' said Jake, and left to see what the problem was. Instincts and experience told him that such noisy activity meant that someone was kicking off about something.

Doing up his hi-vis jacket, he approached a nurse coming towards him.

'Is everything OK?' he asked.

'Yes, we've had to get an MI crash team in for a chap brought in after a road accident.' She eyed his uniform. 'I'm surprised you don't know about it.'

Jake's radio sprang into life, cutting off anything else the nurse might have been about to say.

'Tango supervisor 1540. Urgent message. Over.'

'I think I'm going to find out now.' He smiled.

The nurse returned the smile and walked on. Jake bent his head down towards his radio and told them to go ahead.

'1540, we're in attendance at a serious collision on the A5, north of Watford Gap, reported as a 10/30. Can you attend?'

'Affirmative. Who have you got at the scene?'

'Half of Tango Mike One and Mike Five have booked their arrival.'

'Copy that. I'll take the other half of Mike One up there with me.'

'All received, Sarge, out.'

Jake returned to Prentice, who was talking with the pretty young blonde nurse he'd just spoken to. Jake thought Prentice looked a little flushed and couldn't decide whether it was because of his ordeal or something else. Jake watched Prentice give the nurse his business card and quickly write something on the back. His eyes sparkled as he engaged with the nurse. Jake decided that it was the latter. Prentice glanced over towards Jake, who indicated that they should leave.

'I'll be out in a minute, Sarge. Just need to sign the discharge sheet.'

Jake nodded. He guessed he could let the lad off. He still remembered what it was like to be young and filled with confidence. And policemen and nurses always did have some kind of bond.

He'd liked Prentice from the first time they'd met at Fulborough Wood some twelve months before. Fresh blood, fresh ideas, fresh talent. All waiting to be tapped into. Enthusiastic about his new role on the Road Policing Unit, and obviously his evenings out.

But as Prentice was the newest officer on the shift, he needed to make sure that Prentice's practical skills while out on the road were up to scratch. Despite his ordeal during the night, Prentice was far too awake for Jake's liking. Adrenaline keeping him going he thought and assumed that he'd not had that much sleep, but he seemed to be coping well without it. He knew from his own experience that the fatigue would hit him like a double decker bus later. Something that at his age he wouldn't be able to cope with at all. What he did know was that sometime soon Prentice was going to have to give up the story of his eventful birthday party.

En-route to the collision, Jake thought about Prentice sitting next to him. He glanced towards him.

'This'll be your first fatal won't it, Chris?'

'On the unit, yes. Seen plenty of 10/30s on area, as I told you at my interview.'

Jake reflected for a moment then said, 'I'm going to put you as OIC then. You ready for that?'

Jake flicked on the siren to warn a driver hogging lane three of his approach as he waited for a response from Prentice.

Eventually Prentice said, 'Sure, no problem.'

'So, in the last twelve months you've been to your first murder and now your first fatal as the Officer-In-Charge.'

'Seems that way. Still, Dad taught me a lot about how to cope with the trauma. He'd seen enough of it with his time on the force.'

Jake nodded.

They spoke briefly a little more about his father, as Jake navigated carefully to the scene of the crash.

Christ! What a mess! It never failed to amaze Jake that anyone could walk away from a car crash alive. Although in this case, they already knew that there was at least one person who was dead.

Jake fervently hoped that Prentice's coping strategy would be robust enough to help him through what he knew he was going to find.

The two policemen clambered out of their Land Rover Discovery patrol car and walked towards the scene. He could feel Prentice's nervousness.

'You going to be OK?' checked Jake.

'Of course.'

Jake wasn't so sure as he looked at the smashed-up car, which he identified as a Nissan Qashqai.

'How many fatals have you been to then, Sarge?' murmured Prentice, surveying the scene before him.

'Lost count. Been to a few on this road though.'

Jake watched Prentice quickly wipe his hands on his trousers. Nerves. Jake looked around him. He'd been to collisions on this road many times and very few of them had been minor.

The road here was bounded by trees on the right and followed the bend in the road, on which they were stood. There was a high hedge on the left that afforded no view of oncoming traffic. As it crested the hill, it quite rightly had double white lines down the centre. Jake looked skyward. Darker clouds were building and a late autumn mugginess pervaded the quietness of the scene, as the three emergency services went about their work.

'Does it get any easier?' Prentice asked Jake as they approached the mangled car.

'No, not really. You just, compartmentalise. If you know what I mean.'

'Yeah, I think so.'

They saw Reg Johnson, standing talking to a fire officer, next to the Qashqai. Reg introduced Jake to him, who then went off and answered his phone.

'Reg, I've brought Chris up with me. He can crew with you for the rest of the shift.'

'Thanks, Sarge. Thought I might get away from his enthusiasm for the day.'

'No such luck I'm afraid, Reg,' Prentice said.

'I'm putting him down on the sheet as Officer In Charge.'

'Baptism of fire then?'

'I went to a few when I was on Incident Response, but generally it got left to RP. Now I'm here, on RP, so I suppose from the point of view of being my first to deal with, yes.'

'OK,' Johnson said, 'let's get one thing straight. It's Traffic, not RP or roads policing.' He gestured air speech marks as he said roads policing. 'Or whatever name they decide later. To me it'll always be Traffic.'

Prentice shook his head. Jake just smiled. He'd known Johnson as a traffic cop even before he joined the unit. He was a well-worn portly five-foot-six traditionally orientated traffic cop with thinning pepper-pot hair and the typical cynicism of a copper with nearly twenty-nine years' service.

'Bloody typical, init,' Johnson said. 'I picks up me "Truckers Salad" at Rothersthorpe and then get sent up here, before I could even get it to the table.'

'God's sake, Reg, stop whingeing. Not as if you need it, is it?' Jake smiled.

'I had to grab two pieces of toast and stuff me bacon between them, wasting another quid. Only used to have to pay two bob, y'know,' Johnson continued to grumble.

'Let's call it inflation and leave it at that.'

'Bloody old dinosaur,' Prentice said as a joke, as they went to inspect the vehicles.

They arrived at the crushed car. Taking in the sight before them, Jake asked Johnson to update him on the situation.

'Who's been taken from this vehicle, Reg?'

'Male passenger very poorly, may go 10/30. Two kids, boy and a girl, both with non-life-threatening injuries. Female driver is still in situ. Paramedic has pronounced life extinct.'

'What injuries did the male have, do you know?'

'Head.'

'Wasn't he the guy we saw at the hospital who'd crashed?' Prentice asked.

'Possibly. Don't forget to check that out, Chris. What about the kids then, Reg?'

'The girl was still in her booster seat, but the boy probably wasn't wearing a seat belt and got thrown forward.'

'OK, Reg. Thanks.'

'I'll go see if I can get anything out of the drivers of the other vehicles.'

Jake nodded.

He peered inside the car with Prentice. What they saw made Prentice retch a little. Jake saw him take a deep breath to calm himself and try to hide his response.

'Looks as if the airbag inflated, but didn't do its job,' Prentice noticed.

'That could be for a number of reasons. Unusual though. We'll get an evaluation from the collision investigators.'

Jake saw that the driver's chest was crushed, the steering wheel having been pushed against it, breaking ribs, puncturing the skin and probably the lungs, allowing her to bleed out. Her head was slumped forward, her hands still gripping the steering wheel.

Johnson approached Jake. 'Just got a quick idea as to what's happened from the truck driver. He's a bit shook up, but I think he'll be OK, once the water fairies have cut his legs free.'

'You do have a way with words for our colleagues, Reg.' Jake remarked. Reg just smiled back at Jake. 'How'd this happen then? What's he saying?'

'Apparently, the bulk-tipper artic was travelling south when the Qashqai appeared to accelerate up the hill and slammed into the side of his truck, stuffing itself between the rear axle of the cab unit and the front axle of the trailer. No sidebars to stop it going under, you see. He braked heavily and the fourth axle rode over the front of the Qashqai, eventually spitting the vehicle out into the path of the rigid sixteen tonner that smashed into its side. The impact pushed the Qashqai back into the first lorry which had come to a stop, crushing the Qashqai between the two of them.'

'That'll probably answer the question about the airbag,' Jake said to Prentice, who nodded. Traumatic all the same, especially for the kids. What about the tipper driver?'

'Minor cuts and bruises, he'll be OK. He's sitting in my car, still a bit shocked.'

'OK, take an initial statement from him, breathalyse and drug test?'

Johnson nodded. He turned to Prentice.

'Make sure we get somebody down to the hospital for the kids and the father, get an ETA for the collision investigator, and make sure the scene is locked down for her.'

'Sarge.'

Jake walked away from Prentice as he instructed him to take details. As he did so, his attention was drawn to the back of a dark-haired woman, who approached Prentice. He took a step closer to them to catch the conversation and moved back towards Prentice. By the time he'd got to him she was walking away. He thought about calling her back, but decided to ask Prentice instead.

'Who was that?'

Prentice turned to his sergeant. 'A doctor in the tailback of cars walked up to see if she could help.'

'Really, did you get her name?'

'Sorry, sarg, no.'

Jake watched the woman walking away. Something told him that it didn't feel right, but he put it out of his mind.

7

They strolled together arm in arm in Victoria Park. The breaking autumn sun was warm with a breeze that Jake saw tugged lightly at Kirsty Kingsfield's long red hair.

He glanced toward her. He knew that look on her face. 'You shouldn't still be beating yourself up about this, Kirsty.'

'I know Jake, but I can't get over the fact that if it hadn't have been for Parker, my husband might still be alive.' She pushed some stray hairs away from her face.

In the twelve months since Jim Kingsfield's death, at the hands of Bingham Tyler, Jake knew that all her tears were gone and the only emotion that remained was regret. Regret that nobody saw it coming. Regret at the incident, years before, that started a chain of events that no one would have believed. Back then, Kirsty would have been unable to comprehend that she would be walking in a park, arm in arm, with him. Of course, he'd not told Kirsty about the ongoing nightmares he was having about Tyler and everything that happened. He knew that wouldn't be fair on her. She'd had enough to deal with.

As they walked, Jake was determined to continue to support her, despite being told by his boss to put some distance between them. He argued that his role as her Family Liaison Officer didn't just finish after the inquest was done. He could see that she was an emotional wreck. He felt that he needed to be there for her during her darkest times. There had been a drift towards alcoholism that he had helped her avert. There had been days of depression when she had not wanted to see or talk to anyone – only him. And then there were the days when she didn't want to go to work, to cut up dead people. A job he knew she'd been drawing away from. A job that, as the senior forensic pathologist at the hospital, was cruelly taken away from her. Jake thought that this was the most callous of things to do by her employer, in her time of grief. But most of all, Jake knew that she couldn't reconcile the fact that Stephanie Parker was the catalyst for Kirsty's trauma.

'This isn't Stephanie Parker's fault,' he said.

'But how can I think otherwise? I know we've spoken about this before, but I just can't bring myself to look at her in any other way.'

'You can't blame her for this. Jim only knew her in the early years of his service. Nobody could have known and nobody can be blamed for what happened or for how things turned out.'

'I know, but he obsessed about her disappearance. We had conversations about it. I never thought it would lead to… ' Kirsty's voice trailed away. Jake knew that the whole Tyler incident had left Kirsty with an open wound. Although she masked it well now, it was always just gnawing away under the surface, which is why he could do no other than stay by her side. To support her when she needed him. He was also acutely aware that his own feelings for her needed to be thrown into this emotional maelstrom. He needed, no, wanted, to make her smile and laugh again, but knew that was still a long way off.

'Stephanie Parker is not here and she's not on anyone's radar. And she shouldn't stay on yours, Kirsty.'

'I know I'm a little paranoid about it, Jake. This feeling just won't go away. I suppose I need to blame something or someone and she is the only one directly involved that I can hold on to.'

Jake was quiet for a moment. 'You know that there have been many incidents that continue to haunt me, as I am sure that there are many autopsies that you would prefer to forget?'

She nodded slightly.

'Our jobs put us in front of bad stuff every day. It's what we signed up to. And we have to find a strategy to cope with it. I know this situation is a little different for both of us, but you have to realise Kirsty, that one day you will wake up and instinctively know that you've put it away in a box in your head, and be able to think about the good things and not the trauma.

'One of my younger officers asked me this morning how I coped dealing with fatal road accidents, seeing dead people and dealing with their relatives.'

'What did you tell him?'

'I told him what I told you at the start of all this. How do you cope with the dead? How do you cope with doing what you do, day in and day out? You hide it away, in here,' he tapped his head, 'and you have to hope that it stays hidden away. The thing is, that stuff happens in life to bring it all back again. It's like,' he paused, 'taking LSD ten or twenty years ago, then having a flashback when you least expect it.'

'But how long does it take? How long have I got to put myself through this. I try to forget about all the bad, Jake. I really try. I don't want to forget Jim, but all I see when I think of him is his burnt watch and wedding ring the officer showed me as identification. I feel I'm losing the good memories that Jim and I had, only to be replaced by what I saw on that day.'

Jake could see that Kirsty was both frustrated and tearful. 'Let me tell you,' he said, gently turning her head towards him. 'It never goes away. The feelings only subside with time and then you are left with the good memories.

'You know, I remember the face of every dead person I have ever seen, in the situation in which they died. As a young cop it was terrifying, it kept me awake at night. We didn't have a welfare department then, we had to deal with it in our own way. Find a way to block the bad out. They were there, every time I closed my eyes. Believe me when I say that over time it becomes easier and their images may fade from your conscious thought, but they are still there – locked away.

'In fact, it's a bit like those remains found at Fulborough Wood, which still recline in your mortuary,' Jake said, trying to change the subject a little.

'It's not my morgue anymore,' she whispered.

'To me, it'll always be yours, Kirsty.' Jake smiled at her and she reciprocated, but her smile faded quickly.

They continued walking in silence, until she slipped her arm out of Jake's, when they reached an empty bench. Jake handed Kirsty her packet of sandwiches that they'd bought from the hospital restaurant.

The sun glinted off the river and the tops of the boats in

the marina, as they sat in contemplative silence, eating their sandwiches. Jake could see that Kirsty was thinking about Jim again. He'd learned to recognise the signs of her deep thoughtfulness about her husband over the last year, along with the turning of her wedding ring, which she had refused to remove after an explosive argument with her father.

'Look,' Jake said lowering his voice as a couple walked passed them and turning towards her, breaking the silence, 'this whole Parker thing. You can't let it consume you.' He took her hand and held it lightly in his.

She looked away. There was a pause before she replied. 'You know it's difficult for me, Jake, and I know you understand, don't you?'

Jake wondered whether he should continue with the next part of the conversation. He knew how she might react.

'I do, yes, but I also know that there comes a time when you need to, well… let it go. You know, you've done so well these last months and this is the only thing that seems to be holding you back from getting on with your life.'

Kirsty removed her hand from his, and looked him in the eye, before saying quietly, 'I don't have a life, Jake – it ended when Jim died.'

Jake saw a small tear forming in one of her eyes and, in an attempt to distract her, he held up both hands in surrender.

'Hey, sorry but… ' He tipped his head to one side and smiled. Her gaze softened.

'You're right, of course, and I'm glad you've been at my side, even if you do say things that I don't want to hear.' She finally returned his smile. 'It's so very difficult, and it can't have been easy for you either. I forget that he was your friend and colleague. I'm so wrapped up in my own grief and sorrow.'

Jake nodded slowly.

'Even my month in Spain didn't help much,' Kirsty continued. 'Belinda is only my age and she was so kind and considerate, but she spent most of the time fussing around me like an old mother hen.'

They both laughed at the lighter moment, but that was lost when Jake's phone rang. He glanced at who was calling and answered it. 'What?'

He listened. 'I said I'd be there on the date we've already arranged.' Jake terminated the call as quickly as he'd answered it.

He sighed deeply and looked over towards the marina.

'Are you OK?' Kirsty asked.

'Yeah… but I think lunch is over I'm afraid.'

'Duty?' she asked.

'No, the ex, always manages to interrupt me getting on with my life. We're trying to arrange to hand over the keys of the house to the estate agent. When she can't make it we re-arrange. And she's been incommunicado since she left. I can never get hold of her and neither can the estate agent.'

'How many times have you tried?'

'This'll be the third time. The agent isn't bothered, but when I can't make it all hell breaks loose, pisses me off, it really does.'

'Can't you just hand the keys to the agent?'

'I could I suppose, but if I'm honest, I'm a little reluctant to let it go.'

Kirsty stood, but said nothing.

'Come on, I'll walk you back to work.'

8

The command corridor at police headquarters is generally a hushed environment. The corridors to the offices of the command secretariat had deep pile blue carpet and grey walls, interspersed with scenic views of Northamptonshire, past chief officers and the odd Major Crimes, one of them being the fire in the mid-eighties at British Pepper and Spice.

Detective Inspector Fletcher Randall took time to look at the photos, as he waited to see the Assistant Chief Constable, Colin Marland.

It was Randall's first day as a Detective Inspector and his first day in a new force. He'd taken advantage of an advertisement to apply for the Detective Inspector's role in Northants. Most of his service had been with Thames Valley Police and living on the Northamptonshire/Buckinghamshire border, he didn't even have to move.

Randall was 5'9", of stocky build, and liked to keep himself fit, but it wasn't an obsession. He wore a pair of in-vogue unframed spectacles, a moustache, and had standard-length light brown hair. He'd joined Thames Valley Police after spending time in the Army. He'd met his wife, Annabelle and lost her, a front-line army medic, after only having been married for three years. She died under fire while attempting to administer to the wounds of his platoon, who'd come under attack while on active service.

Randall was invalided out of the Army as a result of his wounds, which were obvious from the long scar on the left-hand side of his face and, when the weather was cold, a limp on his right side from shrapnel embedded in his hip, close to his spine.

Applying to join the police was a long shot, but he managed to get through the assessments. At twenty-five he was surprised when they took him on. Getting a promotion to Inspector in the short time that he had been in the job was another bonus, but living alone he'd become a bit of a bookworm, so spent his time studying for his promotion to Sergeant then to Inspector. As an officer in the army, he thought his new bosses wanted to get him up the ladder as quickly as possible.

Being promoted into a job vacated by the murder of Detective Inspector Jim Kingsfield he knew, probably better than most, about jumping into a dead man's shoes.

Randall stood in front of the full-length mirror in the corridor and adjusted the plain tie he had decided to wear on his first day. The red of the tie stood out against the grey pinstripe suit he was wearing. He squirmed a bit, as he adjusted himself. He didn't like wearing suits or a collar and tie. After the formality of the Army's Officer's Mess, he much preferred to dress down whenever he could. But not today.

As CID in his old force, he spent most of the time in polo shirts and jeans, which matched his personal dress style.

But of course, as he'd been promoted and got two stars on his shoulder again, he realised that he was going to have to set an example to the officers under his command – whoever they might be.

He heard the door to the ACCs office open, followed by laughter and another senior officer wandered out. As he passed him, he acknowledged him with a brief nod, before striding off down the corridor.

Right then, he thought, ready or not, and walked towards the open door, only to be confronted by a small portly man of about 5', who waddled away down the corridor.

'Back in a minute – need a pee.'

Randall stood open mouthed as he passed him leaving him standing at his door. He turned around to the office opposite the ACC's, which he discovered was his Personal Assistant.

'Is he always like that?' he asked of the woman sitting behind the desk.

She smiled. 'He's in a good mood today, otherwise he would have just ignored you.'

'Is that supposed to comfort me?' he smiled warmly at the PA and she returned the smile.

'I assume you're DI Randall?'

'You assume correctly.'

'Take a seat. I'm sure he won't be long.' She indicated a seat opposite her desk. Randall walked into the medium-sized wood-panelled office, which had the smell of fresh polish, reminiscent of a museum, and took the seat offered. He glanced around. The sun was streaming in through the window and he watched flecks of dust floating in the sunlight.

'Can I get you a coffee, water or something?' the PA asked.

'No, I'm fine, thanks.' Randall felt like he was sitting waiting for the headmaster to return to give him a good caning. He smiled awkwardly at the secretary again, as he heard Marland coming down the corridor.

'Do you want to come into the office then?' Marland called.

Randall thanked the PA as he left her.

'Take a seat,' Marland barked, ushering him to his much larger office. The office was like the PA, wood-panelled, but with a large bay window overlooking the fields behind headquarters. Shutting the door, he did what he was told.

'Now, Detective Inspector… ' Marland shuffled some papers on his desk, before he found the one he wanted, '… first, I'd like to welcome you to Northamptonshire Police and your new role as Detective Inspector.'

'Thank you, sir, it's good to be here.'

'I'm not going to beat about the bush, Randall,' Marland gabbled in his thick Derbyshire accent, 'do you understand that you will be replacing one of our officers who was tragically murdered last year?'

'Yes, sir, I understand that.'

'You may well encounter some resistance. He was a popular man, a maverick at times, but nonetheless a good detective.'

Randall said nothing.

'If you do encounter inappropriate behaviour because of this, you are to come directly to me at once. Do you understand?'

Randall said nothing.

'Straight away?' Marland looked at him purposefully.

'Yes, sir, straight away,' acknowledged Randall.

'Good, that's that settled then. I've arranged for you to meet our new Detective Chief Inspector at Major Crimes.

He's only been with us for a couple of months – he's an American, on loan for a little while – some exchange thing arranged by my predecessor. He'll fill you in a bit more about how things work around here.'

Marland paused and sat forward in his chair, looking at Randall directly. 'There is one thing.' He glanced at the papers on his desk. 'A cold case that I want to start you on. I've told the DCI that I want something done about it, so he is fully up to speed.'

'A cold case? Old cold or recent cold, sir?'

'We think it's certainly within the last – say – fifteen years.'

Randall listened to Marland explain about the female remains discovered in Fulborough Wood. Identity unknown. DNA was degraded, but there was nothing to test it against to get any reliable information. It was assumed that the death of the woman was caused by Bingham Tyler.

'So we need to get a handle on that.'

'Right, sir, I'll look into it.'

'OK then, and good luck.' Marland stood and shook Randall's hand as he left the office.

That was interesting. Not one question about where I'd come from, why I wanted to come here. Answers he had ready just in case.

Randall asked the PA the route to the Major Crimes Team and made his way down two corridors, before turning right and through the main Incident Room. Randall found the DCI in the corner office. He continued to reflect on his brief encounter with Marland, and couldn't decide whether he liked him or not, as he entered the office of Captain (DCI) Chuck Freeman.

Freeman was a black, six-foot ex-American-football-player, invalided out of the game fifteen years previously.

His hair was cropped extremely short, almost bald, but with obvious signs of grey around the temples. He wore a badly fitting greyish blue suit, which seemed to be at bursting point, a white-and-blue-striped shirt, the collar of which he couldn't do up because of his thick neck, and a loosely knotted blue tie.

From Randall's point of view, the suit just didn't sit right on the shoulders for some reason. Freeman looked up at Randall, as he walked into his office. He offered Randall a seat and coffee. He almost asked him for some donuts, but didn't want to alienate the big American on his initial meeting.

'First day then?' Freeman enquired, in an accent that Randall assumed was middle America. He certainly didn't come from New York.

'Yes, sir.'

'You can drop the sir bit. I don't hold with all that sort of stuff. Chuck will be fine.'

'Yes, sir.' Freeman glanced at Randall.

'So what did Mr Marland tell you?'

'Very little, actually, just hello and welcome, and that you'd fill me in with what's going on and what I'm supposed to be doing. Oh, and he did say something about a cold case he wanted me to work on, something to do with the Kingsfield death.'

'Yes, I only came into that case after it was all over, but we do have unidentified bones, which we need to put a name to. I'll see that you get the papers.'

'Thank you. What sort of team do I have to work with?'

'They are a good group, but the murder of Jim Kingsfield is still raw.'

'I understand. Were any of them involved in the cold case, do you know?'

'Yes, DC Stevens, now a sergeant. Kingsfield's working

partner was Dave Harte. He's since been promoted to Inspector and moved back to a precinct. There were another couple of guys on the periphery.'

'Right, perhaps I ought to speak to them about it some time – get a handle on what it may be about.'

'Good idea. You perhaps also need to speak to Kingsfield's wife. She's a forensic pathologist at the hospital. Still very traumatised about it. I would go to her via the Family Liaison Officer, Sergeant Jordan. He's Traffic.'

'Traffic? How does a murder end up with a traffic FLO?'

'Long story, but as Kingsfield was killed in his car, it fell to Traffic to do the investigation.'

Traffic? thought Randall, bemused. 'You better talk me through it.'

'I'll tell you what I know, but you need to speak to those who were there as well,' Freeman answered. Freeman then explained to Randall the sequence of events leading up to Kingsfield's and Tyler's deaths.

'Wasn't there some story going about that Tyler had escaped the car before being hit by the train? That even got down to my old force.'

'No, I don't think so. From what I've read, there were enough body parts, confirmed by DNA, that convinced everyone that he was in the car when it got hit.'

'Right, I'll get on to that as soon as I've read the file.'

Freeman nodded, shook his hand and took him to his own workspace.

'When do you want me to meet my team?'

'They'll all be back in here about 16:30, so any time after that. It'll give you plenty of time to settle in.'

9

'Are you going to put us all out of our misery and tell us how you managed to get handcuffed to a lamppost in the middle of the night then, Chris?' Reg Johnson was sitting at a desk with his feet up, mug of coffee in his hand as they were all close to the end of their shift. Prentice had just completed writing the press release for the A5 fatal collision.

'I think he'll tell us when he's ready,' Jake called from his office. He stood and walked out into the crew room. 'Although,' he said smiling, 'we really ought to be told. So we can scotch any rumours.'

Prentice stood up from his work-station and wandered over to the window. He looked out across the Northamptonshire countryside and the setting sun, with his back to his colleagues. Hearing the office door open, he turned to see who it was, smiled, then said, 'It's all his fault.'

Everyone turned to see DS Clive Stevens entering the room.

'What?'

'You were supposed to have watched my back last night, Clive, that's what.'

'I did! You look like shite, by the way.'

'Thanks for that.'

'So, come on then, out with it,' Jake said.

'OK, OK.' Prentice sighed and pushed himself away from the windowsill, sitting down in the nearest chair. 'If you laugh, I'm leaving and never coming back,' he grumbled.

'We won't. We promise.' Stevens said.

'Yeah right.'

Everyone waited in anticipation until Prentice cleared his throat. 'When I got to the bar, Stevens here had already lined up a row of shots. Standing there like he is now, with a big grin on his face.'

'I thought it'd get you off to a flying start,' he said. 'Downed all twelve in quick succession. Quite impressive for one so young.'

'I just got more and more pissed. We then decided to go to the club next door and they continued to ply me with a range of cocktails, shots and beer. I swear I'll never drink so much again. Don't exactly think I'm firing on all cylinders at the moment.'

Jake predicted as much at the start of the day. 'I knew you'd hit the wall sooner or later, Chris,' he said.

Prentice went on. 'Now, as far as I can remember at this point, we staggered out of the pub entrance, colliding with a woman with blonde hair. She looked hot. Short skirt, lovely legs, I seem to remember. I apologised to her in a pissed sort of way, while Clive dragged me from her.'

'Way out of your class,' Stevens commented. 'Didn't want to get you into any trouble.'

'And a lot of help you were. You got just as pissed as me. Neither of us knew what we were doing half the night.'

'The club was dark with a few spinning lights. But it was packed, both of us finding it difficult to get to the bar through the gaggle of scantily dressed women. Eventually we went back to the pub, because it was too busy and you couldn't hold a decent conversation, let alone order a drink.'

'I told Clive that the woman I'd bumped into earlier was sitting on her own at the end of the bar. So, I decided to go and chat her up.'

'I did advise him against it,' Stevens said.

'Yeah, but you bet me a fiver that I wouldn't leave with her.'

'Lost my bet then, you could say.'

'Unfortunately, I can't remember much after that, until I found myself in the street.'

'So, what happened then?' Jake asked, who by this time had taken a chair at an empty desk. Some other officers had also entered the crew-room and were listening to Prentice's story.

'It was when I went to move my arms to pull my coat round me, that I realised I couldn't move them. I was cold. My head was pounding, like the beat base at a rave. I looked around to see if I could recognise where I was. Didn't initially, but thought it might be on the eastern side of town. It was then that I saw that I was,' a beat, 'stark bollock naked.' The room erupted in laughter. 'Yeah, you just laugh at my predicament, why don't you?'

'And what else was there, Chris?' Johnson asked.

Prentice considered the floor for a moment, then said, 'Securing me to the lamp post were a pair of pink fluffy handcuffs.' More laughter. 'I tried to stand up, but I was cold and stiff. Anyway, what really worried me shitless was a group of lads that were getting closer and closer. I knew that before long they would be gathered around me, taking the piss. I tried to pull at the handcuffs, but they wouldn't come apart and I couldn't find anything to undo them with, so I just rattled them on the lamppost. Some house lights came on and I hoped they called three nines.'

'Good job somebody did, or we'd probably still be looking for you,' Jake said.

'You might just have been looking for a body instead,' Prentice moaned. 'They taunted me, kicked me and one pissed all over my back. So, as you can see I'm not exactly happy about it, but at least you can prevent the rumour mill from starting up. So now you know.'

There was silence in the room. The laughter had stopped. The assembled officers beginning to realise how serious it could have all been. Reg Johnson stood.

'Folks, I give you my young crew-mate, "Piston Prentice".'

There was a round of applause, but Jake knew that the incident would probably haunt Prentice for the rest of his service.

10

The central police station on Campbell Square is a white sandstone building. Built in the 1930s, along with the fire station next door. It stands on the site of the Victorian Northampton Gaol. It not only housed the police station on the ground floor, but also the Magistrates Court on the first floor.

Number One court, originally the Court of Assize, would remind anyone of any age of a traditional court of law. It was very Old Baileyesque: oak benches and dock, with the magistrates sitting on a raised dais, looking down on both the accused and the witnesses. The smell of polish and fear permeated the courtroom.

Jake had arrived early to give evidence on a minor traffic matter, situated to the side of the No.1 Court. It was empty, so he went down into the bowels of the station to the canteen. It was small, compared to some canteens. The serving hatch was directly on the left-hand wall as he went in, with a small preparation area behind the hatch. Despite its size, the two kitchen staff managed to produce a fairly decent breakfast, lunch if you wanted it, and an evening meal. That day, Jake opted for a simple bacon butty and wondered how much longer the force would maintain such a service. He knew that eventually it would go the way of other canteens in the county, sandwich and drinks machines and a microwave in the corner.

As he entered the canteen and ordered his butty, he caught sight of newly promoted Inspector, Dave Harte, Jim Kingsfield's old Detective Sergeant. Harte looked uncomfortable in uniform, showing his bright new silver stars on his shoulders. Jake collected a coffee, and went to join him, who looked up, as Jake's shadow fell across him.

'You seem a bit out of place here, Jake,' Harte said warmly.

'No more than you do in that uniform.'

'Tell me about it. I much prefer my suit. Anyway, what brings you here?'

'Traffic court,' Jake said as he sat down opposite. 'The guy probably won't turn up or plead guilty on arrival. That's usually par for the course.'

Harte nodded, but said nothing and kept eating.

Jake took a slug of his coffee. 'So, how are you liking your new job then, Dave?'

'It's OK, if you want to nursemaid new sergeants and probationers. I spend more time doing paperwork, than getting out on the street. Can't believe how much of it there is. Nightmare,' he said, wiping his plate with a large chunk of bread.

'What about the DI role going in CID?'

'Not a chance, not had these long enough.' He indicated the pips on his shoulder.

'Ah, I see, any word on those Fulborough remains?' Jake asked casually.

'No, not a word.'

'Did you know that the new forensic pathologist wants to get rid of them, get them buried?'

'No, I've not heard anything, but there again, I'm not really kept in the loop anymore. Who told you?'

'Kirsty. I said I'd check it out.'

'There's a new Detective Chief Inspector, who's running the department. An American Captain on some exchange scheme. Running it without two DIs, by all accounts.'

'Shouldn't you have been asked?'

'I was. They wanted me to go acting, but I said I didn't want it. Didn't see it as right, stepping into Jim's shoes, you know.'

Jake nodded and took another slug of his coffee, as his bacon butty was placed on the table in front of him. He nodded again in thanks.

'How's Kirsty?' Harte asked. 'I've not seen her since the funeral.'

'She's finding it difficult, as you would expect, but she's coping, just.'

'Difficult losing a partner. I hope I never have to cope with anything like that.'

Jake tucked into his butty and, as Harte was putting the finishing touches to his breakfast, a young constable approached them.

'Inspector?'

'Yes, constable. What can I do for you?'

'You're needed upstairs, sir, something about Fulborough Wood.'

Jake looked at Harte and raised an eyebrow. 'That's just spooky.'

'Indeed it is, perhaps it'll get me back on the enquiry.' Harte smiled and rubbed his hands in mock glee. He collected his kit off the back of the chair and walked towards the door. Before leaving, he turned to Jake. 'Do you want to come up as well?'

Jake thought for a moment. 'I'll see what's happening with this court case then catch up with you.'

Harte agreed, and carried on out of the canteen.

Jake took time to finish his sandwich, mulling over the previous day's events. Andy Thomas the collision investigator had briefly spoken to him at the scene and he was concerned about a number of things that made him and Jake think that the collision was a little out of the ordinary. He'd sent him off to do some digging.

Jake wiped his mouth with a serviette, collected his mug and plate and placed it on the table by the serving hatch. Wishing the canteen staff a good day, he went back upstairs to the court.

The traffic matters were usually held in court number three and, as he approached the open doorway, he was met by the court usher. She told him that the case was to be adjourned. The defendant had called in to say that he was ill. Not being surprised at this information, Jake went downstairs to join Harte.

As he entered the front office, Jake saw a man, who looked like a construction worker, standing the other side of the counter talking to the office clerk.

Harte beckoned him over. 'Apparently, Jake, some suspicious goings-on at Fulborough Wood.'

'Again?'

Harte nodded towards the man standing at the desk, who he turned his attention to. 'I'm Inspector Harte. I was on the Major Crimes unit during that case twelve months ago. You can speak to me and my colleague if you wish?'

The man, who gave his name as Harry Bagshaw, stared at the both of them. 'I suppose so,' he said after a moment. 'Could we talk somewhere more private?' he added, glancing around.

'Sure. Monica, would you put him in interview one for me please?'

Monica nodded and invited Bagshaw into the police station. Jake followed Harte to the interview room on the ground floor. As he sat down, she offered him a drink, but he declined. They both sat down opposite Bagshaw. The room wasn't like the interview rooms in the justice centre, stark and smelling of disinfectant. This room was carpeted, cleaned regularly, soundproofed and hushed.

'I'll record this, if you don't mind?' Harte said holding up two CDs, which he picked up from under the machine.

Bagshaw just shrugged. Jake took a back seat and watched Harte begin the interview. He decided not to interrupt, unless absolutely necessary. After going through the formalities, including stating his full name, Harte asked, 'Mr Bagshaw, how can we help you this morning?'

'First off, I don't want anyone to know who came to you with this information, as it would get me into deep trouble. The sort of trouble that wouldn't end well for me.'

'I see. Have you been threatened?'

Bagshaw nodded.

'For the recording please.'

'Oh, yes, I have.'

'By who?'

'I'd rather not say at this time.'

'What do you want to tell us then?'

'A few weeks ago we were working in Fulborough Wood. His Lordship wanted rid of it, since all that other fuss.'

'Yes, I know. I was one of the detectives who worked on the case.'

Bagshaw looked at Jake.

'I was involved as well,' was all Jake said.

Bagshaw nodded, evidently satisfied. 'OK.'

He went on to explain that Lord Fulborough wanted to destroy the wood and use it for something else. And to dissuade the rubberneckers that came and wandered all over the site in the hope that they would solve the mystery like The Continental Op or Philip Marlowe.

'You like a bit of hard-boiled crime fiction?' Jake asked.

Bagshaw looked towards him. 'Some of it, yes. Anyway, we'd been working for most of the morning, removing the remaining tree stumps and then we found it. At first I thought it was just a roll of carpet.'

'Right. Go on.'

'I was operating the excavator and, as I pulled up this roll of carpet, we saw it was… ' Bagshaw stuttered.

'What did you find, Harry?' Harte said.

Bagshaw looked down at the table and stared at his large hands that lay flaccid and almost disconnected from the rest of his body. When he looked up again, Jake saw that there were tears forming in his eyes, but he quickly composed himself.

'We found a body – a skelington.'

Jake smiled at Bagshaw's pronunciation of skeleton, but was surprised by what he'd said. Another body? More of Tyler's victims? Will the spectre of that man ever go away? The last thing we need is a psychopath's burial ground. The press will be hyping it up and pissing all over the police like they normally do.

'Harry, why didn't you call us immediately?'

'It wasn't my call to make, or the foreman for that matter. He took his orders from the estate manager.'

'That'll be Frank Philpott, if my memory's correct?'

'Yes, right. He and the foreman went away and discussed what to do, then he came back and told us – to bury it.'

'Excuse me? You did what?' Harte said, looking over at Jake.

'And what did you do?' Jake asked.

'We did as we were told.'

'Did you not argue the point. That was the wrong thing to do?'

'There was little resistance. Philpott gave us a grand each and two-grand to the foreman to keep quiet.'

'Who's the foreman?' Harte asked.

'Bloke named Ian Morton. I've worked with him since he took over the company – evil bastard if you ask me.'

'Name's familiar. So, where is your money?'

'I gave it back to Morton this morning. He wasn't happy about it. That's when he threatened me. He had me up against his motor with his fist in my face.'

'If I've got this right then, Philpott paid you all off to rebury the remains of a body you found?'

'Yes.'

'Why?'

'I don't know. Some talk about delaying what Fulborough had planned for the site. But I think there was more to it than that. The look on Philpott's face said it all.'

'Was Lord Fulborough party to this agreement?'

'No, I think it was between Philpott and Morton.'

'How long have you worked for Morton?'

'Morton has only been in charge for three, possibly four years. I worked for the previous owner on and off for most of my life. They were reasonable employers, until Morton got his hands on the whole company. Don't think I'll be working there for much longer particularly when he finds out what I've done.'

'There's no reason for him to find out unless you tell him,' Jake said.

'Why have you come to us now then?'

'Inspector, I have been arguing with my conscience, ever since this happened. I am a religious man. I go to church on Sunday. I couldn't let it fester inside me any longer.' He tapped his chest as he said it.

'Do you have any family?'

'My wife passed away several years ago – cancer – and I haven't seen my son for twenty years. Last I heard he was in Australia.'

'I'm sorry to hear all that, but I can assure you that you have done the right thing by coming here. You realise, however, that by admitting what you've done, you and the others have committed a serious offence.'

'I understand that, yes.'

'I have no alternative in this matter but to arrest you. Do you understand?'

'Yes, I was prepared for this. I've sat for an hour in your car park trying to pluck up the courage,' he gave an etiolated smile.

'Very well. Harold Bagshaw, I am arresting you on suspicion of concealing a body. You do not have to say anything, but it may harm your defence, if you do not mention when questioned, something which you later rely on in court. Anything you do say will be given in evidence. Do you understand?'

'Yes, I do.'

They all exited the interview room, after Harte stopped and retrieved his CDs. As they did so, Harte bumped into the young probationary constable, he'd seen earlier.

'Ah, Aiden, do me a favour and take Mr Bagshaw to the CJC, will you? And book him in for me. He's been arrested for concealing a body.'

Aiden Bentley handcuffed Bagshaw and led him away towards the rear of the station.

'What do you think about that?' Jake said.

'Doesn't it make you wonder what actually has gone on in Fulborough Wood?'

'It makes me question whether there are any more, that's what.'

'I agree. What if Tyler used the place to dispose of all his bodies?'

'We could be looking at remains going back years.'

'Problem is, there would be no reason to investigate.'

'But they'll have to investigate this, surely. If I was Senior Investigating Officer, I'd want to dig up the whole bloody wood.'

'Yeah and that's the point – the case is cold and closed. Why go digging any further?'

'So, what are you going to do, Dave?'

'I'm going up to Major Crimes at HQ, see if I can convince them to look a bit deeper into Fulborough and re-start the enquiry.'

'Tell me how it goes, will you?' Jake smiled.

'As soon as I know something, you will.'

'OK, but I don't want Kirsty involved too much, if at all. She's not ready for it yet.'

Harte nodded in understanding to Jake

'I feel that there will be more turmoil to come up there and it's my duty as her FLO to ensure she is kept away from it as much as possible' as he headed out of the door.

11

Second Monday – Rachel – Two Weeks Later

In the middle of the afternoon, Rachel felt decidedly unwell. Even after her usual nights out with the girls, she had always prided herself on getting to work the following day on time, happy and certainly not hungover. She was only twenty-two after all, and quite capable of staying out late and getting in to work on time the following day.

But she was always careful, kept her drinks covered and never finished them if she had left them unattended. Not that she believed that it would happen to her. The trolls usually went for the pretty blondes or brunettes. She, on the other hand, had short mousy brown hair. She didn't consider herself fat, but knew that she wasn't thin either. She was happy and confident with herself and the way she looked, and that's all that mattered.

As she drove to work, along the Nene Valley Way, she thought again about how, when she'd woken up that morning, she had felt out of sorts. Not bad enough for her to take a sick day. But she felt even worse. She knew that she would get the third degree from Connie about being out on the town the previous night, if she asked to go home. So, she went into work as normal, trying to think of how and why she felt so ill.

She stayed at her desk, not really concentrating on her work. She looked around the office. Her workspace was part of a large, open-plan office with partitions. Even the managers worked on the same floor. There were no special offices for managers or supervisors. It was supposed to ensure that the team worked together. There were motivational pictures on the wall – GOAL, PERSISTENCE and the ones that really pissed her off, 'THERE'S NO I IN TEAM' and 'ASSUME – makes an ASS out of U and ME.'

It was not the job she intended to do when she left school. After all, she got straight 'A's in her GCSEs and should have gone to uni, but couldn't find a place. So she was left on the shelf, a bit like her personal life.

God, my head hurts, she thought. She called to her colleague sitting opposite. 'Hey, Gill, just how much did I have to drink last night? I feel crap.'

'Not much,' Gill responded, keeping her head down.

'What do you mean by not much?'

Gill looked up from her work. 'Erm… you only had a couple of lagers in a bottle, then a load of shots and, of course, the wine before we all went out.'

'That's nothing to what I normally have. Although… shots?' questioned Rachel. 'I never drink shots.'

'So you tell me. You were knocking a few of them back.' She smiled at her knowingly.

'So, why do I feel so bad?'

'Must have been something you ate.'

'But I didn't eat anything.'

'You must have, as you left with that blonde girl. You seemed to be getting on with quite well, if you know what I mean.'

'No, I don't. And what blonde girl?'

'The one in that mini-dress, bit of a looker, probably bent as a nine-bob note, as my old dad would say, but you seemed OK with her.'

'So, what happened? I've no memory of anything that happened last night?'

'She was sitting at the bar on her own and came on to you. You carried on talking and drinking with her, and then left. Don't you remember anything?'

'Nope, not a thing.'

'She must have put something in your drink then.'

'How could she? You know how careful I am.'

'It must have happened either before you left or afterwards. Where did you go?'

'As I said,' Rachel was more frustrated, 'I don't know. I can't remember.' She put her head down and sighed. She rubbed her face and moved her mousy brown hair back from her forehead.

'You were both downing shots, as if they were going out of fashion. The rest of us left you to it. You seemed to be enjoying yourself so much.'

'I must have had a skinful. Christ, I feel really unwell.'

'Where did you leave the blonde?'

'As I said, I don't remember any blonde.'

'OK, if you say so.' Gill left it there and put her head down to get back to work. She had noticed Connie hovering in the background and didn't want to get involved in a conversation with her.

'All right, how did I get home?'

Gill looked up again, glancing around the room to see where Connie was. 'You came back to us just as we were leaving, so we all went home in the usual way.'

'Oh.' Rachel looked at the clock on the wall in front of her. 13.30, its red numerals flickered. She got up from her desk and walked over to her supervisor. She spoke quietly with him then returned to her workstation and, without a further word, left to go home.

Heading out of the Brackmills Industrial Estate, Rachel drove her Fiat 500 out onto the A45 towards Wellingborough, then left onto the Lumbertubs Way.

As she drove along the dual carriageway a bit slower than the fifty miles per hour speed limit, she felt a little drowsy. She took a swig of the Coca-Cola she had open in the cup holder. It didn't do any good, because it was flat and she spluttered a bit as she drank.

Leaving Northampton through Moulton and out onto the A43 heading toward Kettering, she thought she'd soon be back home in Broughton, where she could lie down and recover from her hangover. She reasoned that the journey home should be quick as she got onto the open road. It was usually a tiresome journey, particularly if you got stuck behind a slow-moving vehicle.

Throughout the journey, she felt more and more unwell. Everything was swimming in front of her, in and out of focus. She hallucinated; spiders on the windscreen that she tried to bat off with the wipers. But her main concern was keeping it together until she got home. Feeling panicked, as she passed the Red House crossroads, she felt her feet and hands going numb, her eyelids getting heavier and, as she passed the turning for Walgrave, she blacked out.

She was suddenly awoken by the blare of a car horn. She opened her eyes to see that she had drifted onto the wrong side of the road and a large van was heading directly towards her, the driver with his hand firmly planted on his horn and a look of horror on his face. To Rachel it sounded like a ship's foghorn, blaring away, filling her senses.

She wrenched the steering wheel of the little Fiat violently to the left to try to avoid the van, but it was too late. The van hit the Fiat, spinning it out of control and across the road where the large kerbstone lifted the little car off its wheels and over the barrier.

It slithered and rolled down a steep embankment towards a water filled ditch. Despite her seat belt, Rachel was thrown about the vehicle, smashing her head and smashing the door window, then, as the vehicle rolled, hitting the gear lever, the front windscreen. Door post, gear lever, windscreen. Door post, gear lever, windscreen. Over and over again.

The Fiat came to rest, upside down in the ditch. Rachel was unconscious, hanging in her seat belt. The vehicle slowly slipped further and further into the ditch, but she knew nothing of the dirty water that freely entered her lungs, drowning out her life.

12

There was a time when Jake thought he might like CID, but he'd never been a big one for the gallons of alcohol they managed to imbibe in one session. He preferred to savour his drinks; a whiskey, or a nice wine in a more relaxed atmosphere, as opposed to throwing as much beer down his neck as he could in the shortest time possible. If you didn't fit in with that culture you may as well have given up. Which is what he'd done.

He was still interested in the investigation of serious crime. He did, after all, look after the major collisions and road deaths for the county, until he'd been taken off that duty. Another Tyler legacy. So now, in his down time at work, Jake spent it sitting in his new office, reviewing the never-ending array of statistics that constantly occupied his time. Reviews of officers' traffic offence reports were few and far between unless something had gone wrong, where the officer needed guidance or more frequently, a bollocking.

He did enjoy the cut and thrust of a shift out on the street, doing what he always thought he was best at. He'd be foolish if he didn't recognise the fact that his visit to Ian Morton's place with Dave Harte a few days earlier kept his interest in the Fulborough Wood case alive.

There was no indication of the bribe Morton had taken from Philpott to hide the remains, and Harte wanted to get a handle on the guy before passing it to the new DI. And when his supposed girlfriend turned up with a mouth like a drain, that just made his day.

He sat back in his chair and rubbed his hands through his hair. The next problem was his ex. At this point in his career and personal life, he seemed only to be treading water, with no real chance of moving up the ranks, certainly not after the last twelve months' troubles.

His breakup with Rosie, almost nine months earlier, didn't help his situation either. She had made no outward effort to save their marriage. Yes, she said and did what she thought was right, cooking, talking about work as if nothing was amiss, but he shuddered at the thought of his big, fat brother-in-law trucker getting it on with his wife. It was strange, that even after it was revealed that Rosie was having it away with Gaffney, her sister Elizabeth, Gaffney's wife hadn't even disowned her. It became clear from a conversation he'd had with Rosie that she would be glad to see the back of Adam.

Reaching for his cup, Jake took a mouthful of tea, looked in the mug and turned up his nose. Cold. He opened his top drawer and took a biscuit from the packet that he'd bought from the local garage on his way to work. He flicked his way through another statistical report about speed enforcement targets and casually brushed away the crumbs he'd dropped on it, then picked up a planning report for the forthcoming European goods vehicle check on the M1 later in the month. He threw it back into his overflowing in-tray, not really having any inclination to read it. He sat back and rubbed his eyes. Time to get out on the street.

There was a polite knock on his open office door. He looked up to see Beccy Burnett standing on the threshold. She entered before being asked.

'Jake, got a minute?'

'Always Beccy,' he smiled. Her investigation with the force SIO, Detective Chief Superintendent Colin Marland, before being promoted to Assistant Chief Constable following Tyler's death, was commended for its diligence and professionalism. The sheer number of exhibits from the destroyed police Volvo and the express train filled an aircraft hangar. Their investigation concluded that enough body parts were recovered from the collision to prove, through DNA evidence, that Bingham Tyler was well and truly dead. Even though some witnesses were adamant that he jumped out of the car before the collision.

Beccy sat down in the chair opposite Jake against the back wall of the office. There was a large window behind his desk, over which he had a view of the trading estate, where they now resided.

'Got a quick question for you.'

'Fire away,' he said leaning back in his chair, waiting.

'You're still FLO'ing Kirsty Kingsfield?'

Jake nodded.

Beccy looked around his office and not directly at him.

'Come on, Beccy, you wouldn't have come from your office on the top floor to ask me a question which you could easily have asked me on the phone.'

'Perhaps I just wanted a break?' she smiled.

Jake was sceptical about that. 'I know that look, Beccy. Something's up, so what is it?'

Beccy looked at Jake for a moment. 'How often do you visit her?'

'Not that often.'

She tilted her head slightly and smiled. 'Really?'

'Yes, really. We're not an item you know, if that's what you think. You know I'm not like that. I don't take advantage, do I?'

He gave her a meaningful look, knowing that Beccy knew what the answer to that was.

'It's not me who's thinking that. Personally, I think you'd make a fine couple.'

'Don't go there, Beccy. It's bad enough with one affair in my marriage, let alone two. Anyway, she has no desires on me. I'm just there to help her through the trauma of losing her husband to a psychopath, which was less than twelve months ago – or have you forgotten?' Jake sounded a little terse, which certainly wasn't what he intended. He was not letting on about what feelings he did have for Kirsty. 'I'm sorry, Beccy, but it takes time to recover from such trauma. She just sees me as her confidant, that's all and as an FLO, that's part of my job.'

'OK, I believe you, but… ' Beccy stood to go. 'Just a heads-up, there are certain elements who think you're too close to her, so be careful.'

Jake gave Beccy a mock salute. 'Aye, aye, sir. Noted.'

As Beccy turned to go, there was another knock on the door. Jake nodded to Beccy in acknowledgement and indicated for his new visitor to come into his office as she left.

'In trouble with the boss again, Jake?'

'Don't you start before you've even got through the door, Andy.'

PC Andy Thomas was a forensic collision investigator who had many years' experience in various units on the traffic department. But his best work was that of a collision investigator with the road death unit. He'd been on the unit for six years and was one of the most experienced collision investigators Jake had. When Andy pitched up in any supervisor's office saying he had a problem, then most listened to what he had to say.

Andy was of average height for a copper, fairly fit with black, receding hair swept back that revealed a deep widow's peak. A Londoner, who, having seen the light, decamped from the Met up into 'the sticks'.

'OK. Andy, what's up?'

Andy pulled up the chair Beccy had just vacated, so it was close to Jake's desk, and laid out four files.

'There's definitely a problem with these fatal files, that I mentioned to you a little while ago and I'm concerned,' he said, as he sat down.

'What concerns you, particularly?'

'Well, just so you don't think I'm going mad, I'd like you to read the toxicology reports from all of them.' Andy stood and removed the relevant reports from the folders and placed them on the top of each file which he placed on Jake's desk. 'As you read them,' he continued, 'you will see that alcohol is not a contributing factor in any of these collisions. There is no significance in the location. There is no correlation between the times of the collisions. In fact, there are no correlating factors between any of them, except one.'

Jake spread the four reports out on his desk.

'In fact, for all intents and purposes, these are four unrelated fatal collisions, all within the last two months.'

'Go on.' Jake needed to hear where this was going.

Andy sat back heavily in the chair, which by now he'd

moved to the front of Jake's desk. He took back the files, leaving Jake with the toxicology reports. Holding up each report as he spoke, he gave Jake a review of the files.

'This fatal: M1 Southbound, two vehicles, decapitation, Mazda MX-5 taken out by the trailer of a forty-four tonner. Number two: A6003, Corby, single vehicle leaves carriageway into a tree. Number three: A5 Northbound, Watford Gap, mum dead, dad seriously injured, two traumatised kids. Number four: A43, Gibwood bend, female driver leaves the carriageway ends up upside-down in the ditch and drowns.'

As Andy was explaining the collisions, Jake was carefully reading through the toxicology reports. He looked up. 'Four reports. Four different pathologists. Four different toxicology screens. And?'

'And what anomalies can you see in the reports?'

'I don't see anything that stands out. Nothing to link them that I can see.'

'But there is something – and before you say it, I've checked all our other fatals for the last twelve months. Only these four last fatals have this.'

He pointed to each of the reports on Jake's desk. 'See here, all of them have recorded an 'unknown substance' on their blood toxicology.'

'But it could be a different one for each of them, couldn't it?'

'It could, but I bet you any money it isn't.'

Jake thought for a further moment. 'I really can't see any significance at this point, Andy, unless you have some other evidence. What would you have me do?'

'Take it to Major Crimes?'

'What and tell them that I think we have somebody going around, killing off drivers? I'd get laughed out the office.'

'I still think we have something here, Jake.'

'OK, Andy, I'll tell you what we'll do. Go back to pathology and get one toxicologist to check all the samples again. If it turns out that it's the same substance, then we will go to Major Crimes. Is that OK?'

'That's all I needed, Sarge.'

Andy collected his files and left Jake's office. That's all I need, thought Jake, a bloody serial killer targeting drivers.

13

Jake stood at the wooden gate of his former home and looked around the front garden. In the time that they had both moved out, put it up for sale and received an offer quicker than they expected, the front lawn was overgrown, the hawthorn hedge down the left-hand side of the house needed cutting back and a number of plants had died. It looked unkempt, and, although he wasn't the greatest gardener in the world, at least he knew how to keep it tidy.

He took a deep breath to prepare himself for what he knew was going to be a stressful encounter with Rosie.

He would never forget the day when the chase was on to search for Bingham Tyler, only to discover his wife in the arms of his brother-in-law, at the firm where they worked, Gaffney International Haulage.

Tyler had attacked the staff and stolen a truck. If Jake hadn't been the closest unit to the yard and, out of concern for his wife, got there first, he might never have known about her affair with Gaffney. And if it weren't for the court order to monitise the estate equally, Jake wouldn't be in the position of giving up his house, so she could have her half.

He walked up the driveway towards the brown lacquered front door and let himself in. He remembered how much time it took to decide on whether to paint it a colour or just leave it as natural wood. He smiled, thinking about those better days, before all this trouble.

He entered the light-coloured spacious hallway, a contrast to the darkness of the front door. He went straight upstairs to the bathroom, he needed the loo.

On the day that he was supposed to have come to the house to hand it over to the estate agents, Jake never made it. He'd been called to an emergency on the A14. The estate agent understood and re-arranged. There was no rush from the new buyers. Rosie, on the other hand, was livid. Another nail in his coffin.

'This is typical!' she had screamed down the phone at him, 'typical of the bloody job interfering with our lives.'

He stood looking at himself in the bathroom mirror, her words echoing in his head. The mirror was the only possession left in the room, apart from a thin, faded old towel, draped over the bath. The mirror was screwed to the wall which he really couldn't be arsed to remove.

Over the last few months he had noticed that silver flecks in his hair were making a break for all to see. A sure sign of advancing years, stress or, more likely, both.

His house was empty. He felt empty. Everything that he had strived for over the past twenty years he'd been in the job was virtually gone: the wife; the nice house; the car – yes she'd had that as well. There were good times with Rosie that he preferred to think about, not the last twelve months. Those he would prefer to forget.

'How did it come to this?' he whispered, to his mirror image, as he washed his hands and threw some water on his face. Drying off with the old towel, he sighed deeply, took one last look at himself in the mirror, noticing, and not for the first time, the dark rings which were in permanent residence under his eyes and went downstairs to join Rosie in the kitchen.

'There are many good memories here.' He smiled an unconvincing smile to the estate agent. The agent had come to ensure that everything was in order, before handing the keys over to the new owners.

He saw Rosie standing and staring out of the kitchen window with her arms folded in front of her, a stern look on her face. She was wearing the dark blue skirt suit, which he still remembered her buying. He also noticed that she appeared to have put on a bit of weight. She turned to him.

'Memories or not, can we go now?' Her voice was cold and unemotional.

'Did you ever like living here?' Jake questioned.

'Now is not a good time to ask that, Jake.'

'I just wondered, that's all. I just can't understand how we got here.'

'Really? Do you want me to spell it out for you?'

'We've never exactly talked about it, have we?'

'And you want to do it now?' she snapped.

'I thought that you might have something to say?'

'There's nothing to say – nothing I want to say.'

A disagreeable silence hung in the air.

Eventually, irritated by it, Rosie continued. 'I'll tell you, shall I? I'll tell you why. It's because of your bloody job, that's why. It's the damned police force that's done this to us: the callouts; the late finishes; the early starts; I never saw you!'

'I think that's a little unfair.' Jake tried to quell his anger at Rosie's attitude, 'You knew what you were letting yourself in for when you married me, so don't try to convince yourself that you didn't understand what might happen. Don't keep banging on about my job being the cause of all this. If you hadn't have been shagging your sister's husband, we wouldn't be in this mess, would we?'

'Don't be so crude.'

Silence.

'Would we?' Jake demanded.

'Don't you dare raise your voice to me, Jacob. If you hadn't been away from home all hours of the day and night, I wouldn't have needed to find comfort elsewhere.'

'Comfort – comfort! You are a sanctimonious bitch. I refuse to accept that we couldn't have worked this out, if you hadn't have gone off with him!'

'That's just your opinion,' Rosie seethed.

Jake noticed that the estate agent had moved towards the front door, out of earshot.

'Why, Rosie, why?' Jake asked, quieter now. 'Didn't you want to save our marriage? And is HE so much better than what we had?'

Rosie just shrugged and remained staring out of the window, biting her top lip. Jake thought he saw a flash of emotion, but her eyes were still cold.

'Well?' he asked again softly.

Rosie turned and looked at him, giving him a hard stare. Shrugging again, she turned and walked out of the kitchen, without saying another word.

'Cold-hearted bitch,' he mumbled, as she walked out into the hallway.

Rosie slapped her set of keys into the hands of the estate agent.

The rawness of the situation had got to Jake. It was like somebody opening a file about their life and ripping out the pages one by one. Slowly destroying that which had gone before – destroying both their lives – and for what?

Jake stood and watched Rosie walk away from him, and he moved towards the front door. The estate agent came and stood next to him, both watching Rosie as she walked down the drive. He took a breath to speak.

'Don't,' said Jake, 'don't say a word and just do your job.'

'I wouldn't presume to comment, sir, I was simply going to ask you for your keys.'

'Hmm, sorry.' Jake took his keys out of his pocket and removed them from the ring they were on.

'That's OK, sir. Both of us, in one way or another get to see the bad side of life.'

'I doubt that you do.' Jake eyed the estate agent and gave him his keys. He watched Rosie get into the passenger side of Gaffney's Range Rover. The agent closed the door and Jake made his way to his car. Taking one last glance towards the house, he noticed that the next-door neighbour was looking out of the window. He waved at Jake and gave him the "Do you want a cuppa?" sign, but he declined. The last thing he wanted was to make small talk, today of all days.

14

The following day, Jake was sitting in his patrol car on an observation point, watching the world go by. Large spots of rain had begun to hammer slowly, on the windscreen as the sky darkened. Sitting where he was on the A43 near to Blisworth Hill was a catalyst for an errant driver to brake heavily, on seeing the patrol car, loose control on the wet road and cause all sorts of mayhem. He moved off of his observation point and began a patrol towards Towcester.

He was mulling over the conversation he'd had with his collision investigator, Andy Thomas. He'd sent the blood samples from the four fatals for more testing and was hoping that the results would be "inconclusive".

To him it was only a tenuous connection. He didn't really have the manpower to go to the Superintendent and start a major investigation into four fatal accidents. It would probably mean an incident room there at the new complex, not that there wasn't enough room, he thought, but if Major Crimes didn't take it on?

He realised, of course, that the best person he knew to speak to was Kirsty, but he didn't like to intrude or burden her with his work problems. He felt that she was still mentally delicate and needed to be approached at the right time and in the right place. But this couldn't be put off. If there was a problem, it needed to be identified and resolved quickly. He decided to leave it until Andy had the results. The car phone rang, he pressed the answer button on the steering wheel and listened to the caller.

'Give me fifteen minutes and I'll come over.'

He cancelled the call and wondered what the Major Crimes Team could possibly want with him. He currently had nothing outstanding on the road death board in his office. Nevertheless, he made his way to Major Crimes at Force HQ.

Arriving at Headquarters, he took a detour through the restaurant and grabbed a soft drink from the machine before going up to the Major Crimes suite. He saw that the DCI's door stood open and he was talking to the new detective inspector. Freeman, the American Police Captain, in the UK that made him a Chief Inspector, saw him and waved him into the office.

'Jake, have you met Detective Inspector Fletcher Randall?'

Jake took Randall's outstretched hand and gave it a firm shake. 'What can I do for you, gentlemen?'

'Jake, I know that you were involved in an incident last year with Tyler,' Freeman said.

Jake nodded. Where was this going?

Freeman continued. 'DI Randall here has been allocated the task of resolving the identity of the unknown female found in Fulborough Wood and which we believe was one of Tyler's victims.'

'I understand, sir, but what has that to do with me? I didn't really get involved with that enquiry.'

'Yes, I know, but you are the FLO of D.I. Kingsfield's wife, am I right?'

'Yes, correct.'

'I also understand that you are still in contact with her?'

'I am still her FLO. Yes.'

'I want you to introduce Randall to Dr Kingsfield, so he can look at the remains to try to identify who they belong to.'

'I don't think that we need to be disturbing Dr Kingsfield with this. It's likely to bring back memories that she would prefer to forget, or at least keep suppressed. It may well undo all the work we've done to facilitate her recovery.'

'I understand that, which is why I've asked you to be seconded to this investigation with Randall, until we sort it out.'

'I'm sorry, sir, but I have a full workload and a series of fatal collisions that need to be investigated.'

'I know, but that can be handed onto someone else for the time being.'

Jake, more irritated, continued. 'No, sir. With respect, I'm happy to introduce the DI to the current pathologist, but I don't think that Kirsty, sorry, Dr Kingsfield, is in a fit state mentally and should not get involved!'

'You don't really have a choice in the matter. The decision has already been made.'

Freeman looked away from Jake and saw Kirsty Kingsfield standing in the doorway of his office.

Jake's heart pounded, not only because of the stress caused by the conversation, but because that was what happened every time he saw her. No one knew how long she had been standing there or what she had overheard.

As Jake looked across to Kirsty, he received a radio message informing him that his motorway crew, Prentice and Johnson, had been deployed to a jack-knifed goods vehicle on the M45 at the M1 junction 17. He turned back to Freeman and Randall, who'd also heard the call.

'Do you have to deploy as well?' Freeman asked.

'I'll need to go up soon,' Jake replied.

'Very well,' responded Randall. 'Call me when you've finished and we'll have a chat.'

Jake nodded and went to leave.

Kirsty whispered as he got to her, 'Come over tonight and we'll talk,' then smiled.

Jake nodded again, leaving Kirsty with Randall and Freeman which was not what he wanted to do at all.

Jake drove up to the motorway incident thinking about what Kirsty was doing with Randall and Freeman. He was sure that they must have heard the rumours about them. And they were only rumours, but in the intervening months since Jim's death, Kirsty had become a good friend. He was apprehensive about taking things with her further. He continued to deny any views his colleagues might have about them. Yet deep inside he knew. He knew that it would only be a matter of time, before it turned to more than just a friendship.

Was that what he wanted? Was she just convenient because of his own situation? On the rebound. He couldn't answer either of those questions with any great certainty. He was conflicted, he knew that by his duty to her as her FLO, by his growing closeness and not wanting to take advantage of both their vulnerabilities.

He didn't know what Kirsty thought, because he hadn't asked her or even came anywhere near the subject. There were the affectionate touches, nothing sexual of course; walking arm-in-arm while they were talking, or a comforting holding of hands, but when he was with her he felt like an adolescent schoolboy, flushed with hormones. Inner stirrings he hadn't felt for many years. Perhaps Rosie was right. Perhaps their marriage was over longer than he believed, so there was nothing to save.

15

The invitation Kirsty had given to Jake, as he'd left Freeman's office, turned into dinner the following evening, at Kirsty's apartment and before Jake's nightshift.

Kirsty told him that she was having some unhappy thoughts about Jim again, and about the remains found in Fulborough Wood, since her meeting with Freeman. She wanted someone to talk to and Jake knew that she would always turn to him.

Jake was happy to oblige, and although he was in semi-uniform when he arrived, Kirsty was wearing what she called her pink "Sloppy Joes". She'd cooked chicken fricassee on brown rice. Kirsty invited Jake to sit at the table in the kitchen, which he took after removing his coat, hanging it on the back of the chair. Jake watched in silence as Kirsty put out the food. She wandered over to the table with two plates in her hand and put one in front of Jake.

'Smells and looks good,' Jake commented. Then, as

Kirsty sat down he said, 'We went to a nasty bump yesterday up at the junction seventeen split?'

'Anyone injured?'

'No, just the lorry driver's pride,' Jake joked.

'Funny thing was, Chris Prentice thought he saw a doctor who had also turned up at another collision a few weeks ago.'

'Coincidence perhaps?'

Jake took a mouthful of food. 'I don't know – Prentice didn't think so.'

'What happened then?'

'I was with Prentice at the end of the taper of cones, guiding the traffic onto the hard shoulder. Chris was waving his arms about trying to get the traffic to increase speed past the scene. It wasn't any use, but at least he was trying.' Jake smiled. 'Anyway, as we were watching the traffic, we saw a car pull into the coned-off area and drive towards the rear of the ambulance. The car had a magnetic blue light on the roof. Chris was questioning himself as to where he had seen the woman before and why she was so familiar to him. Then he asked Reg who the woman in the car was. Told us it was a doctor who stopped to see if she could help. Reg thought she was one of these ambulance chasers – hero wannabes.

'Chris was adamant that he'd seen her at a collision before, then remembered it was the road death we had on the A5. Reg thought it was just a coincidence, particularly if the doctor worked nearby.'

'Did you not speak to her?'

'We were about to but she drove off with the ambulance, so I never got a good look at her. Chris was pretty sure about her though.'

They finished the rest of the meal in relative silence, other than the odd word or two.

Jake's mind was all over the place. He knew that there was the possibility of rejection, if he was to ask Kirsty out on a real date. He also knew that if she was waiting to be asked – and that thought had crossed his mind on a number of occasions – then the relationship they had would change but she wouldn't wait for him forever. He had noticed the way that the new DI had spoken to her in Freeman's office and felt that he might have some competition for Kirsty's affections, so he had to act quickly. Not only that, but he knew the job wouldn't like it either.

He deliberately sat in the chair, instead of next to her on the sofa. He casually watched her as she drunk her coffee. Be a man and say something, a voice in his head was saying. But he didn't.

The briefing room for the traffic nightshift used to be a hive of activity at shift changeover. With the new building though, most officers could brief themselves at whatever post they were at, with no real need to come to the hub. Jake surveyed the scene before him as he entered the new briefing room. Long, with chairs in the centre, the room was laid out like a classroom, but most of the officers were sitting either facing a wall or the window at a computer workstation, tapping away on the keyboard or scrolling through information screens. Grey and green metal pull-out trays, stacked eight high, filled the left-hand side of the wall. These trays carried all the officers' workload. Most were stuffed to bursting point, others had stickers on the front – some of which Jake noted were highly inappropriate.

His full complement of nightshift officers consisted of a double-manned traffic car, an armed response car, and a collision investigator. He hoped that nothing major occurred during the night, because he just didn't have the staff to cope with it.

This was the norm, no longer putting two or three area traffic cars out during the night with two or three covering the motorway – not since Highways England took over responsibility. They hadn't any enforcement powers of course, but those upstairs didn't seem to care. It was one less road to worry about. They took away the jobs that officers, they thought, didn't want to do. Not caring that the crews, who actually worked there, wanted to be there and enjoyed the work they did. The result was deteriorating performance records.

He sat down at an empty desk and acknowledged the assembled team, then briefed the shift: a couple of stolen vehicles to look out for; a missing person from the local psychiatric ward; two villains wanted by the Met for Robbery. These were the main items of the day. He was about to allocate areas, when the telephone rang in Jake's office. The officer nearest the door got up to answer his phone for him. He could hear him mumbling something then return.

'Call for you, Sarge.'

'Who is it?'

'Don't know. Just asked for you. Sounded long distance.'

Jake looked curiously at his officer, stood and went into his office. He picked the phone up.

'Hello. Sergeant Jordan speaking.'

'Hello… Jake?'

'Yes. Who is this?'

'Jake, it's me. Steph. Stephanie Parker.'

Jake sat down astonished. 'Oh, where are you? You sound as if you're in a dustbin.'

'I'm at Hong Kong International Airport.'

'What are you doing in Hong Kong?'

'On a layover from New Zealand. I'm on my way back – permanently.'

'Really? You know what's going to happen when you return?'

'I know, but I need to face it. I'll be a couple of days. Perhaps we can talk? I didn't want to just turn up at your doorstep.'

'Right. OK, you'd better ring me when you're ready and we'll sort something out.'

'Sorry, Jake, but you're the only one who can help me.'

'I'm not sure whether I can, but I'll give you my mobile number. Ring me when you want to come in. When you're ready to talk.' Jake reeled off his mobile number.

'Thanks, Jake.'

'You know this isn't going to be easy.'

'Yes, I know, but as I said I'm ready to face it. I'll see you soon.'

He listened to a dial tone for a couple of seconds before he hung up. He recalled that when they visited the pub, the day after Jim's funeral, Parker told them that she had only returned to the UK, after her disappearance, in order to attend her father's funeral. It was he, who had used his contacts in the Foreign Office to get her shipped out to New Zealand. Nobody knew where she was and nobody would even dream she was literally the other side of the world.

When she had left them in the pub, she was still adamant that nobody should know where she was, until she was ready to come back. Now it seemed to Jake that this was the time.

The most important factor was the letter she'd received from Tyler, explaining himself to her. Jake doubted the sincerity of that letter, but Parker seemed to accept it on face value. That was in the past now, and he realised that Parker was going to be put through some real tough times, when she got back.

Although he didn't agree with what she had done and how she went about it, he knew that she needed at least one friend on the force.

His nightshift had been quiet and uneventful and he had arranged to see Kirsty the following afternoon. Sitting in Kirsty's office, still recovering from the shift, he was in a quandary as to whether he should tell her that he'd heard from Stephanie Parker. Knowing that Kirsty's view of her was less than conciliatory, the problem was that, when she did appear on the scene, Kirsty would soon know about it.

He was also annoyed that the DCI had called Kirsty's office and demanded she visit him as soon as possible, without first consulting with Jake. He knew, of course, that he wasn't Kirsty's keeper, but from an FLO point of view, it was only courtesy that he should have been warned – or asked his opinion. Raking over old wounds certainly wouldn't help Kirsty's recovery.

He sat staring down into his mug, watching the steam swirling around the inside-edge, like a wall of death motorcyclist, before it leached from the confines of the mug into the air. Kirsty made a damn good cup of coffee from the machine that she had in her office.

He seemed to recall seeing the coffee-maker in her flat, when he was struggling with Tyler. Funny what you remember…

'Penny for them?' she asked, walking over to him and sitting in the chair opposite.

'Sorry?' was all he replied, still deep in thought.

'And what does that mean?' she said, looking at him, and not without some concern on her face. Jake knew he was subdued and wondered what Kirsty might be thinking of this friend she had sitting opposite her. Jake looked up at her.

'You know, work stuff,' Jake responded with indifference.

'Really? I know you too well, Jake, and can tell when something's on your mind!'

Jake continued to look at her. He was still deliberating whether to tell her about Stephanie Parker, but was more concerned with what had happened in the DCI's office.

'How much did you hear?'

'Not much.'

'How long had you been standing there?'

'Enough to hear you defending me,' she smiled, 'which was nice, and kind, but I don't need you to do it, Jake. I'm a big girl you know. I can look after myself.'

Jake said nothing.

'Sorry if that sounded a little harsh, after all you have done for me, but I have to move on, Jake. I've listened to you and I know I can no longer wallow in the past.'

Again, Jake said nothing, but continued to examine her face, looking for any sign of a 'but'. What the hell, he thought, it's not as if it's likely they'll come into contact, is it?

'OK,' he said, sitting back in the chair. 'I had a phone call last night while I was on duty.'

'Oh, and?'

'It was from abroad. Came in about midnight.'

'For you, personally?'

'Yes.'

'I didn't know you had any relatives abroad.'

'I don't.'

'Come on then. Don't keep me in suspense,' Kirsty also sat back in her chair, waiting.

Jake was reluctant to come straight out with it, which might have given her the idea she knew who he was talking about. 'It was Stephanie Parker.'

Kirsty didn't respond immediately, then murmured, 'Oh.'

Jake glanced out of Kirsty's office window. He got up from the chair and walked towards the window with cup in hand. Leaning forward, he looked skyward. 'Looks like more rain is coming.'

'Yeah, in more ways than one.'

Jake turned to meet Kirsty standing behind him. Too close, he thought. He side-stepped her and wandered back to the chair.

'What did she want?' Kirsty asked, following him.

'She's coming home.'

'When?'

'Lands at Heathrow tomorrow.'

'That was quick.'

'Yeah, she rang me from Hong Kong airport.'

'I hope she doesn't want you to pick her up.'

'No, her mother's doing that, but Steph wants to answer to the big bosses. I think she wants to come back to the force.'

'Will they let her, do you think?'

'I don't know – they can be quite fickle. Whatever happens, she has got to answer for what she did. The book is never closed on those sorts of things.'

'What can she be done for?'

'Misconduct in Public Office, that's a common law offence, punishable by life imprisonment. Then of course there are offences under the Conduct Regs. Failing to appear at court, for one. Bringing the force into disrepute for another, and a shed load of other stuff they could throw at her.'

'It may not end well for her. Why would she want to come back?'

'She told me that she's ready to face whatever she needs to.'

Kirsty was silent for a moment. 'What does she want you to do?'

'Don't really know, other than let the bosses know she's back.'

'Mmm…' was all Kirsty said. It was her turn to stare vacantly out of her office window.

'Are you going to meet her?'

'She's asked, yes.'

'Have you agreed to?'

'Probably. Want to come along?'

'Are you kidding?'

'Just thought I'd ask.' He smiled briefly.

Kirsty moved away from the window and sat back at her desk.

Jake watched her randomly push papers around and put them in piles. He moved towards the front of her desk. 'Look, Kirsty, don't worry about it, or her. I thought it best, that you should know, despite any misgivings I may have had.'

'OK, I understand. Thanks, Jake, but you know how I feel about her.'

Jake nodded and drained his coffee. 'I'd better be going.'

'Right. I'll try not to think about it. Ring me later?' Then she quickly added, 'If you want to talk?'

'Yes, OK.'

He turned to go.

Kirsty got up from her desk and met him at her office door. She took his arm gently. 'Thanks for telling me, Jake.'

'That's OK. No problem.'

'Look, what are you doing tomorrow?'

'It should be my rest day. Why?'

'How would you like to come and see me lecture at the university?'

'I probably wouldn't be good company,' Jake said quickly.

'It'll take your mind off things. And what's going to happen when Stephanie gets back.'

Jake thought for a moment. Is she trying to make it easy for me? Is she fed up of waiting? 'OK,' he said quickly. 'What time?'

'I'll pick you up at 9:30.'

'OK.' He turned back to go, but not before Kirsty kissed him lightly on the cheek. Jake felt himself flush. He left quickly.

16

The auditorium was in the oldest part of the hospital in Billing Road. It had tiered seating for about 200 people. Jake looked around at the walls of oak panelling that reached to just over halfway up the walls, above which hung huge paintings of various important alumni.

'Never been in here,' he said, as they both entered the room.

'It's quite imposing, I have to say. I much prefer it to talking to students in the morgue.'

'How often is that?'

'Not often, but you know I've been looking at doing something else and this just came up at the right time.'

Jake nodded. 'You've taught in here before?'

'Yes, but I like to get in among the students, not me looking up at them all the time.'

Jordan had been annoyed that Kirsty, after Jim's death, was aggrieved with her employer who, while appearing sympathetic outwardly, made it clear they were concerned about Kirsty not being at work.

After she had returned from compassionate leave she was called to see the Chief Executive. A dour, bespectacled, fifty-year-old, hospital administrator.

When he'd removed her from her position with no compassion as to her personal circumstance, she had resolved to find something better to do, preferably somewhere else.

By chance, she had been approached by the university to provide some training to student nurses and doctors, as the university thought that it might take her mind off her recent trauma. It kept coming up in the press and media; some ridiculous speculation by some investigative journalist trying to make a name for themselves who thought they were onto a scoop.

Jake knew that Kirsty hated her situation as it was so well known, never out of the press for more than a few weeks at a time. They had no consideration at all for the grieving widow. On one occasion he told a hack, trying to doorstep her to piss-off, which got him further into trouble. Freedom of speech and all that bollocks, which would be fine normally, but not on that occasion.

Jake thought that the hospital management's attitude was bizarre, but knew that Kirsty didn't have the mental capacity at the time to fight it. People of a certain type like to kick you when you're down, Jake had told her. He was spitting feathers about it and wanted to go and complain to the Commissioning Group, but Kirsty stopped him, before it got them into further trouble.

Jake sat at the back of the room listening to Kirsty. She was very engaging with the students, making sure that they had understood all she was telling them.

She'd been teaching for fifty minutes, standing in the pit in her white doctor's coat, talking to twenty students scattered around the auditorium.

'So, Professor,' asked a student near to Jake.

'Just Doctor, not Professor.' Kirsty smiled. 'Go on?'

'What happens if the religion of the deceased does not allow for a post-mortem to be carried out?'

'That is a good question and quite difficult to answer. However, in such circumstances it is possible for the PM to be carried out using an MRI scanner. There may be some issues for me particularly as a forensic pathologist. It would stop an autopsy being carried out, particularly with a murder or unexpected death. In the end, it is a decision for the coroner alone. And also an MRI PM may have to be paid for by the deceased's family. There is some information in your books and a wealth of information on the internet.'

The student nodded and thanked Kirsty.

'Any further questions?' Kirsty looked around the auditorium. 'No? OK then. I'll see you all next week – don't forget we're at the mortuary and not here. Thank you, everyone.'

The students in the auditorium gathered their bags and laptops and made their way out noisily. Kirsty remained behind, as she tidied her notes and closed down her laptop. Jake waited for her to finish tidying up and saw that she was approached by an older woman, who he'd also seen sitting at the back of the room before he'd sat down.

As soon as her shadow fell across Kirsty's desk, she looked up and immediately recognised the person standing in front of her. 'Tanya! When did you get back in town?'

'Oh, I suppose it's been about six months or so. I've not had time to meet up with old friends, but now things have settled, I thought I'd come and listen in, when I found out where you were.'

'Thanks. What did you think?'

'Very thorough, but as a toxicologist, my examinations tend to be a bit more microbial.' She smiled.

Dr Tanya Nicholls was a tall brunette in her late forties, wearing a dark green suit and white blouse. Her shoulder-length hair was held in a ponytail with a green hairband, and she carried a Burberry, leather shoulder bag. 'Do you want to get a coffee or something? If you have time?'

'Yes, that'll be good. I'm parched after all that talking. I usually bring in a bottle of water, but always forget to use it.' She held up the bottle she'd picked up from the table.

Tanya smiled. 'You're a good lecturer,' she said as they walked out of the auditorium.

Kirsty looked around for Jake and saw him coming down the stairs towards them. He joined them as they arrived at the door. Kirsty checked to make sure she had collected everything.

She introduced Jake to Tanya and explained to her who he was.

They made their way to the hospital restaurant, and the two women chatted idly, catching up with their past news. Jake just listened. It had been a long time since he'd seen Kirsty so animated. Apparently Kirsty had not seen Tanya since leaving medical school, as they had majored in different subjects. Jake offered to get them tea and cake as they found a table and sat down, surrounded by her students studying alone or in groups.

Jake brought the tray of drinks and sat down next to Kirsty and said, 'How long has it been since you've seen Kirsty, Tanya?'

'Yes, I'm eager to know what you've been up to,' Kirsty said.

'You know I went to work for this big American company?'

Kirsty nodded, as she took a sip from her tea.

'I did that for about eighteen months. Awful company, worked you into the ground. Early starts and late finishes, so I wasn't happy. But I stayed out there doing some minor jobs. Married a Yank doctor. Lasted all of five minutes – he was banging some nurse at the hospital, all the time he was seeing me and after the wedding. Took me twelve months to find out about it – and twelve months to screw him to the floor in the divorce settlement. Married again,' she paused, 'I did some time at a crime lab and really couldn't settle. Adopted a daughter! Got back here in the UK about two years ago. Worked in microbiology for King's in London, but now I have this new job as senior toxicologist in the department for this other private company. And that's it in a nutshell – the life and times of Tanya Nicholls!'

Jake smiled. 'What made you come back to the UK?'

'Boredom, and the incessant backslapping that the Yanks seem to be so good at. All that fist punching the air and high fives. Gets on your nerves eventually.'

Jake noticed that seemed to depress her a little. The sparkle had gone out of her eyes, after she'd talked about her divorce.

'You've not done any NHS work then?' Kirsty said, changing the subject.

'Nah – no money in it.'

'Thanks for that vote of confidence, Tanya,' Kirsty mocked.

'You've got to remember that I've not worked in the NHS at all. All my work has been private.'

'And you have an adopted daughter?' Jake said.

Tanya looked at Jake. 'Yes, she's a bit of a handful, even now.'

'How old is she?' he inquired.

'She's twenty-five, going on sixteen,' Tanya laughed. 'But less about me. How about you, Kirsty?'

'It's been difficult over the last twelve months.' Kirsty hesitated.

'Yes, I'm sorry, I saw it all on the news – terrible. How are you coping?'

'There are a few days that are good, but most times it's bad, very bad. Not so much now, but all the same. I have a good friend. He's seen me through the bad times.' She indicated Jake.

'Him?' quizzed Tanya.

'Yes, he's my Family Liaison Officer.'

'Oh, not… ?' Tanya let the question hang.

'No, no, nothing like that. And it's not something I can get into right now, if you know what I mean.'

'Of course, I understand. But would you, you know?' Jordan saw an intent look on Tanya's face as she studied Kirsty.

'I don't know right now. Possibly. He is quite cute.'

'Cute?' exclaimed Jake. 'I am sitting here, remember?'

They laughed.

'I suppose you're married then? The good ones usually are – either that or you're gay.'

Jake cleared his throat. 'I'm divorced.'

'We've supported each other, through our problems, Tanya. So let's leave it at that.'

'He's a free man then?' Tanya responded with a naughty smile and a wink.

'We'll see,' was all that Kirsty replied glancing at Jake.

Tanya studied her watch and eyed them both. 'Well, I've taken up enough of your time. Must be going. It's been really great to catch up, Kirst. Perhaps we could arrange a dinner or something? You know – a girlie night out?'

Kirsty laughed 'Girlie night out? I think we're both a bit too long in the tooth for a girlie night out!'

'Speak for yourself,' Tanya grinned. She paused. 'Perhaps you're right. Dinner then?'

'Yeah, that's more my kind of thing.'

They both stood and exchanged telephone numbers. 'I'll give you a ring,' Tanya said as they exchanged goodbyes and, with that, she breezed out of the restaurant.

As Jake heaved Kirsty's laptop bag onto his shoulder, getting ready to leave, she was met by the university's Dean of the School of Health.

'Kirsty, I hoped I'd catch up with you before you left.' Robert Trevellian was a man of average height in his mid-fifties with receding, greying hair. 'I happened to be passing and saw you in here.' He nodded an acknowledgement to Jake.

'How can I help, Robert?'

'Well,' he said, lowering his voice a little, 'you may be interested to know that the Senate has approved a new full-time post and, along with taking the hospital on as the new faculty of Human Biology, predicated on the success of the courses you have been running, your name keeps popping up to take it on…'

'What do you mean "Take it on"?'

'Why, as Dean, of course.'

Kirsty stood silent and a little shocked. She was not, after all, an academic. She was, when it came down to it, just a mortuary technician with a bit of extra knowledge thrown in.

'What do you think, Kirsty?'

She thought for a moment. 'I didn't think I would enjoy teaching, but it's quite fun and the students are so enthusiastic. I don't think that any of them have missed a session yet. Mind you, they've not seen a real post mortem – that's coming next week.'

Jake watched Trevellian physically cringe. The prospect of a human cadaver being cut up, dissected and pawed over by the students was one that Jake knows all too well. Looking at Trevellian it was clear from his face that it was not something that he would enjoy.

'You don't approve?' Kirsty asked, also noting the look on the Dean's face.

'No, not at all. I just don't want to see it myself, prefer to remain in the land of the living.'

'It's certainly not for everyone. We're bound to get a few drop-out, literally,' she demonstrated a faint with her arm, 'when we start on the real stuff.'

Trevellian cringed again. 'What do you think?'

'I'll give it some thought. I'd still need to do real autopsies, though, to keep my licence.'

'Yes, we realise that. Don't worry. It just means that you'll have two jobs.'

'OK, I'll think about it.'

'Don't think about it too long – Professor.' Trevellian smiled at his use of the title and Kirsty returned the smile.

'Professor – that's twice today you've been called that,' Jake remarked as they walked out of the refectory. 'Mmm, Professor Kingsfield – very sexy.'

Kirsty looked at Jake, smiled and she slapped him playfully on the arm.

17

Mary & Kyle –
Two Weeks Later

Sunday night was a night that Mary wanted to remember, but, for some reason, it was a blank to her. It wasn't very often that the schools' teachers managed to get out of an evening, but it was near the end of term, so they decided to go out and celebrate.

'How were things last night, Mary?' Angela asked, as they travelled along the A45 towards the motorway.

'Yeah, I really enjoyed it. It was good to get out for a bit.' Although she was unsure as to whether she did enjoy it.

'We were all pretty drunk by the end of the night, as I recall. If I remember, we were having such a good time, that some other women gate-crashed the party as well. Nobody we knew, but they joined in.' Angela laughed.

'I'm surprised that we've managed to get everyone here on time this morning. Some of the other teachers looked a bit the worse for wear, I have to say,' Mary added.

'Good job too. How do you think we'll get on today?'

'MK gym team are pretty good, so we'll have to see. I have every confidence in our boys and girls.'

Mary yawned and closed her eyes for a micro-second.

'You falling asleep?'

'No, just tired after last night. I don't think I should have had so much to drink.'

'But you said you weren't going to drink.'

Mary laughed. 'That didn't happen did it?'

They had left the school right on time. Amazingly, everyone had turned up early and enthusiastic about the gymnastic tournament they were going to in Milton Keynes. Even her son, Kyle, had managed to get himself out of bed and was ready to leave the house with her. She thought that the only reason he wanted to be with her today was because of a girl that he had taken a shine to in the year above. Mary smiled. Raging teen hormones.

'What's the joke, Mum?' he asked, as he leaned forward, with one earbud in his ear and the other swaying about in mid-air.

'Oh, nothing – nothing for you to worry about anyway.'

He leaned forward further. 'Can we stop in a minute?'

'Why? We need to get to the venue early.'

'I need to go… '

'Goodness, Kyle. How many times is that this morning?'

'I don't know – nerves, I suppose.'

'But you're not even competing today!'

'Still nervous for my friends,' he said, smiling.

'Or just one friend in particular?'

He grinned. 'Maybe.'

Mary drove the minibus onto the southbound carriageway at junction sixteen. The motorway was already busy with three lanes of heavy traffic. She had only driven a little way when she felt more and more tired. 'I can't understand what's up with me,' she said to Angela.

'You're still a bit sleepy. It'll wear off. Don't worry.'

'I'm just finding it hard to keep my eyes open.'

Mary passed the Northampton services, down an incline, which then rises towards junction fifteen. Traffic was very busy and beginning to slow down, with cars and lorries putting on their hazard lights to warn others behind about slowing traffic.

But to Mary, these lights only confused her. She saw everything out of focus. 'Oh, shit,' was all Mary could exclaim, as her foot hit the accelerator. She was conscious enough to try to stop the minibus hitting the lorry in front of her and managed to wrench the steering wheel over to the right.

Her eyes closed for the final time and there was nothing she could do as she felt her whole body go into a spasm.

Crossing all three lanes, the minibus collided with the central reservation, bounced into the path of another van which pushed the minibus back towards the first lane, where an articulated lorry slammed into the minibus, turning it over, throwing the passengers about, like a washing machine.

The motorway came to a grinding halt and silence befell what was normally the deafening sounds of passing vehicles.

18

The lecture theatre at force headquarters was a large room with tiered seating that resembled the auditorium Jake had attended with Kirsty – only without the paintings and the oak panelling. It was regularly used for briefings, which required multi-agency attendance.

When Jake arrived in the late afternoon, it appeared to have been recently emptied. He'd insisted that all the units attending the motorway smash should be there for a post-incident de-brief. They arrived sporadically and sat talking softly among themselves until Jake brought the meeting to order. He thanked everyone for their attendance and work at the scene and gave a brief explanation as to how they believed the collision had occurred. He went on.

'According to the preliminary findings of the collision investigator, the collision scenario commenced when the school mini-bus went out of control, crossed the carriageway from the near-side lane, and collided with the central barrier. The minibus rebounded and collided with a van, overturned and was hit by an artic. Several other vehicles then collided in the ensuing tailback of traffic. A white van took out a passenger who had got out of another car, and was standing in the lane. Reports from witnesses said the driver was looking down at his phone.

'There were some minor collisions, which we could deal with individually, but we're going to treat it as all one incident. PC Prentice will be the Officer-In-Case. Be gentle with him. It's his first multiple.'

A chuckle went around the room.

'First fatal and now my first multiple – all within a month,' Jake heard Prentice remark to Johnson.

'OK, on a more serious note, the FCI in this case will be Andy Thomas. Unfortunately, the lady driver who died in the collision, we believe, was dead prior to the accident.'

A hand raised. Jake acknowledged it.

'Heart attack?'

'It's possible, but we won't know till the PM.'

'Fortunately, most of the school-children were wearing their seat belts and only sustained minor injuries, apart from one, who is in a critical condition with a traumatic stomach injury.'

A paramedic caught Jake's attention, who indicated for him to proceed.

The paramedic stood and described the injuries using his hands. 'He'd caught his foot under the framework of one of the seats in front of him and, as the vehicle overturned, it virtually ripped off his foot. We could see tendons and bone exposed, when we finally removed him. The seat frame had contorted and come away from the floor. One of the metal legs was twisted upwards and had entered his abdomen. It pierced some vital organs and we were unable to remove the metal leg in-situ.'

The paramedic looked at the air ambulance doctor, who nodded and agreed.

'It was a life threatening injury so it was far too dangerous to do that. If we had we may well have killed the patient there and then,' the doctor confirmed.

The paramedic continued. 'The fire service cut away what they could, then we had to remove him to the emergency department with the pole still in place. He's undergoing emergency surgery now, but the prognosis is not good.'

'What are his chances, do you think?' Jake asked.

The air ambulance doctor replied, 'honestly?' he thought for a moment, 'I'd say 70/30, against.'

'Not good then.' Jake nodded to Prentice. 'We need to prepare for that eventuality, Chris.'

Prentice nodded and made a note in his file. 'There was a kid I saw at the scene sitting on the barrier and texting. What happened to him?'

Jake replied. 'We've spoken to him. He was unhurt, but he did put a video up on YouTube.'

The look on Prentice's face said as much.

'He tweeted it to his mates, before he even contacted his parents. Although he's been advised. He's known for it around the school. Bit of a voyeur, by all accounts.'

Know all about them, Jake thought privately.

Andy Thomas raised his hand and spoke. 'I don't know whether you've noticed already, but the description of the deceased is the same as those we were discussing last week, Sarge.'

'It hasn't gone unnoticed, Andy. It certainly crossed my mind when I saw her. We'll know more after the PM. I want you with me on that, Andy.'

'Roger that,' replied Thomas.

Jake continued to debrief the crews for the next thirty minutes. As the meeting dispersed, Jake called Thomas and Prentice over to him.

'Andy, can you explain to Chris the issue with these other fatals?'

Andy nodded. 'A few weeks ago, we picked up a pattern of road deaths. By sheer chance, nothing that we went looking for. But we noticed that these road deaths were similar from a post mortem point-of-view and the fact that all the deceased looked the same.'

'How do you mean?' Prentice asked.

'They had the same features – dark brown hair in a bob, blue eyes, between twenty and thirty.'

'Surely that's just a coincidence?' questioned Prentice.

'As we thought as well,' interjected Jake. 'But the post mortems all show this unknown substance in the blood, and I bet the toxicology for this collision will be the same.'

'OK, so what are we going to do about it?'

Jake responded. 'If we're sure that this unknown substance is present and if any of the students die as a result of this collision, then we are going to have to hand it on to Major Crimes. I'm not happy to say that we have a multiple murderer out there killing drivers with a new drug just yet, but we haven't got the resources to manage such an investigation.'

'We've put a rush on the tox,' Andy commented.

'So, in the meantime, I want you two to work together to investigate the collision as normal, but keep an open mind about the cause.'

They nodded their understanding and Jake dismissed them.

19

The body of a black male lay on the slab in the post mortem room of the pathology department. Jake noted that the damage to him was apparent, even before any post mortem was started. Both knees were obviously fractured and on the thigh of his right leg was a deep and large red slash, exposing the thigh bone. But as Kirsty had pointed out, his head was not exactly attached to his body anymore, only by muscle and sinew. Industrial accident.

Jake watched her finish sewing up the 'Y' incision. He knew that it would normally have been done by her assistant, Anton, but he'd had the afternoon off. It had always impressed Jake the way Kirsty could put aside all that had gone before in her life to do what she had just done. Even though he knew that deep down it continued to cause her some distress. He looked around as she was finishing up. He knew not to interrupt unless it was necessary.

The new PM room was light, with large panoramic

windows, on the first floor of the pathology department overlooking Northampton Marina. White walls reflected the sun, which made the whole room quite pleasant, if it weren't for that sweet sickly smell that pervaded your every pore during and after each post-mortem.

Jake stood against the back wall of the room watching. She finished her sewing, stroked the man's hair lightly and removed her gloves as she moved towards the door. Jake followed.

'How much of an old friend is Tanya?' asked Jake as they left the mortuary.

'We were at university together. Trained as doctors. She was even my roommate for a little while.'

'Is she a pathologist too?'

'No, she went into toxicology and microbiology.'

'Ah – if she works locally, I may have a little job for her.'

Kirsty glanced towards Jake, as they walked along the hospital street.

Jake saw her looking. 'What?' he said grinning.

'Jake, you never ever have little jobs for any of us.'

'What do you mean by that?' he teased.

'I seem to recall that all these extra little jobs you get us, or should I say me, to do as a favour, turn out to be… not so little, shall we say,' she teased back.

Jake said nothing, only smiled at her. They walked on in silence for a moment.

'What is it then, this little job?' Kirsty said after a few more steps.

'Well,' he said, as he held open the door to the hospital restaurant, to let her go first, 'we've had a spate of fatal collisions, that all show some unknown toxicology, but there are no other related features which tie them together.'

'OK, but explain what you mean by "unknown toxicology"?'

They collected a coffee each from the coffee machine, paid for it and sat down at a table by the window.

Jake outlined the situation brought to him by Andy Thomas. He explained that it was found by his senior collision investigator and that he thought that it was peculiar, particularly when it was found that the deceased all had similar features.

'What types of features?'

'All the deceased were brown-haired, collar-length, almost identical.'

'So, what are you suggesting? That someone's killing off their identical twins?'

'You suggested it, not me.'

'Those unknown substances could all be different, you appreciate that?'

'Yes, I know.'

'There could be substances that we don't know about that are perfectly legitimate.'

'That's fairly slim in this day and age, surely?'

'Yes, but you never know in medicine or human biology for that matter. New drugs are synthesised almost every day.'

'Yes, I understand, which is why I've got my collision investigator to go back and have them all checked again, to see if they are all the same.'

'And are they?'

'Don't know. Still waiting for the result.'

They sat in silence for a moment, deep in thought.

Kirsty looked out of the window of the restaurant and across the hospital estate. The view wasn't perfect and, amongst the other hospital buildings, there was barely any green.

Eventually she said, 'Would you like me to ask Tanya to take a look for you, as well?'

'Only if it doesn't cost me any money.' Jake smiled. 'We're strapped for cash as it is.'

'All I can do is ask, or... we're going to arrange dinner. Do you want to come as well? You can ask her yourself then.'

'Do you think she'd mind? I'm sure you have a lot to catch up with if you haven't seen her for a long time?'

'No, I'm sure it will be OK. I'll ask her first, of course. Don't want just to turn up on the doorstep with you.'

'Why? Do I embarrass you?' he smiled again, something he always seemed to be doing when he was with her.

'Don't be so stupid... ' She grinned. 'And no, you don't.'

'You asking me out on a date then?' he teased.

Kirsty looked down towards the floor, before replying.

'I'm sorry,' Jake said, 'that was, inappropriate.'

'No, it wasn't,' she responded coyly, 'I suppose I am.' She stopped and looked directly at him, searching his face. Jake felt awkward and embarrassed.

They finished their drinks and then walked out of the hospital entrance and across the car park to Jake's patrol car. They stopped, she turned and looked him. Those twinkling green eyes caused a stirring of emotion in Jake. He rubbed a hand across his face.

'Yes, Jake, I'm asking you to come with me to see my friend, as my friend and not as my FLO.' The smile she gave him lit up her face. He smiled back. 'Well?' she asked.

'Yes, Kirsty, I will. And do you know what else? It's nice to see you smiling again without feeling guilty about it.'

'I can't be in mourning forever, Jake.' She said, glancing past him across the hospital estate.

Briefly, Jake wondered whether she might be having second thoughts. 'I know you can't and I'd love to.' At least it would do away with some of the awkwardness usual in the first flush of any romance, Jake thought.

'Great. I'll let you know as soon as I've arranged it. See you soon.' She turned to go, but Jake lightly took her arm and turned her towards him. It was now his turn to peck her on the cheek, as she had to him a few days before.

'Thanks,' she said in a whisper and set off across the car park. Before she crossed the road, she turned back towards him and gave a little wave. Jake got back into his patrol car and drove away. For the first time in a long time, he actually felt happy.

It's not normally in the role of a Family Liaison Officer to fall for his charge, but he'd been seeing and helping Kirsty since Jim's death. He'd seen her at her lowest moments and had grown fonder of her with every encounter. To hell with regulations, if he wanted to start a relationship with her that was his business and sod all to do with the job – or so he thought.

On the way back to the station, he received a radio message from Dave Harte, asking him to visit Major Crimes as soon as he could. A development in the Tyler case.

20

Arriving a few minutes before his two colleagues, Jake got out of his patrol car and walked over to Fulborough Wood. No longer ancient woodland, the trees having been removed by the Fulborough estate. Can't really call it a wood anymore, Jordan thought. As part of the ancient Rockingham Forest the only thing that suggested there was ever a wooded area here were tree stumps and the tilled earth. The damp fresh smell of turned over earth and the cool breeze impacted on his senses and encouraged him to put his collar up. He glanced up at the grey sky, then back along the dry-stone wall that made up the perimeter of the wood. Some of it he saw was broken down, where people, he assumed, had entered the wood. There was no actual entrance from what he could see and what he knew from the files, the locals walked their dogs in the wood and surrounding area. But all that had now gone.

He heard the sound of an approaching car and turned to

see that Randall had collected Inspector Dave Harte in his dirty blue Mondeo car. They got out and all three stood in silence at the edge of the wood and surveyed the site before them. The sky was full of great plumes of grey clouds, being whipped along by winds high in the sky and threatening a downpour at any moment.

'You wouldn't believe it, would you?' said Jake, breaking the silence.

'What wouldn't you believe, Jake?' responded Harte.

'Twelve months ago, when I came here and stepped into this wood, some of the trees here that were probably hundreds of years old, have now been destroyed. And for what?'

'Apparently, Fulborough wants to build some garages for his cars,' replied Harte.

'Certainly looks different. Completely changed the landscape. Couldn't he have put his bloody cars somewhere else?'

'You're a fine one to talk, driving that thing.' Harte pointed to Jake's X5.

'I'm a country boy at heart,' he replied, giving a wry smile.

'Right, shall we get on with it then?' Randall said, who had been silent during the conversation, deep in thought about the view in front of him. The other two nodded.

'Whereabouts was the body found?' Randall asked.

'About seventy yards in from the wall.' Harte pointed in the general direction and waved his hand vaguely, where Chris Prentice had crawled on the floor to find the skeletal remains of what turned out to be female.

'And she was fully decomposed?'

Harte replied, 'Yes, skeletal.'

'And you've not made any progress as to who she is?'

'Not to my knowledge. You have to remember that I got promoted out of the department about a month later and haven't really kept up with the investigation.'

'Did you want out?' quizzed Randall.

'Wasn't given the choice.'

Randall nodded. 'What about access to the wood twelve months ago?'

'Anyone could get in. In fact, most of the locals up the road used it to walk dogs, and kids used to play in it. Nobody seemed to bother, not even the landowner. There was a wall around half of the perimeter, that had been broken down here.' Jake moved to give an idea to Randall where the wall used to be. 'It was an evening that Prentice won't forget in a hurry.'

'And why's that?' asked Randall.

'It was the first time he'd uncovered a murder victim.'

Randall lifted his coat collar to keep away the light drizzle that had begun. 'Always got to be a first time and you never forget it,' he mumbled.

'Amen to that,' Harte said.

Thinking out loud, Randall said, 'So, we've got new information that there is another body buried here and, from what I have seen of the file already, it would seem that the view at the time was that it was the remains of a WPC Parker who went missing. What about other family, siblings, parents etcetera?'

Jake wondered about saying something in the light of Parker's impending return, but thought better of it, so kept quiet.

'I didn't think Tyler had any siblings, other than the stepbrother and stepsister. There were rumours that he had a real sister, but it didn't come out in the ensuing enquiry who or even where she was.' He thought for a moment. 'Can you remember their names, Jake?'

'Yes, I can. Adam Gaffney, the haulage guy.' Jake was going to make a personal comment, but again decided to keep his mouth shut. Harte looked at Jake, but made no comment. They simply exchanged a look.

'Did we do any further background on Tyler after his death?'

'Not to my knowledge. It all got put to bed, job done.'

'Quite spectacularly, I understand.'

'You could say that! Took us four months to piece together the bits, literally,' Jake said.

They moved forward onto the land and aimlessly wandered around kicking clods of earth and rocks, with no real idea of what they expected to find.

'I suppose we ought to do some background on Tyler,' Randall called to Harte.

'Might be able to shed some light on who these remains belong to. And we are only assuming that Tyler killed them both.'

'When are we going to dig?' asked Harte.

'I've arranged for an early start tomorrow. Bagshaw is being brought along to show us where.'

'Does he know he'll go down for this?' Jake asked.

'We've done a deal, as he's turned Queen's evidence, but he still might get a short custodial or even a suspended.'

Jake nodded.

Harte continued. 'Clearly when we interviewed him, he was extremely remorseful for what he had been party to.'

'Church-going man.' Jake kicked another clod of earth. 'His conscience wouldn't allow him to do anything other than return the bribe.'

'Yes, and I think that came across to the CPS, as well. He obviously didn't want to be involved, but got roped in. It's a good job he gave the money back, otherwise the CPS may have taken a different view.'

'As would I,' replied Harte.

After a few more minutes surveying the site, Jake went to walk back to his patrol car. A large pick-up truck rounded the corner as if the driver was in a hurry. It came to a sliding halt, kicking up loose stones and firing them at the stationary police cars. An angry Frank Philpott jumped out. Jake, removing some police tape from the back of the car, looked up and thought that there was something that had put a bee in this man's particular bonnet.

Storming over to the two officers and clearly spoiling for a fight, the man shouted, 'What the fuck are you two doing?' as he charged towards them. 'This is private property and you can leave – now!'

'Ah, Mr Philpott,' said Harte as he walked towards him, 'unfortunately, this is now a crime scene.'

'It can be a fucking film scene, for all I care! You're not doing anything on Fulborough's land. Now, piss off.'

'That's really not the attitude, Mr Philpott. We're here acting on information received and you have no say in the matter,' Randall commented drily.

'We'll see about that.' Philpott lunged at Harte, being closest to him, but Harte took a pace backwards, so Philpott didn't get his hands on him. In the meantime, Jake had made his way over to the group and was standing outside Philpott's view. Harte took a further pace backwards, placing himself in a defensive position.

'I wouldn't come any closer to me, Mr Philpott, and I warn you to stay back. Stay away from me.'

'Really? And what are you going to do if I don't?'

'Then you'll be coming with us to the police station.'

Philpott laughed. 'I'd like to see you try!'

Philpott, was a big man and clearly thought he could get away with throwing his weight around with any one he liked, and used to getting his own way. And Jake was about to give him a wake-up call. Jake recognised the signs of aggression building in Philpott – the flushed face, the clenching and releasing of his big hands, the target acquisition, as his eyes flicked between Harte and Randall, who'd said nothing and kept a distance. But Jake was closing in on Philpott and removed his pepper-spray from his belt. The movement drew Philpott's attention and he swung around to try to grab Jake. But Jake was quicker than Philpott and sidestepped him, as the big man came towards him.

'Stay back!' Jake shouted.

Philpott didn't heed Jake and, without further warning, Jake flicked the top of the pepper-spray and gave Philpott a good dose, hitting him squarely between the eyes.

Philpott fell to his knees, rubbing his face with his hands and screaming all sorts of revenge upon the two policemen. Jake and Harte were on him swiftly and quickly handcuffed him and dragged him into the back of the patrol car.

With Philpott screaming in agony in the back of the car, Harte turned to Randall. 'Thanks a lot for your help.'

Randall just shrugged. 'You seemed to have it all under control.'

'You could have helped a little more than you did, even just saying something to try to calm him down. We're going back to the nick. You can do whatever you want to do.'

'I shall, Dave, I shall,' Randall said with a smirk.

Harte and Jake got into their vehicle, with Philpott by now quiet and with his eyes tightly shut. They drove away from Fulborough Wood.

'Why the hell didn't he give us a hand?' fumed Harte.

'Probably didn't want to get his new suit dirty,' chuckled Jake.

21

Randall didn't like mortuaries. He didn't like peering at the dead, like some sort of voyeur. In fact he liked nothing about post mortems. The iodoform disinfectant smell of the mortuary made him feel like he wanted to puke. He'd managed to grab a coffee, as he entered the morgue for the first time, to try to suffocate that smell. It didn't seem to work.

He introduced himself to the mortuary attendant, Anton.

'You've not been here before then?' Anton asked in the Polish-English accent he had developed since his arrival in the UK.

'No, first time,' Randall replied looking around the office.

'Needs a lick of paint,' Anton admitted.

'Mmm, I can see that. Where to now?'

'Dr Kingsfield is looking at the remains in the PM room on the first floor. Come, I take you up there.'

Randall put his coffee cup in the bin next to the sink, leaving the office, and making their way to the large lift, which took them to the first floor.

'Have you met Dr Kingsfield before?' Anton asked in the lift.

'Yes, but only briefly.'

Anton hesitated for a moment. 'Such tragedy for her recently. It was very sad.'

'Yes, I understand, very difficult to lose a loved one.'

'They were very much in love. I could see that,' Anton remarked, as he adjusted his trademark, bright yellow tie.

'I'm surprised she came back to work so soon.'

'She didn't have much choice in the matter. Between you an' me I think the way hospital management treated her was,' he tried to think of the word, 'diaboliczny – diabolical.' Randall looked at Anton, not quite understanding what he meant.

'What do you mean?' he quizzed.

'They took her away from being boss here.'

'What? Because she was grieving for her murdered husband?'

Anton nodded.

'More like despicable and very cruel,' Randall commented.

'She had a lot of time off. Got very ill. Hit her very hard.'

'I'm sure it did,' Randall said, as he thought of the trauma he went through after the death of his own wife.

'She is very good pathologist, I say that. At least they didn't let her go completely.'

'So, what does she do now?'

'She's on the pathology team with everyone else, but usually specialises in suspicious death, she still does forensics. Strange that she was my boss, which is really how I still see her, great respect.'

The lift door opened onto a corridor with a set of double doors directly ahead. They entered the atrium of the post-mortem suite and prepared themselves for entering the PM room through another set of double doors directly ahead.

Having gowned up, they entered. Randall noticed that it seemed cooler than the rest of the hospital. There were six post mortem tables in front of him. The one directly in front of him had a cadaver on, which another pathologist was working on. He seemed to mumble something to himself, as he cut away something which Randall couldn't see in the chest cavity. On another stainless steel slab lay an old woman in a foetal position with her arm raised, as if saying hello. Anton saw Randall looking at her.

'Can't get her in the fridge until rigor's gone.' He smiled.

Randall walked past the cadaver, trying not to look or think about how she got in that position. The male pathologist also gave Randall a wry smile as he walked on.

Kirsty was working on the skeletal remain found in Fulborough Wood. She thanked Anton. 'Inspector Randall, how are you today?' Kirsty asked.

'Fine, thanks, and it's Fletch.'

'I'll stick to Inspector. For the time being,' she said with a smile.

Randall made no direct reply, but then asked, 'What can you tell me then, Doctor Kingsfield?' he said, emphasising her name.

'These remains have been in the ground a little while.'

'Estimate?' Randall folded his arms in front of him.

'Ten to fifteen years, I'd say.'

'Before Tyler's time then?'

Kirsty looked away from Randall at the sound of Tyler's name, before responding.

'Yes, I'd say so.'

'Male or female?'

'Female.' Kirsty explained that the size of the pelvic bone and its shape made it obvious she was female.

'Cause of death?'

'Blunt force trauma to the head, I would say, but there may have been other factors in her death.'

'Hmm, size and type,' Randall replied.

'Difficult to be precise without some other form of reference, other than it was probably square.'

'Anything else?' Randall asked.

'Not that I can see. There's been some damage caused post-mortem, probably when they excavated her for the first time, then put her back again. I can't understand why they did such a thing.'

'We've got a story from the estate manager as to why. Seems that he didn't want to upset his boss, but I've a feeling he's not telling all he knows. We've just got to figure out who she is and who put her there.'

'Do you think he knows who she might be?' asked Kirsty.

Randall thought for a moment. 'Yes, I have a hunch that he does.'

'We've sent off for DNA and we'll do a bone analysis, so we can give you an idea as to when she was interred. I can also tell you that she'd had a child from the striations on the inside of the pelvic bone.' Kirsty waved a hand vaguely around the pelvic area.

'OK, that could narrow it down a little bit. Not a lot I know, but a bit. How accurate will the bone analysis be then?' Randall asked, peering at where Kirsty had indicated.

'Modern radio-carbon methods can give a result to within eighteen months.'

Randall nodded. 'What about the DNA results?'

'We had a bit of trouble getting a DNA result on the other victim in the wood, so don't hold out your hopes on this one, as it's been in the ground twice as long. We can only find mitochondrial DNA in bone, which is inherited from the maternal side. There are no genetic markers from the father.'

'We'll have to resort to old-fashioned police methods then,' Randall smiled and rubbed the side of his nose.

'How long till we know?'

'Couple of weeks probably,' Kirsty replied and looked away.

'And?'

'And nothing.'

'I see. You're obviously thinking about something.'

'It's none of your business really, but I was thinking that I had the same conversation with my husband a few days before he died, about the other remains.'

Randall looked at his feet. 'I'm sorry,' he said, 'but do you have any further information about those other remains?'

'Not really. We have minimal DNA for her, as I just said. Nothing on any database to give us any ideas. We've been looking at dental records, but it's not a priority, so it'll get done, when it gets done.' Kirsty walked away from the slab and asked Anton, who had busied himself helping the other pathologist, to remove the remains.

Kirsty walked towards the door, snapping off her gloves as she did so.

Randall followed a few steps behind. They went into the atrium, where they both removed their gowns and threw them in the bin with others.

'Anything else I can help you with, Inspector?'

'No, I think that's all. I just needed to confirm how she

died, to understand what I'm looking for,' he paused, 'we could go for a coffee, if you like, if you want to? To discuss the case further.'

'I don't think so. I have a lot to do.'

'Just thought I'd ask.'

They pushed through the doors and walked on together along the corridor towards a lift and in the direction of Kirsty's office in silence.

They arrived at the lift and the doors opened.

Randall held out his hand. 'Nice to meet you, Doctor Kingsfield. I'm sure we'll meet again.'

Kirsty took his hand and shook it. 'No doubt about it, doing what we both do, Inspector.'

Randall nodded, said goodbye and headed into the lift.

22

The apartment that Jake had taken after his separation from Rosie, was on the outskirts of Northampton. Part of a new development. He'd taken the top floor. There was a large landscape window in the lounge that led out onto a balcony. The view from there was unrestricted and looked out over an almost never-ending vista of Northamptonshire countryside. It was a relaxing sight after a busy day at work.

With a westward-facing view, he could sit on the recliner out on his balcony and watch the sun go down with a nice glass of whiskey, feeling the stresses of the day ebb away with the setting sun. Occasionally he would prefer not to be sitting alone.

But that night, he stood in his bedroom. It'd been a long time since he'd dressed for an evening out socially with a woman. Rosie was, when all was said and done, his first love and, after everything they'd been through together, she'd thrown muck in his face. It still hurt him and probably would for years to come.

He straightened his tie, then decided to take it off. It was a social evening not a job interview. He picked up a clothes-brush and lightly brushed the jacket, then took that off as well then gave himself a glance in the mirror before walking downstairs to his car.

He climbed into it and drove away to his first date in years.

As he pulled up outside Kirsty's apartment, he couldn't help but look up at the CCTV camera opposite that had caused so much trouble twelve months earlier. In those twelve months, the camera had been replaced by one that was encased in a grey ball and fixed to look along the road only, as opposed to being able to look into people's apartments.

He sat for a couple of moments, pondering what might come from that evening. Was he doing the right thing? He knew of course that he had an ulterior motive for going with Kirsty, but he could not help but think that this could be the start of something he would be unable to control.

He had concluded a few months earlier that his attraction to Kirsty was more than just that. It had blossomed into a love that he had kept to himself and he had been unable to approach Kirsty, for fear of her pushing him away. But she had been particularly warm towards him just recently, more as a friend than as her FLO.

He knew that he was an inherently shy person, who put on the persona of a macho copper when he had to. Now, he also felt that he might have a rival for her affections in the new D.I. Fletcher Randall. He had seen the way Randall looked at her right from the start. Known that he had visited the hospital on the pretext of looking further at the Fulborough Wood remains. Not once but at least three times, Anton had told Jake on his last visit for another case.

That was not going to happen. The thought of her being with him that night in a social setting was a whole new ball game. He hadn't been this nervous since he was a teenager.

He smiled to himself and checked his hair in the car mirror, not that he had much to check. He thought about the advice his father gave him on his first date with a girl from school. Couldn't even remember her name now, but the last thing his father had said to him, as he left the house, was "No tongues on a first date, Jakey boy." Jake chuckled as he got out of the car.

Walking up to the big oak doors of Kirsty's apartment building, he rang the bell and was buzzed in without a word. When he arrived at Kirsty's top floor apartment, the door was slightly ajar. Memories came flooding back. The last time he'd seen her door like that he had ended up in a scrap with Bingham Tyler in the apartment, after Tyler had taken Kirsty hostage before he ran off.

Kirsty had never left the door open for him. She always answered it, never left it for him to enter on his own. He tapped lightly on the door and called out, 'Kirsty!'

'Come in, Jake. I'll be with you in a moment,' Kirsty shouted from within the apartment.

He closed the door behind him. As he got into the sitting room, Kirsty came along the hallway from her bedroom. Jake just stood staring at her, stunned by the sheer beauty of the woman walking towards him. He saw her in a different light. After all, he'd seen her in her apartment before in all sorts of states of dress during her darker times. But this was different. She wore a slightly flared blue dress, which came just above the knee and a short bolero-type jacket, the whole ensemble accentuating her fine curves. She wore her red hair in ringlets and those green eyes just sparkled as she gave him a beaming smile.

'What do you think, too much?' she enquired, doing a little twirl. He simply nodded, grinning. She walked up to him and gave him a peck on the cheek. Oh God! He felt some stirring emotions he hadn't felt in a long time. He wanted to scoop her up there and then, take her to the bedroom and…

'Jake!'

'Yes, that's me.'

Kirsty smiled. 'You're staring, I've never seen you like this before.'

Jake shook his head as she took his arm. 'Sorry,' he said quietly. He'd fantasised about her before, but not so intense as that night. Perhaps it was the knowledge of not being on an official visit, and he knew that this was going to need a lot of soul-searching and emotional control.

They took Kirsty's car to see her old friend. After hers had been destroyed, she'd told him that she hadn't the heart to sell Jim's Audi TT. It still had the faint smell of his cigars, which he found was a pleasant reminder of him. In the beginning, Kirsty couldn't drive it, because of the memories, but now she seemed to have come to terms with that part of her grief. Part of the healing process. It was good to see her drive it. Jake had offered to go in his, but Kirsty was quite adamant. 'You drive me everywhere,' she said as she got in the car. 'It's my turn to drive you tonight.'

Jake agreed to drive back though, so she could have a drink with her friend. They drove west out of Northampton towards the village of Harpole. High on a hill, having driven through the village, they approached a large, detached house with a white, pebble-dashed frontage, standing in about an acre of land. It had a short, gravel drive, which opened out to a large parking area and double garage. A 'C' class Mercedes Sport stood on the drive, nose in.

By the time they arrived, the light was beginning to fade. They'd travelled mostly in silence. Jake was trying to come to terms with the turmoil of emotions he was feeling as he watched Kirsty driving. Quite efficient. Part of him still wanted just to be her FLO, but a bigger part of him now understood that he wanted more. Wanted to be involved more in her life. Wanted to protect her, to make sure that nothing bad ever happened to her again. He wondered, what was to become of that night and the future.

23

They walked up to the front door and rang the bell. After a minute or so, Tanya Nicholls answered the door. She smiled broadly, a glass of wine in hand, welcoming them in with a double kiss on the cheeks for Kirsty and a fairly firm handshake for Jake.

'Tanya, you've met Jake,' said Kirsty.

Tanya smiled. Jake returned the smile. 'Yes, but all too briefly,' Tanya replied.

'Kirsty has told me so much about you.'

Jake smiled. 'All good, I hope?'

'Oh yes, very much so. Come in and take a seat. You can see I've started before you?' Tanya said, waggling her glass in front of them. 'What can I get you?'

'What've you got?' Kirsty asked.

'It's a nice crisp Chardonnay.'

'That'll do.'

Tanya nodded. 'What about you, Jake?'

'I'll take something non-alcoholic, if you have it. I said I'd drive back, so you two could catch up. I understand from your younger days, that plenty of alcohol was involved, so you've a lot of catching up to do.' He chuckled.

Tanya brought the drinks over to them and invited them to sit in the traditionally furnished lounge. It had a large dresser covering the end wall with a door to the left and a dining table set for four places.

'Expecting someone else?' Kirsty asked.

'Hopefully my daughter. Technically she's not my child – she's adopted.'

'Oh,' Kirsty said, 'when did that happen?'

'It's a long story, but to cut it short, she lost her parents when she was quite young and when she came into the hospital where I worked, we just hit it off. So, I thought, why not? We both wanted it. The problem I have is her bloody boyfriend. He's a bit of a thug – intelligent, but, nonetheless, a thug. I hope she can sort him out.'

Tanya took a seat opposite them. Jake looked at her. There was something about her that was familiar. Different hair. Perhaps it was the charming and relaxed way in which she was talking. He put those thoughts aside and was conscious of the fact that he'd taken the sofa with Kirsty and noticed how close she was sitting next to him.

'How could you both be at university together – training as doctors?' Jake asked.

She smiled. 'I started late. There's what, nine years between us?' she asked Kirsty.

'Yes, something like that. But it didn't seem that way when we were together at university, did it? The stuff we used to get up to! I think you were more of a rebel than I was.'

'I can't believe that,' she said chuckling.

'What does your daughter do?' Kirsty asked.

'She works with me. I'm also her boss.' Tanya gave a little laugh. 'Sometimes it works, sometimes it doesn't, as you can imagine.'

'Indeed,' Jake said. Something in what she said about her peeked his interest.

'What does she do, working for you?'

'She's doing a final year PhD thesis in microbiology, hence the moods. Actually, she's had a blazing row with the thug this evening, so whether she comes down to join us, I don't know. I think she'll just split up with him.'

'And what about him?' Kirsty asked.

'He's got his own business. I don't know what he does. He comes and goes as he pleases.'

'He doesn't live here then?'

'Hell, no,' she said.

They engaged in idle gossip about their lives then and now. Jake found it interesting to watch the interaction between Kirsty and Tanya, laughing together at private little jokes, talking about the other male students in their cohort, wondering what happened to them. And Jake was happy to let them talk, until there was a knock on the door.

'Ah,' Tanya said, 'dinner. I've ordered in. I hope you don't mind.'

'Having eaten your cooking, Tan, I don't mind at all,' quipped Kirsty.

'Cheeky! I've got better over the years, you know. Just had a busy day at work. I can still burn a boiled egg though.' She laughed as she walked towards the front door to answer it.

As they got up from the sofa to help Tanya with laying out the Chinese meal on the table, Kirsty brushed against Jake and took his hand gently. The smell of her perfume, her touch, her sensuality, took his breath away. He could not equate how overwhelming these feelings were having on him. After all this time, why was it happening? He didn't know whether he was going to cope with the rest of the night. He hadn't realised that she had made such a physical impact on him. He was going to have to say something to her. What and how was another matter.

They sat down at the table and Tanya called upstairs. A few minutes later, they could hear Tanya's daughter coming down the stairs. She went directly into the kitchen and said nothing to anyone in the room. To Jake, she was just a blur. In and out very swiftly, practiced almost.

Tanya shrugged it off. 'She has some issues,' was all Tanya volunteered to them for her attitude. She disappeared as quickly as she had arrived and went back upstairs. The bedroom door slammed shut, quickly followed by the heavy beat of drums and some alternative rock music.'

'Dr Tanya Nicholls, what else have you been up to all these years we've not been in touch?' Kirsty picked up the conversation where they'd left off, before the Chinese had arrived.

'It's been quite exciting really. I've been doing some DNA research. I can't go into details, but it was all about getting drugs to work for us in a better way. I really enjoy it.'

'What type of substances are you researching?' asked Jake.

'I'm looking to combat Parkinson's disease.'

'Getting anywhere with it?' asked Kirsty.

'It's a long and difficult process. It's all about getting the drug to work on certain parts of the brain to stop the neurones firing, that, for example, cause the tremors.'

'Is that even possible?' Kirsty asked.

'Theoretically, yes. There are lots of other drug research projects that are trying to tap into effecting certain brain functions, but, as I said, it's a long and difficult process. Generally it takes years.' Tanya offered the bottle to Kirsty to fill her glass.

'Do you work with anyone else?' asked Jake.

Tanya looked at him. 'As I said, I work with my daughter and a team of others at a research facility, not too far from here.'

'You enjoy it then, working with your daughter?' He gave a little smirk.

'Having just seen her performance this evening, I know what you're thinking, but when she's at work, she's a totally different person. I don't know what's got into her lately. She seems to have, well… ' Tanya's voice trailed away.

Kirsty piped up. 'But you're doing some good work though, aren't you?'

'Yes, yes, I am, something for the good of society.'

'Have you worked in this area since qualifying?' asked Jake.

'Yes, Kirsty will be the first to tell you that even during uni, I didn't have the best bedside manner,' she gave a little laugh, 'but I'd always been interested in the molecular structure of the body, particularly the brain.'

'Sounds fascinating.'

'It is,' Kirsty and Tanya said together.

'But Kirsty tells me you have a problem, that I may be able to help with Jake?'

Jake put his knife and fork down and looked at Tanya, then Kirsty. Kirsty gave a little nod, as if giving him permission to tell Tanya about an open case, which in some ways he was reluctant to do. But she was Kirsty's friend, so he was sure it would be OK.

'I can't give you details of the case, but we have a situation with some tox samples from some fatal road collisions.'

Tanya's face darkened. 'Oh,' she said in a lower tone, 'and what's the problem?'

'We've had a series of recent road deaths that have returned a suspicious substance in the bodies and no one we've shown them to seems to know what this substance may be. And we need to identify it.'

'Do you think that this unknown substance caused these deaths?'

'That's what I believe, yes. And before you ask, it's the same substance in every victim.'

'We've had the samples checked and double checked and it's the same,' Kirsty said.

'Have you gone back to the cadavers and checked for elimination over time?'

'Yes, no change, because the body's metabolic systems have stopped, therefore anything that's in the blood, stays in the blood. You know that,' Kirsty said.

'I do, yes, but there have been some drugs recently that continue to metabolise after the body has died.'

'Right. Would that be similar to the body producing alcohol in the blood stream after death, which we have discovered recently?' Jake asked.

'In a similar way, yes. We know that in those cases the microbial action post-mortem could seemingly produce ethanol, because of the blood-glucose increase after death. It's all about hydrolysis of glycogen stores, body temperature, whether there was alcohol in the stomach, and the like.'

Jake waved the palm of his hand above his head from front to back. 'Way over my head, but go on. I'll get Kirsty to explain it later.'

'We already know that certain drugs, like benzodiazepines, are mediated through the bacterial action of the body after death.'

Jake nodded, as he picked at some Kung Po chicken left in the plastic container, listening carefully.

'There have been numerous studies that show all sorts of actions after death at a microcellular level over the last few years,' Kirsty interjected.

Tanya agreed. 'But, it's notoriously difficult to identify whether a substance was there, pre- or post-mortem. Toxicology and the human body has its down-side in cases like this.'

Jake took a moment to reflect on what he had just been told. 'So, how are you going to be able to help, if it's so difficult?'

'The first thing we need to do is analyse the molecular structure of the substance, to see if there is any common ground to work with. Most drugs, particularly these designer recreational drugs you see coming on to the market and sold as legal highs, only need to have one molecule changed to move them from legal to illegal or vice versa.'

'If I get Kirsty to give you one of our samples, could you do something with it?'

'We can certainly try. The company I work for has a huge database of drug types. I'm sure we could come up with some sort of answer.'

'It would certainly help me and Jake if you could,' Kirsty said, 'because, Jake's investigation is going nowhere.'

During the conversation, Tanya's daughter had come down from her room and had been standing, listening to the conversation from the kitchen. Jake hadn't heard her come downstairs. She entered the room and Tanya acknowledged her with a wave of her hand.

'Come and meet my friends, darling,' she said, flapping her hand vigorously. The young woman fully entered the room and shook hands with Kirsty and Jake, and he realised he'd met her before.

'Sorry, about earlier,' she said, 'man trouble. I'm Simone.' She smiled weakly as she introduced herself.

Jake saw that Simone was tall for her age, slim with brown perfect skin, soft and smooth. She had black hair, in light curls, not too long, just about collar length. She was wearing a pair of blue skinny jeans that hugged the contours of her legs and an oversized tee shirt. Above all, there was a defiant attitude between her and her mother.

'That's OK, darling. We all have to cope with that sometime in our lives.' Tanya looked knowingly at Jake. He smiled.

'I know, Mother, but let's not air our dirty laundry in public, if you don't mind,' Simone gave her mother a dark stare.

Jake noticed that once Simone had joined the group, the conversations became more vague, no more discussion was had about Jake's problem, although if she was doing the PhD thesis which Tanya said she was doing, it would probably have been in Simone's interest to talk a little about it. He didn't push it and the rest of the evening continued and finished as amicably as it had started.

'You look perplexed, Jake,' Kirsty said as they left Tanya's house.

Jake looked at Kirsty.

'I didn't say anything in there, but I've already met Simone,' he said in a low voice

'Oh, where?'

'I went with Dave Harte to see the owner of a company who's currently working for Lord Fulborough. The thug that Tanya's talked about was Ian Morton.'

'I don't understand,' Kirsty said.

'Morton was the one who took the bribe to hide that second body at Fulborough Wood.'

'No wonder Tanya's not very happy.'

'It makes me wonder how involved she is with Morton.'

Kirsty nodded slowly, then changed the subject. 'I really enjoyed tonight, Jake,' she whispered into his ear as they got to the car.

Jake's heart raced, pumping blood around his body so fast he could hear it thump-thumping away in his ears. He had some great and some bad thoughts at that time, wondering what to do next, but before he could move around to the driver's side of the car, Kirsty planted her soft warm sensuous lips on his. They moved together, as Kirsty pressed herself harder against Jake with his back to the car door. He gently pushed her away, brushing her hair from her face. He gazed into those deep sparkling green eyes. He was in torment. He could easily take unfair advantage of her when they got back to her apartment.

'What's the matter, Jake?' she whispered. 'This is what you want, isn't it?'

'Course I do, you know that, but… '

'But what?' She leaned into him again and put her head on his chest. Something she had done many times before, but not in this circumstance. He stroked her hair, as they stood in silence just holding each other.

Jake felt Kirsty shaking in his arms and looked down at her and saw she was quietly sobbing. 'What's the matter? Tell me?'

'I miss him so much, Jake, and I want you so much as well. How can that be right?'

The drive home from Tanya's back to Kirsty's apartment was done in silence, the atmosphere electric.

Jake occasionally glanced at Kirsty, discreetly trying not to make it obvious, but he couldn't. He was sure he could detect a smile from her, as she watched the world go by, out of the passenger window.

Despite having been in Tanya's company, he was more than aware of how close Kirsty was to him, while sitting on the sofa. More than aware of the way she leaned in across him to pick some more chicken or rice from the bowls in front of him. And even more aware of that perfume, which sent his senses into overdrive. He had to ask himself whether she was just toying with him. But he knew her better than that, didn't he?

Jake drew to a stop outside Kirsty's apartment. She looked at him and smiled.

'Thanks for this evening, Jake. I really enjoyed seeing Tanya again, after all this time, and I'm glad you came along with me.'

'Yes, it was good, wasn't it? Even if your friend had a wry sense of black humour.'

'She always did have.'

There were a few moments of silence.

'I'd better let you go,' Jake said.

'Yes, I suppose you had.' A beat. 'Do you want to come in for a coffee?'

Jake felt the heat rising in his face. 'Er... better not. On early in the morning.'

'OK. Some other time then?'

Was that an invitation? Jake wondered. 'Kirsty, erm...'

'Yes, Jake, just say what you want. We've known each other long enough.'

Another beat. 'Would you like to do this again – soon?' he whispered.

Two beats. He looked towards Kirsty.

'Yes,' she said grinning, 'I would, just the two of us.'

Jake smiled and visibly relaxed.

'See, it wasn't that bad was it?'

'Bit out of practice, that's all.'

'I know.' And with that, Kirsty opened the door and got out. As an after-thought, she leant back into the car. 'Phone me tomorrow,' she said and closed the car door.

Jake got out of the car and handed her the keys.

She smiled. 'I'm sorry I got a little carried away on Tanya's drive.'

'Nothing to be sorry for, Kirsty. Nothing to be sorry for at all.'

She took a step towards him, kissed him, caressed his arm then walked away. Jake watched her walk up to the front doors of her apartment. He must have stood there for another five minutes with a huge grin on his face before getting into his car and driving away.

24

The following morning, Jake didn't telephone Kirsty. Instead he visited her at the hospital pathology department. He was in a buoyant mood. The evening with Tanya had allowed them both to relax, as they laughed and joked and told stories about work and life in general. It was good to relax in front of Kirsty, in front of them all. In fact he felt better than he had in years.

He'd been kept awake most of the night thinking about Kirsty, her leaning in closer to him. Recalling how stupidly nervous he'd been and how the conversation they'd had was, he knew, about to change the way they saw each other.

But that was the previous night. He pushed the doors open to the pathology lab. The staff there all knew him so they just acknowledged or waved at him, as he made his way to Kirsty's office, humming nonchalantly to himself.

He tapped on Kirsty's open office door and walked in. The smile on his face went when he saw Fletcher Randall sitting in the chair opposite Kirsty.

'Inspector.' Jake acknowledged his rival as soon as he entered. He looked at Kirsty questioning. Randall waved a hand at him, as if giving him permission to enter Kirsty's office.

'Dr Kingsfield here,' Randall said, 'was giving me the low down on the second body we recovered in Fulborough Wood.'

'Oh, right,' was all that Jake could say. He felt that his presence had interrupted something. Not that he had any intention of letting Randall know that of course. He was here perfectly legitimately, but couldn't help feeling becoming trapped into a triangular fight to keep Kirsty's affections.

Why did he feel like this? Why was he being so paranoid? Was what happened the previous night just a drunken tryst? Get a grip.

'Jake,' he heard Kirsty's voice, 'Jake.'

'Sorry, miles away – you were saying?'

'The inspector here was saying that he's going to find it hard to discover the identities of either remains.'

'I have no doubt of that, considering the length of time that they've been in the ground. At least my DBs are still intact – usually.'

'Thanks, Dr Kingsfield for that info,' Randall stood to leave. 'I'll get my team working on it, to see if we can come up with anything else and Jake, perhaps we could have a chat about your involvement in all this in the next couple of days? Get your take on it?'

'Be glad to,' Jake replied unenthusiastically.

Randall turned and left Kirsty's office, slapping Jake on the shoulder as he went. In the doorway, Randall turned back to Kirsty. 'See you later then?' He winked.

'You might,' Kirsty replied.

'What does he mean by that?' Jake asked when Randall had gone.

'He's invited me out to dinner.'

'Oh,' Jake replied, deflated. 'Did you accept?'

'I told him I'd think about it, that's all.'

'It's just that I thought… '

'Thought what?'

'Never mind. It doesn't matter.'

'You're worried he's going to steal me away from you?' She giggled.

'No, no. I just don't want to see you get hurt.'

'You're a bad liar, Jake. DI Randall was telling me that he'd lost his wife and that he could relate to how I felt. The offer of dinner was as a kindred spirit, nothing more.'

Jake nodded slowly, said nothing and pondered his boots. Kirsty went over to him and put her arms around his neck. Some of Kirsty's colleagues were looking towards the office. Jake heard a wolf whistle and some clapping going on behind him. Kirsty smiled, leaned past him and closed the door.

'I think they've all been waiting for that,' she said in good humour. 'I meant what I said last night, Jake. It wasn't the drink, although I'd had a lot. But as I said, I want you to be more to me than just my family liaison… if, and when you're ready to have me. In your own time, with no pressure, and anyway,' she said releasing him and becoming more animated. 'I enjoyed last night. I enjoyed being with you without all that kit on,' she said, gesturing to Jake's uniform, carrying baton, spray, taser, phone, radio, and other stuff that the modern uniformed copper has to lug around.

'I enjoyed it too, Kirsty. Thanks for inviting me.' And you've given me a lot to think about, which he kept to himself.

Changing the subject, she asked, 'What do you want me to do with these samples then?'

Jake cleared his throat. The policeman's armour was

back in place. 'We'll get the SOCO driver to take one of them over to Dr Nicholls, once we have authorisation.'

'OK. How long will that take?'

'Well, I've asked for it to be done today.'

'OK.' Kirsty walked over to her coffee machine. 'Coffee?'

'Please.' Jake plonked himself down in the chair Randall had vacated. He couldn't help but think that he was still going to be in a battle. A battle he was desperate to win, whatever Kirsty thought.

'I went to see Beccy Burnett this morning about using Tanya's company to do some research.'

'And what did Beccy say? How is she, by the way?'

'She's different since her promotion. Hard to think that Beccy was my crewmate not so long ago. Anyway, I had to fight our corner.'

'What was the problem?'

'Two reasons.' Jake took the cup Kirsty handed to him. 'A. It's highly irregular and B. Tanya's not on the suppliers list.'

'Don't they trust you to identify those who can help you or us?'

'Probably not. Either that or they don't trust Tanya or the company, for whatever reason.'

'As much as anyone, I'd have thought you could convince her to allow it.'

Jake took a sip of coffee, looked up and smiled. He tapped the side of his nose. 'She's going to see what she can do – no doubt have a chat with Marland first.'

'He'll refuse, won't he.'

'Not necessarily, if it gets explained to him right.'

'Let's hope so.' Kirsty sat back in her chair and looked at him directly. 'You look worried.'

'What should I be worried about?'

'About me and Tanya.'

'I'd be lying if I told you otherwise.'

'Don't worry about either of us, Jake. I know Tanya. She won't do anything to rock the boat. She's a good doctor.'

'But you haven't seen her for years. She may have changed.'

Kirsty remained quiet.

Jake continued. 'I'd also be lying if I said I wasn't worried about Randall's motives towards you.'

Kirsty glanced out of the window. She turned back to face him, the strain on her face obvious. 'Do you know anything about him?'

'No, other than he transferred in from Happy Valley.'

'Did you know he's ex-Army?'

'No. Is that how he got that scar on his face?'

'I think so. I don't know.'

'I see.' Jake wondered about Randall's motives. Empathy? Understanding? Jake tried not to show his frustration.

'But,' Kirsty said, leaning forward and placing a hand on his knee, 'he knows how you are with me, because I told him. I think he's a gentleman. I think he has his own nightmare to cope with. He said he wouldn't interfere.'

'Unfortunately, I've heard that one before.'

'Do you trust me, Jake?'

'Of course.'

'Then trust me on this.'

It was Jake's turn to look out of the window. Pensive.

'We're OK, you and I, and if it makes you happy, then let's go public about us.'

That drew Jake's attention. 'Really?'.

'Yes, but only when you're ready.'

Jake smiled. 'Dinner then – tomorrow?'

'Yes.'

As Jake left, he said, 'Don't forget that you have to attend Stephanie Parkers tribunal tomorrow.'

Kirsty looked dour faced. 'I don't really know why I've been summoned to attend.' She sat down in the chair behind her desk with a thump.

'She asked you, character witness and to confirm what was said in the pub. Don't worry, it'll be fine. You'll be in and out of the Chief's office in no time at all.'

'Hmm,' was all Kirsty replied.

'Trust me, I'm a police officer,' he said, grinning.

Kirsty returned the smile then waved him away.

25

Emerging from the Chief Constable's office, Jake watched Stephanie Parker approach him, after spending almost five hours in a disciplinary tribunal. He hadn't expected it to last for such a short time, more like a whole a day or even longer. But her solicitor had been extremely elegant in her defence and had clearly won over the Chief early on in her opening arguments.

Jake had been called as a character witness and to confirm the things she had told him twelve months earlier, after Jim Kingsfield's funeral. Jake watched her produce the letter sent by Bingham Tyler about his regret at doing what he did to her. He knew that she regarded them as just words on paper, there was no real remorse in the words, she'd concluded. She couldn't think of anything else, after what he did to her.

She managed to keep her dignity. She didn't break down when she gave her evidence, and remained calm and professional. Jake was dismissed after giving his evidence to the tribunal. He indicated to Stephanie that he would wait outside until the end of the tribunal. Parker was also thankful that Kirsty Kingsfield gave evidence on her behalf, to confirm the meeting between them. Jake knew that Kirsty was not exactly supportive of her and Parker did accept some responsibility for what had happened. Parker said that she was determined to make it up to her if she could, but at that moment didn't know how.

They were both waiting for her in the chairs outside of the Chief's office.

'Well?' asked Jake.

'I'm a little stunned,' replied Parker, who by this time was tearful and had removed a tissue from her small handbag to wipe away some tears.

'Why are you stunned?' asked Kirsty, still sitting.

'I didn't expect the panel to take me back,' she turned towards the Chief's office, as her solicitor also emerged. Parker shook hands with her, thanked her, and confirmed that she would be in touch soon. The solicitor nodded agreement and went on her way. They watched her go before saying anything further.

'So, what have they done to you?' asked Jake.

By now Jake and Kirsty had stood, Kirsty putting on her jacket, helped by Jake, ready to leave with them.

'I've been posted to Daventry. Told that I've got to do my probation again. Only it's been extended to thirty months and I've been fined the equivalent to six months' wages.'

'Wow, expensive,' commented Kirsty.

'Yes, in more ways than one, Kirsty. It means I've got to work six months virtually without pay.'

'But they'll only take it in instalments, won't they?'

'No doubt I'll find out soon enough.' Stephanie gave Kirsty a brief smile.

Frowning, Jake asked, 'Is that what you wanted?'

'I don't know what I wanted, Jake. I was expecting to get thrown into jail for bringing the force down or something worse.'

'Surely they realised that you did what you did out of fear?' Kirsty said.

'If they did, they didn't mention it to me!'

It was the fear and intimidation of being murdered by Bingham Tyler that kept Stephanie Parker away from Tyler's rape trial. Then her father packed her off to New Zealand to keep her out of the way. There was the letter Bingham had written to her supposedly apologising for his actions against her which Jake thought was completely bogus. He knew that Tyler had no remorse or empathy for anyone other than himself. And Parker had got away with the whole thing lightly that was for sure.

'They are notorious for not telling you everything, but it'll stay on your file forever,' Jake said, 'When do you start?'

'Monday. Doing a week's induction here to go through the changes to the force.'

Jake and Kirsty nodded and then Jake asked, 'And what's your mum going to say, do you think?'

'I think she'll be disappointed. In all honesty, I don't think she wanted me back on the force. She would have preferred it if I'd come back to a more sedentary lifestyle.'

'She'll support you though, won't she?' enquired Kirsty.

'Outwardly, yes,' responded Stephanie. She didn't sound convinced though.

The group was silent, as they made their way out of the force headquarters and into the rain. They stepped in line as they walked towards their vehicles.

Breaking the silence, Stephanie cautiously asked, 'What's happening between you two?'

'Oh, you know… ' replied Jake smiling, 'same old, same old…'

'You two… ?' The question hung in the air as Stephanie waggled a finger between the two of them.

'We're taking it slowly,' replied Jake without thinking.

Stephanie smiled. The kind of smile, at least to Jake, that meant she'd probably noticed his attraction to Kirsty. By all accounts, everyone had already made that observation.

The three said their goodbyes in the car park and parted company.

'Didn't expect that,' Jake said to Kirsty, as they watched Stephanie walk away.

'What didn't you expect?'

'That she'd still be in the job.'

'Really?' exclaimed Kirsty.

'No. I thought they'd kick her into the weeds.'

Kirsty looked at Jake. 'Do you think that low-cut dress had anything to do with it?'

Jake chuckled. 'That's a bit cynical, isn't it?'

'You know me. Anyway, what about "we're taking it slowly"?'

'I'm sorry. I said it without thinking. I didn't want to get into it with her and you're right. Let's set the record straight, so we don't get this innuendo all the time.'

Jake looked across the car park to see the new DCI striding towards them. As he got closer, he said, 'Sergeant Jordan, can I see you in my office – now, please?'

Jake looked at Kirsty and shrugged. 'I'll see you later,' she said, and walked off towards her car.

Jake discovered that while Parker's disciplinary hearing was in progress, DCI Freeman had been having his own disciplinary matters to contend with. Jake followed him into his office. He sat down heavily in the chair behind his desk and rubbed the top of his balding head, looking at the three officers standing before him. He gave them a good hard stare before speaking. Jake took a seat in the office behind Randall, Harte and Stevens.

'I never believed I'd be doing this over here,' he drawled in his Mid-American accent. 'I've got three more months to do, and, before I go, I'd like to leave a cohesive team behind me, but all I'm getting is constant friction between you three trying to play one-upmanship. Just put your dicks away and try to get on with the job.'

Randall went to say something, but Freeman raised this hand, 'I don't want to hear it, Randall. How long have you been here?'

'A month, sir.'

'And in that time, have you made any progress?'

'No, because I keep coming up against the brick wall that is these two!'

'What do you mean?'

'Have you spoken to our traffic colleague?' He indicated Jake behind them.

'No, this is a CID matter, not Traffic.'

'But,' Freeman said in frustration, 'he in particular, may have useful information. He was heavily involved.'

Randall turned to look at Jake. He indicated "well" with his hands. He grimaced and turned back to Freeman.

Randall paused a little before saying anything. 'This ever-present reference about Jim wouldn't do it like this, or Jim wouldn't do it like that, and we've already done that. It's really beginning to piss me off.'

'Harte, what have you got to say for yourself?'

'I just feel the investigation is going in the wrong direction. We've got a signed confession from Bagshaw.

We've lifted Philpott, although he "lawyered up", as you would say, and forensic has come up with nothing at the wood, other than those second remains. I don't know how he worked elsewhere, but it just doesn't cut the mustard here.'

'What the hell are you on about?' Randall rounded on Harte. 'I invited you onto this investigation as a courtesy. I'm beginning to think that I made a mistake. Just because you worked with Kingsfield in a certain way doesn't mean to say that I have to work the same way!'

'No, you just don't fucking work, do you? You get me and Stevens here to do all the donkey work, while you sit behind your desk on your arse all day. I'd got the measure of you when we arrested Philpott and you never lifted a finger to help.'

'OK, OK, quieten down the both of you. You're supposed to be senior officers, not two high school teenagers.'

Randall and Harte turned their attention to Freeman.

'Both of you, it seems, have a problem working together, so this is what's going to happen. Harte, you're going back to Division.'

Harte went to protest but the stare he got from Freeman was enough for him to bite his tongue.

'You, Randall, need to get off your butt and find our second Jane Doe's killer, which means doing some foot-work.' A beat. 'Have you seen this Lord Fulborough yet?'

Freeman pronounced Fulborough as Fulborrow.

'No, sir.'

'Why?'

'Not really made himself available to us.'

'And that's stopped you because?'

'He's never been available to talk to. We get the run-around.'

'Have you been up to the estate?'

Stevens pitched in. 'Yes, sir, we've been once, but he wasn't on site.'

'Then you'll just have to make him available to us.'

'You can't just go around arresting the biggest land owner in the county, sir,' Stevens protested.

'And why's that?'

'We've got no evidence he was involved – no probable cause.'

'What about, what do you say here, helping the police with their enquiries?'

'We can try, but he'll bring a lawyer with him.'

'So be it. Just do it.'

'What about the other remains?' Jake pitched in.

Freeman looked at Randall, as if inviting him to speak.

'I've spoken to Dr Kingsfield,' Randall started, but Stevens interrupted him.

'I'm sure you have,' he said, under his breath.

'Pardon?' Freeman asked.

'With respect, sir, but Randall here seems to spend more time at the hospital hitting on Dr Kingsfield, than anything else he does.

'How much time?' Jake asked.

'A lot,' Stevens replied.

'They're legitimate enquiries,' postured Randall.

'Really? I wouldn't go there if I were you,' exclaimed Harte. Jake smiled. Harte knew.

Freeman gave a sigh. 'Jesus, it's like dealing with testosterone-filled teenagers. I'd never have expected this from Her Majesty's Constabulary.'

'Oh, this is only the tip of the iceberg,' said Stevens, trying to lighten the mood.

'Right, OK. Harte back to Division, you're off the

case. Randall, investigate the job, not Dr Kingsfield, and Stevens… '

'Yes, sir?'

'Just get out of my sight.'

'Yes, sir.'

He waved them all away, then sat forward, leaning on his desk shaking his head in his hands.

Jake stood as the three of them left, 'Is there anything I can do to help?' he enquired.

Freeman looked up from his desk and rubbed his face.

'How would you like a transfer?' he asked. 'You seem to like doing CID work.'

'Thanks, sir, but no thanks. I'm happy where I am.'

'So, how come your name is all over the place?'

'I just got caught up with this twelve months ago, by being Kirsty's FLO.'

'You like her. I've heard rumours.'

Jake said nothing.

'And Randall does?'

Jake looked directly at Freeman and in Randall's defence, he said, 'Randall needs to get to know the force. He's new, like you. He needs to get to understand the people, the local force culture. I'm sure you know what I mean.'

'Yeah, I do, but keep us informed of what's going on with you.'

Jake nodded and left Freeman to worry about his new DI.

26

In the foyer of Northampton Central Police Station, Jake stood with Randall. He'd asked him to attend to assist with the enquiry, following the rather heated meeting with Freeman the previous day. But Jake was pre-occupied with three things going on in his life. One, the spate of unusual road deaths. Two, Kirsty. And three, the man he was standing next to.

It was obvious to him that the DCI wanted his input on the seemingly never-ending story surrounding Fulborough Wood. Not that it had anything to do with him. He felt that he was bound to get roped in, whether he liked it or not. It was best, he thought, to roll with it and see what happened. But, he didn't know whether to trust Randall. Yes, he was new to the job and their encounters to-date had all been a bit prickly.

'What's this all about?' he asked.

'I'm seeing Lord Fulborough,' Randall said, without looking at Jake. He kept his eyes on the front door.

'Right, and why do you want me?'

'You've met him, I understand?'

'Yes, so has Dave Harte. Why not use him? This is his station.'

'He's on his rest day, and I needed somebody who'd had dealings with Fulborough before. What's he like?'

'He can be an obnoxious bastard, cantankerous.'

'Let's hope he's having a good day then.'

They looked towards the main entrance as the door opened, producing a corridor of white light up to the front desk.

Short in stature and plump through good living, despite only being in his mid-thirties, Lord Barrington Fulborough was already greying and his hairline was receding away from his bushy eyebrows. It made him look older than he was. He was with his lawyer. A tall swarthy-looking European man which, as they stood there, made them look like Little and Large, a nineteen eighties comedy duo.

Fulborough, looked towards Randall and Jordan. Fulborough's face darkened as he strode up to Jake. 'What's the meaning of demanding my appearance here? Don't you know who I am?'

'Of course I know who you are! And I understand you are here at the request of Detective Inspector Randall?' Jake said, pointing to Randall.

'You have no rights to demand my attendance at a police station,' Fulborough fumed.

'We have every right, sir, especially as we're investigating an apparent murder on your land. Now, if you'll come with me, we'll get the matter over with and you can go on your way.'

Jake noted that Fulborough was upset at being called into a police station and the look on his face showed his disapproval. He looked towards his lawyer, who said nothing and simply nodded.

As they walked into the station towards the interview room, Fulborough said, 'I know nothing as to what has gone on. I was shocked to hear that you had arrested my estate manager.'

'If he'd have been cooperative instead of charging at us, it wouldn't have happened, would it?' Jake commented.

Fulborough made a guttural sound at Jake, like a growl. They entered the small front interview room where he and Harte had interviewed Harry Bagshaw. With all four of them now in the room, it looked overcrowded.

'Before we start,' Fulborough began – making it clear to Randall and Jake that he was not used to being ordered around by the local police, 'I'd just like you to know that I am a personal friend of the Chief Constable and I find it quite outrageous that you have demanded I attend a po-lice station.' He spat out the last few words.

'If you had made yourself available when other officers visited your estate, then this situation may not have occurred,' Jake said.

Fulborough made that guttural sound he'd made to Jake earlier. Randall, had in the meantime sat down opposite him, calmly arranged the papers from the file he had brought in with him.

Randall cleared his throat before speaking. 'Lord Fulborough, we are making some preliminary enquiries, so if you'd calm down, I'll explain to you what it's all about.'

'You'd had better do so.'

Randall smiled. 'Can I get you a coffee, tea, cold drink, before we start?'

'I'll do without, thank you. The sooner this is over, the better.'

Eventually, silence fell in the room, only to be broken by the solicitor, who demanded that the interview be recorded.

'Interviews are recorded as a matter of course nowadays, standard procedure.'

'Really? Well, my client has nothing to say at this point.'

'You don't know what I'm going to ask him.'

'We have an idea. He's spoken to his estate manager.'

'I have no doubt that he has,' Jake said.

Randall glanced at Fulborough, waiting for a reaction. His face gave nothing away.

'I just hope he passed on all the information and not just that which favoured himself.'

Fulborough harrumphed, the solicitor sighed loudly in a pissed off sort of way.

'Let's get on with it then, shall we?' Randall said. 'Tell me about Fulborough Wood.'

'Not a lot to tell really. It's just a wood, until I got rid of it.' Fulborough grinned.

'And why did you do that?'

'It was becoming… ' He paused for a moment. '… a tourist attraction.'

'Oh. How do you work that out?' Jake asked.

'Since that body was found, people come to gawp at it, amateur sleuths, trying to find new evidence to crack open your case.' He pointed at the both of them in turn.

'Do you not like them doing that then?'

'Doubt that they'll be able to now.' Fulborough again smiled and sat back with his hands locked behind his head.

'What do you intend to do with it?'

'I have planning permission to build on it.'

'Build what?'

'Garages, probably, to house my classic car collection.'

'Do you have many?'

'Enough.'

Randall shuffled through some papers in front of him. 'Did you know, or were you remotely aware of the fact, that a second body had been found in your wood?'

'Not until Philpott told me, no.'

'You have no idea how it got there?'

'No.'

'Our investigations so far show that the remains may have been in the ground for up to fifteen years.'

'Lets me off the hook then.'

'What hook would that be?' Jake asked.

'That I murdered the woman.'

'I didn't say that the remains were female.'

Fulborough looked at his solicitor, his face still giving nothing away. 'Philpott must have told me.'

'He didn't know either, which brings me to the question as to how you know.'

Fulborough flushed slightly and moved uncomfortably in his chair.

Finally moving his arms from the supposed superior pose, from behind his head. He placed them on the table in front of him and picked at one of his fingers. A reaction at last, thought Jake.

'There had been rumours.'

'About what?'

'My father.'

'What sort of rumours?'

'A long time ago, my father was believed to have had an affair with one of the estate workers.'

'Go on.'

'This is all conjecture. There was never any proof, you understand.'

'What happened to this woman? I assume it was a woman.'

'Oh, yes, it would definitely be a woman. As far as I am aware and was later told by my father, he'd paid the woman off and she left.'

'How long would this be?'

Fulborough raised his eyes to the ceiling, thinking. 'Fourteen or fifteen years ago.'

'You would have been a teenager at that time?'

'Something like that, yes.'

'Did you see this woman or know her?'

'Yes, I knew of her. She worked in the estate office.'

'Doing what?' Jake leaned forward in his seat.

'I don't know exactly. She was a bit of a looker from what I remember. The raging hormones of an adolescent boy notices these things.' He smiled again, as if he felt more comfortable talking to them. The aggressive attitude had ebbed away a little.

'Any idea what she did around the office?' Randall questioned.

'Just seemed to be there all the time. Office manager I think. I don't really know.'

'What about your own mother. Do you think she knew?'

'I think she had suspicions. She knew that Father always had an eye for the ladies. Power and land get them excited.'

'Including you?'

Fulborough's grin was cold and he said nothing.

'So, would it have been enough for your mother to kill her, perhaps?'

'No, Virginia wasn't like that.'

'Do you believe that either of them could have killed her?'

'I really don't know. I doubt it.'

Randall opened the file he had in front of him. 'How long has Philpott been working for you?'

'About twenty years.'

'Could he have done it? He has the right – temperament, shall we say?'

'I suppose so. He's a big lad.'

'Is it possible?' Jake re-iterated.

Fulborough sat forward conspiratorially. 'I've never liked the fellow personally.'

'Would you ever fire him?'

'If the opportunity came along I would, yes.' Fulborough sat back in his seat. He looked across at his solicitor who had not said a word, but had been writing copious amounts on his brown leather embossed note pad and using a very expensive ink pen.

'What about these remains then?' Randall said, bringing Fulborough's attention back towards him. 'Do you have a photo of her?'

'I may have an old one somewhere.'

'Can you find us a copy?'

Fulborough looked across at his solicitor, who nodded lightly.

'Did you know her name?'

'Avril, I think.'

'What about a surname?'

Fulborough shook his head. 'I'd have to think about that, I can't recall ever hearing it.'

'OK, it's obvious that the remains found in your wood is not specifically down to you, but it would be much better, if we had your co-operation during our enquiries. We're trying to find out who both remains belong to.'

'I understand that, but it's still an inconvenience. I can't do anything with that land until you've finished with it.' A little of his aggression had resurfaced. Jake wondered whether he had some issues in that regard.

'As soon as we have, we'll let you know. One final question – there is evidence that this woman had given birth. Do you have any knowledge about that?'

'No, never heard anything.' Fulborough hesitated. 'Look, I'm sorry that we got off on the wrong foot. It's not every day that you get two bodies found on your land.'

'Very well, but we may need to speak to you again.'

'I understand.' Fulborough stood to leave, as did his solicitor.

Randall showed them out of the station and the officers watched them walk back to his solicitors car, a Porsche Cayenne.

'Do you believe him?' Jake asked.

'I think that he knows more than he's letting on, that's for sure. He knew the remains were female and we haven't told anyone that yet. Not even the press.'

'If he was a child when all this was going on around him, he may only have put together snippets of information and come up with a completely incorrect solution.'

'Possible, but I bet any money he knows a lot more. What we need is DNA, or evidence of Fulborough's or Philpott's involvement. There's stuff going on up there that makes me very suspicious.'

'A proverbial upper crust "can of worms" it would seem.'

27

The realisation that they had a multiple murderer on their hands became obvious, after Andy Thomas had received the new toxicology reports from the motorway collision and he'd immediately told Jake.

PC Thomas's concentration on rendering the scene from his laser scanner was such that he did not hear Jordan enter his office. Thomas had been the only one in the office, the silence only interrupted by the occasional burst from the Airwave base unit on top of a filing cabinet in the corner, of their new spacious and airy office. It still had that new building smell of paint and plaster. The grey industrial carpeting was beginning to form track marks from the constant comings and goings of officers and staff with mucky boots. Thomas turned to Jake as he tapped him on the shoulder.

'What! Bleedin' hell. You wearing Jesus creepers? Skulking around offices?'

'I thought I'd made enough noise, Andy, but you were so engrossed in your pictures.'

They glanced at the screen with a line drawing of the collision slowly appearing.

'OK, perhaps. What can I do for you?'

'I've just seen the tox reports from the motorway fatals,' Jake said as he took a seat opposite Thomas.

'Yeah. That unknown substance has popped up again.' Thomas rubbed his forehead. 'What do you think we ought to do about it? You said that Major Crimes wouldn't even look at it.'

Jake stood and paced the office, glanced out of the window and turned back to Thomas. 'I don't think we have a choice, Andy. We don't have the resources to deal with something like this. We've six deaths, all suspect, standing orders don't give me a choice. Whether they like it or not, Major Crimes have got to take at least some of it on.'

'And they'll tell us that they don't have the resources either and they'll want to know which budget it's coming from. We've had this discussion before. You'll be lucky if you get any support for it.'

'But we've got to try. The same unknown substance in six different blood samples, in six different locations, at six different collisions. What other assumption can we come up with other than the fact that it may have been administered by the same person or group of people?'

'It seems that we certainly have something going on here. What about Dr Kingsfield, could she help, as she's your friend.'

'Andy, I'm her FLO, not her boyfriend,' exclaimed Jake, exasperated. 'Jesus!'

Thomas looked at Jake with a wry smile. 'You can't fool us, Sarge, it's common knowledge.'

Jake raised an eyebrow. Said nothing.

'I'm surprised that the bosses haven't said anything to you already.'

Jake thought about the visit he had recently had from Beccy Burnett. 'Why should they?' Jake asked defensively.

'You've committed an FLO sin, you got involved.'

'It wasn't supposed to be like that.'

'Look, Jake, I've known you for a long time, and believe me, I understand where you're at, but you are both quite high profile, considering what you've both done in the past.'

'To be honest, Andy, I don't really care. They can say what they want.'

'That's right – don't let the bastards grind you down.' He smiled.

'Which bastards are we talking about?' Chief Superintendent Burnett stood at the door to the office.

'Oh, you know, ma'am,' Thomas said.

'Don't worry, PC Thomas. I knew what you were talking about anyway.'

Jake looked at Burnett, questioningly. 'We know. The whole bloody force knows.'

'Except Randall, it seems,' he said without thinking.

'I told you to be careful, didn't I? I gave you fair warning, but you didn't listen.'

'Anyway, what are you doing down here, ma'am?' Thomas asked.

'I was looking for you, Jake, but caught onto your conversation. Seems we have a problem with these collisions, don't we?'

Jake invited Burnett to sit down at the desk opposite, as he recounted the information they already had, along with the occasional interjection from Thomas.

'So, we've got to add the motorway collision as well?'

'That's about the size of it.'

'What do you need to do?'

'We want resources and the only way we are going to get that is by handing it on to the detectives. It should be put on HOLMES. That's the only way we're going to correlate information, particularly about the toxicology.'

'I doubt very much whether Major Crimes will set up a HOLMES profile for us to work on. But they may give us some manpower. It seems to me that we have an issue we need to resolve and I agree that the only way to get to that point is to involve them.'

'Do you think they will go for it?' Thomas asked, fiddling with his picture.

'We can but ask, Andy. Let me make a few phone calls.' She went to leave the office, then turned to them both as an afterthought. 'I assume that the strange toxicology is now confirmed?'

'Once we've heard back from Dr Nicholls, we'll have a better understanding, but yes, by all accounts it is.'

Burnett nodded, then indicated for Jake to walk with her. They walked in silence, until Jake could not wait any longer.

'Are you not going to say anything then, about what you heard?'

'Pointless me saying anything, about that which you already know.'

'Christ, does everyone know then?'

'If I know, they must know. I did warn you.'

'I understand that, but you have to believe that it's a natural progression – two single people, working together to overcome a difficulty. It's not a crime, you know.'

'I know that, Jake, because I know you,' she said, stabbing a finger towards his chest, 'but that's not what

155

everyone else sees. You've been told to back off, not just by me, but the ACC as well.

'It's natural, and Kirsty and I will be making it public soon.'

'I'm sorry, Jake, but I may not be able to stop the process that's started.'

'What process?' Burnett found an empty office and indicated for them to go in.

'What process, Beccy?' Jake asked, more frustrated than angry.

'Professional Standards are onto it.'

'It's got bugger all to do with performing seals. Why?'

'There's been a complaint.'

'From who?'

'I'm not at liberty to divulge that information.'

'Fuckin' Randall – just because he's been sniffing around.'

Burnett kept quiet.

'I take it from your silence that I'm right?'

'I'm not saying you are, but you were her Family Liaison Officer. For God's sake, Jake, you've broken the rules. FLOs have been disciplined for doing what you're supposedly not doing. So I'm telling you to desist.'

'I'm sorry, ma'am, but I cannot.'

The use of the ma'am word towards Burnett, shook her, Jake could see that. He knew, it would instantly change whatever relationship they'd had as a crew. Up to now, he'd seen her as his ex-crew-mate. But this indicated to her that she was not going to get any further with him. He could see from her face, that whatever she was going to do next would hurt her as much as it would hurt Jake.

'Look, Jake, I don't have any other options here, friend or no friend. The reason I came to find you was to inform you that PSD want to interview you about it. They'll be contacting you to make an appointment and they'll want to make it soon. In the meantime, dependent upon the results of their investigation, we will decide as to your posting. You are also taken off all FLO duties.'

'Including Kirsty?'

'Yes, especially Dr Kingsfield.'

Jake stood, opened-mouthed, at what he had just been told. He sat down heavily in the nearest chair and shook his head. Fuck…

'I'm sorry, Jake,' was all Burnett could say as she left the office.

Jake sat there for a few more minutes thinking about what Burnett had said to him before standing and going to the locker room. He'd had enough and, glancing at his watch, decided to go home. No overtime today.

Jake stood in front of his locker and sighed. He removed his coat hanging on the open locker door. Part of him said it would be all right and that he'd be able to get away with it when they heard the circumstances, but the other part of him knew that he'd really pissed off the bosses and his chances for any advancement. What with him just missing out on another discipline over the Tyler affair twelve months earlier, his long-term plans of any type of advancement were truly up in smoke now.

He knew that what he had done was against the rules, but he had been with Kirsty all this time supporting her. The expectation that nothing would happen was a naïve view, if ever there was one. But the job worked in black and white, or so everyone thought. Policemen are not robots. And it was about time that management realised that.

Perhaps it was for the best. In any case, it didn't matter who he had a relationship with if he wasn't on FLO duty with her. In fact, he felt a little relieved that he need not try to keep what was obviously a well-known secret anymore.

Unlike the other lockers in the room, the insides of the doors were usually adorned with pictures of family, and in the case of single officers, the current love of their lives or fantasy. He'd removed the only photograph of Rosie he'd had in there, when they separated. He stood gazing at the marks on the door, where the picture used to be.

'Penny for them?'

Jake looked up to see Andy Thomas, whose locker was in the same aisle as his. A brief smile crossed Jake's lips. 'No, not today, Andy. Thanks.'

'Sorry, mate,' Thomas said. 'Shitty decision on their part.'

'Yeah, it's probably for the best.' He shrugged on his coat, said goodbye to Thomas, and left.

28

He'd arranged to see Kirsty that evening, and now sat outside her apartment. His recent euphoria had degenerated into depression. A feeling that he'd not had in a long time. What was he going to tell her? What was he going to do? He had come to realise that the affection he had for Kirsty was something more than just friendship. It was a deepening love for everything about her, her very essence. He couldn't suppress the feelings he experienced every time she was near him. But he didn't know whether she felt the same. They were close, yes. Got even closer the other night, but he'd put that to one side for now. It was probably the alcohol in her that was talking. The fact was that he wanted to get closer – was that wrong of him? If he continued the conversation they'd started, what are the chances that it would destroy what they had? Or would it bring them closer together? Whatever the case, now that he'd been removed from FLO supervision duties, he had to tell her, come what may.

He got out of his car, pulling his jacket around him to keep out the autumn chill. He looked towards the darkening sky. A storm's brewing, he thought, in more ways than one.

Kirsty invited him into her apartment. Jake could smell something cooking and realised that he was quite hungry.

'Thought I'd do a chilli.'

'Smells good – I'm starving,' he said, as she walked back towards the kitchen. She was wearing a pair of old blue jeans and a faded, black tee shirt with the slogan 'Pathologists do it on a slab' on the front. Jake smiled. She seemed happy and he wasn't looking forward to what he needed to tell her and how his day ended. He'd leave it until they had eaten. But sitting together on the sofa, he decided to start off on another tack.

'So, have you seen Randall for dinner yet? You said he'd asked you?'

Kirsty glanced across at him. 'No. And between you and me, I won't be.'

'Oh, why's that?'

'I don't know. I just find him a bit full on.'

'Full on. What? In a stalker sort of way or his magnetic personality?'

'I hadn't considered the stalker angle, but he does seem to spend a lot of time at the morgue.'

'Perhaps he's a secret goth,' Jake joked.

Kirsty smiled. 'No, it's just that he seems to be trying too hard, almost creepy, but there is something about him that I can't get a handle on. Do you know what I mean? I think he thinks that we have something in common because of our personal circumstances. You know the loss of Jim and his wife.'

'Yes, I think so. Perhaps he still needs some loss counselling, but it seems to me that he's the sort who'd rather put a brave face on it and slug it out with himself. My conversations with him have been stilted, to say the least, but he's new to the force, still finding his feet. I'm sure he's OK really.'

Silence fell for a few moments, then Jake said, 'You need to know that two things happened today, neither of them good.'

'OK, should I be worried?'

Jake looked towards her and paused, before he said, 'I got pulled from FLO duties and officially I am no longer your FLO. They're going to allocate another one. If you want one they said.'

'What! Why? I don't want another FLO, if it's not you.'

'It's because they think we're in a relationship. It's the rules.'

'That's a ridiculous rule.'

'They seem to have made their mind up and remember, I've been told to keep my distance from you on more than one occasion, so the performing seals want to interview me.'

'But that's stupid.'

'I know that, you know that, but they don't. You know that doing FLO and getting too close to the person you're supposed to be looking after is a big no-no. Most of the time it's not a problem, but when one of your own gets involved, there is a natural responsibility to do more. You know?'

'It's stupid, if you ask me,' said Kirsty folding her arms across the front of her indignantly.

'I know, which is why I told them I wasn't going to stop. Somebody reported me and I think I know who it was.'

'Randall?'

'Can't really say if he's that sort of cop.'

'Couldn't you tell them we're just good friends?'

'It'd be no good.'

'It's not as if we're sleeping together, is it?'

Jake flushed. Kirsty smiled. Jake felt his colour rise and his mouth go dry. He couldn't speak for a moment. Had she just invited him into her bed?

Kirsty chuckled. 'Look at you, Jake. You're like a teenager with a crush on a girl.'

'Perhaps because I have,' he mumbled, 'don't tease.'

'Now why would I do that?'

Don't blow this, Jake thought. He'd not been involved in this sort of thing, since he was dating Rosie. He was out of practise. 'You know how I feel about you?' he said modestly.

'I have an idea, yes.'

'How long have you had this idea?'

'A little while, I guess.'

'And you didn't say anything?'

'No, I was waiting for you.'

Jake thought for a moment. 'But is it right, not from the job's point of view, I couldn't care less about that, but the two of us – Jim's wife…'

'Widow,' Kirsty corrected. 'It's not as if we're having an affair, is it? We're grown-ups. We both need to move on. I know that I'm still coming to terms with Jim's death. He'll always be a part of me. He will always be a part of us as well, but I am sure that if he's watching, he'd be happy for us.'

Jake sat up from the sofa and brushed his hand through his hair, looking at the floor. 'Kirsty, I would be more than ecstatic to move our relationship forward.'

'Oh, behave, Jake. You sound as if you're on a management course. Just tell me plainly how you feel.' She gazed seductively at him.

All the conversation was in good humour. There was nothing to hide. He cleared his throat and sat back looking at her, studying her face, the green eyes which seemed to sparkle every time she looked at him, also surveying his face. The light from the lamp behind fell on her red hair, almost presenting itself as a halo around her head. He took a deep breath, before he spoke.

'I've known it for a long time that I was falling in love with you. And, yes. I am like an adolescent – it's been a little while since I did this sort of thing you know.'

'But that wasn't so bad, was it?' Kirsty said, jumping up from the sofa and bringing back the half-empty bottle of red wine. She refilled their glasses.

'But, how do you feel? You must have men falling over themselves to tell you that.' He gave a nervous laugh.

'Yes, they are, but they're not you.'

'Is it the right thing though?' He still felt unconvinced.

'Look, Jake, you want to be with me?'

He nodded.

'I want to be with you, not only because of everything you've done for me in the last twelve months, but because you've not forced it. I've always known you liked me even before Jim died, and I respect the fact that you have been more than professional during my traumas. But nature takes its course. I like you Jake, and I am very fond of you, but you can understand that I cannot say, at the moment, that truly I love you, even though my heart may be telling me otherwise. I am a scientist, after all.' She smiled.

'In time then?'

'Yes, in time. You know that Jim was the world to me. I loved him and I gave him my heart. We were soulmates, until he was torn away. It's not like divorce or a separation. Tyler tore us apart, a breaking asunder of two people, who had vowed in a Christian church to spend the rest of their lives together.'

'No, I understand that, I certainly do and I'm not saying

that we should jump into bed straight away. It will take time. These things do, but I'm just happier now that you know how I feel and we'll see how time progresses us. I'm in no rush.'

'And that's why I like being with you, Jake, because you don't push. You're just happy for us to be together.'

Raising their glasses, Jake said, 'To us then.'

29

Wednesday – Ian Morton

Stanwick Lakes had been, for many years, a gravel pit, extracting sand and gravel for local building works. As all the gravel had been extracted it had been developed into a series of lakes for fishing, recreation and now parts had been redeveloped as a retail outlet. The area was flat and in the early autumn, the sun shimmered off the water with a relaxing glow, as one stood and watched it set.

Standing on an outcrop of land, just north of the lakes, Ian Morton watched his team putting the finishing touches to the hedgerow they were laying for the local farmer. He'd agreed with him to do it some months earlier, but it was only now that he'd got around to it, just in time for the end of the season.

He stood with his hands in the pockets of his overalls and was speaking to his foreman, giving him instructions for the completion of the job. They finished speaking on a joke to which they both laughed loudly. Morton walked away from his employee with a wave and a smile, kicking at the grass as he walked back towards his pick-up. He was in a good mood. As he got back into his pick-up. He shut the door with a loud bang that caused a flock of birds sitting on the water behind him to take flight.

She had been sitting in the truck since he'd picked her up from home. She wanted to spend the day with him as she had the day off, she told him. That was all well and good for her, but he still had to work. She nevertheless insisted that she should spend the day with him.

Settling into the driver's seat, he started the engine, looked over to her and smiled. They continued with the conversation they were having before he'd arrived at the lakes.

'Well?' he said. 'Did you get what I needed?'

'I've got some of them,' she said, cryptically.

'Where are they?'

'They're safe, where no one would look for them.'

'OK. When will you get the rest?'

'Tomorrow, probably.'

'Take them to the house then.'

'What are you going to do with them all. It'll be a hell of a cocktail?'

'I just want to get rid of some vermin, that's all.'

'I just hope that she won't notice.'

'What's the likelihood of that?'

She shrugged. 'Depends.'

'On what?'

'Whether they do an inventory check.'

'Would they?'

She shrugged again. Very helpful, Morton thought.

Driving back onto the A45, he headed towards Northampton,

past the new commercial centre on a site he remembered used to be an outdoor ski-slope. They travelled on towards Wellingborough. She had been quiet, sitting next to him and fiddling with her phone.

'I'll tell you what,' she said, suddenly, 'let's go back to my place.'

'What happens if she comes home?'

'No, my place, I rent a semi.'

'Really? Where?'

She tapped the side of her nose. 'I'll direct you, when we get nearer.'

'And what do you want to do there?'

'Whatever you want.' She leaned across and rubbed Morton's thigh, then thrust her hand between his legs.

Morton looked at her and smiled. 'You don't need to go to your rental.' He grabbed her hand and kept it between his legs.

'Ian, I'm not a slut and I'm certainly not giving you a blow job in this dirty old bucket.' She smiled. 'Later maybe, but not here.'

Morton turned his face down in a fake sulk. 'I'll hold you to that when we get to wherever we're going.' He released her hand as they approached a roundabout, then continued on in silence. He had a smug look on his face thinking about what might happen when they got to her place. He was determined that he was going to get his end away. That was for sure.

Closer to Northampton, she gave Morton directions to her rented house on the estate.

The house was a small semi-detached, in the middle of a council estate. The fronts were dotted with grey and green refuse wheelie bins with big white numbers painted on them. None of the open-plan gardens had been maintained. Most were overgrown with high grass and nettles. Morton saw the remnants of a broken multi-gym sitting, rusting by a front door, and he didn't understand why people didn't look after their gardens. If they asked him, he'd do it for them. He made a mental note to do a leaflet drop there.

She told Morton to park on the hardstanding outside the house. They walked up to a white PVC front door. She unlocked it and they both went in.

The place was dark. The curtains were closed. He saw that there was very little in the way of furniture. And only the essentials in the kitchen.

'How long have you had this place?'

'Couple of years.'

'You've never mentioned it before.'

'You don't know everything about me, you know, Ian.'

Morton wandered around after taking his boots off. 'Not done much with it then?' He smiled.

'I come over here to get away from you-know-who.'

'Does she know you've got it?'

'Of course not.' She took off her coat and hung it over the bannister.

'It may look like a crap hole downstairs, but why don't you go up to the bedroom, and see what I've done there.' She directed him up the stairs with a wink.

Morton thought that she was taking him to a whole new level, a house of her own, a secret from Her. He smiled as he climbed the stairs and entered the bedroom.

A huge double bed dominated the room. There was a built-in wardrobe. The door was open. He glanced inside, just a few clothes. He slid the door shut and walked into the en-suite bathroom. It was small and only had a shower and a sink. The shelf above the sink had a few essentials. The shower needed a good de-moulding. He could offer to do that for her.

He turned and walked back into the bedroom. The walls were a light shade of yellow. It brightened the room, for the bedroom window seemed small and looked as though it had never been cleaned on the outside. Morton could hear her downstairs in the kitchen.

He sat down on the bed and felt the springiness of it. He'd taken his boots off downstairs, which was good, as the mud would only have messed up the thick cream-coloured carpet.

He swung himself up onto the bed as she walked in, carrying two mugs. 'Have you not got anything stronger?'

She smiled. 'I'm sorry, no. The cupboard is bare, like you should be by now.'

'I thought that I would give you that pleasure,' he teased.

She smiled and gave him that incredibly sexy pout he'd come to love. 'As you wish, but drink your drink first,' she instructed, as she sat on the bed and passed him his mug. They both drank in silent anticipation and she made no attempt to rush him. He liked that. He didn't like to do things in a hurry.

She stood and went and stood by the window, as if waiting for something.

Morton continued to drink, but as he did so, he felt as if he'd actually had too much alcohol. He couldn't understand it. 'Are you shurr you din' put anyfin in this?' he slurred.

She turned to him. She looked as if she was shocked at what she saw, but he couldn't tell as two of her swimming together, with psychedelic lights exploding behind. He slumped down onto the bed, spilling what was left of his drink. He tried to sit up. She came over to him. He was sure she was telling him to drink up. He was trying, but he couldn't lift his arms. They felt as if they were being weighed down with concrete, like his eyelids. 'P'raps I need to shleep,' he slurred.

'Yes, you do.'

30

The medical development facility, operated by a US corporation, was situated in the grounds of one of the newest UK hospitals in Coventry. The two-storey building was light, airy and predominantly made of glass. As Jake and Kirsty drove towards the facility, the sun reflected off the glass, making the whole building light up like a beacon in front of them.

They parked in one of the visitors' spaces and entered through the rotating doors. The reception area was cool and spacious. There was an atrium behind the reception desk. It had an ornamental pond with running water that trickled and burbled gently, giving everywhere a sense of calmness. It had a high glass ceiling, revealing the sky above. There were a few tables and chairs, where people could sit and talk or conduct business meetings. The sun sparkled off the running water.

There were two lifts on either side of the pond with glass frames showing the occupants. They moved up and down silently, the doors sliding open smoothly with a light hiss.

They were expected and were quickly shown up to Tanya Nicholls's office, on the first floor, where they were offered refreshments and told to sit and wait for Tanya, who was in the laboratory.

Jake wandered around the medium-sized office. More glass. Not a lot of privacy, as he looked out of the window across the hospital grounds. He was still looking out when Tanya arrived.

She sat down behind her desk, a little out of breath. 'Sorry. I just wanted to check out something, before I spoke to you.' She swept a lock of hair behind her ear.

'Good news?' Kirsty asked enthusiastically.

'Yes, I think so.'

Jake sat down next to Kirsty. 'And?'

'It seems that it is some sort of drug with GHB as its base component.'

Jake glanced at Kirsty. 'The date-rape drug?'

'Yes, it would seem so. Very very clever, whoever did it. Someone with a deep understanding of microbiology.' Tanya smiled. It wasn't warm like the smile he'd seen recently. It was almost smug, which raised a question in Jake's mind, but he dismissed it.

'No wonder we didn't know what it was,' Kirsty said.

'I know, but what gets me is that if GHB was its foundation, then the amount of time involved in these deaths, you shouldn't have found it at all. You need to remember that Gamma Hydroxy Butyrate has particular qualities that make it perfect for use, as you've said, in assault cases. GHB is one of the few drugs that crosses the blood-brain barrier without anything chemically needing to happen first. We know that it is similar to the Gamma Amino Butyric Acid – GABA, that the body produces naturally, so any changes in the make-up of GHB itself would have to take into consideration how it would react with the body.'

'So, what if, whoever made the drug got the formula wrong? Might that account for the fact that we can still find it in the body?' Kirsty asked.

'Anyone playing with the synthesis of any drugs has a period of, shall we say, trial and error.' That smile again, Jake noticed. 'But that still doesn't account for why it didn't disappear in the blood.' A look of concern crossed Tanya's face.

'Perhaps,' offered Kirsty, 'the person doing this is not such an expert, after all?'

Tanya raised an eyebrow. 'Possibly.'

Jake sat back in the chair, thinking. 'So, if it's a new synthesis of GHB–'

'Which it seems to be… ' interrupted Tanya.

'Then you should be able to identify how it has been changed, surely?'

'In theory, yes.'

'I sense a but,' Kirsty said.

'There is a big but.' Tanya sat forward leaning on her desk with her arms out front, forming a triangle.

'What is it?' Jake asked.

'In order for us to find out how its new synthesis works, we need to do a bit more research. We need to understand what happens when it's in the body to be able to do what it does.'

'How long will that take?' asked Jake.

'We don't know. What we have done is identified that one of the new molecules has a resistant shell. Now, this is very difficult to synthesise without having the right equipment and the scientific knowledge to do it. What we don't know is what happens when that breaks down.'

'We do know, don't we. It sends drivers, and only drivers apparently to sleep, when they are behind the wheel. They die. They crash.'

'But why only when they are driving?' Kirsty directed the question to the two of them. Tanya was the first one to answer.

'It has to be specific to react with certain neurotransmitters in the brain, perhaps those associated with driving. It's like these drugs I am working with for my Parkinson's research.'

'What neurotransmitters?'

'That's years of research, Jake.'

'We don't have years to wait, Tanya. We need some pretty swift answers.'

'I can't see how we can work any quicker, not without more funding.'

They sat in silence for a moment.

'Look,' said Tanya eventually, 'I'll see what I can do, but I can't promise anything. However, what I can tell you is, that in order for this drug to work, it has to act on those voluntary movements controlled in the motor cortex in the brain and–'

'That's the rear portion of the frontal lobe,' interrupted Kirsty.

'Yes, that's right, the primary motor cortex – you probably see them more than me.'

'You could say that,' agreed Kirsty, 'but doesn't that require stimulation from other parts of the brain?'

'Correct – which is why whoever has re-synthesised this drug has a far deeper knowledge of how neurotransmitters work in the brain than I do, or perhaps anyone else here.'

'So, how do we move forward?' asked Jake, who had been sitting quietly watching the two women talk medicine that was well over his head.

'We can do a bit of work here, but it's going to take

time.'

'Which we've already said we don't have. There is an expectation that this person will strike again soon.'

'We can't have that now, can we? OK, I'll do my best.' That smile again.

'That'll have to do then, but you need to let us know as soon as you get anything.'

'I'll give you a ring, Kirsty, as soon as I have something.'

The two left Tanya's office and made their way back to the car. Jake was sombre, thinking. Quiet. His copper's instinct was on high alert. Something was not right.

Kirsty took his hand lightly, bringing him around from his thoughts. 'Everything OK?'

'Yes, fine – if she can't help us, I don't know what we can do.' What Jake had decided not to tell Kirsty, was that he was convinced that Tanya knew more than she was letting on. And that disturbed him.

As Jake got back into their car his phone rang. He answered it. It was Randall.

'Have you got Dr Kingsfield with you?' No pleasantries, just launched straight into it.

'Yes, we've been to see Dr Nicholls, about my enquiry. Not that I had to tell you that. Why do you need her?'

'Yes, we do.'

'Where?'

'Fulborough Wood – we've got another body.'

31

By the time Jake and Kirsty arrived at Fulborough Wood, the area had been sealed off and officers were meticulously searching the area. Scenes of Crime had arrived with their incident vehicle and had begun to erect a SOCO tent to cover the body. The sky was grey with thick clouds threatening more rain, so the race was on to get the tent erected before it started, to protect the body and its surroundings.

Jake saw Randall talking to Freeman and other officers in a huddle, on the edge of what used to be Fulborough Wood. Randall saw them and waved them over.

'What have we got?' Kirsty asked as they joined the group.

'White male – mid thirties – looks as if he's been laid out,' Randall said, 'he's about a hundred yards in.'

'Is the body complete?' asked Kirsty.

'If you're asking whether the body is decomposed, then the answer is no. For all intents and purpose, it's.' Randall thought for a moment, then said, 'Fresh.'

'That makes a change,' Jake said.

'Right, let's go and have a look.' Kirsty walked off towards the SOCO van and climbed in. She came out wearing a SOCO suit.

Jake joined her. 'Are you going to be OK?'

'Yes, Jake, I'll be fine.'

'Only – I thought – you know – the location and everything.'

Kirsty nodded. 'Don't fuss, I'll be OK as long as I stay focussed.'

They continued to walk towards the completed SOCO tent over the body.

'Focused or not, I'm going to stay with you, OK?'

Kirsty nodded again. 'This is déjà vu, for me. Twelve months ago I was doing the same thing, only with my husband. You've parked in the same place he did. I changed into a SOCO suit in the same van, and he walked with me, like you're doing up to the scene. It's as eerie as it is disconcerting, Jake.'

'Do you want me to go then?'

'Part of me says yes, but the stronger part says no.'

'We should really get the other pathologist to come out.'

'Can you see Randall being up for that? I don't think he'd be very happy.'

Jake smiled. 'No, could you just imagine the look on his face if we suggested it?'

Kirsty shook her head. 'Better get on with it then,' she said quietly.

They could hear someone walking up behind them. They both turned to see Randall approaching.

As they got closer to the scene, Kirsty stopped and put her head down.

'Everything all right?' Randall asked behind them.

Jake turned to him and nodded as he passed them, as Randall walked on towards the SOCO tent.

Kirsty raised her face toward the sky. The rain had started quite heavily. Jake watched. Kirsty gave a big sigh and looked up into the sky. She let the rain wash away the tears that nobody else saw, except Jake. He touched her arm lightly and smiled, but said nothing. For there was nothing to say between the two people whose paths had run parallel and close for so long that no words needed to be said at this point. Both knew that what they were doing simply required the resolve of professionalism. The time to cry would come later. She smiled back at him briefly.

He knew that this was an emotional rollercoaster. Her love for her husband and the closeness between them must be a torment. Jake hoped that she would be able to put it all out of her mind and concentrate on the job. Just for a little while.

Kirsty entered the tent. Randall had already moved inside out of the rain and he beckoned Jake into the tent.

'May as well join in, Jake,' he said.

Jake stepped in immediately recognising the corpse as that of Ian Morton. His presence seemed to make it even more humid, with the rain hammering on the roof of the tent, reminding him of the times he'd spent under canvass in the rain.

He watched Kirsty bend down towards the body. She removed her recorder and spoke into it. 'Body is that of a white male. Laid on his back with his arms down by his sides. Feet together. Dark hair appears to have been combed and was neat. Eyes closed. Clean shaven.'

Kirsty looked up at Randall. 'I think this has this been staged. What do you think?'

Randall shrugged.

'To all intents, you may think that he's just asleep, if it weren't for the pale blue tinge to his skin.'

'It does make you think that whoever dumped him here, did so with some reverence, or…' he paused, 'love.'

Kirsty nodded. 'Possibly.' She lifted the body's eyelids and looked into both of his eyes with a pen torch. 'Pupils fixed and dilated. No petechial haemorrhage meaning he wasn't asphyxiated.'

She went back to her observations. 'Hands are calloused, as if he did hard labour, but not very often. Dressed in a green Dickies overall, brown caterpillar boots, a green gillet. Under the overalls a thick jumper, farmer's shirt, blue jeans. Any belongings on him?'

'Not looked yet. Thought we'd better wait for you.'

Kirsty asked the SOCO to come into the tent to photograph the body in situ. The SOCO continued to take photographs, as Kirsty searched the body methodically. She retrieved a wallet from the back pocket and gave it to Randall. There were some keys in his gillet pocket which she also gave to Randall.

'Nothing else on him,' she said.

Randall nodded, as Kirsty watched him open the wallet with his gloved hand.

'Any I.D?' she asked.

Randall searched the wallet and removed a driving licence. 'Driving licence – name of… '

'Ian Morton,' Jake said.

'How did you know that?'

'Dave Harte and I interviewed Morton, about him and his workers taking backhanders from Philpott for hiding the second body here.' Jake waved vaguely towards the entrance.

'So he should be in the system then?'

Jake nodded. 'Whatever the case, it gives you a head start.'

'How come?'

'Philpott knows him. Lord Fulborough knows him and Ian has a girlfriend.'

'We'd better get onto it then,' Randall said, as he moved towards the tent entrance.

'Why would he be left here?' Kirsty quizzed. 'It's as if someone wants to tell us something. The body is almost in the same place as the one we found twelve months ago.'

'Does that concern you?' Randall asked.

Kirsty took a deep breath before she answered. 'No. Why should it?'

'No reason,' Randall said nonchalantly. 'What about time of death?'

'Looking at the body and rigour, I can't be precise – within the last thirty-six hours, I'd say. I'll know more when I've done the PM.'

Randall said nothing.

'I can't see any cause of death externally,' she added, 'no marks on his neck or hands, nothing under the nails, as far as I can see. Nothing on the body, so I'll get him to the morgue and see what we can find.'

'Thank you, doctor. Can we move him?'

She nodded. Randall turned and retired from the tent. Kirsty heard him giving instructions. She stood then took one last look at the body before leaving the tent herself.

'Are you OK?' Jake asked her.

'Yes, but would you take me home, please?'

He nodded. As they walked back towards their car, Kirsty told Randall that she'd do the PM, first thing in the morning. Jake thought he seemed rattled by that, but the last thing she was going to do was jump when he wanted her to.

32

Jake had been informed that Freeman was putting together an enquiry team and to get himself over to the briefing room. The latest find at Fulborough Wood appeared in some way to be linked with his collection of road deaths and that Burnett and the ACC wanted Freeman to start a full enquiry.

A team of traffic officers and detectives gathered in the briefing room to discuss this new information that had come to light.

As Jake entered the room, Randall acknowledged him and noted the obvious demarcation between traffic and CID. The detectives were sitting on the left of the room close to the windows. The sun shone brightly making that part of the room warm with the haze of dust swirling about slowly. All the traffic officers sat on the right of the room. Jake went and sat down with his colleagues, next to Kirsty who was engrossed with her phone. She looked up as he sat down and smiled at Jake.

Randall began the briefing and after the preliminaries introductions, said, 'For those of you who have just joined the investigation, I'll give you a brief run-down as to where we are. As of yesterday, this enquiry has been given a high priority status. It appears that someone out there is determined to drug and kill people, which seems random. Dr Kingsfield has just confirmed that the blood toxicology of the victim, Ian Morton, is the same as those deaths in which Sergeant Jordan is investigating. He and his team from roads policing initiated this enquiry, following a number of fatal collisions, the toxicology of which showed some unusual results. And, before anyone asks, all the collisions are unrelated, as far as we can see. Six or seven collisions have been identified.' He turned to Jake to confirm the number, who nodded in agreement. 'These collisions took place in various parts of the county, but the latest one involved the multiple collision on the motorway a few days ago. I'll hand you over to Sergeant Jordan to continue.'

Jake stood and joined Randall at the front. 'From what we can make out so far, these collisions all involve women of a certain age and a particular appearance. The ages are between twenty-five, the youngest, and the oldest, thirty-six. All the women had dark brown hair, cut in a bobbed style.'

DC Fred Martin raised his hand.

'Yes, Fred?' said Randall, acknowledging his detective.

'Boss, if you say that all the women were of a particular type, do we know whether they were single or married?'

'Both,' replied Jake quickly.

'No pattern there then.'

'Nothing we can see at present.' Jake went on. 'What we do know is that CCTV has confirmed that all the victims were seen in clubs and pubs in the town centre the night before their deaths.' Jake was acutely aware, as he spoke, that

Chris Prentice was squirming a bit in his seat. Jake continued his briefing, knowing how some of the information may be embarrassing to Prentice, but it had to be said nonetheless.

Kirsty stepped up to talk about the toxicology angle which didn't take too long. Jake could see that she was uncomfortable talking to the group, even though most of the detectives knew her.

As Kirsty sat down, Sergeant Stevens spoke up. Jake looked at him, expecting some sort of quip, but he simply asked, in a matter of fact way, that took Jake by surprise, 'If they've been seen on CCTV in the town, have they looked to see if they were with anybody or has the same face popped up in the vicinity of our victims?'

'We're still on that, Sergeant,' Randall responded. 'The forensic computing team are looking through hours of footage. Hopefully something will come out of it.'

Stevens nodded. Jake, in the meantime, had put photos of all the victims up on the big TV screen at the front of the briefing room.

'All these victims,' he said, pointing to each of them individually, 'have families of some sort or another. The most distressing of these collisions also involved the son of the last victim, who lost his life in the minibus being driven by his mother, so the family are doubly traumatised. We've allocated FLOs to these families.'

'Have we checked their mobile phones?' Fred called out. 'Bound to have taken a selfie or some other snaps of their boozy night out surely?'

'I'm glad you brought that up, Fred. The answer to that is yes, particularly for the last victim.'

A picture appeared on the screen showing two women, apparently the worse for wear, who had taken a selfie somewhere out in the street. They could see one of those horrible coloured doors behind the pair leading to a nightclub.

As the picture was displayed, the colour in Chris Prentice's face drained and he sat low in his seat. This reaction was not lost on Jake or Randall. Randall looked at Jake – neither spoke but both had an idea of what Prentice was thinking.

'So, if anyone recognises the blonde in the photo, they had better come and see us.' They both looked at Prentice.

'But if all of your victims have so far been women,' Stevens asked, 'how come we have a dead male?'

'That we can only surmise,' Randall said, 'it's possible that he may have been an experiment – in the similar vein as young Prentice here.'

A chuckle went around the room. Prentice simply sat with his head bowed. 'Or,' Randall said as the room came to order again, 'he may have got in the way of our murderer and until we find out who it is, I hope there will not be any more.'

'There are a few leads on that,' Jake said, 'which we'll let you have now.'

After distributing tasks, the briefing ended and everyone left, except Chris Prentice.

'I thought you might stay behind, Chris,' Jake said.

Prentice nodded. 'I think you know what I'm going to say.'

Jake gave him an encouraging look for him to continue. After a short pause, Prentice said, 'I think the blonde in the photo was the woman who – you know…'

'I thought as much,' Jake said. 'Would you recognise her in the club again?'

'Of course – I'd hope she'd recognise me as well!'

'Not unless you were naked,' smirked Randall.

'Yeah, right, thanks for that, boss,'

'At least we have a lead,' Jake said.

'A slim one,' Randall added.

'So, how are we going to capitalise on this information, Inspector?'

'Any ideas, Prentice?' Randall asked, turning to him.

Prentice shook his head.

'No,' said Jake slightly more animated, 'but I have. An idea which might draw our killer out in the open.'

'How?' Prentice and Randall asked in unison.

'I recently gave evidence at a disciplinary tribunal… '

'You're not going to suggest, Parker,' Kirsty pitched in, finally drawing herself away from the picture on the screen.

'Got it in one!' Jake said smiling.

'But why?'

'She wants to prove herself.'

'She won't be proving much, if she ends up dead!' Kirsty retorted.

Jake looked at Kirsty for a second or two, trying to work out what to say next, but was interrupted by Randall, before he could say anything.

'She wouldn't have to do it, if she didn't want to.'

'No, but I'm going to go with her,' Prentice said.

'How's that going to work then, if she only targets lone females?'

'Ah,' said Prentice, 'she doesn't. She waits for people to approach her. That was my downfall – long legs and a short skirt, sitting alone at the bar.'

'Not that you remember anything of it,' smiled Jake.

'I don't remember the getting handcuffed bit, I'll agree.'

A silence descended in the room while they contemplated their next move.

'Well,' Randall said, breaking the silence, 'it seems that this is all we've got, so let's run with it.' As he stood to leave the briefing room, he turned to Jake. 'Go talk to Parker, Sergeant,' he said, as he disappeared out of the briefing room.

Jake watched the big black iron gates swing open, as he waited to drive into the rear yard at Daventry police station. It was a modern, square, red-bricked building of three storeys, built in the 1960s. Jake remembered seeing an old photograph of the place taken in 1965 and it looked fairly new then.

The yard was small, barely large enough to park eight or ten patrol cars of various sizes at any one time. Fortunately for him, most of the patrols were out, so he found no difficulty in parking his BMW estate.

Out of the car, he sidestepped a large foamy puddle that had been left behind by someone who'd recently cleaned a car. He swiped his card across the reader to get in and walked through the station and down a corridor to the front office. He asked the female counter assistant where PC Parker could be found, to be told that she was upstairs in the canteen on her break – a rare thing, Jake thought – if only.

The canteen was on the first floor. It had succumbed to the force's desire to do away with station canteens and although of a fair size, it had been reduced to a self preparation area for the street cops who wanted to make their own food, (if they ever had time), or just hit the chocolate and coffee machine. A large panoramic window showed a view over the town centre and the superstore car park. He found Parker sitting in the corner, eating sandwiches from her sandwich box and reading a dog-eared Police magazine, some years old.

She looked up, as he approached her. She smiled warmly. 'Hi, Jake.'

Jake could just about still make out the faint New Zealand accent that Parker had picked up while she was out there.

'And what brings you here?'

'I've come to see you, and to ask you something.'

'Not just to check up on me then?'

Jake smiled. 'No, I've come to offer you a job.'

'I can't, Jake. Remember? I'm only just into my thirty-month re-probation.'

'Re-probation or reprobation, as in reprobate?' Jake smiled.

'Reprobate is right, the way I've been treated.'

'What if I can help you?'

'Oh, how?'

'We need somebody for an undercover operation, a sting. We also need somebody that wouldn't be sussed out as a copper, someone neutral, unencumbered by police procedure.'

'Oh, so you think I'm neutral and unencumbered?'

'At the moment, yes.'

Parker chewed on her sandwich before answering. 'What's this job? And how does it help my situation?'

'We need somebody to go into a nightclub and...' Jake faltered.

'And what?'

'Pick up a suspect.'

'What? As in arrest?'

'No, as in "pick-up".' Jake's eyes danced as in a "you know" fashion.

Parker smiled, getting the message. 'What's this guy done then?'

'It's not a guy.'

She took another bite from her sandwich. 'I'm a bit insulted, Jake. I don't follow Sappho of Lesbos, you know.'

'I know, but we think she does.'

'So, what, I wait for this woman and then try pick her up?'

'No, hopefully she'll pick you up, if you are the right, type, shall we say.'

'And what type is that?' Parker put what was left of her sandwich back in the box, looking intently at Jake.

'You'd have to wear a dark brown wig, unless you want to dye and cut your own hair.'

'It wouldn't be the first preference, I have to say.' She took a drink from a can sitting next to her lunchbox.

Jake smiled. 'So, do you want to help us out then?'

'You'll have to give me a bit more information first.'

Jake sat down in the low easy chairs opposite Parker after taking off his hi-vis. He sat back and folded his arms, looking at Parker. 'Are you sure you're happy to do this?'

Parker nodded, took another drink.

'I understand this woman we are after doesn't want to take women to bed.' Jake squirmed a little, not knowing how Parker would take the next bit of information. 'This woman…' he paused, 'drugs her victims, puts them in their car and lets them drive, usually ending up involved in a fatal collision.'

Jake agonised over the information he'd just given her and it was obvious to Parker from his face. She remained quiet for a moment, and took a peak into the sandwich she had just picked up. She looked across at Jake.

'You want me to get drugged up then?'

'Hopefully it won't come to that, because we'll get to her before she does it. There'll be a full team to back you up.'

'Will anyone be with me?'

'One of my officers, who, shall we say, has had experience of this woman.'

'What sort of experience?'

'Let's just say that it was a public embarrassment for him.'

'So, he has a motive to find her?'

'He wants to see her locked up, yes.'

'How many women has she…?'

Picking up where Parker was going with this, Jake clarified. 'Definitely murdered? She may be responsible for the deaths of several people while driving their cars and yesterday's body found out in Fulborough Wood.'

'Jesus! What is it with that place?'

'Yeah, I know.'

'How does that work then, this drug thing?'

'We think a new kind of drug has been developed that only works on certain parts of the brain and only when you drive.'

'Is that even possible?'

Jake sat forward. 'Kirsty says it is, and it's very sophisticated.'

'When do you want to do this?'

'As soon as possible, probably this weekend.'

Parker nodded slowly. 'And what about my boss here?'

'ACC Marland is looking after that.'

'And what happens to me if I survive all this?' Parker asked. 'A lamb to the slaughter,' she added.

'No guarantees, but your case will be reviewed with a view to reducing your probationary period.'

Jake watched, as Stephanie stared out of the window towards the town centre. He looked in the same direction and saw a woman on the pelican crossing stop halfway to pick up a toy her child had thrown out of the buggy she was pushing. He could hear the tantrum from the child, even behind the glass of the police station canteen. Parker turned back to Jake, solemn-faced.

'And back to Northampton – please?'

Jake nodded.

'Can I think about it? I don't know whether I'm ready for undercover operations.'

'I'm sure you'll be fine and I know you can do it.'

Jake looked into Parker's lunchbox as Parker went to pick up her half-eaten sandwich. There were a few chocolate biscuits in the corner of the box. He stood.

'Don't be long making a decision about this, Stephanie,' Jake said. 'I can only give you till tomorrow. Ring me, OK?'

'OK.' Parker took a bite out of her sandwich. 'Seems I might be indebted to you again Jake – if I take the job.'

Jake simply nodded slightly, leant over her sandwich box and nicked a biscuit. He smiled. 'Not good for you, chocolate.'

'No worse than being drugged by a murdering psychopath,' Parker countered in good humour.

Jake waved the biscuit at her as he went to leave, and smiled. 'Indeed,' he said, leaving Parker to think on.

33

The restaurant at force headquarters was virtually empty when Jake arrived just after eight AM, the following morning. Randall, was sitting in the corner by the window tucking into his breakfast. He acknowledged Jake as he entered the restaurant.

The restaurant had long tables with utilitarian easy clean table tops, it was bright and the smell of cooking permeated from the kitchen area as he placed his order for a bacon sandwich.

While he waited, Jake poured himself a coffee from the machine at the end of the counter. By the time he'd done that, the bacon sandwich had arrived, which he paid for then wandered over to Randall and sat down opposite him.

Jake bit into his bacon sandwich. Randall was knee-deep in a greasy, fried breakfast, wiping up egg and bacon fat with a thick chunk of white bread. Stuffing the bread in his mouth, he licked his fingers, quietly belched his satisfaction and scrutinised Jake, while taking a great gulp of coffee.

'Do you make a habit of it. Fletcher?'

'Make a habit of what, Jake?' Randall said, wiping his mouth with a serviette.

'Going around picking up or hitting on female colleagues?'

'I don't know what you mean.'

'You couldn't get it on with Dr Kingsfield, so now you're hitting on PC Parker.'

'No, it's not the sort of thing I do and I'm insulted that you think that.'

'Really? That's not what Parker told me this morning.'

Randall stared at Jake then just shook his head.

'I spoke with her yesterday, as we agreed, and then she tells me this morning that you went and saw her last night to try to convince her to join our operation.'

'I didn't want her to miss out on the opportunity to get in the bosses' good books, that's all.'

Jake leaned across the table, speaking almost in a whisper. 'That's bollocks, sir, and you know it. She would have come round eventually.'

'Eventually is a long time away and we need her, Sergeant.' Randall sat back and folded his arms. He looked around the restaurant. 'Is she in then?'

'Yes, no thanks to you. Did you not think that I could secure her assistance?'

'No, it's not that. I just thought that it would reinforce what you asked her.'

'So, you reinforced it, by taking her out for a drink.'

'What was wrong with that? She could have refused.'

Jake said nothing.

The restaurant was beginning to fill up with a group of officers on a training course, sitting around them, so their conversation was no longer private.

'What's she going to do?' Randall asked after a moment.

'She told me this morning that she would do the undercover job, so long as she had full back-up.'

Jake looked around the restaurant, acknowledging a couple of colleagues as they walked past.

'OK. And what about Dr Kingsfield in all this?' Randall asked.

'She's not in it, is she? And I don't want her involved.'

'But if she insists?'

'Then, for her own safety, we should ensure that that doesn't happen.' Jake stopped chewing on his sandwich and looked at Randall. 'She's been through enough, Fletcher. It wouldn't be wise to get her involved. She's a scientist, not a copper.'

Randall nodded slowly. 'You have a thing for her, don't you?'

'More than you will ever know. Do you?'

'I do, yes, but as a colleague – nothing more. We have things in common, that's all I want to say. Anyway, by all accounts, Dr Kingsfield has made up her mind.'

'Yes, but it wasn't for the want of trying your luck, was it?' A beat. 'What things in common?' Jake asked as an afterthought.

Randall looked around the room before answering. Jake noticed Randall touch the wedding ring on his finger. He looked directly at Jake. 'Let's just say that we've both lost people we've loved and you… you lost your job over her. Now just another shift sergeant.'

'You win some, you lose some – there'll be other opportunities. Anyway, it's all about doing things that are right and not necessarily worrying about the job. I've done nothing wrong. I can't help it if the job is so blinkered, that they can't see, that if they put two people together, after a time something is bound to happen.'

'You sound bitter. Was it worth it?'

'Yes,' Jake responded, without hesitation.

'Did you know her before her husband's murder?'

'Vaguely, professionally.'

'Ah, admiration from afar.'

'She's a good pathologist, you know.'

'Why didn't the hospital keep her in her position then?'

'You'd have to ask them that.'

Randall sat back in his chair, then leaned forward, while Jake finished eating his sandwich, washing it down with what remained of his mug of coffee.

'I've decided that I like you, Jake. You're a good copper.'

'That's very condescending of you, but I don't need your approval.' He smiled. A cold smile.

Randall gave Jake a huge grin, the first time that Jake had seen his face break from the dour looks he normally had. They both stood, then Randall held out his hand. Jake took it.

'Go and enjoy your life with Kirsty, Jake. From what I hear, I think you deserve it.'

There was a momentary silence before Randall spoke again as they walked out of the restaurant together. 'How are we going to catch your killer? After all, that's what we've come here to discuss, isn't it?'

'I think we need to put Prentice in with Parker, but separate, so that he can ID her to the rest of us when she turns up.'

'What intel have we got about these other women, dates, times etc?'

'Commonly, a Sunday night, although the A5 one was a private party, we think she may have crashed, so to speak. Don't really know how our perpetrator got into that one, but my guess is that it'll be over a weekend, which makes me think that whoever is doing this works during the week.'

'Do you think that we'll be able to set something up for this weekend?'

'If Parker and her boss agree, I don't see why not.'

'How long do you want to run the operation?'

'Till we catch her.'

'And practically?'

'No idea – two, three weekends, maybe.'

'OK. I'll draw up some plans.'

'I'll arrange for some extra cars in town, just in case she does a runner.'

Randall nodded. They walked in silence.

As they got to the car park, Randall said suddenly, 'You know, Jake, I'm not chasing Kirsty. I was, I'll admit that, but it's plainly obvious to me that she has eyes for you and nobody else. The conversations we've had feature you quite prominently, enough for any man to understand that she's not available, if you get my drift.'

They stopped walking. Jake looked directly at Randall. 'Thank you for being honest, Fletcher, but…' Jake smiled, 'you better not go after her. Traffic's arms are very, very long!'

Randall guffawed as they went off in their separate directions.

An hour later, when Jake had spoken and cleared the operation with Beccy Burnett, he walked into the incident room. As he stood on the threshold, he felt strange. It was peculiar, that he saw uniformed traffic officers in deep conversation with detectives.

He knew that there was a traditional split between the two departments. The view amongst some of the elder statesmen of the detective world, was that a constable was promoted to the detectives and demoted to traffic.

With the advent of extended road death investigation, the two departments were inexorably drawn together, so much so that there were even two detectives allocated for use by the road death investigation unit.

He stood near the door and watched his officers and Randall talking to another detective. He didn't know what to make of Randall. One minute he was friendly and willing to engage and the next a dark mood would come over him, making him appear introspective – thoughtful or distant maybe. Colleagues had quickly learnt not to cross him, when he was in one of those moods.

Jake had made a few enquiries about Randall discreetly with his counterpart in Thames Valley after his comment in the restaurant about him having things in common with Kirsty. The source told him that Randall had only been in the job for about ten years, but moved up the ladder fast. However, something had happened, which had stopped him. And Jake hadn't managed to find out why he'd been discharged from the Army either. He assumed it was something to do with that scar on his face. But there again, he could be looking at it all wrong and, if the guy was doing his job, did he need to worry about it?

Randall saw Jake standing by the door and called him over.

'Well?'

'All OK, all sorted. We're on for Friday, as discussed.'

'Splendid! Let's go catch us a murderer,' Randall said, rubbing his hands.

34

Friday
Lord Fulborough

Standing in the estate office, Barrington Fulborough waited for the arrival of his manager, who he had summoned as a matter of urgency. Fulborough was, to say the least, more than angry at Philpott. Not only did he dislike being instructed to attend a police station, but he also disliked being deceived, allowing Philpott to think that everything went OK with the wood-clearing job, when clearly it hadn't.

He knew that Philpott had been with the estate for a good twenty years, but he had never liked him and thought him more a thug than a manager. He had forgotten the number of times his father had argued with him about upsetting the staff, because of his arrogant attitude.

But this was different. The man had deliberately concealed the remains of a human being, so he could get the job done. Thinking that no one would find out about it was a presumption beyond belief.

Fulborough was savvy enough to know that you couldn't keep that sort of thing quiet for too long. People talk. He was determined to find out who had told the police about this and was determined to see Philpott gone. Today. After all, the reputation of his family was at stake, and if the press got on to it?

He'd sent all the office staff home early, so that he would have the place to himself.

He looked out of the window onto the rain-soaked gravel yard to see Philpott in his 4x4 come sliding to a halt outside the office door. His attitude and posture were clear to Fulborough. This was going to be a stand-off.

Philpott barged into the office, letting the door slam behind him. 'You want to see me?' he growled.

'Yes, sit down.'

'I'll stand.'

'Please yourself.' Such an air of superiority, thought Fulborough. We'll see about that!

'I need to know what's going on?' Fulborough demanded.

'There's nothin' going on.'

'So, why have I spent hours with the police talking about the remains of a body found in the wood you're clearing?'

Fulborough could see that Philpott was caught off-guard, thinking this meeting was about something else perhaps.

'I'm not sure what you mean?'

'It's obvious, isn't it? I've just been interrogated by a detective about a body found in my wood, which you failed to tell me about.'

'I left the contractors there. This is the first I've heard of it!'

'That's crap and you know it! Why did they tell me that you knew all about it then, tell me that?'

'They told me that they dug up an old rug and I told them to bury it.'

'So, they did tell you, or were you there at the time, Frank?'

Fulborough could see that Philpott was considering his options – lie or tell the truth. Lying came easily to Philpott, he knew that, but if his job was on the line, he might come across with the truth.

'Well?' Fulborough reiterated. 'You tell me the truth or you're out of a job!'

Philpott glared at Fulborough. 'You can't do that! The old Lord saw to that.'

'He's dead and I can. Now tell me the truth, Frank.'

Philpott walked over to the office window and glanced out of it, before rounding on Fulborough. 'You wouldn't understand, if I told you the truth. What was I to do? You've been banging on about the fucking place for twelve months. Any delays and you'd have been on my back for not getting the job done.'

'Yes, Frank, but there are limits. I have a reputation to uphold not come right down to your level and into the gutter.'

'Is that all you're worried about? Your bloody reputation? Jesus, Barry.'

'You still haven't answered my question – did you find a body; simple answer, yes or no?'

'Yes.'

'Did you put it back in the ground?'

'Yes, we did, and I paid the contractors to do it!'

Fulborough stood from behind the desk he had been sitting at and rubbed his hand through what hair he had left, shaking his head. He walked around the front of the desk and stood in front of Philpott. 'Who is it?'

'How the fuck should I know?'

'You've worked on this estate for long enough to know where all the skeletons are buried, literally, it would seem, so don't lie to me.'

Philpott didn't answer, but in the back of Fulborough's mind, he was trying to recall something that had the estate buzzing years earlier, when he was a child. He just couldn't recollect it and it worried him.

'The police told me you had been arrested. Is that why you've not been about for a couple of days?'

'They took me in, yes.'

'And?'

'I've been charged and bailed.'

'With what?'

Philpott reached into his inside pocket and withdrew a charge and bail form. He handed it roughly to Fulborough, almost throwing it at him. Fulborough read it.

"Charged that Frank, Philpott did an act, namely to assist in the disposal and concealment of the body of an unknown female, with intent to impede the apprehension or prosecution of an unknown person, who had committed the offence of murder."

Fulborough looked up at Philpott. 'Jesus, Frank, you could go down for this.'

'Not a chance – got a good lawyer.'

'Whom I'm paying for, no doubt.'

'If you want me to keep quiet about who it is, yes.'

'You know who it is?'

'I have a good idea!'

'And the one they found last year?'

'Probably…'

'I'm sorry, Frank.'

'For what?'

'I'm not going to pay for your defence.'

'You want me to go to the old bill then?'

'You can please yourself. You're in enough trouble as it is.'

Philpott took a step closer to Fulborough, who stood his ground.

'I'll bring you and your fucking reputation down with me if I do! I've worked here for twenty years. You can't just get rid of me!'

'Watch me, Frank. You're fired! Now, get off my land.'

Philpott lunged at Fulborough, but, heavy as he was, he managed to duck out of the way of Philpott as he came at him, anticipating Philpott's reaction. He wasn't prepared, though, for Philpott's quick recovery, as his elbow struck Fulborough hard on the back of his head. Fulborough went down, cracking his head on the corner of the desk. As he landed, Philpott gave him a heavy kick to the head, knocking him unconscious. Another kick in the back and head ensured that Fulborough wasn't going to get up in a hurry.

Philpott didn't check to see whether he was alive or dead. He left the office, locking the door behind him. Then he got in his 4x4 and raced out of the estate.

35

At the Fulborough Hall estate office, the scene was in the process of being locked down by uniformed officers who had already cordoned off the office. Randall had been dispatched to the scene after it was reported by a member of staff as they got to work, that Lord Fulborough was found unconscious in the estate office. The staff had gathered themselves in the estate yard, a large square of gravel parking area bounded by box hedging on one side and what were converted stables on the opposite side. The office was directly ahead, in front of the main entrance, with a large green stable door, both halves of which stood wide open, blue police tape swaying lightly in the breeze. A couple of the female staff were openly weeping as most had worked for the Fulboroughs for many years.

A single SOCO was going about her business, taking photographs of the scene, and the ambulance was just leaving, as Randall, Stevens and Martin arrived. Randall got out of the car that Stevens had parked next to the SOCO van. He walked over to the van, found a pair of overshoes and entered the estate office.

'What's happened here then?' he asked the SOCO.

'Lord Fulborough was found here,' she said, indicating the side of the manager's desk, 'when the staff arrived this morning. He was lying on his side with his back against the desk. How he managed to survive the night is beyond me – got a nasty gash to his head.'

'Hmm, what did the paramedics have to say?'

'I don't think they were very confident about his survival, but they spoke to one of the uniformed officers.' Click, flash.

'Have you found anything of significance?'

'Not yet, no.' Click, flash.

'Why are there no others SOCOs here?'

The SOCO put her camera down on her SOC box and got down onto her knees near the desk, with a torch, as she searched underneath it. 'It only got reported as an assault, not a possible murder scene, but I've updated my manager,' she said as she surfaced from underneath the desk.

'Right. I'll give him a ring anyway. We need to treat this as such, just in case he doesn't survive.'

The SOCO nodded and returned to her photography. Randall left the office, removing his overshoes. He threw them in an evidence bag and sealed it up. As he was doing that, Stevens walked over to him.

'Any luck with the staff?' he asked.

'No, not yet. The office manager hasn't arrived. Apparently she starts late on a Thursday and Friday.'

'Did they say anything that would help us?'

'Only that Fulborough sent them all home early yesterday.'

'Any reason for that?'

'They don't know.'

Randall rubbed the scar on his face, thinking. 'Do you think that this may be something to do with those bodies we found in his wood?'

'I'd bet my boots on it, guv.'

'Let's get the ball rolling then and treat this as a murder from the outset. I'll speak to Freeman. You get more SOCOs in and let's cordon the yard. Move everything and everybody away that wasn't here last night, before we lose any more evidence.'

Stevens turned to go.

'Oh, and let's get some more uniforms down here to stop anyone entering the estate – and find me Frank Philpott.'

Randall was already on the phone to Freeman.

By the time Freeman had arrived, the scene was as secure as Randall could have made it. Freeman gathered his CID and uniform officers in the mobile police station, which had been set up in the entrance to the estate.

'Right, we all here?' announced Freeman. The talking subsided and everyone turned their attention to him.

'As far as we know at this point in time, Lord Fulborough is still alive. What we don't have is a motive or any other reason why he was attacked, although we are working on some theories. We have officers at the hospital waiting for him to regain consciousness, if he does. We need to interview all the staff again, particularly those who found him. We're looking for any bit of information. Leave nothing to chance. Our first priority is the recovery of any physical evidence, now that we have extended the cordon. Anybody got anything else?'

Fred raised his hand and Freeman indicated for him to continue.

'I've spoken to some of the staff,' he said, looking in his notebook, 'The office junior arrived first at about seven a.m., but didn't have a key, so she had to wait for the key-holder to arrive. If she'd have looked through the window, she would have seen Fulborough lying there, but she never got out of her car until a key holder arrived. The senior estates manager was the first to pitch up.'

Freeman nodded. 'He was the first to find Fulborough, along with the officer junior?'

'Correct.' Fred said.

'Did he say where Fulborough was?'

'Just opened the door and there he was,' pitched in Stevens.

'Very funny, Clive,' remarked Fred. 'They saw him lying by the desk. Thought he was dead, checked for a pulse, then called the ambulance. She's very shook up about it. I've had her taken home and said we'll get a statement later. I don't think she can add anything of significance anyway.'

'Fred, thanks for that update. Inspector, any news on the whereabouts of Philpott?'

'No, but we've put out an all-ports warning. What you would call a BOLO, I think – what does that mean anyway? Oh, and we've updated the Auto Number Plate Recognition database. We'll find him, no doubt about that.'

'Right, let's all meet back at Headquarters at 18:00 and see how far we've got. And Randall?'

'Yes, sir?'

'BOLO means, "Be On the Look Out".'

Randall smiled and nodded to the DCI. As the room dispersed, a young PC entered and went up to Randall.

'Sir, I think you need to come and speak to the office manager, who's just turned up, She has some information I think you'll need.'

36

Freeman sent Randall and Stevens out with the constable and across the yard to see the office manager. She was standing with a WPC, with her back to the wall. In one hand, she had a cigarette, which she was pulling on rapidly. In the other hand was a small handkerchief, with which she kept dabbing her eyes.

Randall wondered whether the tears were because of the cigarette smoke that swirled around her head or genuine sadness for what had happened. The WPC introduced the woman as Marjorie. She was in her late sixties, with short black hair, obviously coloured. But despite this, she wore a knee-length, floral skirt and black leggings, and a sense of up-to-date fashion.

Randall introduced himself and Stevens and asked her what she knew. Before she answered, she dropped her cigarette stub and lightly stood on in to put it out.

She looked up at Randall, her eyes bloodshot where

she had been crying and cleared her throat. 'Late yesterday afternoon,' Marjorie began, 'Barry, Lord Fulborough, came into the estate office. He usually comes in at least once a day, not like the old Lord, who we never saw from one week to the next.'

'What does he do when he visits?' asked Stevens.

'He just comes in to see how we are. Welfare check, he calls it, but sometimes he has other things he wants us to do. But he just wants to see if there are any problems on his estate. Taking an interest, you know.'

'And was yesterday any different?' asked Randall.

'Well, yes, he was a bit agitated.' She looked past Randall into the distance, eyes still watering.

'Do you know why?' Randall moved into her eye-line and asked again. He had a good idea as to why, but asked nevertheless.

'He didn't say directly. I got the impression it was something to do with the wood.'

'How agitated was he?' Stevens asked.

'Very. I've never seen him like that. He usually takes most things in his stride. Very calm.'

'So he never gave any indication?' Randall said.

'No, but what he did say was that he was unhappy with Frank and I think he wanted to get rid of him.'

'What do you mean, get rid of him?' Stevens asked.

'He's been wanting to give him the sack, I think, ever since the old Lord died. They never did get on. I think he was looking for an excuse to fire him.'

'So there has been friction between Frank and Lord Fulborough?'

'Yes, all the time, since he took over the estate.'

'Marjorie, it's important to our investigation for you to give us all the information you can, so we can find whoever did this, and resolve the identity of those remains in the wood. What sort of friction are we talking about?'

'I don't like to say.'

Randall looked at Marjorie and was about to say something, when Stevens said, 'We know there are probably some loyalty issues here, but, as DI Randall has said, we need as much information as you can give us – any little thing, even if you might think it's not relevant.'

Marjorie looked between Randall and Stevens and wiped her nose with the handkerchief. Nothing was said for a moment, the silence only interrupted by the twittering of a blackbird in the trees around them.

She gazed at the floor, then said quietly, 'Frank has said in the past that he knew where all the family skeletons were.'

'What did he mean by that?' asked Randall.

'I really don't know.' Marjorie looked away.

'How long have you worked for the estate?'

'Most of my life. I started as a stable hand with the old Lord. He was much younger then, of course. A handsome man, with the world at his fingertips.'

'And how did you get on with him? By all accounts he was not a man to be trifled with.'

Marjorie looked away again, nervously tapping her foot, before answering. 'I got on with him very well actually. It wasn't until his first wife died that he became that grumpy old goat that everyone hated. But I didn't hate him. I knew what he was like under that harsh exterior.'

'What does that mean, Marjorie?' asked Stevens.

Marjorie looked directly at Stevens. 'I wouldn't still be here, if it weren't for his mentoring.'

Randall cast a knowing look at Stevens, who raised an eyebrow.

'What happened yesterday, Marjorie? We need to know. What can you tell us?'

Randall saw that Stevens was getting a little agitated himself at this interrogation, which appeared to be getting them nowhere.

'After Barry had been in the office for a little while, he went outside and made a call on his mobile phone.'

'Did you hear what was said?'

'No.'

'Anything at all?' Stevens said.

'He raised his voice only once.'

'And said what?' Randall asked.

'Something like, get yourself over her now or immediately.'

'Do you know who he was talking to?'

'No, but after the call, he came into the office and sent everyone home.'

'Why?'

'He said that he wanted a private meeting with Frank.'

'And you all went home?'

'Yes.'

'What time was that?'

'About four thirty.'

'What time do you normally knock off work?' Stevens asked.

'Sixish – depends what's going on.'

Randall looked at Marjorie for a moment then said, 'OK, Marjorie, thanks very much. We'll get an officer to take that statement from you now if that's OK?'

She nodded. Randall instructed the WPC to take her to the mobile police station to get a statement from her and to make sure she was looked after. The WPC walked away with Marjorie. Randall waited until they were out of earshot.

'Mentoring, my arse,' Stevens said smiling. Randall looked at him. 'Oh, come on boss! You didn't believe that the old Lord would tutor a stable hand, honestly, did you?'

'I suppose not, but the aristocracy have always been quirky, so I don't know what to believe.'

'Right, quirky, that's for sure.'

'No, but if I read this right, the old Lord was a bit of a Jack-the-lad. We know that these second remains had been in the ground for about fifteen years. What if there had been some liaison that went wrong and it's nothing to do with the Tyler guy anyway?'

'Possible, but the only person that we know who may have any further information is Philpott and he's on his toes.'

'I think he might just be glad to talk when we get him in. Let's find this guy before he disappears into the woodwork for ever. I knew I should have kept him in when I had him.'

37

Her

It was difficult. She knew that. She placed the glass of red wine down on her desk and opened her diary. "This is the only way anyone will know about what I've done and what I am about to do," she wrote. "I've managed to keep my obsession under control for the last couple of weeks, but the need, the overwhelming desire to continue developing my drug, is almost tangible. I'm so close to finalising its structure. So close to finally being able to put my past behind me and conclude my business in this world.

"I know that I'm not going to survive this. In fact, I have no desire to want to survive after all this. I couldn't spend the rest of my life in a ten by eight prison cell. I'd go even more madder than I am.

"Why do I feel guilty? It's never worried me before. It's right that I should seek vengeance upon those who cause pain to others. Pain to ME.

"I've taken so long to build my laboratory. Why should I

not use it for my own ends? It's MINE. I still can't understand how I've managed to get away with it. All this equipment and I've not paid a penny. It's all on the company. They've never even suspected. They've got no IDEA.

"I know the company accountant is suspicious, but I can keep him sweet. I think he fancies me anyway, that's for sure."

She put her pen down and stood, stretched and rubbed the small of her back. She removed the keys to her laboratory from the top drawer of her desk. She collected her wine glass and refilled it with the bottle on her desk, then went to her laboratory. A few steps away from the door, key in one hand and the ever-present wine glass in the other, she took a step closer. It was enticing her to enter. Her mind drifted off, remembering the occasions she had tried out her new drug in the town centre.

She'd decided that she didn't like the town. It had changed so much in the time she'd been away. A wine bar where a bank used to be. Nightclubs fighting for custom from the passing stags and hens. The only place to come to try my new drug, pissed-up girls ripe for the taking. She smiled to herself.

She went back to her desk and continued writing. "One of the girls I looked for had a problem. She walked off with my bottle of water, the stupid bitch, so high on crack she didn't know what the fuck she was doing. Forced me to go chasing after her the following morning to see if it worked. My only regret is that she had her husband and her kids with her. I don't want to kill children – the husband though – collateral damage.

"The crash was explosive. Never seen anything like that before and I was so close." She stopped writing and rubbed the top of her nose, as the images of her own collision came flooding back, the tornado, the semi, driven by a woman high on amphetamines and who took her husband and child. She carried on writing.

"Funny that the cop I went to help was actually in the club the following week. I couldn't help it. Well, he approached me. I saw him – leering at my legs when I got off that stool. But I got my own back. Gave him good dose, and handcuffed him to a lamppost. Not seen anything on the news, so I assume he got away." 'Ha!' she shouted.

She went to grab her glass of wine, but knocked it over her desk. She swore loudly and mopped it up with some tissues she filched out of the top drawer. She looked at the lab keys again. Stroked them. In two minds.

Do I or don't I?

It was just an ordinary door. It wasn't fortified, re-enforced or anything like that. It was just a locked white door. But to her it looked different today for some reason. Perhaps the drink was playing a trick on her. She shook her head. 'What am I doing? I've made my decision. I'm safe,' she whispered to herself and turned on her heel and walked back to her lounge, where she re-filled her glass and flopped back down on the sofa with a great sigh.

Some hours later, when the bottle was empty again, she found herself standing at the lab entrance. But not her own lab. The lab at work. How she got there she had no idea. She shrugged, swiped her card and input the six-digit access code. The night watchman looked up, surprised to see her.

'You finishing late or starting early?' he asked.

She didn't respond, just gave him a happy wave, as she walked past his desk. She didn't want to say anything, because she knew that she would make it obvious that she was drunk. At least I know I am, she thought. The night watchman just sat down again, not worried.

She entered the lift, which took her up to the first floor. The door pinged open. The upward movement of the lift made her a bit dizzy. She staggered out of the lift and sat down heavily on the floor. The automatic lighting came on and she closed her eyes to shield them from the brightness. The clock on the wall said two a.m. She sat there, unable to move and closed her eyes.

When she opened them again, she cursed herself for falling asleep for an hour. The lights had gone off and she was in darkness, but the early August dawn was expectant. She got up from the floor, feeling a little better for her catnap. She sauntered over to the pharmacy, where she used her card to unlock the door and went straight to the vials of drugs she needed.

She put the drugs into her pocket and left the pharmacy. 'I'm so close to getting it right.'

As she drove back home, she considered that if she tried that weekend and if it worked the way she wanted it to work, she'd be more than happy. Perhaps then, the obsession would go away. She could even sell it on the net maybe. She smiled to herself as she abandoned her car on her driveway. She couldn't say that it was parked.

She went straight to her laboratory without further delay, spurred on by the thought that she could at last finalise her new drug, but first she needed a drink.

Her obsession with completing the right synthesis of the drug had returned after she realised that it would be tragic if she had come so far, yet not to see a conclusion. She didn't see herself as the competitive type, but once she had decided to do something, there was very little that anyone could do to change her mind.

"I did feel a bit guilty, when I realised that a youth had died in the motorway accident, but that wasn't my fault," she wrote in her diary. "How could I know that her victim drove school minibuses? I only found that out when she'd kept her usual eye on her victims. And do I care really? No, it was down to the driver to make sure that she did nothing to put her passengers in danger. Once the drug had been administered, it was too late anyway."

She shook her head to rid herself of these guilty thoughts as she closed her diary.

She spent the day working on her drug. Nobody ever asked her where she was, so she downloaded the new structure into her computer from the memory stick and completed synthesising its amended molecular structure. She hoped that this was the last iteration and that the drug was now complete in all its forms.

She felt excited. She felt she was near the end. She knew she'd never be caught. This prospect increased the adrenaline that kept her going through the night.

While the drug was cooking, she managed to down a bottle of her favourite Chardonnay, with a frozen pizza she cooked in the oven, topped off with some Vodka. I do know how to live it up, she thought, as she went back down to her lab to see that the process was complete.

Decanting the clear liquid into vials, she felt happy with her night's work and went to bed at six a.m.

She fell quickly into a deep and restful sleep – her task almost complete.

38

The officers from traffic and CID had been instructed to arrive at Force Headquarters lecture theatre for a briefing at 17:00. As they gathered, they only knew that they were in a search for a multiple murderer. Nobody had said anything to anybody other than Prentice, who was dressed in his civvies and sitting in the front row. Randall and Jake were conversing quietly at the front, waiting for the officers to arrive.

'Is your man up for this, Jake?' asked Randall.

'Of course he is. Why do you ask?'

Randall looked across at Prentice. 'He's not done any of this before, I take it? I'd be a bit apprehensive if I were him. It's like sending Daniel into the lion's den.'

'He looks a bit pale, I'll give him that, but he's a good copper. He'll do fine.'

'I just hope he doesn't cock it up. We've only got one chance at this, you know.'

'I'm well aware of that.'

Most of the officers had arrived when the double doors at the back of the room opened and Stephanie Parker entered.

'Always one for a big entrance,' muttered Jake. All eyes were on her, as she walked down the steps to the front seats and sat near Prentice, who, like all the other men in the room, Jake noticed, were gawping at her.

'Shut your mouth, Chris, or you'll catch flies,' he heard her say to Prentice, as she sat down. 'Have you never seen a girl in a skirt before?'

'Not as short as that,' he commented.

Jake smiled.

'Oh, this,' said Parker, looking down at herself and arranging her skirt demurely. 'It's just something I threw on for tonight's little escapade.'

Prentice could do nothing but nod in agreement. Jake had sent Prentice off to have a preliminary meeting with Parker a few days before at the station, but then, of course, she was in uniform. What he saw that evening was distracting, to say the least and she'd even dyed and bobbed her hair to make her look like the other victims.

Randall brought the briefing to order. 'Right, ladies and gentlemen. This is Operation Winkle.' Some CID officers laughed and looked towards Prentice. Randall continued. 'I don't choose the names. It's what they tell us.'

The group laughed. All except Prentice.

'The aim of this operation is to find, or shall we say, winkle out, our murderer.' Randall smiled at his own joke. 'Sergeant Jordan will fill you in with the details later, but for now you need to be aware that we have two undercover officers in the club, PC Chris Prentice–'

Some of the group jeered in good play.

'–and WPC Stephanie Parker from Daventry Area. Chris is the only one who has seen this woman and we all know the outcome of that meeting.'

More jeering and japing. Prentice flushed and looked at the floor. He was comforted by Parker's hand tapping his thigh in sympathy.

'Now we know that she frequents the clubs and bars in the town centre, so Prentice and Parker will be in these clubs, but acting individually. Prentice will ID the woman when she arrives. If she arrives. Parker will make herself known to her. We know that previously she has targeted women. She approaches them and engages in conversation. At some point, she slips a Mickey in their drink, then invites them to go home with her or offer to drive her home. It is important that we catch this woman before she slips anything into Parker's drink, so we'll need to approach her in the club. As we don't know which club she is going to frequent it needs to be as covert as possible. Stevens, Martin and myself will be in the main club. We'll follow Prentice, wherever they end up. There will be CID officers in each of the clubs, as allocated on your operational order. You all have her picture, so we need to move swiftly when and if she makes her move on Parker. Any questions?'

'What if she doesn't make a move on WPC Parker?' Fred Martin asked.

'I'm sure that WPC Parker and PC Prentice will be able to ensure that she does.'

Randall looked at the pair. They nodded. Jake took over from Randall, who told the gathering that the Road Policing crews would be stationed in and around the town.

'It is hoped that we'll be able to identify the car she drives, as we have no intelligence on that. We need to rely on observations. Area officers working the town have also been given a photograph of the woman, so they will also be on the lookout. The vehicle needs to be stopped, before she gets to her destination, if Parker is on board, but we hope that it's not going to come to that.'

'Right,' said Randall, 'you've all got your assignments. Let's get out there and find her.'

The room dispersed noisily, leaving Parker and Prentice with Randall and Jake. They stood and moved towards them.

'Please make sure you have our backs?' Parker pleaded.

'You're going to be fine. We'll make sure that no harm comes to either of you. There's still time to back out if you're not feeling up to it,' said Randall.

Parker gave Randall a telling smile. 'Really, and what would you do if we did?'

'Panic, of course,' Jake joked.

'So, we're committed, come what may?' responded Prentice.

'You'll be fine, I told you – trust me I'm a detective.'

'Yeah, that's what I'm worried about Sir,' smiled Prentice. Turning to Parker, he said, 'Come on, Steph. Let's go do this.'

39

Friday
Stephanie Parker

The club was stifling and not something that she was used to, so Parker stepped out of the club and onto the street. She needed to get some air. She looked at the sky and took big breaths – cool and fresh. She found herself shivering and couldn't decide whether it was the nerves of the operation or the freshness of the air… as fresh as it could be in the middle of a Midlands town. The sky was clear as she stared upwards thinking of the wide and open spaces she had left behind in New Zealand.

She couldn't believe that Kirsty Kingsfield had turned up at the bar. She could put a mocker on the whole operation. How could she be so stupid? She took another deep breath and exhaled.

'Stuffy in there, isn't it?'

Parker turned to see the woman, who she'd bumped

into on her way out of the club. Had she followed her out? She turned to see a redheaded woman leaning against the door. She could see now, under the streetlights, that she was the woman that they were looking for. The only difference was the colour of her hair and she'd dressed down for her next victim. Or so it seemed to Parker.

'Noisy as well,' Parker replied, nervously.

'I come here regularly and it never gets any better.'

'Why do you come here then?'

'Oh, you know, it's what you know, really. Can't be bothered to go anywhere else.' The woman gave her a brief cold smile.

Parker went to walk back into the club.

'Are you going back in?'

'Yes, why?'

'Are you with anyone?'

Parker hesitated. 'Erm… no.'

'Only I saw you talking to that man sitting at the end of the bar.'

'Him?' She laughed. 'I've only just met him, when I went up to get a drink.'

'Right. I think I've seen him here before.' She smiled again.

'I wouldn't know.'

'You're not from around here?' she asked, still blocking Parker's entrance back into the club.

'Easy enough to guess that,' Parker said, beginning to find her confidence and making her accent heavier.

The woman then stepped aside to let in a party of people, pushed out of the way by the bouncer, who waved them away from the door. The woman ignored him. 'Australia?'

'New Zealand.'

'A place I've always wanted to go.'

'Really?' responded Parker, sounding bored.

'Yes, perhaps we could have a drink and you could tell me the best places to visit? You know, off the beaten track – non-touristy?' The doors closed and they were left on their own again. A moment's silence. 'Can I buy you a drink then?'

'If you want to,' Parker moved towards the door.

'Not in there, too noisy,' the woman said. 'Let's go next door.'

Parker stood for a moment, not knowing what to do. Yes, they needed to catch her, but they also needed to know where she was.

'Why not go back in there?' she asked, pointing to the door.

The woman took a step forward and with a scheming whisper in her ear said, 'I recognise a couple of people in there, that I don't particularly want to say hi to.'

'Ex-boyfriends?' Parker laughed nervously. Had she clocked Kirsty, or Prentice?

'No, ex-girlfriends,' she smiled, but Parker heard the hardness in the other woman's voice. Parker was becoming more and more fearful, that her backup wouldn't be able to keep up with what she was trying to do, but realised she had to go along with it. Reluctantly, Parker moved away from the door with her. She slipped her arm around hers, pretending they were two old mates.

They walked to the pub at the bottom of the hill, making small talk. Parker didn't take much notice, speaking only, she hoped, in the right place.

It was quieter than the club – loud talking, but no thumping music. The pub was in semi darkness decorated with distressed pine furniture and a flagstone floor. It wasn't too busy. A group of men were gathered around the bar drinking and being loud about it. A young couple in the

224

corner talking quietly and a couple of other small groups of men and women dotted around the floor space in front of the bar. Others came and went in quick succession

The woman took Parker over to the bar and ordered two double Vodkas for them both. Parker hated Vodka, so at least she would be able to hold on to it for a little while, without having any refills.

After they had ordered, they found a secluded table. The woman sat down close to Parker and said, 'That's better. Hi, I'm Fiona.' She held out her hand.

Parker took it and they shook hands. 'Steph,' she replied, releasing her grip quickly.

Parker looked around the pub to see if she could spot the two CID officers that were supposed to be in there. She couldn't see them.

Parker was beginning to panic. I could be done for, if they don't know where I am. I'll make an excuse; go to the loo or something like that. Before she went, she put a beer mat on top of her drink to cover it over.

'Don't trust me then?' Fiona said, watching, as Parker got up.

'I don't trust anyone.'

'That's a good thing in a place like this.'

Parker left and went into the ladies. She retrieved her mobile and sent a text to Randall's phone '999' and left the phone on, as agreed.

Parker returned to the table and made the decision to sit opposite the woman, asking whether she could change her drink.

'You really don't trust people, do you?' said Fiona.

Parker shook her head.

'I've been here all the time and nobody has touched your drink.'

Parker looked at the beer mat, convinced that it had been moved, then looked back at Fiona.

'Honest,' she smiled. That smile again was less than friendly.

'Anyway, tell me about yourself, Steph. When did you get into England?'

'Only been here a couple of months,' she said looking around the bar.

'Really? How are you finding us?'

'Overcrowded!'

'Yes, I can understand that, too many immigrants sponging off the government.'

'I'm an immigrant, if you don't mind.'

'Yes, but I assume you have a job?'

Parker nodded. She expected the next question to be as to where she worked and quickly made something up. The small talk continued for some fifteen minutes or more and Parker did not touch her drink during that time, or do much listening to Fiona.

'Come on, drink up, the night's still young.'

'Well, I'm not keen on vodka to be honest,' Parker said. Instantly Fiona's demeanour changed from being the friendly girlfriend. She leaned forward and looked directly, menacingly, into Parker's eyes.

'No,' she said, pushing the glass towards her. 'I insist!'

'Why?'

'Because I want you to, and what I want, I usually get.'

'But I don't want to,' said Parker, pushing the glass back and standing up to leave. Fiona stood quickly. She moved out from her side of the table and blocked Parker's exit.

'Sit – down!' Fiona hissed.

Parker stood her ground. 'I'd like to leave now.'

'I don't want you to go.' Fiona took a pace forward, her face inches from Parker's and placed a hand on her shoulder, pushing her back down into the seat. A man standing at the bar saw what happened and came over to them asking if Parker was all right.

'It's OK,' Fiona said, 'just a husband and wife tiff, she'll be okay in a jiffy.'

The man looked at Parker and back at Fiona, shrugged and walked away. Fiona sat down so close to her that she was unable to exit from the table. Sliding closer to her, Fiona said, 'We have such a party planned for you tonight and tomorrow, so I insist that you drink the vodka that I've paid for.'

Parker looked at her and then around the pub. Nobody was paying them any attention now. Fiona could have stuck a knife into her there and then and nobody would have even paused to look. Parker looked back at her. She was holding the drink and thrust it towards her.

'Drink!' she growled.

Parker took the glass and sniffed at it. 'What have you done to it?'

'Nothing more than being able to enhance our evening together, now – drink!'

Parker put the glass to her lips, at the same time looking around the pub for her back up. Fiona grabbed hold of the glass to ensure that it stayed at her lips. She tried to put the glass down and stand up. Fiona pushed her down again, Parker falling heavily onto the seat.

'What happens if I throw this at you, as I should,' Parker said.

Fiona stared down at Parker, then she picked up her own glass, smashing in on the table. It drew some attention but she indicated to everyone that was an accident.

'Perhaps,' she said, her nostrils flaring, 'you'd like me to smash this into your face instead.'

Parker glanced around uneasily to see if she could find some way of getting out from the table. Still nobody was paying any attention. How that sort of thing could go on in a crowded pub and nobody come to help? What sort of country was this that she had returned to? She was blocked in the corner of the seat with Fiona looming over her with the glass and that Vodka. She felt unable to do anything now, but acquiesce to Fiona's demands and she drank the liquid. Perhaps she could spit it out, into her face, and she held it in her mouth. That would get somebody's attention, surely?

'And don't even think about spitting it out,' Fiona said, as if reading Parker's mind. She swallowed.

'There, that's better. Shall we go?'

'Go where?'

'You'll see.' She got up and manhandled Parker out from behind the table. Parker's clutch bag got left on the seat with her phone inside. She wondered why Fiona wanted to move her so quickly. Perhaps the drug Fiona had given her was not working in the way it should be. I could make a run for it, she thought, but her legs weren't moving properly. Fiona was dragging her out of the pub. Where's my back up. I didn't see them. Lights were swimming in front of her eyes, she felt weak and unable to coordinate her limbs. She had to rely on the woman dragging her. Who is she? I don't know her.

'Everything all right, love?' the waiter said, as he passed.

'Yes, fine. She's had a bit too much, that's all.' Fiona said dragging Parker towards the doors.

The waiter grunted and walked on.

Help me! Help me! Please. But nobody could help Parker for her screams for help were only in her mind.

40

'Where the hell are they?' Randall ranted down his phone. He was standing outside the club with a finger on one ear and his phone to the other.

'She can't have just disappeared. Get your arses into gear and go and find her.' Randall continued to listen to what he was being told.

'Jesus fucking Christ how the hell did that happen? Look, I know her phone is still on. She sent me a three nines text, so get somebody on to search the mobile network and ping her phone.'

Randall terminated the call and rubbed a hand through his hair, exasperated at what had happened. He thought perhaps that he was partly to blame. He should have been watching her, instead of babysitting Kirsty Kingsfield. Nobody saw Parker leave, apart from Prentice, who, by the time he got outside, saw that they were gone.

'Shiiiiit!' Randall shouted, as he slammed his hand against the door.

As he did so, Jake rolled up in his patrol car, opened the passenger side window and shouted to Randall, 'What's up?'

Randall stepped out of the cover of the club doors and put his head into the open window of Jake's patrol car. Nighttime revellers were all about Jake's car, jeering. One guy bumped into Randall as he walked past.

'Careful, mate. He got the bird in response. She's only gone fuckin' missing, that's what's up.'

'How did that happen?'

'I'm still working on that, but if I find out somebody's not done their job, I'll have their balls in a sling.'

'Get in!' ordered Jake. Randall jumped into Jake's car and he powered away from the club, through the town.

'Do we have any idea where she was last seen?'

'Prentice said that she went outside for some fresh air and appeared to be followed out by a red-headed woman, but by the time he got out of the club, they'd gone.'

'She's changed her appearance again then?'

'It would seem so, yes.'

'So where do we go from here?'

'We'll get a trace on her phone, but that tends to take a while.'

'Can we hurry it along?'

'In progress.' Randall stared out of the window, as Jake moved the car slowly through the town, to see if they could see Parker somewhere.

The force radio crackled into life. 'Tango supervisor 1540.'

Jake answered.

'1540, are you still in town?' the female operator enquired.

'Yes, yes.'

'Can you attend St Peter's Way car park and speak to two PCSOs on duty there. They think that they have information pertaining to your search.'

Jake glanced at Randall, who was still staring out of the car window, searching every face he could see. He was going to make damned sure that whoever was responsible for this abduction was going to pay for it. Jake could see the hard lines on his face, and the scar that seemed more prominent in the half-light of the patrol car.

A few minutes later, Randall and Jake were out of the car talking to the two PCSOs. They told him that they had seen a woman in the car park earlier in the evening, acting suspiciously. Not that they had anything concrete about her. She just didn't seem to fit with what else was going on around them at the time.

'What did she look like?' Randall asked.

'Red hair, dark trousers,' the first PCSO responded.

'No, that's not her. The photos show her as blonde.'

'You're not mixing her up with our pathologist?' asked Randall.

'No, I've met Doctor Kingsfield,' PCSO number two said. 'It wasn't her.'

'She wouldn't be here anyway,' Jake said.

Randall looked at Jake, with a grin on his face. 'Er… actually she is. She turned up at the club.'

'Where is she now then?' Jake asked defensively.

'Gone off with Stevens, looking for our suspect and Parker.'

Jake turned his attention back to the PCSOs. 'Anything else you can tell us?'

'Yes, she got into a blue Ford Focus, with another woman, who looked as if she'd had a skinful.'

'How long ago?'

PSCO number one looked at her watch. ''bout thirty minutes.'

'Christ, she could be anywhere by now.'

'Tell me you got the registration.'

'Yes, sir, I did,' said PCSO number one. She passed Jake the details and he was on the radio straight away circulating it.

'At least we know what car she's in.'

'If it's her,' commented Randall.

They thanked the two PCSOs and made their way back across the car park to their car. As they were about to get in, Stevens arrived with Kirsty. The two CID officers parted company to search in their own vehicle, while Kirsty got into Jake's patrol car.

Jake looked at her sternly. 'What are you doing, Kirsty?'

'I suppose you're going to give me a lecture as well?'

'I know that would be futile.'

'Correct.' Kirsty grinned.

'What did Randall say?'

'Told me off for turning up, then asked me if I wanted a drink.'

'What!' Jake shook his head. 'Is there no shame in the man? Obviously doesn't know that you don't drink.'

'He does now.'

'Man's gotta do his homework if he wants to impress a girl,' Jake said in a "Dirty Harry" accent.

Kirsty smiled. 'Sounds like a quote from somewhere.'

'No, other than the accent, poorly done I might add – and Jake's rules for an easier life.'

'Be difficult. They change every week.'

He gave a short laugh. 'So why are you here? I told you what was happening in confidence.'

'I have a theory, but I wanted to tell you first.'

'A theory about what?'

'Our killer.'

'Come on then, hit me with your blinding case-cracking theory,' he said, as he drove out of the car park.

'You know when we went to see Tanya, she gave us a list of so-called suspects for you to investigate?'

'Yes, I remember.'

'I found it strange that she didn't put her own company on the list.'

'Perhaps she thought that they were beyond investigation, as we had gone to them with a problem.'

'I thought that, so I decided to do some digging.'

'Digging into her or the company?'

'Both. I looked on some websites about her and the company. Did you know that she is a 40% stakeholder in the company?'

'No, but why should that be significant?'

'When we went to see her, she told us she was just an employee and that she'd taken the job when she returned to the UK.'

'That's right. I remember.'

'Turns out that the US arm of the company was involved in some scandal, developing mind-altering drugs, which either activated or deactivated certain neurotransmitters in the brain. Apparently, fourteen of their supposed volunteers died over a period of eighteen months, and since that time it turns out that ten of them died in road collisions, which have not been explained satisfactorily. But interestingly, her daughter, who we met, is not actually the wayward child we were led to believe. She works for Tanya as a major contributor to the research programme.'

'All sounds a bit far-fetched to me, a bit sci-fi. Mind-altering drugs causing drivers to crash? I can't believe that for one minute.'

'OK, think about this then. Tanya told us that the drug was based on the date rape drug GHB. Yes?'

Jake nodded, keeping his eye on the road.

'What does GHB do to you?'

'I don't really know. I've not tried it.' He chuckled. 'I'd have to ask my drug recognition trainer for that.'

'Let me tell you. GHB is a mind-altering drug. It affects your ability to remember what's happened to you, because of the way it works on neurotransmitters in the brain, so it's not so far-fetched.'

'You think the daughter's to blame?'

'I'm not sure, frighteningly, it could be either of them.'

'It clearly can't be the daughter because our suspect is white.'

'But she could easily pass for a well-tanned white woman, if she changed the colour of her hair.'

Jake slowly nodded in agreement. 'What happened to her company?'

'The US company closed down and the regulators over there seized all their assets.'

'When?'

'Have a guess.'

'Two years ago?'

'Right on the button.'

Jake pulled the patrol car into a junction and manoeuvred the vehicle, so it was parked just out of sight of approaching vehicles and sat thinking for a moment.

'Shit, so we've given her all our evidence,' Jake exclaimed suddenly, 'so she can do with it what she likes.'

'She didn't have it all. Remember? We kept some back.'

'Do you think that's why she's been stalling?'

'It pains me to say it, but yes.'

They sat and took on board the revelation that one of Kirsty's friends could be their murderer. It didn't bear thinking about.

'Do you know what really riles me up, Jake?'

Jake shook his head sombrely.

'I thought she was my friend. We were in uni together. Christ, I don't half pick up some crap.'

Jake saw the tell-tale signs of tears welling up in Kirsty's eyes and the turning of her wedding ring.

'Come on, Kirsty, we don't know. We're only surmising. Perhaps Tanya is still your friend?'

'But what if she isn't?'

'Perhaps we ought to find out.'

'How's that going to help?'

'One, it'll put your mind at rest, and that's all I'm concerned about by the way. And two, we'll get the evidence we need to close the case.'

'I can't see Randall going for it.'

'Randall isn't going to know, until he needs to.'

'Look, if we go over to Coventry tomorrow to see her…'

'But we can't just pop in on the off-chance.'

'Of course we can. There are always traffic cars at the hospital. We can say we've just been to see a victim of a road death. It wouldn't look suspicious.'

'But you don't normally take a forensic pathologist for that sort of thing.'

'Perhaps you went to converse with a colleague and I just happened to be going your way?'

Kirsty hesitated. 'OK, that might work.'

41

Saturday
Stephanie Parker

Parker woke up with a start. She felt cold. It was still dark. She tried to look around, to see where she was. She didn't recognise anything in the gloom. She realised she was on a bed and tried to move her right arm. It had been handcuffed to a heavy steel and cold bedstead. She gave it a tug. Useless, she knew, but...

She thought it might be early dawn. The curtains were not very heavy and had some sort of floral pattern reminiscent of the style of the nineteen eighties. It produced a jaundiced hue to the room, but not enough to get a good look around. A dark and yellow hue, a strange and eerie combination.

She leaned up on her elbow. The room was what her mother would call a box-room. Big enough for a single bed, with little space for furniture. The walls were a plain magnolia, no pictures or ornaments on the wall. There was a small bedside table, on which stood a jug of water and a small, kidney-shaped stainless steel bowl. The sort they use in hospitals. An empty syringe lay in the bottom of the bowl.

Realising how thirsty she was, she tried to reach the water jug with her free hand, but couldn't quite reach it.

It seemed strange to her that, despite being handcuffed to the bed, she was under the covers. With her free hand, she looked under the covers. She was still wearing her bra and knickers, but she also saw that her top and skirt she'd worn the night before had been folded neatly and placed at the bottom of the bed, almost motherly.

But was it the night before? How long had she been here she asked herself? She looked towards the bedroom door, which was in front of the bed. She could see a light from under the door and called out.

'Hello? Hello? Can anyone hear me? Hello!' There was no response. She lay back on the bed and wondered what was going to happen to her next, determined to make an escape as soon as she could.

Then she heard a key in the lock of her prison.

42

Randall, Stevens, and on the instructions of the DCI, Jordan, stood in front of Freeman at half past midnight. Freeman was in a foul mood and he was about rip them all a new one.

'What in friggin' God's name happened tonight? I've had Marland and the Chief on the phone to me, ripping me a new arse, as to why I've lost one of his officers. I was invited over here to see how you Brits are supposed to have the best police force in the world, but at this time I'm finding that hard to comprehend. The advertising doesn't do justice to the crap that I'm getting from on high. So, what's the story, Randall? And it's a friggin' Sunday morning now.

Freeman's raised voice was heard outside his office and probably down the corridor. He stared angrily at Randall for an answer.

'One minute she was in the club, the next minute she was gone,' responded Randall.

'What, she just vanished like a puff of smoke? Where has she gone, Randall? Where?'

'We don't know, sir.' Randall cringed a little.

Jake had to smile inwardly, seeing Randall being brought down a peg or two.

'I've also had the Daventry Commander on, wanting his officer back and I've had to tell her we've lost her.'

'We're doing all we can at this point to secure her whereabouts,' Stevens said.

'Secure her whereabouts? Jeez, I'm beginning to think that you constabulary boys couldn't organise a, a... '

'Piss-up in a brewery?' volunteered Stevens.

'Yeah, that'll do. So, where are we now with this shit-storm?'

'We've got an all-ports warning out for the car. Both descriptions, her new description and Parker's. We're also looking at CCTV footage for last night in the street and surrounding area. CCTV picked up her car leaving St John's car park a few minutes after we discovered her gone, then again on Victoria Prom and onto the Bedford Road. We pinged her phone and we found it in the pub just down the road from the nightclub, in her handbag.'

'So she's no way of contacting us, wherever she may be, or whoever she may be with.'

'She's resourceful – she'll find a way.'

'I fucking hope she does,' Freeman snarled. 'Do you think she'll have been taken far?'

'Personally, I think she's still in town somewhere,' Randall said.

'I agree with that,' Jake affirmed.

'Hmm, seems to me that a couple of, what do you call them?' Freeman paused momentarily. 'Ah, hobby bobbies, did better than you in discovering the vehicle she was abducted in.'

'They were PCSOs, sir,' Stevens volunteered again.

'I really don't give a shit who they were, they obviously had their eyes on the ground, didn't they?'

'Yes, sir,' Stevens acknowledged glumly.

'And where were the two officers, who were supposed to be in the pub she was abducted from? Tell me that?'

'It seems that they had stepped outside of the pub for a cigarette.'

'Did both of them have to go at the same time? They're not women who have to go to the john in pairs, y'know.'

'I'm dealing with them, sir. Both of them realise that they made a mistake.'

'Yeah, made a mistake that could cost an officer her life. I hope you've told them that they're on... what you call a fizzer?'

'In no uncertain terms, sir, yes.'

'You were both in the club?'

Randall and Stevens nodded.

'Where were you, Jordan?'

'All Saints, static obs.'

'Did you see them?'

'No, you can't see the club doors from that position. My other officers had a better view from the bottom of the hill.'

'Did they see anything?'

'No, they got called away to a serious RTC about five minutes before it all kicked off.'

'Did you replace them?'

'Couldn't get a resource there quick enough, before we realised she'd gone.'

Freeman rubbed his face, before returning them to his hips. 'Do we have anything to go on?'

'No,' said Randall.

'Erm... I'm not so sure,' butted in Jake. They looked

towards him. He was unsure of whether he should give them details with which Kirsty had confided in him, but it was clear that Freeman was desperate for some good news.

'Last night, Dr Kingsfield turned up at the club.'

'Why?' asked Freeman curtly.

'She wanted to tell me a theory about these collisions and the other ongoing line of enquiry, you know about this unknown substance.'

'What has this got to do with Parker's disappearance?' queried Randall.

'If you hear me out, sir, I think it's highly relevant and, above all, I think it's a good theory. We don't have anything else, do we?'

'Tell us,' Freeman said, as he sat down.

Jake went on to explain Kirsty's theory to the three of them. At the end, they sat in silence, waiting for a response from Freeman. He leaned forward, rubbed his forehead and pinched the bridge of his nose, sighing.

'Really, that's all we've got?'

'It's a start.'

'It's a fuckin' fairy tale, that's what it is. Dr Kingsfield should stick with the dead and let us deal with the living. Now get out, all of you.'

Outside Freeman's office, Stevens said, 'That went well then!'

Randall growled. 'You better get your arse into gear then Clive and get me some answers. You, Jake, can do what you traffic boys do, which clearly isn't detective work!' and he stormed off along the corridor. Jake made a move to follow him to the exit, Stevens held him back.

Speaking in a low tone, he said, 'Look, Jake, I don't know about you, but I think Kirsty's theory is a runner. We both know her better than these two imports and she wouldn't have said anything, if she didn't feel it was significant.'.

Jake nodded. 'I'm off to do what us traffic boys do, Clive.' Jake gave him a quick wink as he walked off in the direction that Randall had taken.

'I've got your back, Jake, just in case.'

Jake thanked him, as Stevens turned and returned to the incident room.

43

Sunday
Stephanie Parker

There was no way of knowing how long she'd been unconscious. They'd come and drugged her again. She tried to prevent them from sticking the needles in by struggling as much as she could, and got a slap around the face, several times.

Parker was frightened now about what was going to happen to her. The drugs they'd given her were, in all probability, going to kill her, if what Jake had told her was anything to go by. Was that their intention? Neither of them who brought her food or water ever spoke to her. Never said a word to her, ever. Just looked at her through the disguise they were wearing around their faces. Scarfs tied around their heads, so she couldn't even get an idea about them. All she could see were their eyes, burning into her, behind masks that reminded her of those old black and white TV programmes, where the villain always had a band of light accentuating the evil in their eyes.

One thing she was determined to do, if she ever got out of there, was remember those eyes, that was for certain. She'd lost a sense of how long she had been held in captivity. It could have been days or even weeks. The drugs she had been given made her drift in and out of consciousness, and causing hallucinations and muscle spasms. She felt even more powerless to resist the injections being given to her, the more they gave her. Every time she tried to resist, the other one would come into the room and hold her down. Then she'd drift off to sleep, only to wake up in darkness and silence. She knew she needed to escape, but how?

As she lay there, she thought about how she had managed to get herself in that position. What was she doing, agreeing to Randall's suggestion that everything would be OK and that there would be plenty of backup every step of the way? Where was the backup in the pub? Where was the backup that should be there, getting her out of this mess. If she ever got out of here she would never again volunteer for such hair-brained schemes. She'd even changed her hair for the operation, so she looked like those other women targeted by the killer, and here she was handcuffed to a bed. Welcome to my parlour, she snorted, and rattled the handcuffs out of frustration.

What she didn't understand was why she hadn't been dumped somewhere, like Prentice instead of using her as a guinea pig. She was pretty sure that one of them was the woman who abducted her, but her disguise and the drugs made her unsure. But she'd know those eyes.

Parker thought about her abduction, the approach of the red-headed woman, after she had moved outside to get some fresh air, then wouldn't let her back in. She must have been watching her in the club, perhaps saw them all arrive then followed her outside. Damn! She should have realised earlier. Paid more attention, that this woman was the one Randall and Jake were looking for. She was put off the scent by the red-hair and conservative dress style. They'd expected her to look like some blonde bombshell. By the time she realised who she was, they were in the pub and she was desperate to let Randall know. She hoped that he had received her text that she had pinged across to him. He should have pinged it back by now. She'd tried to look around the room for her purse, but couldn't see it. She must have dropped it in the pub, which meant that Randall wouldn't be able to find her, even if he did try to respond to her text.

She sat up on the bed. In the jaundiced darkness, it was difficult to see and she fumbled around until the silver tray with the syringes in, went crashing from the bedside table and onto the floor. She lay down, the sound of the crash still ringing in her ears. She expected somebody to come in to find out what the noise was. She closed her eyes, heart pounding and her breath shallow, waiting.

Nobody came. Despite her mind being fuzzy from the drugs, she tried to get to the tray that had fallen on the floor. She knew that there were a needles and syringes in the tray. Leaning out of the bed, she scrambled around on the floor with her free hand. She found the tray and felt inside it. It was empty. Of course it would be – it's not as if the needle's going to stay there when it fell, stupid.

She carried on searching with her hand. At the limit of her outstretched hand, she felt the body of the syringe plunger, but she couldn't quite get hold of it. She stretched with her feet to see if she could reach it. The handcuff, pulling tightly against her left hand, sent pain shooting down her arm and into her shoulders.

Stretching with her feet and her free hand, she eventually managed to get a hold on the syringe. Drawing it closer to her, she grabbed hold of it and felt elated. All she had to do now was pick the handcuff lock with the needle, if she could remember how to do it.

She was unsure of how much time had passed since trying to pick the lock. She remained conscious of the fact that her captors could return at any moment but she continued picking at the lock. Then. Free. At last.

She quickly slipped on her top and skirt, still folded at the bottom of the bed. She moved towards the door, as quietly as she could.

She turned the door handle, slowly. It squeaked a bit that seemed to echo around the room. She froze. She expected it to be locked but it wasn't. How wrong they were to think that she'd not try to get away.

She opened the door a crack and peered out. Dark. She opened the door some more and stood listening for any noises from downstairs. She looked around the hallway. It wasn't carpeted, just plain board. She slowly made her way out into the hall with her shoes in her hands, which was only lit by the light coming in from an outside street lamp.

Standing at the top of the stairs, she could hear talking. Waited. Then realised it was the next-door neighbour's television. She realised that she'd been holding her breath and relaxed with a great sigh. She looked in the other rooms. One had a large double bed, and a soft carpet, not like her wooden floor. The other room was locked. She crept down the stairs. A floorboard creaked and she stopped for a moment. Her breathing was fast.

At the bottom of the stairs, she looked around the corner of the balustrade into the darkness of the kitchen. She moved forward towards the lounge door that she found ajar. She peered in. It was also in darkness. It was empty. No guards, just silence.

Putting her shoes back on, she was fully convinced that there was nobody in the house. She switched on the light in the hallway, which provided enough to be able to see the rest of the house.

Feeling more confident that she was on her own, she made a quick search of the house. Looking for anything that might give away who her captors were.

In the kitchen, she found a bowl with a set of car keys and put them in her pocket. Lucky. She switched on the kitchen light, and rummaged around to see what evidence she could find. Under a small pile of papers and till receipts, none of which gave any indication of where she might be, or who may have abducted her, she found an envelope.

She looked closely at it. Oh shit.

44

Sitting in the collision investigation office reviewing a file, on Sunday morning, Jake heard the phone ring. He ignored it, a little irritated, as it came at a place in the file where he needed to get to grips with the physics of collision investigation, in this case, the complex calculations of momentum exchange. He needed to try to get the fact that Steph Parker was missing out of his head, as it was an all-consuming worry.

He had been put off talking to her mother as he didn't really know what to say to her. In the end Randall decided to go and pay her a visit at home, and by himself. By all accounts, she was spitting feathers at the news, blaming anyone she could find for losing her daughter.

It reminded him a little of his father's response when he joined the police. Jake never thought much about his parents. In fact, even when his mother still had all her faculties, he never really got on with them.

Jake reflected that they weren't the type of family, who spent their lives in each other's pockets. Never close, in the true sense of the word. It was difficult for Jake to describe the type of relationship he'd had with his mother and father. He only wished he'd had better conversations with them, but his father was always very aloof – lukewarm – towards his son. If you believe the experts, an only child is usually doted upon by overbearing parents, but not him.

He heard the way some of his colleagues talked. The way they went on about their own children of varying ages. Yes, some of them who had teenagers moaned about them, particularly if they could see them going off the rails and spending their life grunting at you as opposed to having a conversation – hormones, the doctors would say. Just bloody ignorance, as far as Jake was concerned. But there was still the understanding of a love between fathers and their offspring.

Jake was different. He took a different view to most about the role of parents in a family. The lack of childhood love and closeness to both parents made him unwilling to have children of his own. And, after discovering that he could not have them anyway, it was a large burden off his shoulders.

The only time he remembered his father being overcome with emotion was when his mother was given the diagnosis of early onset dementia. She was just forty-five and the ten-year struggle put a strain on his relationship with his father, right up until his mother died, aged fifty-four. A day he remembered vividly.

Having joined the force when he was twenty, in the millennium year, the only reaction he got from his father was, "I suppose you'll get a good pension, unlike your mother and me." No "well done" or "congratulations". The rest of the extended family rallied around with congratulations, but it was clear from his father's reaction, that he saw his son becoming part of the establishment, whereas he, on the other hand, had been the union convenor for Wilberforce and Stack, a local and globally renowned boot and shoe company.

Since his father's redundancy and the pitiful pay-off he got after so many years service, he'd become even more insular, more withdrawn in himself after the passing of his wife.

Jake thought fifty-four was no age to shuffle off, even if she did walk out in front of a number sixty-three bus in the Kettering Road, one bright August afternoon in 2012. She believed that she was meeting one of her make-believe friends on the other side of the road. Jake wondered what had been in her mind at the time. What if she had just one lucid moment and decided to end her misery and that of her husband? Strangely, a mysterious witness came forward to state that she mentioned seeing somebody she knew coming out of 'The White Elephant' pub. Jake wasn't convinced. Funny how the friend didn't come forward. He preferred to keep his own counsel and think that it was probably suicide. The coroner recorded an accidental death verdict and that was that. He certainly wasn't going to rake up the past.

The relationship with his father became even more strained after the death of his mother, to the point where they had not been in contact with each other for more than a year. He hadn't told anyone about it, of course, and that was the way he wished it to stay.

Jake was extracted from his reverie when Andy Thomas called him to the phone. 'Randall,' he mouthed to him as he took the phone. Jake listened. Said nothing, then put the phone down.

In a private room at the hospital, Randall and Jake watched as the nurse made Fulborough comfortable. She smiled at them. 'Don't be too long now, he's still very weak.'

They acknowledged the nurse and Randall thanked her. He drew up a chair and sat down beside Fulborough's bed. Jake pulled up a chair on the other side of Fulborough.

His eyes were closed. He was pale and his two bruised eyes were an island of red and blue against the pale deathly green hue of the rest of his face. Jake had seen this coloured face before – usually on the dead, so he knew that Fulborough was probably not long for this world. They needed to get as much information out of him as they could, because there might not be a tomorrow.

'Barrington,' Randall said quietly, 'can you hear me?'

Fulborough's eyes, dark and bloodshot, flickered open. He looked towards Randall. Whether he could actually see him or not, neither of them had any idea.

'Tell me what happened, Barrington.'

Fulborough's voice was deep and gravelly. 'Met Philpott, wanted to talk about those remains, being buried, not happy, didn't tell me.'

'What happened in the office?'

'Argued, because he didn't tell me, what, happened.' Fulborough clearly found it difficult to talk and was in pain.

'You argue a lot, according to your staff.'

'Yes, don't like the man, felt it was a good, time, to fire...'

'And did you?'

'Yes.'

'Then what happened?'

'He hit me and I fell, don't remember any more.'

'You're lucky to still be alive.'

'So I've been told, but I don't actually think I'm hundred percent at the moment,' he tried a smile.

'Do you know anything about these bodies in the wood?'

'Yes, I do know a little, history.'

'Are you willing to share it with us?' Jake spoke for the first time. Fulborough turned his head towards the sound of the new voice.

'Suppose it's about time that... ' Fulborough winced with pain, as he tried to move his arms. 'Sorry.'

'That's OK. Take your time,' Randall said.

'I suppose you need to know about them. It all started a long time ago, when... I was a... boy... growing up on the... estate... '

Twenty minutes later, Randall and Jake were walking away from Fulborough's room, stunned by what they had been told.

'Can you believe that?' Jake asked. 'After all these years! And nobody had any idea, until today.'

'Yes, it is an interesting story, but at least we have a few more questions to put to Philpott when we find him. We can work on him and I think we'll have enough to hold him.'

'Indeed there is,' remarked Jake. 'I'd like to see him go "no comment" on that little lot.'

45

Late Sunday
Stephanie Parker

Parker read the contents of the envelope she'd found in the kitchen. She folded up the envelope and stuffed it in her skirt pocket, and fished out the car keys she'd pocketed earlier. She hoped that the car to which the keys belonged was sitting on the drive outside the house.

It was still dark outside. The clock on the oven flashed 22:19. She continued to wonder why her captors were not in the house and questioned why she'd been left alone on her own. Surely they knew that she would try to escape at her earliest opportunity – or perhaps they were so sure that whatever they had given her was going to keep her quiet for a long time.

She moved towards the front door and tried the lock. It was a double-locked PVC door, one of those white ones, which seemed to grace every house she'd seen on certain estates in Daventry, since her return to the force. Windows at the top half of the door, with a swirly, flowery pattern on frosted glass, and plain white plastic for the bottom half. She realised that without a key, she wouldn't be able to get out, unless she had one of those big black door keys the Support Groups use for raids on houses. And she suspected, in amusement, there would not be one of them in the house.

She went to the back door. Same type of door, same type of lock. Her captors must have known that if they kept those doors locked, she'd never be able to get out without assistance. She walked back into the kitchen and searched further to see if she could find some keys. Then checked the windows – double glazed uPVC – locked. Then she went into the sitting room and ferreted around in there for a few minutes. Checked the windows, they were the same. But she could not find any keys anywhere.

She was beginning to panic, so close to being free. She stopped and stood in the middle of the room, thinking about what she could do next. Where would they hide front door keys? She saw that the old sofa was littered with pizza and take-away cartons, abandoned, as if the occupants had left in a hurry. The wastebasket was full of empty bottles. The occupants obviously drank excessively.

This whole experience was almost surreal, laughable, if it weren't for the fact that she'd spent most of the time full of some sleep-inducing drug.

She hadn't checked the hallway for keys. Perhaps on the table hidden somewhere? But she was sure there wasn't a drawer in the table. She went and had a look anyway. As she stood in the hallway, she saw a set of vehicle lights pull onto the driveway. Damn. I'm not getting this far to be put back in that room, she thought, and switched out the light.

She decided to make her escape, when the front door

was opened. She stood in the shadow behind the door, intending to surprise the first person who came in.

The car lights went out and the hallway was plunged into darkness. She had the car keys in her hand and every intention of using them to put her captor down.

She saw a shadow coming up to the door, having the gait of a woman, and Parker readied herself. She saw the shadow lift her hand to put the key in the lock and the door opened. When the door was halfway open, Parker slammed the door into the woman. The door hit home with such force, that she fell back against the wall. Parker ran at her before she could get up from the floor, whereupon she punched her hard in the face. The woman shied away from Parker, but she punched her again and kicked out striking the woman's leg. She cried out, but Parker was already out of the door and heading for the car. She unlocked the car and climbed into a dirty old Ford Focus. It took a couple of tries to get it started, by which time her captor was hobbling towards her.

She wrenched it into reverse gear and shot backwards off the drive, catching the wing of the car the woman had arrived in.

Parker left the estate and recognised the Wellingborough Road. She knew that she was near to the Weston Favell Police Station and quickly drove towards it. When she arrived, she found that it was in darkness. "Closed. Only open between 09:00 and 17:00," said the sign on the door. 'Fuck! Who the hell closes police stations in a town this size?' she shouted at the door and ran back to the car.

She sat in the car trying to decide what to do next, thinking about where she would find somebody, then realised that there might be someone at Jake's station, so she made her way towards it. She drove from Weston Favell onto the Lumbertubs Way to join the A45 towards the motorway.

Quite unexpectedly, as she moved into the third lane, she felt extraordinarily tired. How can I be so tired, she thought, with all the sleep I've had? Her eyes felt heavy and she had difficulty keeping them open. Her body convulsed and she gripped the steering wheel so hard, it left indentations where her fingers were. She tried desperately to keep her eyes open, under the realisation that she was losing control of her body. Her foot was planted heavily on the accelerator pedal as it went into a spasm, and the vehicle was increasing speed.

She tried with all her remaining energy to lift her left foot onto the brake pedal to slow the car down. As the Focus approached the Barnes Meadow flyover at over seventy mph, she failed to negotiate the left-hand bend. The car mounted the central reservation and collided with the barrier, where it rebounded across the road into the nearside barrier, spinning out into the road again, losing momentum as it crashed backwards into the central barrier, coming to a halt.

Parker was unconscious, but her left foot was still on the brake pedal.

46

At eight a.m. on Monday morning, Jake was contacted by the on-call traffic collision investigator, informing him that WPC Parker had been found in a Ford Focus on the A45 having, 'fallen asleep at the wheel' was how he described it cynically. He was told that she had some serious injuries, and was unconscious.

Jake's first thought was for her mother Emily and he rang her almost immediately he'd received the news.

'Do you want me to come and take you to the hospital?' he asked her.

'I'm perfectly capable of getting there under my own steam, thank you.'

'I'm sorry. I thought I'd just ask.'

'I told your Inspector Randall the other day that I am not at all happy with her being back on the force, so I certainly don't need your assistance with my daughter. I'll make my own way, thank you very much!'

She put the phone down without a further word. Jake looked at the handset and grunted as he put the phone back down on its cradle.

As he stood in the incident room with Randall and the others, he couldn't help but feel a little responsible for her state. He should never have suggested her involvement to CID and certainly wouldn't again.

It had been two days since the operation had lost her, so standing in the incident room on Monday morning didn't have the usual cheery banter between everyone, and the room was subdued. Another week of road policing coppers working with detectives – a marriage made in hell.

But it wasn't, was it? Parker could have been killed in that single vehicle crash. What would he have done then? What would he have told her mother and what retribution would she throw at him? She clearly blamed him for bringing her back into the service, and made no secret of the fact to everyone she spoke to.

By all accounts there had been too many deaths, injuries and domestic upheaval that could all be linked back to Bingham bloody Tyler. All the shit in his life over the last twelve months could be traced back to him. Still reaching out from beyond the grave.

'Jake!'

'Yes, sir?'

'Are you with us this morning?'

'Only just, sir.' He smiled at Freeman. It was only reciprocated with a scowl. No sense of irony, these Yanks.

'What do we know then?' Randall asked, a little irritated, turning to Jake.

'According to my collision investigator, Parker lost control of the vehicle, just before Barnes Meadow flyover, travelling west. She was found unconscious at the wheel.

Whether that was as a result of the collision or what may have been administered to her, we don't yet know. I've asked Dr Kingsfield and her team to make the blood tests a priority. What we can say with certainty is that, before the collision, Parker realised what was happening and managed to put her left foot on the brake pedal. In fact, we think that her body went into some sort of spasm. Her left foot was so hard on the brake pedal, that she bent it to almost breaking point, while her right foot was just as hard down on the accelerator. If it weren't for that, there's every chance she'd have gone over the flyover and into the river below.'

'Do we think she'd been drugged?'

'We're fairly certain of that if we consider the MO of all the other collisions we're investigating. We've sent some blood samples to our outside specialist as well, to see if that can come up with some answers.'

'I'm sure that we're all relieved that constable Parker has survived this ordeal, despite what happened on Friday night,' Freeman said.

'CCTV?' queried Randall.

'We're on that, nothing yet. The A45 cameras will no doubt pick her up, but it's where she came from we need to know.'

Randall nodded. 'Right then, let's get out there and find whoever did this.'

'Yes, sir,' replied Jake with a mock salute. As if we're not doing that already.

He needed to go and see Parker in the hospital. He had got her into this mess, so he'd damn well make sure he got her out of it.

Jake stood at the end of Stephanie Parker's hospital bed. Kirsty was doing the doctor thing, checking charts and monitors. They spoke in low tones to each other, almost whispering.

'I shouldn't have got her roped into this,' Jake said.

'You weren't to know what was going to happen.'

'Emily, her mum, isn't very happy she's in here. In fact, she isn't very happy about her being back in the job in the first place. Blames me personally.'

'But it's her decision isn't it, not her mother's. All you did was let the force know she was back. I think her mum's trying to hide her own guilt.'

'Possible, but the job does tend to drive a wedge between families, as I know to my cost.'

'We can only hope that she's going to be OK. She'll be back at work in no time, you'll see.'

Kirsty moved around to the end of the bed and stood next to Jake. She took his hand, looked at him and smiled. He smiled back. 'Don't worry,' she said, 'she's going to be OK. Trust me, I'm a doctor.'

'And when did you change your view about her role in all this?'

'You told me, Jake. I've got to move on. I listened to you.' She leaned closer to him.

'I knew you two would get together,' croaked Parker, without opening her eyes. Her dry throat made her cough.

'How long have you been awake?'

'Long enough,' she said, opening one eye and coughing again. Kirsty moved around the bed and poured some water into glass, helping her to take a drink. She put the glass down on the bedside cabinet.

'I'll get the doctor,' Kirsty said and breezed out of the private room.

'Tell her mum as well. She's in the restaurant.'

Kirsty nodded as she left the room.

260

'I'm sorry, Steph,' was the only thing he could think of to say to Parker.

'At least I'm still alive.' She closed her eyes. 'Christ, I hurt.'

'You were very lucky.'

'Hmm, I knew there was something wrong, when I felt tired so quickly after I got into the car,' she spoke quietly, so as not to start coughing again.

'We'll need to talk about what happened,' Jake said.

She nodded slowly. 'Jake, there is something I need to tell you – I think it's quite important. Something I found at the house.'

Jake leaned in closer to hear what Parker had to say, but was interrupted by the doctor and Kirsty, closely followed by Emily.

Emily looked at her daughter sympathetically and said, 'It's good to have you back, Steph. You had me worried.'

Parker gave a lopsided smile to her mother. 'You can't get rid of me that easily,' she said with another short cough.

Emily turned to Jake. 'I'd like to be alone with my daughter now, if you don't mind, Sergeant.'

'Steph was about to tell me something, which she felt was important, before you came in.'

'I think it's more important to get my daughter back to health, don't you, Sergeant. Whatever it is it will have to wait,' Emily glowered at Jake, irritated by his presence. Jake looked across at Parker. She nodded briefly. He glanced at Emily, who was looking directly at him. Her eyes said it all. She was not going to let her little girl out of her sight again.

Jake and Kirsty left Emily with her daughter. Outside Parker's room, Kirsty said, 'What was that all about?'

'Emily came to the station the other day and we had a conversation about Steph, that's all.'

'I'm assuming that the conversation didn't go well?'

'Not for me, no. I couldn't say about Emily.'

'Still going on about her daughter re-joining the force?'

'Yeah, it's like a stuck record.'

'Hmm… Anyway, I have some good news for you.'

'What's that? I could do with some.'

'Parker's blood sample? We sent it off to have it examined as a priority and it came back. And the other ones that we kept back, after taking some of the samples to Tanya, when we discovered she'd not included her own company.'

Jake said nothing.

Kirsty opened the door to her lab with her swipe card and let Jake go in first. 'They've found a marker on the drug. A marker that identified its origin.'

'And?'

'You'll never guess.'

'Don't tell me…'

'…Exactly.'

'How did they find that?'

'One of the technicians stumbled upon it by accident. It forms part of pre-cursor chemicals, once he had disassembled it.'

'You make it sound as if he's taking apart a light-fitting.'

'Crude, but the same concept.'

'How do you disassemble a molecule?'

'Ah… Wouldn't you like to know?' She tapped the side of her nose.

'I would actually.'

'If you're very good, I might explain it to you one day.'

'Thanks a bunch,' he laughed. Some technicians looked up from their stations, as they walked through to Kirsty's office. Since she'd been taken off her senior role, the office her mentor had given her had been re-allocated to the new Head of Pathology. Kirsty had to move back into her old office in the corner of the lab. It wasn't so plush and grand as the one she'd come from, but there was room for a couple of easy chairs and a table along with a desk that overlooked the hospital grounds. Jake took off his high-vis vest and sat down. Kirsty poured a cup of coffee from the machine and sat down opposite him, handing him the mug. Jake watched her sit. Graceful would be the way he would describe it, and very alluring. He put that thought to one side as she spoke.

'OK then, just a bit of info because somebody is bound to ask.'

Jake sat back in the chair, waiting for an explanation.

'Years ago, some big pharma companies were developing numerous new drugs for a lot of applications, in science and in medicine. It was discovered that chemical markers could be included in the manufacture of a particular chemical, so if, in the future, there was some argument about whose drug it was and, more importantly, what chemicals were manufactured to produce the new drug and where they came from, they would be able to find out from the marker on the molecule.'

'A bit like an author copyrighting their work?'

Kirsty nodded.

'So would whoever manufactured this chemical have known that it was marked?'

'Not necessarily, no.'

'But they'd have a pretty good idea?'

'Depends how far up the food chain they are in the company. So, what are we going to do?'

'I think we need to go and talk to Dr Nicholls,' she said, sitting back in the chair and taking a sip of coffee.

'But won't that give the game away?'

'She probably knows that we're on to her company now anyway, if she's got any sense.'

Kirsty thought for a moment. 'I think I probably added to that suspicion when I asked her why her company was not on the list.'

'I can't believe that she is involved though. It must be someone else in the company.'

'I hope so, Jake. I do hope so.'

'We need to speak to Randall. I suppose I ought to ring him now,' Jake put his coffee down and fumbled around for his phone. Pressing the speed dial for Randall, he waited for an answer.

'Parker's awake.'

'When?'

'About half an hour ago.'

'How is she?'

'Tired and in pain. Her mother's with her.'

'Did Parker say anything?'

'She wanted to, but we were interrupted.'

'When will she be ready for interview?'

'Couple of days, I suppose.'

'Can't really wait that long if we're going to catch your killer. What about tomorrow or later today?'

'You can try, but the doctor may object.'

'OK, we'll see about that. Anything else?'

'Yeah, Kirsty's had a hit on the blood sample we've taken from Parker. Got an idea as to where some of the chemicals originated from.'

'Really?' Randall paused. 'Come and see me when you get back and we'll sort something out.'

'Search warrant might be good.'

'OK,' and he terminated the call.

'Bugger!' exclaimed Jake. 'Why did I have to open my

big mouth? He'll be wanting to take the credit now, I don't doubt,' he mumbled, as he picked up his hi-vis, putting it on. He hesitated, then said, 'Erm… do you… well…?'

'What, Jake?'

'I was wondering whether you'd like to… '

'Wondering what, Jake?' Kirsty said, a little frustrated.

'No, it doesn't matter. Another time, perhaps.' With that, he left Kirsty standing in the middle of her office.

47

Jake and Kirsty entered the wide lobby at Tanya's medical development offices. Jake was out of uniform and in civilian clothes. Although it was his day off, he considered that the investigation was too important to be delayed any further. And, in any case, he hadn't anything better to do, other than depress himself at home.

He collected Kirsty from the university, where she had been meeting with her pathology students. He knew, of course, that other than the fact that she was Tanya's friend, her presence was not necessarily required. But he had got used to her company, which he was sure was not lost on her.

They walked up to the reception, where he flashed his warrant card at the receptionist and asked to speak with Dr Nicholls.

'Do you have an appointment?' the receptionist asked, in quite a surly manner.

'Do I need one?' Jake snapped.

'Dr Nicholls is a very busy woman. I doubt if she could make the time.'

'Oh, she'll make time for us,' Kirsty said.

'And who are you?'

'Doctor Kirsty Kingsfield, forensic pathologist.'

The receptionist raised her eyebrows and picked up the phone. She spoke quietly into it, then replaced the receiver. 'Take a seat over there.'

'Mardy bitch,' Jake grumbled under his breath, only for Kirsty to dig him in the ribs. He smiled.

A few minutes later, Jake saw Nicholls exit the lift and approach them. She was, as usual, immaculately dressed and wearing a doctor's white coat with the company logo emblazoned on the right pocket and her name sewn underneath it.

She shook Jake's hand and gave Kirsty a hug and a kiss on both cheeks.

'This is a surprise,' said Tanya, addressing Jake. 'Didn't expect to see you till next week.'

'We've had a development, that we need to talk to you about,' Jake replied.

'Oh, and what's that?'

'Can we go to your office and talk there first?' bristled Kirsty.

Tanya glanced at Kirsty. Jake noticed that a worried look had crossed Tanya's face briefly, as they made their way to her office.

Offering them both a seat, Jake and Kirsty sat down in front of Tanya's desk.

'So, what's up,' she asked cheerily.

'We've made some of our own developments on that drug we gave you.'

'Really?' Tanya exclaimed. 'Anything that we can help with?'

'I'm sure you can,' Kirsty said.

'I'm going to tell it how it is, Tanya,' said Jake, 'but we've discovered a marker on the drug that was administered to a WPC we put up in an under-cover operation last weekend.'

'What sort of marker? Is your officer OK?'

'Yes, she's fine now, thank you,' responded Jake.

'The marker is one which identifies the manufacturer,' said Kirsty.

'I'm not sure that's possible,' Tanya responded.

'You, of all people, should understand the concept of molecular recognition markers for newly developed drugs.'

'Yes but, this company can't afford the thousands of dollars in costs to register such compounds with the FDA in the US and various other authorities around the world.'

'But you still develop them anyway, with these… ' Jake turned to Kirsty and prompted her.

'Molecular recognition markers,' she confirmed.

'Not all our drugs have MRMs.'

'Which ones do?' Kirsty asked.

Tanya paused for a moment, looking hard at Kirsty. Jake noticed the look on Tanya's face. A look that worried him as to where she thought they were taking the investigation.

'I don't think any of our drugs have MRMs or other isotopic markers either.'

'What are these markers anyway?' asked Jake naively. Knowing what the answer would likely be, he wanted to see who would explain it to him first. There was a short silence, before Tanya sat back in her chair, seeming to relax a little, as she launched into an explanation of molecular recognition markers.

As she spoke, Kirsty also sat back, and Jake saw the brief flicker of a smile cross her face. Jake could see for himself that Kirsty was trying to reel in her supposed friend. Kirsty would make a good cop, Jake thought.

'Well,' Tanya said, 'this sort of molecular marking has been developed over decades and has become one of the most effective methods in secure authentication of pharmaceuticals developed by big multinationals. Along with stable isotopic markers, it has revolutionised the way companies can secure their patents for new drugs. I'm sure you don't want me to go into the technical details at this stage?' She smiled an unconvincing smile at both of them, satisfied that she had batted away any further questions about her drug stock.

'OK, for the non-scientific ones amongst us,' Jake asked, 'what does that really mean, practically?'

'In simple terms, it's intellectual property, copyright, if you like.'

'So any drug which has been marked as such can identify the manufacturer of the drug?'

'In a word, yes.'

'And can this be disputed, say, in a court of law?'

'It would be very difficult. There was a case in Asia a few years ago that proved that those producing the drug were using the manufacturer's product, simply through this marker identification.'

'I see. 100% then,' Kirsty said.

Tanya nodded.

Kirsty rose to her feet and walked over to the window, where she stood and looked out across the hospital grounds. It was raining, washing across the car park almost horizontally.

'Is there anything else?' Tanya asked.

Kirsty turned. 'Yes, we have a technician in our laboratory. He's very bright and he'll go far, I think, but he found something almost by accident.'

'And what was that?' Tanya asked defensively.

'A marker,' Jake pitched in.

'That's a bit of luck then.' Tanya smiled. 'You'll be able to resolve your problem without further input from us?'

'We can indeed,' Jake said.

'The problem is the manufacturer,' Kirsty said.

Jake watched Tanya closely, he could see her flush, the red hue starting at her lower neck.

'Really?' Tanya fidgeted in her chair, looking a little uncomfortable.

Jake nodded slowly.

'How does that help me in what you want me to do?'

'You're the manufacturer,' Jake said.

'I find that impossible. Are you sure your young technician is right?'

'Certain.'

'How can you be certain?'

'Because, as you have just said, it's 100% reliable, a forensic molecular fingerprint, with your company's name all over it,' bristled Kirsty, she walked over to stand behind Tanya's chair.

'I see you've had some highlights done,' Kirsty questioned, changing the subject.

'Yes. What do you think?'

'Hmm, red, it doesn't suit you,' Kirsty took another glance at Tanya's highlights and walked back to her chair where she sat down. Jake could clearly see where that came from. The thought that Tanya could actually be the person he was looking for had, for the first time, crossed his mind.

'So, Tanya, what we need from you is that list of employees you said you were going to give us.'

'Right. In that respect, I've spoken to our company solicitor and I'm afraid you're going to need a warrant before we give out any of our information.'

270

'I see. Are you trying to hide something?' Kirsty said with a smile.

Tanya glanced at Kirsty. 'No, nothing at all. We just need to be seen to be complying with the appropriate laws, before we hand out our employees details. For the employees' sake, of course.' She smiled at Jake, but he saw that it was certainly not the warmth he'd seen earlier.

'I think you're being obstructive,' Kirsty said. 'Friend or no friend, somebody in your organisation…'

'… It's not my organisation,' Tanya interjected.

'It is according to Companies House,' Jake said.

Tanya flushed again, but said nothing.

'As I was saying, somebody in your organisation may be our killer and an abductor. The police will find out who it is, Tanya, so don't be so stupid and let's have that list,' hissed Kirsty.

Tanya glared at Kirsty. 'I thought you were a friend. I was wrong.'

'I'm no friend to people who deceive me, Tanya, and you're clearly holding something back. I don't like that.'

'I think you'd better leave now, Sergeant. The next time you want to speak to me, or my staff, you'd better have a warrant or whatever it is you lot get over here – and my solicitor will be present. I'll see you out.'

Jake and Kirsty remained seated.

'Please – I don't want to have to call security.'

Reluctantly, Jake and Kirsty were ushered out of the building.

By the time they exited the lift, two security guards were waiting for them and escorted them off the premises. After they had left the building, the guards stood at the doors, trying to look hard.

'That was new,' Jake said, as they got into their car. 'I

can't recall ever having been escorted off a premises before.'
He sighed.

'What do we do now?' asked Kirsty.

'We'll have to tell Randall.'

'Do we have to? Can't you just get your own warrant?'

'No, well, I suppose we could, but I think we have our suspects, all 140 of them. My department couldn't cope with that. I'm in enough trouble as it is.'

'I'm not so sure we have 140 suspects. Look?' Kirsty pointed to a woman walking into the building.

'Isn't that Simone Nicholls?' Jake asked, as if confirming it for himself.

'Yes, and what's that bruise on her face?'

48

Later, having returned Kirsty to the hospital, Jake went to visit Parker. When he arrived at her room, he saw that Parker was busy getting dressed, so didn't go in. Her mother was also in the room and listened to the conversation that was going on between them. Not that he normally spied on people, but Emily was talking quite loudly to her daughter.

'You shouldn't be doing this, Steph.'

'I have no option, Mum. These people who took me knew who I was and what I was doing. It's my duty to catch them.'

'Duty – duty – duty! What about your duty to get yourself better? What about your duty to me, your mother? Your antics in this damnable job could have and still could get you killed. Don't you realise that? And what about that detective visiting you? Do they not realise that you were ill?'

'I'm a police officer, Mother. It's my job, antics or no

antics. I have no option. I'm not going to just give up at the first hurdle. And in any case, the DI and his sergeant needed information to find out who did this to me, don't you understand that. Or don't you want them to find out?' Parker finished dressing and sat down to put on her shoes.

Emily walked over and stood in front of her, 'Of course I do, love, but this isn't your first hurdle! Think about that time when you were a cadet and that murder they sent you to. Think about all the trouble that you got into – and think about what your father had to do to get you out of it.'

'Don't bring Dad into this. It was his idea, not mine, to send me to the other side of the world, like packing me off onto the naughty step, but 12,000 miles away.'

'I didn't want him to!'

'But if he hadn't, I probably wouldn't be here now, would I?'

'I suppose so – but – you're not better yet.'

Jake knocked on the door and entered. He apologised for the intrusion.

'I suppose you've been listening outside?' seethed Emily.

Jake raised an eyebrow, said nothing.

'Mum, leave it – I'll manage, don't worry. I tackled a lot worse in New Zealand.'

Parker moved closer to her mother, who by now was standing and staring out of the window. She turned to her daughter, her face softening. Emily glanced at Jake.

'Steph, you know I worry about you. And you know I don't want you to do what you do.'

Jake went to respond, but Emily held up her hand slightly to stop him.

'But, I will be here for you, whatever you decide.'

'All I need, Mum, is your support when I need it. There's only two of us now and we need to be able to give each other strength and comfort in times like these, whether we like what we're doing or not,' she smiled. 'I don't want to end up not talking to you.'

'That'll never happen, love.'

They hugged each other, tears welling in Emily's eyes. Parker pushed her away gently.

'Come on, Mum, take me to work, please.' She turned to Jake, then back to her mother. 'And please, don't be so hard on Jake.'

'You like him, don't you?'

Jake grinned at her and again was about to say something, but Parker stepped in this time.

'Yes, but not in the way you're suggesting. Jake was the only one who listened to me, when I got back to England. Anyway,' she said, looking at Jake and laughing, 'I think he has the hots for Kirsty Kingsfield.'

Jake rubbed his chin, not really knowing how to answer that. He smiled at them both. He was going to offer to take Parker, but felt that mother and daughter needed to be together.

Emily smiled. 'I hadn't noticed,' She winked at Jake. A thaw?

Having said goodbye to her mother, and asking her to collect her later, Parker hobbled into the Road Policing Operations building. Signing herself in, she asked where Jake's office was and how to get there. The desk clerk rang his office, then told her where he could be found.

She took the lift to the second floor. She managed to get to Jake's office, where he invited her in. She sat in the chair Jake indicated.

'You shouldn't be out of hospital yet,' he scolded.

'Glutton for punishment, I suppose.' She smiled briefly. 'You sound like my mother.'

'Hmm, how do you feel?'

'Bloody awful, but I needed to get out of that place. Never been a great lover of hospitals – boring!' She shifted slightly in her chair to get more comfortable.

'Why didn't you just go home?'

'I needed to give you the information we spoke of, that I found at the house, where I was held captive.'

'Why give it to me?'

'Randall isn't exactly my best buddy at the moment; he told me when he visited that there were supposed to be two detectives in the pub she took me to.'

'And where were they?' Jake asked, sitting down.

'They pissed off for a fag, or so it seemed. By the time they returned, the damage had already been done and I was being dragged away to her car. The one I smashed up on the A45.'

'But it was my cock-up as well. I should have stationed myself closer.'

'But Randall and his detectives were in the club, not you. He should have had my back and he failed.'

'I understand how you must feel.'

'I think,' she continued, 'that you have a fair idea who this person is?'

Jake slowly nodded. 'Possibly,' was all he said.

'Perhaps a certain drug company?'

'Possibly,' he said again.

Parker reached into her bag and took out a plain, unaddressed envelope. On the envelope, Jake saw the company logo. She handed it to Jake, who took it from her. He opened it.

'This is an acquisition request for controlled drugs.'

Parker nodded. 'Any you recognise?'

'I recognise precursors that metabolise into drugs found in some of our victims and in your blood sample. I'm sure Kirsty would be able to identify the others.'

'Look who the requisition is from.'

Jake looked to the bottom of the page.

'Signed by Doctor Tanya Nicholls, it would seem.'

Parker sat with her arms folded.

'It doesn't mean to say that she's involved, but it does seem to be a smoking gun, I have to say.'

'Could be somebody in her employ?' Parker suggested.

'It's possible. But it could also be someone a bit closer to home.' Jake didn't want to reveal to Parker who they saw at the company the day before. Not just yet anyway. He picked up the phone and dialled Randall's office. When Randall answered, he said, without any preamble, 'We need to do a raid on Tanya Nicholls' company.'

'Why?' was the curt reply.

'I have some information, which may lead to our suspect.'

'What sort of information?'

'Positive proof that this company or its employees are developing clandestine drugs of a particularly nasty nature.'

'Where did you get this information from?'

'Parker.'

'Are you at the hospital?'

'No, she's in my office.'

'I'll come over,' and rang off.

Fifteen minutes later, Randall blustered into Jake's office. 'What's this all about?'

Jake showed Randall the contents of the envelope Parker had given him. He looked at it briefly, glanced at Parker, and handed it back to Jake.

'Means nothing to me.'

'These drugs are part of the make-up of the drugs that have been killing my drivers.'

'Doesn't mean to say that this company is involved.'

'No, but it's a bloody good lead, don't you think?' Parker said.

'Mmm, maybe, but it's not enough to go and raid the place. Anyway, it's not even in our county.'

'You don't think?'

'No, I don't think.'

'What more do you want then?'

'Caught red-handed in the biscuit jar would be good.'

'Catching someone actually stealing the chemicals would call for a massive operation, much more than just raiding the place.'

'We need something more concrete, sergeant, not just a drug requisition sheet.'

'Which was found in the house where I was held,' Parker interrupted.

Jake was getting more and more frustrated by Randall's attitude over the investigation. In fact, Jake was beginning to understand why the two departments found it difficult to get on with each other. 'This is the best piece of concrete evidence that we've found,' Parker said.

'Tell you what,' Jake said at last, 'leave it to me. I'll sort it out myself. And when we're right don't come cap in hand to me wanting a piece of the action.'

Randall stuffed his hands in his pockets, huffed and walked out.

'Typical! When we want help from CID, we have to

fight for it, yet when they want help from us, we jump to it like good little soldiers.'

Parker looked at Jake and grinned. 'I knew I'd made the right decision.'

'Now all we've got to do is work out how to get into the building without a warrant.' They both sat thinking.

'Perhaps you won't have to,' a voice said from outside his office. 'I told you, I've got your back, Jake,' said Stevens as he entered the office.

'How did you know Randall was here?'

'I'm a detective,' he said grinning.

'So what do you suggest?'

'Why don't you go and wait outside her house? You know where she lives, don't you?'

Jake nodded.

'Well then, job's a good 'un, wouldn't you say?'

'Not that easy, surely?'

'Happens all the time.'

'But I can't recognise any of my captors, unless I see their eyes,' Parker said.

'Didn't you hit one of them, when you escaped?'

'Yes,'

'Enough to hurt them?'

'Yes.'

Time to come clean, Jake thought. 'When Kirsty and I visited Tanya yesterday.' Stevens looked quizzically at Jake. 'Don't ask. When we left or, more correctly, when we were thrown out...'

Stevens looked at Jake. 'Ah, we'll make a detective of you yet, Jake.'

Jake just shook his head and continued. 'We saw Simone Nicholls enter the building and she had a right shiner.'

'Which side?' Parker asked.

'Right.'

'With a cut?'

Jake nodded.

'That's her then. It's got to be. Too much of a coincidence otherwise, don't you think?'

'Indeed it is,' Stevens said, 'I think that's enough to at least bang on her front door and convince our illustrious leader.'

'No, Clive, he had his chance. Leave it to us.'

'And me?'

'Yes, and you, but only if you're sure it won't get you into more trouble.'

'Trouble, is my middle name,' Stevens said.

They agreed on a plan of action. Parker couldn't get involved, because of her injuries, but when it came to doing an identification parade, she'd be there, no doubt about that.

'What I can't understand,' Parker said, as she struggled to stand up and was helped by Stevens, 'is that there were two of them. I'm convinced that they were both female, but they never spoke. I got the impression that they were a bit out of their depth, didn't really know what to do with me.'

'So, we're looking for an accomplice for Simone Nicholls.'

'It would seem so,' Stevens said.

'We'll have to ask, after we've arrested her, won't we, Clive?'

49

Jake and Stevens wasted no time in trying to find Simone Nicholls. They parked outside Tanya Nicholls's house and waited for her to return. Jake had decided not to tell Kirsty what they were doing. He didn't want to compromise what friendship she had left with Tanya.

But he couldn't get the nagging feeling out of the back of his mind that Tanya was somehow involved. And he was sure that Kirsty probably had the same feeling after their conversation in Tanya's office. Something that was said at that meeting picked at his brain, but he couldn't remember what.

He and Stevens sat in an unmarked BMW saloon, secreted in a farm gateway a few yards from Nicholls's house. They could just about see her driveway.

Stevens sat in the passenger seat, stuffing a burger into his mouth. The aroma of the burger made Jake's mouth water and he realised how hungry he was. He should have taken Stevens' offer, when he invited him to partake.

'Right,' Stevens said, licking his fingers, wiping them off on a paper towel, 'you can't beat a great, greasy burger, can you?'

'Just don't get grease all over my upholstery, Clive, or the Super'll have my balls in a sling. This is a new car, remember.'

'And very posh it is too.' He stuffed the container back into the plastic bag and put it down in the passenger well. 'Wish we had cars this posh. Ford Focus is about it – and diesel at that,' grumbled Stevens.

They sat in the quiet of the evening; waiting and watching the sun go down.

Stevens broke the silence. 'Tell me about Dr Kingsfield and you?'

'There's nothing to tell.' Jake kept his head looking out of the driver's side window. He could see Stevens' reflection.

'That's not what I heard.'

'What did you hear, Clive?'

'That you were shagging her.'

Jake turned toward him. 'I'm not and she's your friend as well, you know.'

'Yes, I know, sorry, a bit crude of me, but you do seem to spend a lot of time together. It's been noticed.'

'We're friends, Clive. Just because a bloke likes the company of a woman doesn't mean to say he's, as you so crudely put it, shagging her.'

'But, if you look at the statistics, it's only a matter of time.'

'So what if it is?'

'Nothing, only you're a divorcee, and…'

'Don't remind me.'

'And she's a widow, both single. So what's the problem?'

'I don't see a problem, but the force does.' Jake pointed to his Sergeant stripes on his epaulettes. 'Hence these still,' he said, tapping them.

282

'Ah, so it's the force then? Not your reluctance to take it a step further?'

'Clive, I've just finished a bloody messy divorce. I don't know whether I want to commit to another relationship at the moment.' He decided to be economical with the truth on this matter, until it was necessary to admit the way things were.

'Does she?'

'I don't know.'

'Haven't you asked her?'

'We've had a conversation.'

'And?'

'We're going to take it slow.'

'I find that hard to believe.'

'Look, Clive, I like her. I know that. The whole bloody force knows it too. But I'll do things in my own time.'

'Just don't leave it too long, OK?'

'Do I need your permission?'

Stevens shook his head.

'Anyway, changing the subject, what's happened to the Clive Stevens' great sense of humour?'

Stevens held his face front and quietly replied, 'I grew up.'

'What sort of answer is that?'

Stevens was quiet for a moment, while he took a gulp of what was left of his coffee.

'As a colleague of the same rank,' he said, 'I'll tell you, but only you. Both of us have been through the ringer over the last twelve months.'

Jake nodded. 'You could say that.'

'Jim Kingsfield was a good friend. A real friend. And you don't get many of them in a lifetime, if at all. He took me under his wing, when I joined CID as a DC and he was my DS. I was the best man at his wedding with Kirsty. They were a fine couple. Both suited each other really well, and what happened was an absolute tragedy. Did you know, it hit me hard, harder than I ever thought it would? Spent six weeks on the sick, three of them at Flint House, on rehab.'

'I didn't realise, Clive. I thought you were just... Clive, if you know what I mean.'

'Yeah, I understand, but it sort of knocked the wind out of my sails, you know. Before I was known as the office joker. I still make the odd joke here and there, but as I said, I grew up. I understood that this wasn't a game. Colleagues – friends – get hurt. I'd never had anything like that in my service up to that point, up to Jim's death... ' His voice trailed away, and Jake looked at him. He thought he could see his eyes watering a little.

'I only knew him as a Probie. We went our separate ways. Funny old life, the way it brought us back together, if only briefly.'

'Yes, you don't know what life has in store. Before Jim's death, my attitude was live it, do you know what I mean?'

'Yes.'

'But you know what they say, "shit happens",' he said, trying to lighten the mood. The sun had gone down and the interior of the car was also cooling. Jake did his jacket up, started the car and put the heater on.

'You really like her, don't you, Jake?'

'Yes, I really like her.'

He nodded. 'Do me a favour will you?'

'If I can.'

'Look after her, look after her well – for Jim's sake – will you?'

'I will do that, Clive, as long as Randall keeps his nose out.'

'I'll make sure he will.' Stevens pointed out an approaching car.

'It's Tanya's Merc,' Jake said.

'And Simone's in the passenger seat. I wonder where her car is?' He grinned across at Jake. 'Let's go and find out, shall we?'

Jake pulled out of the gateway they were parked in and drove the few yards to Nicholls's house, parking across the drive, to prevent them from using the car to escape, if they were so inclined. They got out of the car and approached Simone Nicholls. Tanya was just putting the key into the house door lock, when she turned and saw Jake.

'I told you that the next time we met, I wanted to see a warrant.'

'We're not here to talk to you. We're here to talk to Simone.'

'Why do you want to talk to me?' Simone asked.

Before they could answer, Tanya said, 'She's an employee of mine, so the same stands.'

'Not on this occasion, Dr Nicholls,' Stevens said.

'And who are you?'

'Detective Sergeant Stevens, Major Crimes Unit.'

Nicholls looked aghast at Stevens and shot a menacing look at Jake. She was clearly uncomfortable with two policemen standing on her drive, but Jake wondered whether she was going to make more of a fuss.

'Don't worry, Mum. Just call our solicitor, will you?'

Tanya came towards her daughter. 'Are you sure about this?'

'Yes. Don't worry.'

'Simone Nicholls, I am arresting you on suspicion of murder, grievous bodily harm and abduction. You do not have to say anything, but it may harm your defence, if you do not mention when questioned, something which you later rely on in court. Anything you say will be given in evidence. Do you understand?'

'Yes, and you'll regret it.' Simone answered with a threatening voice.

Tanya went to say something, but Jake interrupted her. 'It would be in your interests, Dr Nicholls, to keep quiet.'

Stevens placed the handcuffs on Simone and marched her towards the car.

'You haven't heard the last of this,' hissed Nicholls. 'You're making a big mistake.'

'I'm sure we are,' mumbled Jake, as he got into the car.

50

Randall sat at his desk reviewing action messages. A large mug of coffee steamed to one side, within reach of his outstretched hand. The heavy rain, which seemed to be a feature of the autumn, continued to pound on his office window. The occasional flash in the distance was enough to warn everyone that the storm was coming. It was still hot and muggy, even in his office. He would have loved to open the window, but knew that would mean getting as wet as if he were standing outside.

The light had faded so much in his office that he had to put on the desk lamp to the left of his computer screen. Flicking through the messages, nothing of importance screamed at him.

He thought that the two most important cases on his desk, Jake's car crash killer and those UIDs in the morgue had become stagnant. Randall needed to inject some life into them, but if nothing was coming in, there was little he could do. Perhaps a section on Crimewatch might help the bodies-in-the-wood scenario. He made a note to speak with media relations to see what they thought.

The interview with Parker had revealed nothing, other than that worthless piece of paper that was floated at him. Although he thought that Jake might be right. There might be something in it after all. He made another note, on his list. Then there was the search for Frank Philpott, which seemed to be doing nothing either. That was an important task. Another all-ports warning and some press coverage might be best for that as well. CCTV perhaps might reveal something. He'd get Stevens to look into that, when he came in. Another note. Then there was Lord Fulborough. Randall needed to speak with him again, but the hospital wasn't playing ball. Another note.

He drained his coffee and stood from his desk, stretched and looked at his watch. It was just gone 08:00. He'd been in the office for a little over an hour. Time to reflect before the rest of the team arrived. Adjusting his tie, he decided to go to the restaurant for another coffee and to wash down a butty.

As he made his way to the restaurant, he reflected on his time with Northants since his arrival and promotion from Thames Valley. He still felt a little lost. His integration into Northants had not gone as smoothly, as he would have wished. He seemed to have made too many enemies already in the short space of time he'd transferred in. He knew that he was not the most amiable of people. His time in the army built a suit of armour that very few were able to penetrate, and only if he let them, which wasn't often enough.

He tried with Dr Kingsfield, but her allegiance was to someone else, that was obvious. In a way he could understand why she'd been a little aloof. Her husband, after all, was a

Detective Inspector, so Randall was probably barking up the wrong tree with that one. He genuinely wished her success in building her new relationship with Jake. Perhaps he ought to tell them both, one day.

The death of his own wife made him understand what Kirsty Kingsfield was going through. Life had been difficult enough for him, brought into focus when he got himself blown up and his medic wife died trying to save him. He'd become insular, he recognised that, and thought that, by moving forces, he'd have a better chance of returning to the way he saw himself. The way he was when he joined the army. He rubbed the scar on his face, as the memories of that day flooded back. Sometimes they were difficult to hold at bay.

By the time he'd finished his remorseful thinking, he had arrived at the force restaurant, where he ordered a sausage sandwich and a coffee. He picked up a paper, which had been abandoned on one of the tables and sat down to read the headline

"Police Woman Abducted In Failed Sting Operation. Special report by our staff reporter."

Bloody press office! They could have held that info back. Really not necessary to blast his first failed operation all over the press.

Some minutes later, his phone rang and, wiping grease from his hands, he answered it. It was DC Fred Martin.

'Yes, Fred, what's up?'

'Good news, boss!' he exclaimed down the phone.

'About time. I could do with some.'

'Frank Philpott was picked up a hour ago in a traffic stop on the M55 in Cheshire.'

Finally a bit of good news. 'That's great, where is he?'

'At Chester nick. Been lifted for breach of bail conditions.'

'Ah, we told him not to leave the county.'

'We did, and he did,' Fred said.

'Right. Are they doing him for anything?'

'Only some minor traffic offences. They said if we want him, we'll have to go and fetch him.'

'Right, speak to the CI. I'm on my way back to the office.' Randall wrapped up what was left of his sandwich and made his way out of the restaurant. 'Then arrange for you and someone else, probably a uniform, to go up with you to bring him back.'

The news Randall received about Frank Philpott's breach of bail, was a good start to the day, just for a change. Good news had been difficult to come by in both enquiries.

He made his way back to the incident suite with a bit of a spring in his step. As he entered the suite, that spring soon disappeared, as he saw ACC Marland talking to Freeman.

Freeman looked over to Randall and beckoned him over. He tried to think about what he might have done to warrant a visit by ACC Ops.

He exchanged pleasantries, as he approached Marland, who looked at him with a face that he couldn't really read. Was it good or bad that he was here? he asked himself, as he approached.

'Ah, Randall, how are things progressing?'

'I think we've had a spot of luck. Frank Philpott, caught in a traffic stop in Cheshire and currently residing at Chester nick for breach of bail conditions.'

'Somebody going to get him, I hope.'

'Fred Martin and a uniform are going up. In fact, I hope they've gone by now.'

'Good work, Randall.' He turned to Freeman. 'I understand that there has been a bit of friction between the department and Jordan?'

'Nothing we can't handle, sir,' replied Freeman, glancing at Randall, in a 'how the hell did he hear about that?' sort of way.

'Right, give him all the help he needs. We've got to foster good inter-departmental relations, in these times of austerity, you know.' The smile that crossed Marland's face was not what Randall would call warm.

'He does tend to go and do his own thing, sir,' Randall called out as Marland walked away from him.

'You have to give him the benefit. After all, he is a black rat,' Marland said, stopping midstride and turning back towards them both.

'A what?' quizzed Freeman.

'Black rat – traffic cop. You not heard the expression, since you've been over here?'

Freeman shook his head.

Marland took a couple of paces back towards them. 'When I did my time in the Met, traffic cops were called black rats – because they eat their own.'

'Really? Never heard that before.'

'It moved out into the provinces and most traffic cops are referred to as black rats. The Met even set up a charity to help orphans and bereaved children of serving officers and others. What started as derogatory to our white-hatted colleagues has been turned into something for good. On the other hand, I wouldn't let them catch you with too much beer in your belly!' Marland guffawed at his own joke.

Randall and Freeman simply smiled politely.

Marland excused himself, told them to keep up the

good work and retired from the suite. Freeman indicated to Randall to follow him into his office. He shut the door.

'What's going on with Jake?'

'He had a hunch about who he might think was involved in the deaths he's investigating.'

'And?'

'And I didn't think it was worth running it.'

'Why?'

'It was just a hunch, based on a piece of paper Parker found in the house where she was held.' Randall stuffed both hands in his pockets.

Freeman sat down behind his desk. 'What was in this piece of paper? he asked eventually.

'It was requisition for certain drugs.'

'And you didn't think it was important?'

'No, not at the time.'

Freeman indicated for Randall to sit in the chair opposite his desk. He rubbed his face and looked directly at Randall. 'What if I tell you that he's made an arrest?'

'When?' That got Randall's interest. He sat up further in the chair, and adjusted his glasses.

'Last night.'

'You knew about it?'

'I did, yes.'

'Only after it had happened, I'd guess?'

'Correct.'

'Why didn't you let me know?'

'Your phone was off.'

Randall was not happy and he was sure Freeman could see it in his face. He stood, then paced the office. 'Who?'

'An employee, where we sent our samples for a second opinion.'

'What has he said?'

'She – and the interview is still ongoing.'

'Don't you think that I should be handling the interview?' Randall was becoming more and more frustrated by this conversation.

'No, let him get on with it and we'll pick up the pieces.'

'Great.' Randall stuffed his hands back in his pocket and turned to leave.

'You should have listened to him, Inspector,' Freeman said as Randall opened the door to leave. He paused for a second, but made no comment as he walked out. He was more interested in getting Frank Philpott into an interview room, than worry about a traffic cops problems. In the meantime, he needed to go and speak to Lord Fulborough. He looked around the office.

'Where's Stevens?' he growled. He got some blank looks and head shakes. He phoned him. It went straight to answerphone. 'Never mind, I'll go on my own.'

51

Arriving at the hospital, Randall asked to see Lord Fulborough. The doctors agreed, but only for a short time. Randall walked into the private room, a room not too dissimilar to that where Parker was previously. Fulborough was awake, drifting in and out of sleep from the different cocktail of medication he'd been put on. He opened his eyes and watched Randall find a chair in the corner of the room and dragged across to Fulborough's bed and sat down.

'Are you awake, sir?' he asked.

'I am.'

'I need to get some information from you. We have Frank Philpott in custody.'

'Good, you can tell him from me that he's fired,' Fulborough's voice was low as if talking through a mouthful of gravel.

'I'll be sure to mention it. Are you up to talking to me?'

'For the moment, yes.'

'So, Lord Fulborough… '

'Barry, please.'

'So, Barry, can you tell me what happened that evening?'

Fulborough shifted his weight and tried to sit up further. He indicated to Randall to reach for the glass of water on the bedside table. Randall stood and gave Fulborough the glass, from which he took a drink. Randall took the glass from him then placed it back on the table. Fulborough laid back, wincing with pain.

'I was angry, it has to be said. I found out about him hiding that second body in my wood. It was bad enough finding one twelve months ago, let alone finding another one.'

Randall sat back in the chair and steepled his hands. He didn't want to interrupt, now that Fulborough had started to talk.

'I wanted to speak to him, to ask him why he'd done it. I know that I wanted to get on with clearing it, because I'd been on his back to get it done. But I didn't want him to break the law. I'm not that sort of person – law-abiding. I may be a bit of an arse sometimes, when things don't go my way, but I would never condone breaking the law. It was my father who walked the line of criminality – and I know that Philpott was almost his henchman. He used to do things that my father wanted without father knowing, if you understand what I mean.'

Randall nodded. 'Go on.'

'There's a story, a fable, if you like, about these remains.'

'Why have we not heard this before?'

'Family secrets.'

'Hmm, we all have them. But surely if it was well known, somebody else would have spoken out about it before now?'

'No, we kept it close to our chests. I didn't even find out about it, until after my father died. Philpott told me, in a way that suggested there would be a lot of trouble if I said anything.'

'You're going to tell me now, are you?'

Fulborough nodded. 'I am, yes, because he doesn't work for me anymore, as far as I'm concerned. In any case, I am not beholden to one of my staff, however long he's worked on the estate.'

'Do you want to make a formal statement?'

'I suppose so,'

Randall removed his phone from his pocket, clicked on an app, and set it to record. 'If you don't mind,' he said, glancing down at the phone. Fulborough shrugged.

'When you're ready.'

'The story goes that father became besotted with a young stable hand. A pretty girl, by all accounts, but from what I can make out, a bit unhinged. father would not leave her alone and one Sunday morning after he had returned from the hunt – pissed as usual – there should be a legal limit for riding a horse too.' He smiled. 'Anyway, he took her in the stables when everyone else had left and raped her. Nine months later, she had a baby girl. It was always a thorn in his side. She blackmailed him for thousands, so she'd keep her mouth shut. She went off with another chap and had a son by him, but she continued to blackmail father.'

'Did he ever report it?'

'No. Would have been his worst nightmare.'

'What happened then – to his Lordship, I mean?'

'He drank himself to death.'

'But carried on paying this woman?'

'Oh no. He stopped doing that, when she mysteriously disappeared.'

'Really? Was she reported missing?'

'As far as I am aware, father instructed Philpott to report

her missing. Whether he did or not is anyone's guess. No doubt, you could find that out from your records.'

Randall nodded. 'Go on.'

'The rumours, of course, didn't go away and everyone believed that Philpott had done her in for father.'

'Do you believe that?'

'I wouldn't put it past him, but you have to understand, I was just a boy. The rumours, however, never went away.'

'Do you think that the body in the wood – the second one – is her?'

'It would explain why he never wanted anything to do with the wood, calling it "his special place", wouldn't it?'

Randall nodded slowly, thinking. 'What about the other remains, which we found twelve months ago?'

'That's where the story gets even more intriguing. Again, it's all rumour, but the remains you found twelve months ago are believed to be her daughter.'

'How do you work that one out?'

'My office manager, Marjorie, also had a bit of a thing for father. They were seen together on more than one occasion. One day he was out with her, when he got a message from Philpott and they rushed back to the estate. You'd have to ask her the rest.'

'But these remains have only been in the ground for about five years?'

'Yes, that would be about right.'

'And the remains we found recently, about fourteen to fifteen years, give or take?'

'Yes, that seems about right as well.'

'What happened to the daughter?'

'They, and I mean her and her stepbrother, lived in Northampton, both got into the social system, after their mother disappeared.'

'What happened to all the money she had from your father?'

'We assume she spent it. I don't know.'

There was a knock on the door and the nurse entered.

'I'm afraid I'm going to have to ask you to leave, Detective Inspector.'

Randall acknowledged her with a nod and held up five fingers. She nodded and retired.

'What I can't understand, is why would the old Lord be chasing woman at his age?'

'Money pit, they wanted a bit of his, my, estate. He was quite dashing in his younger days, always had women around him. Just couldn't give it up, I suppose.'

'And what about your mother?'

Fulborough looked hard at Randall and, for the first time, saw a flicker of emotion in him.

'I would prefer not to speak of my mother.' He cleared his throat, then mumbled, 'More family secrets, of which you do not need to know. Nothing relevant to your investigation anyway.'

Randall nodded and stood to leave. 'Very well then.' He picked up his phone and switched off the recorder. He thanked Fulborough for his frankness and walked towards the door. He opened the door and turned back to Fulborough.

'One thing, do you know the name of Lord Fulborough's disappeared moll?'

'Oh, yes – Avril Tyler.'

52

Jake and Stevens sat in interview room seven in Northampton's Criminal Justice Centre. The room was small and soundproofed, with dull pinkish tiles and was no more that twelve by eight feet in size.

In the centre of the room was a desk pushed endways against the wall. On the table was a double-deck CD recorder, above which was a computer screen. A bluetooth keyboard and mouse sat on top of the CD deck. Next to the unit was a box of unused and sealed CDs, ready to be placed in the machine. Instructions to the officers were stuck to the top of their side of the desk.

They sat on one side. Jake had in front of him a file of documents in a manila-coloured folder. Opposite him Simone Nicholls sat, staring hard at them both.

'What the fuck am I here for?' she demanded.

'All in good time, Miss Nicholls,' Stevens replied. 'Once we get these CDs in the recorder,' holding them up and waving them in front of her, 'everything will be explained to you.'

Nicholls said nothing, but continued to stare hard at both of them, sucking her teeth occasionally and looking skywards.

Jake went through the preliminaries, reminding her that she was still under caution and agreed that she had declined a solicitor at this time. He explained that they were investigating the abduction of WPC Parker the previous Friday night and other matters.

'Tell me what happened last Friday night.'

'Nothing happened.'

'Did you do anything last Friday?'

'No, I worked till late at the laboratory.'

'How late?'

'Late.'

Jake looked her in the eye. 'How… late?'

'Very.' Nicholls looked away.

'That doesn't tell me anything.'

'That's all you're gettin'.'

Stevens looked at Jake. 'Last Friday a policewoman was abducted from a club in Northampton town centre. She was taken to a house, where she was detained against her will, until she managed to escape.'

'And what the fuck has that got to do with me?'

'Explain to me how you got these bruises.' Jake pointed at Nicholls's face.

'I fell over.'

'Where?'

'At work.'

'So, there will be a record of your accident.'

'Which is a legal requirement,' Stevens put in.

'I suppose so, somewhere.'

'Did you need hospital treatment?'

'No.'

'It looks like a nasty gash.'

'I'm a big girl. I can cope.'

Jake opened the file in front of him slowly. 'Tell me what you do with your mother?'

She sighed and folded her arms in front of her. 'I'm an analyst.'

'What do you analyse?'

'Drugs, samples, anything I'm given.'

'By?'

'My mother.'

'I bet that can get difficult?'

'Why should it?'

Jake read the top document briefly of his file. 'You're adopted, aren't you?'

'Yes. What's that got to do with anything?'

He read the sheet of paper, headed New York Police Department. 'Your biological parents weren't very law-abiding, were they?'

'So what? I am.'

'Tell me a bit about them. Do you remember them?'

'Nothing to tell. All I know is that my old man was shot by the cops.'

'With good reason, it seems.'

'That's your opinion.'

'You don't like the police then?'

'They stop people from being free. Doing what they want.'

'You prefer anarchy then?' snorted Stevens.

'You wouldn't know what that was, unless you'd lived in New York as a child,' she sneered.

'So what was it like?' Stevens asked.

'When you have parents who both take drugs, walk

around carrying a gun, shooting people and when you ask why, you get a beating. That, is my anarchy.'

Jake glanced at Stevens. 'So you were brought up in "The Hood"?'

'Yeah, and?'

'I think you're a bit of a rebel.'

Simone remained silent and looked skyward again. Then bit her nails. Jake thought that she looked a little more nervous. Some of the edge was falling away to reveal something else, but he wasn't quite sure what.

'Do you own a blue-grey Ford Focus estate?' Stevens asked.

'Yes.'

'Do you know where it is now?'

'No, it got stolen.'

'When?'

'A few days ago.'

'Have you reported it to us?'

'Pointless.'

'I see. Can you confirm that you live at this address in Eastlands, Northampton?'

'That's what I told you.'

'We have in our car pound a Ford Focus estate, blue-grey, with you as the registered keeper.'

'So you found it.'

'We did indeed. It was involved in a collision.'

'Is it damaged much?'

'Written off, I would say.' Jake said.

'It was an old heap, not worth much anyway.'

'When was the last time you drove it?'

'Friday, for work.'

'Didn't you wonder why it wasn't on your drive?'

'As I said, it got nicked.'

'The car was involved in a collision that injured our missing WPC. She was driving it.'

'So the cops nicked it. I always knew you were thieving fuckers.'

'Where did you park your car?'

'Outside the house.'

'The one on Eastlands?'

'Yeah, where else would I park it.'

'Indeed. OK. Let's move on. How is your relationship with your mother?'

'My relationship is perfectly fine, thank you. She brought me up to be a good girl.' Simone said coyly.

'Would you do anything for her?' Jake asked.

'Of course.'

'Even if it meant breaking the law?' Stevens said.

Nicholls hesitated, then said, 'No comment.'

'Would that go as far as murder?'

Nicholls exploded. 'What the fuck are you saying? You've got nothing, you're just fishing.'

Nicholls stood and wandered around the room. Her arms were down by her sides, flexing her hands as if she was preparing to fight with one or both of them.

'Come and sit down, Simone?'

'Fuck off!' she shouted and continued to pace until Jake got up and went over to her, trying to calm her.

When they had all sat again, Stevens asked, 'Where were you at two a.m. on seventeen this month?'

'Probably at home, in bed.'

'Where were you at four a.m. on the twenty-first?'

'The same. I'm not an early riser.'

'OK then, where were you eleven a.m. on the twenty-second?'

'At work, I would assume.'

'Do you get much time off?'

'When I want it, yes.'

'Because your mother is your boss?'

Nicholls nodded.

'Respond for the recording, please.'

'Yes!'

'You see, our difficulty is that on this date and a few more, your identity card was used to enter the controlled pharmacy. Your card, your pin number, how do you explain that?'

Nicholls said nothing.

'Well?'

'I don't know,' she said quietly.

'Why don't you know?'

'I just don't – perhaps my card was stolen!' she shouted.

'Like your car?'

'Yes,' a beat, 'perhaps somebody copied it.'

Jake produced an identity card from the folder. He showed it to Nicholls. 'Is this your card?'

'You know it is – you took it from me when I got here.'

Pointing to the base of the card at the rear, he said, 'This number here is the unique identity number for your card.'

'So?'

Jake removed another sheet from his folder, which contained a list of numbers on a printout.

'When we executed a warrant, we asked for details of access to the pharmacy. You see there have been a number of fatal road collisions, where a drug has been found in the bodies of those who have died, which we could not account for. Analysis of the drug – by your company and our pathology department – identified that certain chemicals contained isotopic recognition markers that identified its owners as the company you work for. Now, how is it possible that your card was used to gain access to the precursor chemicals to make up the drug, which ended up in several individuals who have died and PC Parker?'

'How's that got anything to do with me? I'm just an employee.'

'But you know who, don't you?'

'No comment.'

'We have a number of options here,' Stevens said. 'You can tell us what your involvement with all this is, you can say nothing and we'll draw our own conclusions, or we can charge you with six counts of murder and still draw our own conclusions.'

'Murder!' exclaimed Nicholls. 'What hat did you pull that out of? I'm here because of that cop. Nobody ever mentioned murder.'

'You see, Simone, we can associate those dead drivers with the same drug as found in PC Parker. You're a bright girl. You'd come to the same conclusions, wouldn't you?'

Nicholls didn't reply.

'Do you know Ian Morton?' Jake said.

Simone shook her head. 'No.'

Jake glanced at Stevens then said, 'Did I not see you at his workshop with another officer?'

'I don't think so – we've never met.'

'Really, so how come his death was caused by the same drug that killed my drivers and nearly killed my policewoman?'

'No comment.'

Jake tried another tack, 'What does your mother do at the company?'

'She's the chief chemist.'

'How long has she been doing that?'

'Since we moved back here.'

'That would be about two years ago?'

'Yes.'

'Does she have access to the controlled pharmacy?'

'Of course she does.'

'Does she have access to your card?'

'No, why should she?'

'Could she get a copy of it?'

'I doubt it. It's strictly controlled.'

'What did your mother do before you moved back here?'

'I don't know.'

'What do you mean, you don't know?'

'Exactly what I say. She only adopted me when she moved to New York.'

'Did she not tell you about her life elsewhere?'

'No.'

'Did you even ask?'

'Of course.'

'And what did she say?'

'She told me it was a period of her life that she would prefer to forget.'

'What about her childhood – did she talk about that?'

'Not much, only that she was born here in Northampton and went to doctors' school in London.'

'Don't you think that – unusual? You not knowing her life history?'

'Look, what's all this about my mother? She's hardworking. She has done everything to bring me up as best she can, as a one parent-mother.'

'How old were you when you were adopted?'

'Six.'

'How did she get to know you?'

'I got taken into the ER, with my parents on the night they died. Family services were going to put me into the system, but she took pity and arranged that I stay with her. I don't think I want to answer any more of your questions.'

'Obviously you don't have to, but it would help us further with our enquiries.' Stevens said.

'How did Ian Morton die, Simone?' Jake asked.

Simone remained silent for a minute or so. Jake could see that she was thinking hard. Perhaps weighing up her options. Will she hang her mother out to dry? he wondered. Is she that calculating?

Nicholls looked down at her hands which she'd placed on the desk in front of her, palms down, and her freshly bitten fingernails. She looked at Jake then Stevens, both of whom sat waiting for Simone to answer the question. Willing her to come clean.

Simone sighed. 'Will it help me if I tell you?' she said calmly.

'It may go in your favour with the CPS,' Stevens said.

Jake saw now that Nicholls had changed her attitude. Perhaps there was something in this fishing expedition nether he or Stevens expected. 'That depends on what you want to tell us,' Jake confirmed.

Nicholls thought for a moment. 'I don't know everything, you understand?'

'But you know some things.'

Nicholls bowed her head. 'I do, yes.' A pause, a sigh. 'I killed him, Ian Morton. It was an error, I didn't mean to do it.'

53

'How so?' Stevens asked.

'Mum had told me to try out the new formula on him, but I gave him too much. I hoped that it would loosen him up a bit, make him a bit more laid back. He was so tensed up all the time. Particularly after he found those remains in the wood. I just tried to help him relax, that's all.'

'Who made the drug?'

'Mum, she'd been working on it for years?'

'Why?'

'She just told me it was revenge for what happened before she went to New York and adopted me. She felt that I didnt need to know. And not to have two people on the same quest as her.'

'How did he die, Ian Morton? What went so wrong?'

Simone looked at the floor. Tears were forming in her eyes when she looked up. 'I sent him upstairs to the bedroom. I was going to use something stronger, but I didn't have anything in the house. So I made him a tea and slipped a vial of the drug into his tea. I realised something was wrong when he seemed to have a fit. He lay down on the bed. The look in his eyes, I will always remember. A combination of fear and anger at what I had done to him.

'I tried to soothe him and tried to stop the fit, but I couldn't. Then he just stopped breathing. I tried to revive him but it was no good. He'd gone.'

'Did you try calling an ambulance?'

'There was no point. In any case, they'd find out he was drugged.'

'But the pathologist would find that out during the post mortem in any case.' Jake said.

Simone said nothing.

'So what did you do then?' Stevens asked.

'I panicked. I didn't know what to do, so I took him to the wood and laid him out nicely. He would have liked it there. He actually resented Fulborough for clearing it. He was a good man really.'

'So to recap,' Stevens said, 'You used your mother's drug concoction on Ian Morton which killed him, and your mother has been making drugs that kill people.'

'That's about it,' Simone said soberly.

'Do you wish to have legal representation for this now? If so, we'll suspend this interview further until they arrive.'

'I suppose I ought to.'

'Very well. We'll continue this interview shortly, after a search of your address.'

As they left the interview room, Jake got a phone call from Randall.

54

The coolness of the light wind following the overnight storm swirled around Randall like a fan. It was still warm enough for him to take off his jacket and it was slung over his shoulder. He had arranged to see the Fulborough Estate office manager at home, without the distraction of work. He'd collected Jake, who he thought could help by providing some background if needed.

Marjorie lived in an end of terrace cottage on the outskirts of Northampton. The town he saw was creeping ever closer to the village and he wondered how long it would be before it was swallowed up like Weston Favell or Dallington, two places he'd visited before, both of which would have been quite picturesque, had they been left alone. Randall was always amazed at how town planners managed to swallow up little villages, without seemingly any thought about what the residents wanted. He smiled inwardly, thinking about the beginnings of Milton Keynes and how that had become England's answer to New York, all straight lines and 42nd Street.

The front door of the cottage was painted green with a large brass door knocker. Entering through the small immaculately dressed front garden, he banged on the door. It was immediately opened. Marjorie stood before him in a green apron and gardening gloves.

'I saw you coming from the back garden,' she said.

She invited them in and removed her gloves, tossing them on the end of the large pine kitchen table, and inviting them to sit. She scurried around the kitchen, making tea and small talk, while Randall and Jake made the right noises at the right time. Eventually, she sat down at the table opposite Randall and looked directly at him.

'How's Barry?' she asked.

'Doing well, I think. You've not been to see him?'

She shook her head.

'How do you get on with him?'

'Very well. He's different from his father.'

'A case of having to be, so I understand.'

'The old Lord's style was very different. Different times, different everything really, but I got on with him, no problem.'

'I understand that he had a bit of a way with the ladies?'

'He had women after him, yes, but he never went to pursue them. It wasn't lecherous at all.'

'What way is it not lecherous then?' Jake asked.

'I'm sure I don't have to explain it to you,' she grinned knowingly.

'What do you know about his wife, for example?'

'First or second?'

'First.'

'She died in child-birth.'

'Unusual for this day and age, isn't it?'

'It was thirty years or so ago.'

'And what about Barry? Who brought him up?'

'His second wife. There was a nanny, of course, and us girls in the office.'

'Did he have much to do with his father?'

Marjorie thought for a moment. 'He wasn't a doting father, that's for sure, but he didn't go without.'

'And what about your relationship with the old Lord?'

Marjorie flushed. 'Whoever said there was a relationship?'

'Barry seems to think so.'

She became a little uncomfortable and looked down at her mug. 'I'd rather not go into that, if you don't mind, except to say that he was fine and generous to me over the years. We didn't step out together, if that's what you mean. It was more... casual.'

'But you worked your way up to office manager?' Jake cut in.

'Yes, but not on my back, I'll have you know,' Marjorie replied.

Randall gave Jake a knowing glance.

'What do you know about Avril Tyler?'

A pause. 'Ah, I wondered when you were going to get around to her.' She stood, went and leaned her back against the kitchen unit, watching Jake and Randall.

'Well?' Randall said.

'She disappeared.'

'We know, but why?'

'Nobody knows.'

'You were close to him.'

'He didn't tell me everything.'

'But you must have heard something, being that close to what was going on around the estate surely?'

'Rumour has it, that she blackmailed him over getting her pregnant. She said she was raped by him, but I know she was all over him, giving him the come on.'

'And he obliged?'

Marjorie nodded.

'Did you say anything to her about this… liaison?'

She glanced out of the window, before answering. 'Not my place and I just worked in the office then. I haven't been the office manager all the time. I told you that.' She took a sip of her tea.

'What do you know about her disappearance?'

Marjorie came and sat down again. 'Nothing, really. When she'd had the child, she stopped working here. She used to call in occasionally with her, but then stopped. By that time, about a year or so later, she'd had another child by someone else, a boy.'

'What happened to her then, do you think?'

'Nobody seems to know – or if they did know they weren't telling.'

'Like who?' Jake asked.

Marjorie looked at Jake, thinking about what to say. She bit her bottom lip, while trying to work it out.

'Like who?' mirrored Randall.

'I don't know whether any of this is true, you understand.'

'We recognise that stories may change over the years, handed down from person to person, but you are the only employee at the estate who has been there for any length of time.'

'Other than Frank, of course,' she countered.

'How long has he worked out of the estate office?'

'I don't know. Got to be twenty/thirty years at least, probably more.'

'He started early on then, like Avril?'

'Yes. They may even have started about the same time.'

'The Fulboroughs tended to keep their staff then?' Randall moved his position slightly to regain eyes contact with Marjorie. She'd moved to look through the kitchen window into the middle distance.

'Only those who they wanted to keep. The old Lord was ruthless about getting rid of those he didn't want around.'

'Like Avril?'

'That was different.'

'In what way?'

'He liked having her around him.'

'Even after she'd had his child?'

'Yes, but like Barry, he didn't have much to do with her.'

'A girl?'

'Yes. Didn't you know?'

'We thought it would be one or the other.' Randall smiled at his own joke. 'Where is she?'

'She disappeared with her mother.'

'Really? What sort of time scales are we looking at here?'

'Well, Vanessa was born around eighty three, eighty four time, when Avril was quite young, seventeen I think.'

'So, when her mother disappeared, she went as well?'

Marjorie nodded again and took another sip of tea. She'd kept it cupped in her hands throughout the interview.

'Did you ever see them again?'

'No,' Marjorie paused for a moment, 'you don't think that those two bodies you found are them, do you?'

'We can't say at the moment.' Randall wouldn't give any more away.

'You've got this DNA thing that you use now? Surely you'd be able to find out?'

'We have no DNA to compare it with, unfortunately.'

Randall watched, as he saw Jake writing furiously in the

back of his notebook. Jake showed it to him. Randall looked at him and read the note, then looked back at Marjorie.

'Thank you, Marjorie, you've been very helpful. We may need to ask you some more questions later. Would that be OK?'

'Yes, Inspector, that's fine. Anything I can do to help.'

Randall and Jake left Marjorie.

By the time he got back to the car, Jake was already on the phone to Kirsty Kingsfield.

'Kirsty, did we ever do a DNA comparison for the remains found in Fulborough Wood?'

'Yes, both of them,' Kirsty replied.

'Did we get a match?'

'No, we haven't compared the two though.'

'Why not?'

'Haven't been asked.'

Randall looked again at Jake's hand written notes in capital letters. "HER NAME WAS TYLER. WE HAVE BINGHAM TYLER'S DNA!!"

'Did we run a DNA comparison between both remains and Tyler?'

'No, we didn't have a reason to.'

'You have now. Can you arrange it?'

'Yes, we can do that.'

Jake terminated the call. He looked around at Randall and smiled. 'I'm glad I brought you along, first decent break we've had in this case. Good job!' he said, smiling while starting the car.

55

Randall sat with Martin across the table from Frank Philpott in an interview room at the Criminal Justice Centre. Philpott appeared relaxed and unconcerned, possibly under the misapprehension that his boss was going to bail him out. Randall had a file in front of him, with some damming evidence against Philpott – or that's what he'd make Philpott think anyway. The interview room was hot and stuffy and the silence between them hung in the air like a muggy evening before a storm. The background noise of the CJC was the only intrusion. After reminding Philpott that he was still under caution, Randall started by relaying Lord Fulborough's comments about Philpott.

'I went to see your boss this morning.'

Philpott sat in silence, stony-faced.

'He asked me to give you a message.'

Still no reaction.

'He said to tell you that – you're fired.'

Philpott shifted a little in his chair as a look of thunder crossed his face. 'He can't do that!' he roared.

'I think he can. And he has. And he has every right to do so after what you've done to him. What did you expect to happen? That he'd take you back as if nothing had happened?'

'But I've worked there all my life!' replied Philpott ignoring the question.

'So he tells me.'

'He's not heard the last of this. He doesn't realise how much I know.'

'Oh, I think he does, that's why you've been sacked. Other than knocking him unconscious and leaving him to die.'

Philpott folded his arms in front of him and said nothing.

'So, let's do the easy bit first, shall we?'

'If you want.'

'Tell me why you assaulted Fulborough.'

'The man's a wimp, not like his father,' Philpott sneered.

'Is that a reason?'

'Under the circumstances it was the right thing to do and – satisfying.' He smiled.

'You think so, do you? Do you always resort to violence when you don't get your own way?'

'Not always.'

'So why that night?'

'I was angry.'

'At what?'

'Him. For not having enough balls to leave things alone.'

'About the remains, you mean?'

Philpott nodded.

'For the recording, please?'

'Yes, about the remains.'

'You don't think that finding skeletal remains in the wood necessitated calling the police?'

'No comment.'

'Did you not think we'd find out anyway?'

'If they'd done the job and kept their mouth shut, nobody would be any the wiser.'

'You mean the workers you paid off?'

'Right.'

'But you can't trust them can you? Because one came to us full of remorse.'

'More fool him. I knew he was the weak link in the chain, but I didn't think he'd drop his mates in it as well.' Philpott sat forward. Randall thought that he might be getting somewhere with him.

'He recognised that it was wrong and obviously has higher moral standards than you.'

'If you say so.'

'I do say so, because it's not the first time, is it?' Randall looked down at his folder and looked back up at Philpott.

'I told you I know where all the secrets are on that estate.'

'Did you know about this particular secret, when you started excavating?'

'Yes.'

'But you said nothing – you didn't let on?'

'No.'

'You had it all worked out though, didn't you? In case they came across the remains? The bribe to keep them quiet about putting it back?'

'No comment.'

'You fought with Fulborough, because his morals are higher than yours.'

'He didn't want me to conceal the remains.'

'So you hit him – hard.'

'Yes.'

'And left him to die.'

'No – I didn't know he'd be there all night. I thought he'd come round and go home with a headache.'

'You gave him quite a wallop.'

'Sometimes I don't know my own strength.' A smile flickered across Philpott's face.

'Who do those remains belong to in Fulborough Wood?'

'No comment.'

'But you know who both of them are, don't you? The one we found recently and the one we found twelve months ago?'

'No comment.'

'I'm not playing games here, Frank. You will need to talk to me at some stage. Is this how it's going to be?'

'Seems that way.'

'What can I say to you that would allow you to give me the information that I need?'

Philpott thought for a moment, but said nothing.

'Look, Frank, we need to clear up a fifteen-year-old riddle. If my information is right, these two people.' Randall removed three photographs, two of the skeletal remains and one of Ian Morton, placing them on the table in front of Philpott. 'These people need to be laid to rest, properly and not left in an unmarked grave in some churchyard in Northampton.' He paused, before asking, 'Who's Ian Morton?' Pointing to his picture.

'The contractor working on the wood.'

'Did you pay him off?'

'Yes.'

'How much?'

'Two grand.'

'To keep him quiet?'

'He obviously didn't keep quiet though, did he?'

Randall leaned back in his chair. The silence hung for a moment, Randall hoping that Philpott would fill it. Tap, tap with his pen, as if going to write.

'There's nothing I can tell you without compromising myself.'

Randall smiled.

'If you help us, I'll put in a good word for you with the CPS. Tell them that you've co-operated fully and, after all this time, to show some leniency. I can't promise it, of course, but I'll tell them.'

Philpott remained silent for a moment, seemingly studying his hands.

'Well?' Randall asked, a little frustrated.

'OK, OK, I'll tell you what I know, but I want a solicitor now.'

'Thank you, Frank, that's all I want. And I'll get the duty solicitor in here as well. Is that OK?'

Philpott nodded. 'But you have to understand that I was working under orders from the old Lord, for fear of losing my job, work that I've loved all my life.'

'I understand that, Frank, but it doesn't make you immune from the law.' Randall studied Philpott. He seemed to have relaxed a little, as if the heavy burden he had been carrying around with him for years was about to be lifted.

Randall called a temporary halt to the interview, to wait for the solicitor.

56

Randall thought about how the next interview with Philpott and his lawyer would be best served. How to get the information he wanted in the shortest amount of time. Randall knew that Philpott would try to shift the blame for the deaths onto the old Lord, because neither could contest it. And in any case, the passage of time either at the house or the burial site was too long to reveal any new forensic evidence. Of that he was certain. There had to be someone other than Marjorie who remembered something about it. And he wasn't sure that Philpott would actually bump off his contractor, Morton? When Marland told him that the case was puzzling he wasn't joking and with the death of Morton added into the mix, had to mean that they are connected in some way. But how, that was the question.

He decided to go and talk to Kirsty Kingsfield about the remains of both women. A possibility that there was a connection between the two. He made a phone call and arranged to meet her later that afternoon. He glanced at his watch – lunchtime. But he couldn't take another HQ lunch again, so he decided to take a break and perhaps pay a visit to the town. He'd never spent a lot of time in Northampton, so he decided to have a wander around the town centre to clear his head ready for Philpott's next encounter.

Leaving HQ, he went and parked in the Grosvenor Centre car park, next to the eye-sore that used to be the bus station, but was now a piece of unused wasteland.

The mall was typical of most town centres. All the big names were there, pedestrianised areas, but it was interspersed with smaller closed and boarded-up shops. Those doors were adorned with adverts for a forthcoming circus coming to the town, some party on the racecourse, and some graffiti of which he had no comprehension.

He walked into a baker's and bought a sausage roll, an apple turnover and a coffee. The baker's had chairs and tables in the mall, so he sat down to eat his lunch and watched the world go by. He checked his emails on his smartphone, which revealed nothing of importance, so he pocketed it and concentrated on people-watching.

A couple of old men walked by, with small shopping bags, one leather, one canvas. A gaggle of young women, all with phones in their hands, chatting happily, an idiot on roller blades, and a girl in a black hoody and black trousers. So different from his time in the military and what he saw of society in the Middle and Far East.

He sighed as he thought about his wife. Managing only to block memories while he was working, the minute he relaxed, they came flooding back. He could only imagine that Kirsty Kingsfield had to be going through the same trauma. He knew it would never go away, but hoped, over time, that it would get a little easier.

Brushing some crumbs from his jacket, before he moved away from the table, he walked back towards his car. He'd managed to park his pool car near to the entrance, but, while making his way towards it, something felt wrong as he emerged onto the car park landing. A prickle at the back of his neck, the sort he used to get on patrol, where his instincts came alive.

Something was wrong. He slowed his pace, all the nerves in his body preparing him for fight or flight. That primordial response to survival. He clenched his fists as he got closer to his car. Before he got to it, he was swiftly approached by the female in a black hoody he'd seen in the centre. Randall was ready and deflected her with his arm. The force pushed her back towards his car. She raised her hands in surrender. With his fists raised, Randall asked what she wanted.

'I don't want to hurt you!' the woman said.

'You won't get the chance. Why approach me, as if you were going to?'

'I didn't know what else to do.'

'You could have been more pleasant.'

'I'm not a pleasant person.'

'I wouldn't know that, would I? And I'll ask you again, what do you want?'

'You're Randall, aren't you?'

'Depends who wants to know.'

'Your lot have arrested Simone Nicholls?'

'I haven't arrested anyone.'

Jake, Randall thought, been going off half-cocked again. 'What's she been arrested for? And how did you know I'd be here?' Even I didn't know I'd be here, mused Randall.

'I happened to be in town.'

'But we've never met.'

'I have my methods,' she grinned.

'And?'

'And what?'

'What do you want me to do about it?'

'Release her.'

'I don't even know where she is being held,' he lied.

'You'd better find out.'

'Or what?'

'Somebody may get hurt.' And with that, she removed a syringe from her pocket.

Randall looked at it. 'What's that?'

'I'll show you!' The woman lunged at Randall and stuck the syringe with full force into his chest. Randall grabbed hold of her and pushed her away, before she could get all the contents of the syringe into him. With the woman's back against the car, Randall hit her hard around the face with a punch. The woman and the syringe fell to the ground, but she was up and away, running fast.

Randall tried to run after her, but some of the drug was beginning to have an effect. He took a couple of steps and dropped to the floor. His legs wouldn't move. It was as if they had become lead weights. He managed to sit up against the front wheel of the car. Taking the police radio out of his inner pocket, he pushed the red assistance button, before he passed out.

He awoke with Freeman standing over him. The lights of the Accident & Emergency Department at Northampton General Hospital were extremely bright and hurt his eyes. His senses were flooded with the coming and goings of the department, as he lay there and wondered whether it was an effect of the drug he'd been given. He looked down towards his legs to see if they were still there. They were, but somebody had stripped him down to his underpants.

'I hope they haven't destroyed my suit. It's the only one I've got,' he said, smiling weakly at Freeman.

'What happened to you?'

'I should ask you that. I've no idea.'

'What do you remember?'

'Black hoody, black trousers, female. Asked me why we'd arrested Simone Nicholls, then stuck a needle in my chest, if I didn't arrange her release.'

'Why?'

'How should I know? I don't even know who Simone Nicholls is.'

'Jake and Stevens arrested her late evening for those road deaths he's investigating.'

'No wonder I couldn't find Stevens when I wanted him.'

'He's doing the paperwork with Jake.'

'Has he released her?'

'No, she's in court in the morning.'

'But now we've got something else to put to her.' Randall started to get up. 'Get my clothes, would you, sir?'

Freeman pushed him lightly back down on the trolley. 'You're not going anywhere for the moment. Take a day or two to recover.'

'Can't do that, boss, too close to solving a real crime.'

'Oh, and what one would that be?'

'Fulborough.'

'I see. Come and see me tomorrow, but take the rest of the day.'

'That's great, sir, as it's gone 18:00!'

Freeman smiled and went to leave. 'Tomorrow, 09:00, my office,' he said, as he breezed through the curtains.

Randall rested his head back on the starchy white pillow. A little sleep would be good, and he closed his eyes while putting together the day's events.

57

Kirsty's mortuary assistant, Anton, knocked on her office door in the pathology department of the hospital. She beckoned him in and told him to take a seat. He declined. He had in his hand an A4 envelope that he had opened and had come directly to her office once he knew the contents.

'What is it, Anton? You look a bit shocked.'

'Yes, not shock, but strangeness – I think that's the right word – the results of DNA tests we did on Fulborough remains…'

'What do you mean – strange?'

'Not right – something wrong.'

'Let me see.'

Anton gave Kirsty the envelope and she removed the contents. Two sheets of A4 paper. She looked them over, glancing from one sheet to another. Her eyes widened, when she realised what she was looking at. The evidence before her would blow the Fulborough case wide open.

She thought she'd better talk to Randall as it was his case. She thanked Anton and told him that she would deal with it. She went back to her desk and went to pick up the phone, when it rang. She answered it quickly, eager to deal with the caller and get the DNA results back to Randall. But before she could speak, Tanya screeched down the phone.

'Your boyfriend has arrested my daughter.'

'Tanya, what do you mean? Arrested?'

'Bloody obvious; my Simone has been arrested.' Tanya was very agitated and breathing heavily.

Kirsty told her to calm down and tell her what had happened. 'OK look, where are you?'

'I'm at home.'

Kirsty looked at her watch. It was just past five o'clock. 'I'll come and see you later. I can't get away right now.'

'Right, I'll see you later. Please, Kirsty, she didn't do this. You need to tell Jake.'

'Let's talk later then.' Kirsty put down the phone. She sighed, rubbing both hands through her long hair. She tied it up in a quick ponytail, while still staring at the DNA reports. Then she rang Randall. It went straight to answerphone, so she left a message, unaware that he'd been attacked and was along the corridor in A&E.

It was almost dark when Kirsty managed to get away from the hospital. She was annoyed that Randall had not returned her calls, after the fuss he made about getting the arrests as soon as possible. She thought about contacting Jake, but it wasn't his case. From what he had told her recently, there had been a difference of opinion between them about the investigation that Jake was conducting. She knew, of course, that the collisions were important to clear up, but there seemed little evidence from a scientific point of view that was making itself known.

As she stepped out of the hospital, there was a light autumn breeze. A balmy evening, one which she would have preferred to spend with Jake, rather than having to go and see Tanya, even if she was a friend.

Tanya had sounded distraught, when she had rung her earlier, but it wasn't her place to go running to Jake to get him to release Simone, even if he had arrested her for some reason. And there must have been a reason.

She thought about Tanya's company, as she drove towards her home. There was something in the back of her mind, that all was not right. And she had become defensive about her company when she and Jake last visited her. She wondered whether going to see her was a good idea. But Tanya was her friend, wasn't she? She couldn't see that she'd do anything to her, would she?

As she drove onto Tanya's driveway, she saw that the lights of the house were on. Her Mercedes was parked just as it was when they'd visited before.

She parked hers next to Tanya's and, as she got out, the front door opened to reveal Tanya, in a housecoat and dishevelled state. Her hair was all out of place, with no makeup, as if she'd just got out of bed. It didn't take a lot of observation from Kirsty for her to realise that Tanya was drunk – not just drunk, but very drunk.

Standing on the threshold she invited Kirsty in. Her speech was heavily slurred and she had to use the doorframe and the wall to keep her balance.

'Good heavens, Tanya! You look terrible.'

'I'm goin-g out of my mind wizsh worry about my Shiiimone,' she said as she staggered down the hallway towards the sitting room.

'You'd better sit down before you fall down.' Kirsty helped steady her, as she moved into the sitting room and plonked herself down on the sofa, sitting with at least a fifteen-degree list to starboard.

'How much have you drunk today?'

'Dunno, a… lot.'

'I can see that. I'll go and make you a coffee, strong and black, to see if we can sober you up.'

'I don't want shobering up,' she mumbled.

'I'm going to, whether you like it or not.'

'Pleash youshelf.'

Kirsty made her way into the kitchen and looked through the cupboards for coffee and mugs, while she waited for the kettle to boil. Finding the mugs, she removed one but by taking it out, she spotted a small container with a glass vial inside. Looking closer, she saw the container was marked with the company logo and that it contained a clear liquid.

She completed making Tanya's coffee and taking it into the sitting room, she saw that Tanya was still listing on the sofa with her eyes closed. Just as Kirsty put the cup down next to Tanya, her phone pinged with a text message.

'WHERE R U. NEED 2 TLK'

She quickly responded.

'@ TANYAS, SHE'S P****D, WORRIED ABT HER.'

Jake's response was almost immediate. 'OK, WILL C U THERE SOON.'

58

After Randall's ordeal the previous day, he finally managed, with Martin, to resume the interview with Philpott, who appeared relaxed sitting next to the duty solicitor, a young dark-haired man with a shiny grey suit that probably needed to see a dry cleaners. Randall thought that the young solicitor was more nervous than Philpott appeared, as he constantly chewed the top of his government-issue pen.

'Did you speak to the lawyers?' Philpott asked.

'Yes, I did.'

Philpott shrugged. 'I don't really care whether you did or not.'

'Why, a change of heart?'

'No, a relief.'

'A relief? You've certainly changed your tune since both of your recent arrests.'

Philpott took a great gulp of air before replying. 'People know me as a hard man. You know I've got convictions.

Petty stuff. But I've never been into what I would call the big crimes and I've been carrying all this knowledge about the old Lord for years. Things he'd got me to do – illegal things, which had turned me into the man I am today. Enough is enough. I'm really sorry, that I lashed out at Barry. I can get pretty het up sometimes. He's done me no wrong since taking over the estate from his father, and, in a way, it was a relief that he didn't ask me to do things – other than grease the palm of the council about the wood. But those things happen in business anyway, don't they? There were things that the old Lord asked me to do, which I would prefer not to remember.'

He stopped and watched Randall insert two DVDs into the recording machine and enter details on the display screen – who he was, who Randall was and whether it was just an audio or audio and video recording. After going through all the preliminaries, Randall reminded Philpott that he was still under caution and that he didn't have to say anything.

Philpott asked, 'Where do you want me to start?'

'What about at the beginning? That's usually the best place,' Randall replied.

Philpott looked around the windowless interview room, with its battleship grey walls, isolated against letting sound in, or out. Virtually a sound-proofed-booth, where every noise made was hushed. He could make as much noise as he wanted and nobody outside the room would hear, not even through the heavy sound-insulated doors. The lighting was cold and harsh – and it was hot.

'You look a bit flustered, Frank,' Martin said.

Philpott pushed his shirtsleeves back. 'I'm not used to being inside and it's stuffy in here.' He sat back in his chair. 'Did you know that I've got an agricultural and horticultural degree?' he asked Randall.

331

'No, I didn't. Is it relevant?'

'Yes. I started work on the Fulborough Estate, I was nineteen, as a groundsman, doing all the heavy work – moving stuff around the estate on a tractor, feeding the animals, that sort of thing. After I'd been there for a little while, Fulborough suggested that I go to college, get an education, some formal qualifications, if I wanted to stay in agriculture. He sent me to Moulton Agricultural College. I enjoyed it. It was good fun and I like to be outside, you know?'

'He paid for it, did he?'

'Yes, all of it.'

'Didn't you think that was a bit strange?'

'Not really, he could be quite philanthropic. He sent others to college as well, not just me.'

'What happened when you got your degree?'

'I got a bit of a promotion to a team leader and worked my way up from there.'

'You were on your way up the agricultural ladder, so to speak?' Stevens said, smiling.

Philpott nodded, without smiling or even acknowledging the funny side of Stevens' comment. 'Yes, and I knew that I would be grateful for him to keep me on as long as I needed, if I played my cards right.'

'How has this got anything to do with my investigation?' Randall asked.

Philpott leaned forward, pushed his chair back from the desk and rested his elbows on his knees. 'You see, other members of the group he educated were Avril and Marjorie.'

'Really, what did they do?'

'He sent Marjorie to college to do secretarial studies and Avril to do equestrian studies. He thought they had promise. What I didn't know at the time was that it was a way of keeping Avril quiet, after what he did to her.'

'What did he do to her?'

'He had a bit of a thing for her. Avril was a pretty girl in a plain sort of way, if you know what I mean. I remember that it was a Sunday morning. The day of the hunt. We went through the usual rituals at the start, drinking, rounding up the dogs, and all that other shit.'

'You don't agree with it?'

'What? Fox hunting?'

'Yes.'

'I've never been a supporter. I may be aggressive towards my fellow humans, but never towards animals. I could never see the point of a pack of hounds ripping a fox apart. One or two foxes in a day. How's that going to cull the population?'

Randall made no comment and raised his eyebrows at that. Unusual for a farm worker not to support hunting. 'So what happened?' he said after a moment's silence.

'It wasn't until they got back. I never went with them, obviously, but Avril came out of the stables and started on the horses with the other stable hands. After a little while, everyone drifted away. The guests went up to the house and Avril was left on her own, finishing off in the stables, before going home for the day.'

'She, or you, weren't invited up to the house then?'

'God, no, we're just the hired help. No such luxuries for us.'

'But his Lordship was still in the stable yard?'

'Yes, he was hanging about, supposedly checking things were OK.'

'But?'

'But I thought he was hanging about deliberately waiting for everyone to go, leaving him and Avril on their own.'

'Where did you go?'

'I got called up to the top field. One of the sheep had got itself tangled in the fence.'

'How long did it take you to get there?'

'About ten minutes, I suppose.'

'Leaving Lord Fulborough alone with Avril?'

'Yes.'

'Then what?'

'I got to the field and the sheep was all right.'

'A ruse to get you out of the way?'

'I think so, yes.'

'What happened when you got back?'

'As I got back into the stable yard, his Lordship was coming out of one of the stables. He looked a bit dishevelled and was – adjusting himself – if you know what I mean…'

'What did he do, when he saw you?'

'He strode over to me and told me, in no uncertain terms, that I had not seen anything. I hadn't actually. I just put two and two together afterwards.'

'Did you see Avril?'

'Yes.'

'And how was she?'

'Timid.'

'What do you mean by that?'

'Withdrawn, non-communicative.'

'Did you ask her what happened?'

'Yes.'

'And what did she say?'

'She refused to talk to me and went home.'

'What do you think happened?'

'I think he had his way with her.'

'You mean he raped her, or had consensual sex?'

'Raped, yes.'

'Why?'

'Because of how she became.'

'What happened to her?'

'His Lordship sent her away to college for a year.'

'Knowing she was pregnant?'

'Probably. It did seem strange, that she got sent away.'

'Did she speak to you about it?'

'Not directly.'

'Meaning?'

'She felt that talking to anyone about it would have been a betrayal.'

'Who did she think she was betraying?'

'His Lordship and the trust that he had put in her to keep her quiet, and, of course, her education. Up to that time she was not a well-educated girl.'

'But you're sure she was raped?'

'I don't see it as anything else.'

'We have it from a witness that she was giving his Lordship the big come-on?'

'Ah, you've been talking to Marjorie. There was a rumour that they'd been having an affair, but I never saw anything like that. The common feeling around the estate was that what they did was not consensual from her point of view.'

'But nobody knows for sure?'

'No, not really.'

'When did Avril leave his Lordship's employment?'

'She never did officially. His Lordship kept her and her baby, Vanessa, at arm's length. Again, there was talk of Avril blackmailing him for money to keep her mouth shut about what happened.'

'What do you think?'

'He didn't seem to resent paying her off for all those years. Perhaps, in his mind, he was paying for the upkeep of the baby.'

'Even after she'd had another child?'

'Yes, even then he kept paying until…'

'Until?'

Philpott sat back, folded his arms. 'One night, some years later, Avril and the two kids seemed to have fallen on hard times. She started doing drugs and whoring. I don't know the full details, but she went to him and demanded more money.'

'And did he give it to her?'

'No.'

'Why?'

'He told me that she'd had enough of his money to shoot up her arm and wasn't going to get any more.'

'How did that end?'

'Badly.'

'How badly?'

'The worst type. It was a Friday evening. His Lordship was in the house on his own, when Avril turned up at the door with the two kids in tow. By all accounts, there was a blazing argument and he hit her. She fell, but was able to get up, telling the kids to run away. He grabbed her by the throat and squeezed the life out of her. When I arrived, she was lying on the library floor.'

'Did you check to see if she was alive?'

'Yes,' he shook his head then looked down at the floor in front of him. 'She wasn't.'

'Did you think his Lordship was capable of such an act?'

'No doubt in my mind, after working with him for all those years, he could be a right bastard.'

'Where were the children?'

'They left the house. They were found in the stables later that night.'

'Who found them?'

'Two of the young groundsmen. They called the house and spoke to me. He then called the police and told them that they were intruders and didn't know who they were. So they got taken away.'

'Didn't you do anything to help them?'

'More than my job was worth. I regret it now, of course, knowing what happened later.'

'What happened later?'

'That's another story, for another day perhaps.'

Randall let that go for the time being. 'What happened to Avril?'

Philpott stumbled a little, as he tried to compose himself. Randall saw that Philpott seemed to be haunted by some of these memories and probably didn't want to drag them up.

Philpott took another deep breath. 'His Lordship ordered me to dispose of Avril's body.'

'Did you tell him that was wrong and that he should call the police? Accept the consequences?'

'He was more worried about being found out – by his second wife.'

'You buried Avril, didn't you?

'Yes, I did. In Fulborough Wood. Where she was found.'

There was a short silence, as both took in the revelation. Philpott clearly reliving the scene.

'You must believe me, Inspector, that I did not kill Avril. I only...' He wiped a big hand across his face. '... put her to rest.'

'You didn't want to do it, did you?'

'No.'

'You were close to her, weren't you?'

'Yes, I actually told her not to go to the house that night. I knew that if he'd been drinking, he'd be in a foul temper.'

'A bit like you?'

'Yeah, but I don't have to be drunk!'

'After you had disposed of the body, what happened to you?'

'I entered into an agreement with the devil. I agreed not to discuss Avril's disappearance, ever. And he promoted me to deputy estate manager with a hefty pay rise and eventually estate manager.'

'Do you regret what you did?'

'Yes.'

Randall leaned forward and switched off the DVD after closing down the interview. Philpott was escorted back to his cell.

The cell door closed on Philpott. Randall looked through the hatch. Philpott looked diminished, dirty and repentant. It is amazing, Randall thought, how a police cell can reduce a man to his emotional component parts.

59

Kirsty sat down opposite Tanya with her own coffee cup, after rousing Tanya and putting her coffee in her hand. She took a few sips, but it wasn't enough not to let her fall asleep again. Kirsty managed to get her mug out of her hand before she spilled it all over the sofa.

'Why on earth have you got yourself in this state, Tanya?' Kirsty asked herself, not expecting any answer.

Tanya was slowly coming around. 'You don't know much about me, do you, really?' she slurred.

'I know enough.'

'Izz been three long years, y'know.'

'What has?'

'Sinz the crash. Three years of mourning my husband and my boy, a depression, deep, inside, me.' She thumped at her chest. 'Three years of never watching Randy Junior grow up, to take his place in the world, of which I could be proud. Wish all the crap dished out to me as a kid, I want'd some revenge and youz arrested my Siiimo…' Tanya collapsed onto the settee.

Kirsty wondered what she was talking about. She tried to rouse her again. She couldn't let her sleep with all that alcohol in her body.

Kirsty went back into the kitchen to make some more coffee. While she was in the kitchen, she removed the vial from the cupboard and put it in her pocket. She wanted to know what it was and had a deepening suspicion, that it was something to do with the drugs that Tanya was investigating for her and Jake.

She was just leaving the kitchen, when Tanya stood in the doorway, clearly not as drunk as she had been making out. 'Come and sit down for a moment, Kirsty. I'm afraid I can't let you leave, until I get Simone back.'

'Oh, why?'

'To start with, you can return my property, which you have in your pocket.'

'I don't know what you mean.'

'The vial, Kirsty. Don't treat me like a fool.'

'I was looking for mugs and coffee to get you sober, but you've been having me on, I see. Why?'

'I wanted to know how much you thought you knew?'

'I didn't know anything, until I found it. Here.' Kirsty removed the vial from her pocket. 'What is it, Tanya?'

'A new drug the company is working on.'

'The company, or just you?'

Tanya glared at Kirsty and pushed past her into the kitchen. Opening the fridge, she poured herself another glass of the white Chardonnay she'd been drinking. It only filled the large goblet halfway.

'Shit,' she mumbled and quickly downed the glass then threw the empty bottle into the trash. It clattered and fell in amongst the other bottles.

Kirsty could do nothing but stare at her friend. It was as if she had forgotten that she was there with her.

Grabbing a whiskey bottle from the kitchen unit, she filled the glass with the amber liquid and took a big slug of the drink. She closed her eyes.

She looked directly at Kirsty. 'You know, I always knew, that once you had found out about those drugs, you'd come running to me for help. Go to your friend, you no doubt told that boyfriend copper of yours?'

Kirsty went to reply, but Tanya swiftly walked over to her, pushing her against the kitchen unit and clapped her hand over Kirsty's mouth.

'You're going to listen to me,' she hissed, 'without saying another word.'

Kirsty nodded. Memories of Tyler's abduction in her apartment flooding her mind. She started shaking. She tried to keep calm. She tried not to cry. Tanya stood back from Kirsty.

'Don't' you go all weak and feeble on me, Kirsty,' Tanya jabbed a finger towards Kirsty.

'But you don't understand,' Kirsty said, composing herself.

'I understand all I need to, you on the other hand do not, so I'm going to tell you why I would do this to people I didn't even know,' said Tanya.

Kirsty kept quiet, in the hope that Jake might get there soon.

'I'm being pulled in two ways. One way to do the right thing and stop at these collisions which I orchestrated and conform to my hypocratic oath. And another was still to seek revenge for everything shitty thing that has happened to me in my life. Why did I do those things? What's possessing me? Other people don't go around killing people, just because their family died at the hands of a drugged-up driver.'

Kirsty said nothing.

Tanya smiled. 'I have, of course, questioned my intentions, but after my husband and child were killed by a lorry driver, who was also high on amphetamines on a tornado-driven highway in Indiana, I couldn't believe it when both of my families had been destroyed by drugged up drivers. So you can certainly see my predicament.' A cold smile. 'The fact that I am a microbiologist helped my cause better than I could have hoped.'

Kirsty could keep quiet no longer. 'But…'

'… Shh – be quiet, I said. It's my turn.'

'I will not be quiet!' Kirsty said.

Tanya slapped Kirsty. 'You will speak when you are spoken to and not until. Children are seen and not heard.'

'I'm not your child.' Kirsty received another slap. Instinctively, Kirsty retaliated and slapped Tanya hard around the face.

'How dare you,' Tanya screamed and went to strike Kirsty again, but she moved out of the way and backed ot of the kitchen. She rubbed her face and glared hard at Tanya. Kirsty tried another tactic. 'Tell me about your parents.'

Tanya came towards Kirsty with a raised hand and Kirsty moved away again and the threatened assault didn't come. Tanya pushed past Kirsty and sat down on the sofa. She seemed as if the question about her parents had subdued her a little.

'We'd all driven up to Alton Towers, somewhere I'd had pestered Mum and Dad to take me for months. We went there one Friday during the holidays. I didn't know that I'd signed their death warrant. All I wanted to do was enjoy the rides. I blame myself. Guilty as charged. As I got older, I discovered that Mother was pregnant with my brother, so not only did I feel guilt and anger about their deaths, but also for snuffing out the life of my unborn brother.'

342

Kirsty looked at her watch. Tanya saw, but said nothing. Simply carried on with her story.

'We had a good day. The sun shone. We had ice-cream. We played in the old castle. We went on some rides – Mum knew I shouldn't, but I was tall for my age and managed to get away with it. We were all happy that day.'

She stared off into the corner of the room for a moment in remembrance.

'On the way home, we had a sing-song. I can't remember what we sung, all I knew was happiness – the whole family was happy, no bad words between any of us.'

Kirsty saw that Tanya's eyes had begun to water. She was going to make a move to leave, but she wanted to hear the end.

'When we got near to home, Dad left the motorway and drove towards Northampton. We were nearly home. We were so close to home. It happened so quickly. The sun that had shone down on us all day was to be our downfall. Never mind the fact that the female driver was pissed and drugged-up, although she claimed she never saw our car, because the sun was in her eyes.

'I found this out later as well. The fact that she was doing seventy in a thirty, as her car slammed head on into the front of our car. She only had minor injuries and cleared off from the accident. And not once did she ever show any remorse for what she'd done, standing in the dock with a smug look that she really needed wiping from her face, with an axe.

'She only got two years. One year for Dad and one year for Mum. I only realised later on, as I got older, trying to find out exactly what happened. But the simple fact was that she was driving pissed and drugged. How to screw up a kid in one easy lesson. I was never the same. I wanted my revenge, but it seems I am now more than an avenging angel.

'The police knew she had a habit. They knew of her. She was on their system, but they couldn't stop her driving. She just wouldn't quit. The only good thing to come out of it all was that I discovered that the driver had been found dead in some abandoned houses a few years after she came out of prison, having shot herself up with heroin. Too strong for her and killed her almost instantly. That was judgement upon her.'

There was silence in the room.

'So, there you have it.'

'And what about what happened in Indiana?' Kirsty asked, thinking that the longer she could keep her occupied, the better. She was beginning to wonder where Jake was.

'I don't want to go there tonight,' Tanya said.

'In that case, Tanya, I'll be going then.' And Kirsty marched towards the front door but Tanya blocked her way. 'I've told you you're not going anywhere. I wouldn't want you to end up like Simone's boyfriend.'

'Oh, and who was that – or can I guess?' Kirsty bristled.

'Your third body in that wood, I think,' laughed Tanya.

'So, what's the problem with me leaving?'

'Well, I need to know why your boyfriend has arrested Simone.'

'How should I know? I'm a doctor, not a copper,' Kirsty replied, trying to move closer to the door.

'He tells you things, doesn't he?'

'Nothing to do with work, unless it's something we've been working on together.'

'Like this little drug problem you've got?' she said, holding up the vial and shaking it in front of her.

'Yes, like that.'

'So, I'll ask you again, why has he arrested Simone?'

'Probably because she's in on your illegal activity as well,' she scolded.

Kirsty received another slap around the face. 'Don't be insolent.'

'You like a bit of violence, do you?' Kirsty spat, wiping a small amount of blood from her mouth.

Tanya went to hit her again, but was prevented by Kirsty holding up her arm stop it.

'You've got a nasty temper,' Kirsty said. 'Didn't see any of this at university, did I?'

Tanya smiled coldly.

Kirsty knew that it was now even more important that she tried to get away from her. She felt threatened and frightened, by the way Tanya had turned from the woman she met again a few weeks earlier to someone she no longer recognised as her friend. She had been wrong all the time. Jake had been wrong all the time. If she was the killer of those drivers, they'd given her all the evidence for her to dispose of and get away with it. No, she had to get away. Tanya and her daughter were in it together.

It all made sense now – the reluctance to help, stalling the results of the samples they'd given her, trying to prevent a search of the premises and staff records. It all made sense. Jake had not told her he was arresting Simone, out of support for her friendship with Tanya she supposed. As far as Kirsty was concerned, there was no more friendship as of this moment. Tanya's attitude towards her had changed. It was aggressive and angry. She had to get out of the house.

'As I can't help you, Tanya, perhaps it would be best if I leave you now.'

'No!' Tanya exclaimed. 'You know too much,' she growled. Tanya appeared to have a constant manic smile on her face. 'If you put two and two together, and I think you have, you'll know what's occurring here.'

'Tanya, this is stupid. You can't keep me here.'

'Actually, I can,' said Tanya, taking another step forward. Kirsty could see that she had taken something out of her pocket. Realising what it was she ran back into the kitchen and tried to get out of the back door. But Tanya was closer than she thought and had grabbed at her hair. Tanya dragged her backwards and kicked Kirsty's legs from under her and she fell to the floor, with Tanya still holding on to her hair. Pain shot through her head as Tanya knelt down by the side of her. Kirsty struggled and tried to get up, but Tanya plunged the syringe into Kirsty's neck.

Succumbing to the drug, Kirsty felt her eyes watering as her body went into a spasm. She couldn't move. She thought she shouted at Tanya that Jake was on his way but couldn't be sure. This cannot be happening again. In her mind she was crying, her eyes closed.

The only thing she knew was that Jake was on his way.

60

Jake and Prentice approached the house on Eastlands. As soon as they drove into the cul-de-sac, Prentice looked at Jake. 'I know this place,' Prentice said.

'I bet you do,' Stevens said with a smile. He was sitting in the rear seat of the traffic car.

'Have you got the keys, Clive?' Jake asked.

'I have.' He jingled them in front of him.

Prentice drove onto the drive of the little house. The police van pulled up behind them and four other officers got out. Jake went up to the front door and unlocked it. Pushing the door open, he looked in and saw an uncarpeted hallway and stairs on the left of the hall. Both the kitchen and lounge doors were on the right, with an under-stairs cupboard.

Jake entered the premises with Prentice, Stevens and the other officers in tow. He told the other officers to start upstairs.

Sparse and mismatched furniture was in the rooms. 'It's as if nobody really lives here,' Prentice said.

'Just used to bringing people back to experiment on them,' commented Stevens.

The kitchen sported all sorts of empty takeaway cartons, a kettle, toaster and a small table-top fridge. Stevens opened the fridge and gagged at the smell. 'Milk's off!' he said and closed the door. But then he opened it again. Something was not right with the contents. Removing the bulging milk carton that looked as if it were going to explode at any minute, he saw a small plastic box at the back of the fridge. Removing it, he took off the lid and beckoned his colleagues over. Inside was a tray of vials full of a clear liquid.

'I think we've found what we're looking for,' Jake said.

'I'll bag it up, but we need to get SOCO in here as well now.'

Jake nodded and Stevens left to make the necessary arrangements. Jake rifled through some kitchen draws. One had some knives, forks and spoons liberally thrown in, along with some plastic accoutrements. He looked into another draw, an unpaid gas bill, electricity bill, some delivery notes, in the name of Simone Nicholls. Still, he thought, they might reveal something. He bagged them up also. As he walked from the kitchen to the lounge, one of the officers searching upstairs called to him. He went upstairs and was shown a small room with a bed and table. On the floor was a stainless steel kidney bowl with three empty syringes scattered about.

'Looks as if this is where they kept PC Parker,' the officer said to Jake.

'It does, so let's withdraw and wait for SOCO. DS Stevens is on to that, as we speak.'

The officer nodded and they left the house to wait for scenes of crime.

About thirty minutes later, a SOCO van turned up and Jake explained the situation and what they were looking for. He handed over the two exhibit packets to them for safe keeping and left them to it.

In the time they had been in the house, night had fallen and the calm evening had turned into rain. Jake remembered that he had to visit Tanya's house. It might give him some of the extra evidence he needed, he thought, so he told the other two that he needed to make a detour and they made their way to Tanya Nicholls's house on the opposite side of town.

Jake saw Kirsty's Audi TT parked next to Tanya's Mercedes and he parked behind the Audi. He told his colleagues that he needed to check whether all was OK and to wait in the car.

He rang the doorbell. Tanya opened the door.

'Where's Kirsty?'

'Sorry. Not here.'

'That's her car there.' He pointed to the Audi, but as he did so beckoned for his colleagues to join him. 'Can I come in anyway?'

'No!' shouted Tanya and she shut the door in Jake's face. He went back to the car and asked for the same van who'd helped him at Simone's address to attend Tanya's house.

'What's up?' Stevens asked.

'I wasn't allowed in.'

'Why?'

'Something's going on. Tanya answered the door in a state I've never seen her in before, and she failed to acknowledge that Dr Kingsfield was in the house. Kirsty's here, I know it. That's her car.'

'When she looked out, she looked the same as the description of the woman who attacked the DI earlier.'

'You think it was Dr Nicholls?'

'I reckon.'

'Why don't we just break down the door and go in?' asked Prentice.

'We do have reasonable grounds,' Stevens replied.

'To save life, prevent injury,' Jake said.

'Seems reasonable,' Stevens said, 'if you think that Dr Kingsfield is in there and being held against her will.'

'I do,' Jake said. He got in the car and moved it back onto the road. As he did so, he saw the van approaching with its blue lights flashing. He explained the situation to the officers, as they put their protective overalls on. Jake told HQ what was happening, but before getting a response, he decided that the situation in the house could be deteriorating and had to go in anyway.

One of the officers approached the front door with the big red door key and smashed through the door with shouts of 'Police!' and 'Stay where you are!'

A few moments later, the officer came out. 'They've gone.'

'What do you mean they've gone?' Jake demanded.

'Nobody in the house that we can see.'

'Keep searching, they're somewhere inside.'

Jake went in. He was trying to remember the layout, from when he had visited with Kirsty. He was sure there was a cellar. The house was certainly old enough to have one. He searched the house from top to bottom. The only room he was unable to get into was the study. The door, which was locked, was made short work of, again.

One wall of the study was floor to ceiling in bookshelves. Nothing like the type of shelving you'd find in a stately home library, but cheap, bending under the weight of books and journals. There was a desk with an iMac computer, a printer and a photocopier in the corner. But toward the far end was another door, made to look as if it was part of the wall. A crude disguise.

He opened the door and revealed a short corridor down a slope with another door at the end. It was locked. He withdrew and sought his other officers, explaining the presence of another locked door.

It was just an ordinary internal door and he felt that the people he was looking for were behind it. He called out. 'Can anyone hear me in there?'

Silence.

'Unlock the door now or we will break it down.'

Silence.

'Final time. I won't ask again.'

Silence. Jake indicated to the officers to break down the door. It splintered with ease under the weight of two officers, and opened to reveal a fully equipped laboratory – and Kirsty lying on the floor. Jake rushed to her side and knelt down. He felt for a pulse. Slow and regular.

'She's still alive, Jake.' The voice came from the darkest corner of the laboratory. 'If it wasn't for the fact that I once considered her my friend, she'd be dead by now.'

'Why, Tanya? Why did you want to hurt Kirsty?'

'I didn't... no, couldn't, let her leave. She knows too much. She's put it all together. Bright girl.'

'I need to get to the hospital, Tanya.'

'No, not yet. She'll be fine. I made an antidote for my drug, just in case anything happened to me or my Simone. She'll be fine in a few moments, no after effects.'

'Other than the trauma, of you hitting her, by the look of the bruise on her face,' Jake commented. He stood up from Kirsty's side, fists clenched ready to pounce on Tanya.

'Did you attack DI Randall?' He called.

'Yes.'

'Why all this then?'

'It's a long story.'

'I think we'll have plenty of time.' Jake moved towards the voice. 'Will she really be OK?'

'She'll come round in a few minutes.'

'Then you'd better come with me,' Jake said, as he took a step closer.

'I can't do that, Jake.'

Suddenly the dark corner lit up brightly, as a door was opened onto a floodlit stairway, which Tanya fled up. Jake chased after her and called to the other officers to seize her, but she managed to get into her Mercedes and screech off the driveway, clipping the police van as she did so. Jake called it in and went back to Kirsty, who was sitting up and being comforted by Prentice and Stevens.

'Tanya's on her toes,' Jake said. 'Call an ambulance for Kirsty, while I go after her.'

'Not without me,' Kirsty said groggily.

'You're in no fit state, Kirsty, you can't.'

'Nevertheless, I am coming.'

Jake sighed. He knew not to argue.

By the time they'd got onto the road the force helicopter had traced the Mercedes and followed it from overhead. It was not being driven erratically or at any speed. Ground vehicles were in the area and picked up Tanya heading towards the A43. Jake was listening to all this over the force radio. Then came the news that the car had stopped near the M1 on the over-bridge at Rothersthorpe. A ground patrol was soon on the scene and stopped a short distance from Tanya's Mercedes.

By the time Jake and Kirsty arrived, Tanya was standing on the bridge, the wrong side of the safety barrier. The situation was not helped by the growing intensity of the rain, accompanied by the relentless rumbling thunder and lightning. Jake got out of his car and approached Tanya.

'Don't come any closer!'

'You don't really want to do this, Tanya.'

'I have no option. I'm not going to prison.'

'Better prison, than this type of ending. We can help you. Help you recover from this.' He was shouting against the rain, wind and thunder.

'You wouldn't understand.'

'How do you know that?'

'I just do!'

'But if you don't tell us, how can we help?'

'There is no help for me, not now, not ever.'

Jake felt a presence by his side and found Kirsty standing next to him, trying to protect herself from the wind and rain.

'Let me try.'

Jake nodded.

'Tanya, come back over the barrier. We can talk?'

'I've nothing to say, Kirsty. I'm sorry about what I did to you.'

'But it's no way to end up like this.'

'I can't. I just can't go on. It's been years of suffering. My life's work has only been to seek revenge. But I know now that was wrong. So you see, I have no alternative. This is the best way.'

Jake could see that Tanya was crying and trying to wipe the tears and rain away from her face, while holding onto the safety barrier with one arm.

Jake had requested the Traffic Officer Service from Highways England to stop the traffic on the northbound carriageway, but they seemed to be taking their time about it. He looked towards the northbound traffic and saw some orange flashing lights approaching with some blue mixed in. Finally.

The traffic came to a stop, held back by the traffic officers and the police car some five hundred yards away from the over-bridge. Already, he saw that people were out of their cars, taking pictures. Vultures, he thought, and hoped that the rain ruined their photos.

Tanya saw that the traffic had stopped. 'No!' she screamed. 'Why have you done that?'

'To prevent ruining those drivers' lives if you do this, Tanya. Think about that. About what you would put them through. Think about it, Tanya. You are a doctor. What about your Hippocratic oath about doing no harm. Think, Tanya. Think.' She started to move nearer.

'No closer, Kirsty.'

'But I want to talk to you, Tanya. I can't hear you above the wind.' She took a step closer. Tanya didn't make any further comment, until Kirsty was about ten feet away.

'Can you hear me now?'

'Yes, I can. Come back over the fence and we can talk.' She started to cry again.

'I miss them, Kirsty.'

'Who do you miss?'

'My parents, my son, my husband.'

'Make me understand then.'

'I told you that my son and husband died in a car accident, but what I didn't say was that it was all my fault.'

'How can it be your fault.'

'Because I was in the car when it happened. We knew we shouldn't have gone out in tornado weather. It's my fault they're dead. It's my fault I grew up without my parents.'

'You can't blame yourself for any of that, Tanya, you just can't.'

'I can, and the only way to get rid of my demons, is to get rid of myself.'

'If you do that, are you not thinking of Simone? You'll be leaving her alone. No mother to turn to. She still needs you as much as you need her.'

Tanya turned to Kirsty. As she did, her foot slipped, but she held on. Kirsty went to grab her, but she shuffled away still on the edge of the bridge.

'Do you really think she'll still need me?'

'Of course she will.'

'But I've got her mixed up in this – vendetta. It was I who told her to try it out on her boyfriend, Ian. I needed to stop and rid the world of drugged drivers, but ended up just making more of them, causing families to end up in the same situation as myself.'

'You won't be able to help anyone if you're dead. What if you can carry on your work legally?'

'That's not going to happen, is it? We'll go to prison for the rest of our lives for what we've done.'

'You have some special circumstances. Perhaps they'll give you a reduced sentence, if you cooperate and come with me now.'

Tanya stood thinking, crying, looking out onto the stationary traffic, stopped in both directions. Jake had managed to manoeuvre himself across from the other side of Tanya, approaching from her right.

'I know you're there, Jake.'

'OK I'll just stand here.' Jake indicated to Kirsty to try to grab her.

Tanya turned to Kirsty, took her hands off the safety barrier and mouthed, 'I'm sorry.'

As she leaned over, Jake rushed forward and grabbed her as she fell. With Kirsty and the help of other officers, they pulled Tanya back over the safety rail.

Tanya lay on the footpath. She was sobbing. She rolled over and pulled herself into the foetal position. Her breakdown now complete. Kirsty moved to comfort her friend, holding her in her arms as she cried herself to sleep.

61

When Randall got out of the hospital, his first reaction was to go and kick Jordan's arse, while at the same time asking Stevens who he thought his boss was. But a visit to the DCI in the Major Crimes office convinced him that was probably not the best course of action.

His final interview with Philpott and another visit to Barry Fulborough revealed an even more intriguing story. Along with a conversation with Stevens and Fred Martin about the Nicholls's. A story that he was now about to reveal to the DCI.

When he arrived at his office, Freeman suggested that they have the conversation out of earshot of others in the incident room. They made their way to the conference room, where Randall was convinced he was going to be given a right bollocking.

In the middle stood a large oval-shaped table that was almost as big as the room itself. Randall was surprised to see Jake, Kingsfield, Stevens, Parker and the collision investigator, Andy Thomas, in the room.

'How are you feeling?' Jake asked.

'Better, no thanks to you.'

'What have I done?' Jake exclaimed.

'It was your suspect, who attacked me.'

'She wasn't a suspect at the time. Still, at least you had a rest,' Jake smiled, trying to make light of the situation.

'I've seen plenty of hospital wards,' he said, touching the scar on his face, 'I really didn't need the rest.'

'But you look so much better for it, boss,' Stevens chipped in.

'Don't you start, Clive! I've got my own bone to pick with you.'

'Me?' Stevens replied, gesticulating towards himself.

'Yes, me.' It was no good. Randall couldn't keep up the hard DI image anymore and chuckled at Stevens.

'Anyway,' Freeman said, 'how are we with putting these two cases to bed?'

Randall sat down at the table and poured himself a coffee from the pot someone had brought up from the restaurant. He took a sip and sat back in his chair.

'Philpott squealed, once he realised he'd got no option, despite protestations from the solicitor. And a conversation with Barry Fulborough tied together all the loose ends. We've charged Philpott with concealing the two bodies. Both of the remains have now been identified, thanks to the DNA evidence presented by Dr Kingsfield.'

He looked towards her and smiled, and she thanked him.

'So, who do those remains belong to?' Stevens asked.

'If you were here, instead of galavanting off with traffic, you'd know, wouldn't you, Clive? In fact, I think I'll put you in for a transfer.'

'Not on your life, boss. I'm happy here. Anyway, it's far too dangerous, all that high-speed stuff. I'm more of a sedate sort of chap.'

Everyone chuckled and threw a few more insults towards Stevens.

'Right, the remains that were found about twelve months ago were Vanessa Tyler, aged twenty-four. She was the daughter of Avril Tyler and Albert George Fulborough, 16th Earl of Fulborough.'

'You're kidding me!' Jake said.

'Not at all, Jake. It seems ludicrous, but when you consider that Avril Tyler was raped by his Lordship, hence the paternal line, it becomes obvious.'

'We did a DNA test on Barry Fulborough that confirmed the familial line,' Kirsty put in.

'How did Vanessa die so young?' Jake asked.

'That's where your lot come in. You remember the PM report on Vanessa's remains, provided by Kirsty? It recorded an open book fracture of the pelvis. The most common cause for this type of injury is… '

'… Motorcycle,' Andy Thomas muttered.

'That's correct, Andy, and that's exactly what it was.'

'But her hyoid bone was broken as well,' Kirsty added.

'Correct again, but I'll come back to that. What you won't be pleased to hear was that her death was caused by her brother.'

'Who is?' Jake asked, having already guessed the answer.

'Bingham Tyler.'

Kirsty shuddered and looked down. 'Am I ever going to get away from that man?' she whispered to Jake, who took her hand to comfort her. But he didn't remove it straight away. This action was noticed by all the others in the room.

'How did that happen?' asked Parker.

'Apparently, according to Philpott and he's the only one we've got to rely on for this information – how much is fabrication I don't know, but Vanessa was a bit of a tearaway. Good tearaway, if there is such a thing. She wasn't a criminal, there is no record of her. But she rode a motorcycle regularly, given to her by her father in a roundabout sort of way. One day during the summer, she had her younger brother Bingham on the back and he was encouraging her to go faster and faster. Close to Fulborough Wood, she lost control and collided with a tree, causing her horrendous injury.

'But there was nothing else broken,' Kirsty said.

'And in regard to that, if Bingham didn't do what he did then, she might still be alive.'

'Don't tell me, he choked her?' Jake said.

Randall nodded.

'So, he always was a little shit!' Kirsty said, with vehemence in her voice.

'I'm sorry, Kirsty, this must be a bit hard for you.'

'I know, but at least I know that he's dead as well.'

Freeman, who had sat quietly up to that point listening to the story said, 'So how did Vanessa get into the wood?'

'Philpott – he buried her in the same place as her mother.'

'Why would Philpott help Bingham?'

'That's easy. Philpott was Bingham's father.'

'Hold on a minute,' Jake interjected. 'So the woman who was murdered back in the nineties, that you, Steph and Jim went to wasn't Bingham's mother.'

'Correct,' Stevens said, 'Our information was that she was only the foster parents. Her husband killed her in a fit of rage He's doing a full term somewhere up north.'

'What a tangled web. Why didn't he look after him after Vanessa's death?

'Instructions from the old Lord, if he wanted to keep his job.'

'So he had no further contact after that accident?'

'Not as far as we're aware.'

'This all sounds incredible,' Freeman said. 'The sort of thing you'd see on the television.'

'Truth is stranger than fiction – to use a cliché,' said Stevens.

'I know, but this is just one family, all of whom are dead as the result of the action of one Lord,' Freeman said.

'Indeed.'

Jake sat thinking. 'What if Bingham didn't die at Fenton's Folly? For a psycho, he was quite bright.'

'But we picked up all his bits, didn't we?' Kirsty said.

'We picked up sufficient to determine that he was in the vehicle at the time, but remember, the traffic Volvo was destroyed, after being hit by the express train, travelling at about a hundred miles an hour. We didn't find any large pieces of body, which I found quite unusual.'

'Jake, please don't go there,' asked Kirsty.

Jake still had hold of her hand and squeezed it lightly.

'What are you saying, Jake?' asked Freeman.

'I don't really know, other than perhaps the whole family is not dead. What if Philpott knows that his son is not dead and is keeping him in hiding?'

'Really?' exclaimed Stevens. 'I can't see that. The bastard disintegrated in the crash.'

'You're probably right, Clive. It's just my overactive imagination.'

'What about your fatals then?' Randall asked, moving on the discussion.

'We discovered that the people we asked to check out the drug were the people who were committing these crimes.'

'There was only ever one person. Dr Tanya Nicholls. She convinced her daughter that it was for the greater good. She even got Simone Nicholls to try her drug out on her boyfriend, Ian Morton – the contractor for Fulborough Wood. So she left him there for us to find. She admitted that in her other interviews with Stevens and Fred Martin.'

'But who made the drug?'

Kirsty sat up and leaned on the table, letting go of Jake's hand. 'Tanya made the drug at the laboratory in her house, with drugs she had stolen. She had been working on it for years, as a way of seeking revenge for the drug driver who killed her parents and her own family.'

'Seems a bit drastic,' Parker said. 'She ends up providing the drug by spiking people's drinks in the first place?'

'Yes, but it seems she did some research first,' commented Jake, 'checking on her victims to see if they were of the drunk-driver type. She admits that it got out of hand and it became an obsession, but she was conflicted between her Hippocratic oath and the need to avenge the death of her son and husband when she worked in the States. That in itself was enough to make her a killer it would seem. Revengeful obsession overtook the persona she really was, a caring doctor.'

'Is she a psychopath?' Stevens asked. 'Like Tyler?'

'When we were at university together,' Kirsty said, 'she certainly didn't show any signs of psychopathy. I think that the years of mourning the death of her family took its toll on her mind. It's a delicate balance after what had happened to her, but nobody saw that or, if they did, they did nothing about it. I don't think that she's a psychopath in the true sense of the word – but I'm not a psychologist.'

'How does Simone fit into all this, after they abducted Steph?' Stevens said.

'She became so caught up with Nicholls's work I think she had to choose. But, if you recall, Simone has a nasty streak in her as well.'

'She was from "The Hood", originally,' Freeman said. 'Not a nice thing to do, to drag your kids into this.'

'She was getting more and more mentally unstable and had become an alcoholic, trying to drown her unconscionable actions – to forget what she had done. She became frustrated that the drug was not doing, what she wanted it to do.'

'And what did she want it to do?'

'She wanted to activate your sleep mechanism, but only when you were driving,' Kirsty said.

'Almost impossible, I would say,' Jake said.

'Yes, Jake, but she nearly made it.'

'Pity she couldn't have put her talents to better use for the good of society.'

'Clearly, she was never the same, after her family died and that life-changing event altered the way her life was to go.'

Freeman stood. 'OK everyone, I think we're about done here. Good job, all of you.' He went to leave the room.

As he got to the door, he turned back to face Randall. 'And Randall?'

'Yes, sir?'

'Welcome to Northants Police!'

62

Two Weeks Later

'The Berrywood Psychiatric Hospital is formed out of the decommissioning of the St Crispin's mental institution, originally called Berrywood Lunatic Asylum, and the mental handicapped hospital, The Princess Marina. It is a modern psychiatric institution with state-of-the-art facilities for treatment and recovery for adults and older people in a safe caring environment. So says the website.'

Kirsty was reading the information from her smartphone, while en route to the hospital with Jake.

'I've never actually been there, other than to drop people off at reception,' Jake said.

'Not the sort of place I go to either,' said Kirsty, as she replaced the phone in her handbag.

'What are you expecting this afternoon?' he asked.

'If I'm honest, I don't really know. An explanation? A reason? I don't know.'

'Have you made enquiries about her current state?'

'I rang this morning. I get the impression that she's on plenty of psychiatric medication, so we probably won't get much out of her.'

'How has she been described?'

'What do you mean?'

'Is she psychopathic, schizophrenic, both, or what?'

'They say she's not a psychopath and she doesn't hear voices in her head telling her to do things – like Tyler did.'

'Just deeply disturbed then?'

Jake watched, as Kirsty played with her wedding ring. Always at the mention of Tyler.

'It would seem that way. Are they prosecuting her for all those road deaths?'

'Yes, they will, but they're waiting to see whether she is fit to stand trial.'

'That could be ages.'

'Yes, it could. It depends on how she responds to treatment. She only needs to be cognisant of what's going on and what's happening to her.'

'It still may take time.'

Jake pulled into the car park and they walked to the main entrance. A bright and air-conditioned reception area was to the right of the main doors with seating in front of it and a small café. Jake showed his badge to the receptionist and they were offered a seat to wait for the doctor to take them to Tanya.

A few moments later, a short overweight man in a white doctor's coat approached them.

'Are you here to see a patient?' the doctor asked.

'Yes, we are,' Kirsty replied.

'What's the name of the patient and I'll see you get taken up to the ward?'

'Tanya Nicholls.'

'Thank you, I won't be a moment.'

'Oi – Bob,' the receptionist called out and came out from behind his work station and took Bob by the arm. 'Come on, Bob, back to the ward with you.'

The receptionist turned to Kirsty and Jake. 'Sorry about that, delusions. He thinks he's a doctor, but he's harmless.'

Jake and Kirsty chuckled to themselves.

'Just our luck,' Jake said quietly, as the receptionist put Bob in the lift, and a tall elegant woman, also in a doctor's coat, approached them.

'Dr Kingsfield?'

'Yes.' Kirsty stood.

'Are you a real doctor?' Jake said, teasing and also standing.

'Yes, I'm Dr Dixon, and I see you've met Bob! She turned back towards the lift.

'We were certainly taken in by him.'

'He has that effect. Actually, he spends so much time reading medical texts, he's probably a better doctor than I am,' she grinned. 'Come on, I'll take you to see Tanya.' They followed her.

Tanya had been put in the community day room on the female ward. There was a large picture window that presented the same views of the rolling Northamptonshire countryside, that Jake had from his apartment. The sun had warmed the room and there was comfortable seating with coffee tables spread around. In the corner was a machine which dispensed coffee or tea, depending on what cartridge you put into it.

As they entered, Tanya was standing looking out of the window. She turned and smiled at Kirsty, walked over to her and gave her a friendly hug. She shook Jake's hand politely.

'This is what my life is to be,' she commented, as Dr Dixon left the room and locked the door behind her.

'It didn't have to be this way. You shouldn't have done what you did,' Kirsty said.

'You should have left me on that bridge.'

'I couldn't do that, Tanya. You're the last person I want to see in my mortuary.' She smiled.

Tanya offered them a seat and got them both a drink.

'I'm fully cognisant, Kirsty. They've put me on a cocktail of drugs to keep me calm, but most of it's just counselling. Things I've not spoken about for years.'

'Would you like to tell us?

Tanya looked at Jake.

He held up his hand. 'Off the record.'

There was a faint acknowledgement from Tanya.

'How did you get like this, Tanya?' Kirsty asked.

'I wanted to avenge the death of my son and my husband, Randy. I felt that the world had thrown me one hell of a curved ball, what with the same thing happening to my parents as well. And on both occasions I blame myself. But I didn't want to make it obvious. I'm not a psychopath. I just wanted to be subtle and insolvable by you lot,' she said, pointing to Jake.

He didn't react, thinking better of it.

'Revenge, vengeance. This is not like you.'

'Yes, it always has been, but I concealed it well.'

'You did indeed. I had no idea. When did it start?'

'While I was in America, after the accident, working with the company that developed new drugs. I saw my opportunity to do what I wanted to do. It had been my total driving force since. That's all I ever wanted to do.'

'Why didn't you put your talents to better use?' Jake couldn't resist but ask. Tanya shot him a glance that said it all. Keep your mouth shut, Jake.

'When I was in America, I discovered a way of combining the molecules of specific drugs to ensure a specific reaction.'

'But chemists have been doing that for years.'

'Yes, but I was able to make it resistant to being broken down, until activated by certain parts of the brain, motor functions, amygdala, you know. It took years, but eventually I had the basis for a drug, using pre-cursors of GHB. So I came back to the UK and tried it out. In some cases, it worked well, but more often than not, it didn't. I had to monitor my subjects from afar.'

'Hence you being noticed at the scene of a number of road deaths, in Simone's car, as it turned out?' Jake said.

Tanya shot Jake another look. He thought she was going to say something but just nodded.

'But why drugs?'

'Because a drugged driver killed them. Once I'd made my mind up, nothing was going to stop me.'

'You got frustrated, though, according to Simone,' Jake said.

'Yes, I wanted to move things along. I felt that time was running out. I didn't want to wait any longer. I had plans for SOMA-D. To sell it on the internet and make some money.'

'SOMA-D? queried Jake.

'Don't you read, Sergeant? SOMA was the drug used in Aldous Huxley's 'Brave New World.' I just added the 'D' for driver.'

Jake raised an eyebrow, but said nothing.

Kirsty continued. 'So you knew these subjects were likely to kill themselves in a road collision?'

'Yes, that was the idea.'

'But they had no idea that they were…' Kirsty thought

for a moment. '… driving dead.'

'They didn't, no.'

'You were so convinced that you were doing the right thing?' Jake said, more irritated now than sympathetic.

'Yes, and if it weren't for your decoy, I'd still be doing it.'

'How did you know that Parker was a plant?'

'She stuck out like the proverbial sore thumb, as soon as she got in the club.'

'You were already there?'

'Yes.'

'Why didn't we see you?'

'Because I made sure you didn't.'

'What did you intend to do to her?'

'Keep her to try various versions of the drug.'

'So how did she get away?'

Simone convinced me to let her go, so we arranged that she could get away, but as she was still full of the drug, we could see how she reacted when she drove.' She paused. A sinister smile crossed her face. 'And it worked too.'

'I thought you were my friend, Tanya. I don't understand how the death of your family could make you do what you have done. Lots of families suffer this sort of trauma or worse. They don't go around killing people. I don't want to go around killing people because some psycho took my husband!'

Jake saw a flicker of anger cross Tanya's face, but it soon went away. Probably the drugs she was on, Jake assumed.

'I had lots of friends, for a time, but then I got fed up with them. I got fed up with people. I got fed up with those at work. I got fed up with my daughter and her boyfriends. I even increased the dose she gave to Ian, to see what happened. She thinks she killed him, but actually, I had a hand in it as well.

'You know, society is sick. We're all sick. People are

becoming ignorant plebs, too worried about their image on social media, instead of being caring. We've become seekers of fame, without the fortune. I saw on the internet the other day, they let me play for an hour a day, a group of holiday-makers on a beach, passing around a live dolphin that had washed ashore taking effin' selfies. What sort of society have we become that makes a group of people think that's right? Tell me that? What I've done is just helping society to get rid of those undesirables. Those people, who put other's lives at risk by driving drugged up.'

'But you drugged them, Tanya.' Jake said in frustration.

'But they were all druggies anyway weren't they.' A cold smile.

'The kid in the minibus wasn't, was he!' Jake stood. A beat. 'And that still doesn't answer Kirsty's question.'

'I just need you to help me out here, Tanya,' Kirsty said. 'I've had enough to deal with over the last twelve months. I didn't expect a friend to end up as a murderer.'

'I don't see it as murder. I see it as a release.'

'Yours or ours?' Jake said, beginning to pace the room.

'Mine.' She looked angrily at Jake.

'So?' Kirsty said.

Tanya thought for a moment, then sat down opposite her and relaxed into the chair.

'So, when I first moved across to the States, I went to work at the headquarters in Indiana, near Bloomfield. There I met my husband, Randy. I rose through the company, ending up as a VP, as did Randy. I married and we were happy, then Randy Junior came along and I was happier still. Then one day we had to go out. We lived on Tulip Drive, a few miles north of the city line. It was early afternoon and a tornado warning was in force. Tornado Alley, that's what they call Indiana. We knew that we should not have gone out in that weather. We were told to stay indoors or in tornado shelters. We went anyway. Randy was a native of Indiana and said that it would be OK. Nothing had ever happened to him out in this weather. Life had to go on, didn't it?

'But the visibility was so bad. There were hailstones battering the car and the rain was almost horizontal. We were turning at a crossroads and didn't see the semi that took us out, before we even realised what had happened.

'They both died instantly. I was seriously injured with a broken pelvis, two broken legs and was in a coma for nearly three weeks. They didn't even tell me that my husband and child had died, until I asked after them when I came around. That was the first question I asked – where's my family?'

Tanya took a gulp of her coffee. Jake could see that the recounting of the story was hard for her, but she continued, steely eyed. He sat down again.

'It wasn't until the court case that I found out that the driver had been driving for nearly twenty hours without a break and was high on methamphetamine and didn't even see us. She blamed the weather as the cause of the collision. An effin' woman in a truck killed my family.'

'What did she look like?' Jake asked.

'Like all the women I targeted with my drug, dark brown bobbed hair.' Tanya smiled, but it wasn't a warm smile; it never reached her eyes.

'The truck had hit us at nearly seventy miles an hour. Pity it didn't kill her as well – would have been better if it had.'

'But why do it over here?' Jake asked.

'The company got into a bit of trouble. We had to move our operations from the US to the UK. I'm sure you've already found out why.'

Kirsty nodded.

'Was that why you asked me that question about my involvement in the company, when you came to see me?'

'Correct,' Jake said.

'I'm really sorry that you've ended up in this state,' Kirsty said.

'Didn't expect anything else after you… "saved" me.'

'Do you want me to visit you again?' Kirsty asked.

'I'd prefer it, if you didn't.'

Kirsty looked at Jake, indicating that they should go. It was clear that Tanya was not going to allow them to get any further understanding, as to why she'd done what she'd done.

They left the hospital and, as they drove out of the car park, Jake said, 'She could have been so much more.'

Epilogue

The intimate restaurant situated along the Wellingborough Road in Northampton was where Jake decided to take Kirsty on their first real date. He pulled out the dining chair to allow her to sit down at the table, when he revealed to her that he had never been to the restaurant before, so he had no idea whether the food was good or not.

Kirsty's eyes wandered around the interior, purple contrasted by a lighter purple, almost lilac decor. Small intimate tables took centre stage with a raised dais at the far end of the restaurant with bench seats to sit groups of people, some of which were occupied.

'It looks OK to me,' Kirsty said, smiling at Jake. Jake touched her hand resting on the table to draw her attention to the approaching waitress and she took a menu from her. She quickly told them what the dish of the day was and took an order for drinks. Jake, a cola, Kirsty, an orange juice.

'At least you didn't suggest alcohol, unlike some I could mention,' she said.

Jake smiled. 'Homework, and previous knowledge, obviously.'

'I don't suppose I can blame him, really. He's new.'

'What do you think of him?'

'Randall?'

'Mmm… '

'I don't know. I can't get a handle on him. It must be difficult to blend into a new force. Not knowing anybody and having the background he has.'

'Do you know how he got that scar?'

'When he was in the army, is what he told me, when he lost his wife.'

'I can see how he could be drawn to you, after what happened.'

'I thought he was after something else.'

'Figures. He probably was and he seems a bit of a maverick to me.'

'You should know.'

'What do you mean by that?' he said, taking a swig of his drink.

'If it weren't for you chasing after Tyler in the warehouse, nobody would have found him.'

'Dogs would have got him eventually. I just couldn't wait.'

'See, maverick. You disobeyed an order from Marland,' she said giggling, 'you bad boy.' She waggled an index finger at him.

Jake raised an eyebrow, thinking, then said, 'In the words of Captain James T Kirk on trial on the Klingon home-world, "occasionally I have disobeyed orders".'

Kirsty stared at Jake. 'I never took you for a Trekkie! All this time we've known each other, not a word.'

'There are a lot of things you don't know about me. Remember, up till now, I've just been your FLO.'

'What are you now then?' she asked demurely.

Jake thought. 'Friend, companion…' He hesitated. 'Lover, perhaps?'

Kirsty lowered her head and studied the table for a moment, just as their food arrived.

Jake looked at her. He used his hand to gently lift her chin. 'All of these, but only when you're ready, Kirsty. You understand?'

'Of course. Whatever happens, I'd like to think you'd always be my friend.'

Jake nodded. 'For ever.'

Throughout the meal they'd talked about nothing in particular, a bit of work, a bit about people in general, but that last comment, before the meal arrived, hung in the air. Jake was worried he had overstepped the mark. This was, when he thought about it, their first real date. Yes, they'd been out to see Nicholls together, but they had another motive. Had he put his foot in it? He couldn't read Kirsty after that comment, so he decided to enjoy the meal with her, come what may.

As they were finishing their dessert, Kirsty looked up, as the front door opened, recognising the man who entered.

'Who's that?'

'The dean of the university faculty, remember, he wants me to go and work for them as a professor of pathology.'

Jake's eyes opened wide. 'Wow, what I wouldn't give for a job like that – professor eh? Cool!'

Kirsty laughed. 'I'm afraid that teen talk doesn't suit you, Jake. You'll be making these silly gestures next.'

'What's wrong with cool – you gotta keep wiv da times!' Jake guffawed.

'Yeah, whateva!' she giggled.

'Here, he's coming over.'

'Ah, Professor Kingsfield,' the Dean of Faculty said, holding out a hand.

Kirsty stood and they shook hands. 'Er, not yet, I think?'

'I have news for you. The senate has agreed and the job is yours. Once we've worked out the terms, you will become adjunct professor of pathology from next month.'

Kirsty smiled.

Jake stood up from the table and introduced himself. They shook hands. 'That's good news for Kirsty.'

The Dean agreed, then made his way to his table. Jake took Kirsty's hand, but she let go and embraced him for the first time in public. Kissed him on the cheek and whispered,

'Come on, let's go.'